"Ellie's books are like ch
Minnesota comfort food
—Ab..., ... bestselling
author of *Just for the Summer*

"The rare book I wanted to start over again the very second I finished it, *Anywhere With You* is a witty, wise, and warmhearted treat. Straight to the top of my favorites pile!"
—Christina Lauren, *New York Times* bestselling author of *The Unhoneymooners*

"The friends-to-lovers romp OF MY DREAMS. Another sharp, poignant turn from Ellie Palmer that plucks at your heartstrings. I can't wait for everyone to read this book."
—B.K. Borison, *New York Times* bestselling author of *First-Time Caller*

"Ellie Palmer has that special gift of creating a laugh-out-loud romp that never shies away from the complexities that make us beautifully human. *Anywhere With You* is packed with wit, warmth, and joy on every page."
—Tarah DeWitt, *USA Today* bestselling author of *Savor It*

"Ellie Palmer's sophomore novel has cemented her spot as an auto-buy author! With overwhelming heart and whip-smart humor, Palmer has crafted a childhood-friends-to-lovers story that had me absolutely swooning. Add this one to your must-read list!"
—Falon Ballard, *USA Today* bestselling author of *Change of Heart*

"Ellie Palmer has mastered striking that perfect balance between humor and heart. This book made me want to quit my job, buy a camper van, and roam the Minnesotan woods!"
—Kate Robb, author of *This Spells Love* and *Prime Time Romance*

"Ellie Palmer writes romances that are pure magic! Her voice and wit and humor always shine, and in *Anywhere With You*, she offers a fresh and tender friends-to-lovers story featuring characters who grabbed my heart and never let go!"
—Naina Kumar, *USA Today* bestselling author of *Flirting With Disaster*

"Delightfully fresh, hilarious, and oh so romantic. Told with thoughtful flashbacks, gorgeous Minnesotan scenery, and a hilarious cast of characters, this is a big love story with so much emotion, which is perfect for fans of Carley Fortune and Abby Jimenez."

—Danica Nava, *USA Today* bestselling author of
The Truth According to Ember

"Tenderhearted but hilarious with razor-sharp banter, *Anywhere With You* is a reminder that it's okay to course-correct your dreams, and that the ones who love us best love us for who we were, who we are, and who we will become."

—Meredith Schorr, author of *Roommating*

"*Anywhere With You* is a deftly penned siren call to lovers of romance, impossible to resist. Palmer's books have something to say, and her outrageously clever voice will hold you captive while you listen. She is an elite emerging voice and an auto-buy author for me."

—Livy Hart, author of *The Great Dating Fake Off*

"With her signature blend of laugh-out-loud hilarity and earnest heart, Ellie Palmer's sophomore romance, *Anywhere With You*, unequivocally cements her as a modern rom-com queen! I cried, I laughed—no, guffawed—and I yearned. The sizzling sexual tension and crackling banter between these two softhearted childhood friends could make even the most cynical reader squeal and kick their feet."

—Melanie Sweeney, *USA Today* bestselling author of
Take Me Home

PRAISE FOR *FOUR WEEKENDS AND A FUNERAL*

"Prepare yourself for a whole five-course forced-proximity meal! Who wouldn't swoon?"

—*The Washington Post*

"Debut author Ellie Palmer is poised to become one of the most beloved voices in the romance genre, mark my words. If you enjoy romance novels with a heavy dose of sarcasm, vulnerability, love scenes worthy of several spicy peppers, and lots of tension, you need to add *Four Weekends and a Funeral* to your TBR list."

—**Scary Mommy**

"An emotionally resonant grumpy/sunshine romance. . . . Alison makes for a deeply sympathetic heroine [and Adam] will tug at readers' heartstrings as he juggles his attraction to Alison with his grief. Palmer also handles tough issues with grace. This packs a punch."

—***Publishers Weekly***

"These protagonists are realistic and likable and have sizzling chemistry. Their banter is amusing and witty, and Alison's interior life is both frustrating and hilarious."

—***Library Journal***

"A cozy affirmation for introverts and homebodies about loss, love, and being enough."

—**Abby Jimenez, author of *Yours Truly***

"I fell all the way for the slow, warm unfolding of friendship and love. I already want to reread this book all over again; it feels like a comfort I will return to many times!"

—**Alicia Thompson, author of *With Love, from Cold World***

"My absolute favorite kind of rom-com, where laugh-out-loud banter, lovable characters, and swoony moments sneakily add up to something deep and beautiful. . . . An incredible debut!"

—**Sarah Adler, author of *Happy Medium***

"Ellie's voice is fresh and real. *Four Weekends and a Funeral* is a story about finding yourself and being brave enough to take ownership of your life, in addition to being a sparkling, heartwarming, and perfectly witty romance. I will read anything she ever writes."

—**Tarah DeWitt, author of *Funny Feelings***

"Ellie Palmer has such a compelling voice—razor-sharp wit wrapped up in beautiful warmth—that every word she writes leaps off the page. The fresh take on fake dating hooked me from the start, and the perfectly balanced mix of serious topics and electric banter made it unputdownable. I'll devour anything Ellie Palmer writes."

—**Jessica Joyce, author of *You, with a View***

Anywhere With You

ALSO BY ELLIE PALMER

Four Weekends and a Funeral

Anywhere With You

A NOVEL

Ellie Palmer

G. P. PUTNAM'S SONS

New York

PUTNAM
— EST. 1838 —

G. P. PUTNAM'S SONS
Publishers Since 1838
An imprint of Penguin Random House LLC
1745 Broadway, New York, NY 10019
penguinrandomhouse.com

Library of Congress Cataloging-in-Publication Data

Names: Palmer, Ellie, 1989– author.
Title: Anywhere with you: a novel / Ellie Palmer.
Description: New York: G.P. Putnam's Sons, 2025.
Identifiers: LCCN 2024042019 (print) | LCCN 2024042020 (ebook) |
ISBN 9780593714324 (trade paperback) | ISBN 9780593714331 (epub)
Subjects: LCGFT: Romance fiction. | Novels.
Classification: LCC PS3616.A33887 A84 2025 (print) |
LCC PS3616.A33887 (ebook) | DDC 813/.6—dc23/eng/20241001
LC record available at https://lccn.loc.gov/2024042019
LC ebook record available at https://lccn.loc.gov/2024042020

Printed in the United States of America
1st Printing

The authorized representative in the EU for product safety and compliance is
Penguin Random House Ireland, Morrison Chambers, 32 Nassau Street,
Dublin D02 YH68, Ireland, https://eu-contact.penguin.ie.

To long-distance friends. We're our own
kind of happily ever after.

Anywhere With You

Prologue

===

My Husband Left Me for the Rowing Machine

Years from now, when I think back to the moment my husband left me for my rowing machine, I hope I forget I was holding the penis straw.

If I'd known where the conversation was headed, I might've set it down. He was just being so casual about the whole thing, explaining that he was ending our marriage the way one might mention a particularly filling soup they'd had for lunch.

When he'd first said the words "I'm leaving," I hadn't believed him.

"Is this a prank?" I'd asked. Or maybe I'd only thought it, which is absurd because Rich doesn't "believe" in pranks the way other people don't "believe" in social media or fabric softener. But what other explanation could there be? This wasn't supposed to go this way. Rich isn't this kind of man. We aren't supposed to be this kind of couple.

But this is real. He's leaving me for a rowing machine, or—rather—the new lease on life it represents. And I'm left holding the phallic party straw.

"Life is a current, Charley," he's telling me as he scrambles around our (former) marital bedroom. "We can't fight it. If we drag our oars in the water, too scared of where we might go, we won't stand still, but drift off course from our destiny."

"Off course from our destiny," I repeat as though he'll hear how ridiculous he sounds if I manually rewind the tape. But how else should I respond to the motivational gobbledygook he's parroting back from this morning's Sunrise EDM Bootcamp? How should I react when the man I chose to build a life with decides to dismantle it brick by brick because a fitness influencer named Evian reminded him of the mere possibility of *more*? The idea of someone, *anyone*, better than me.

I pinch the straw penis between my forefinger and thumb. "We were supposed to finish *Oppenheimer* tonight." I'm blatantly bargaining at this point.

He does his stiff-shouldered inhale thing. As a confrontation-averse Midwesterner, it's the closest he gets to an eye roll.

The vibration of the phone in my pants pocket interrupts Rich's performative exhale and cuts into the gesture's overall effectiveness. The tiny buzz wears out his last shred of patience and empathy for me as the woman he's actively abandoning based on his tenuous interpretation of scripted exercise affirmations.

"Get it. It might be work," he dares me. Is that what this apparent midlife crisis is *really* about?

I take the bait and check my phone—it very well could be work—but I send the call to voicemail when I see it's my sister, Laurel.

"What's so wrong with caring about my job?"

"You hate your job, Charley."

"Everyone hates their job."

"And still, you love it more than me." He lays the statement down like a pair of twos he thinks will win him the game. A little dark brown curl falls onto his forehead. His Clark Kent curl. I liked that curl. Now I hate it. "We've only been married less than a year, and we're already glorified roommates. How long are we supposed to go through the motions?" he asks.

The motions. The words sear into my skin. The way he says it, it's almost as though we're partners—active participants in a ruse to fool our friends, our families, and the state of Minnesota. Only I didn't know we were going through the motions. I thought we were in love.

Sure, we aren't a passionate couple, but we're something better: Stable. Compatible. We want similar lives and like the same shows. *Some* of the same shows. Not *all* the same shows. I can't invest in every *Walking Dead* spin-off AMC feels compelled to produce, but it's important to have separate interests.

Passion is unpredictable. Volatile. Passionate people are driven by impulses and whims. Rich has never done *anything* on a whim. At dinner, he refuses to let Rock, Paper, Scissors determine whose AmEx should get the rewards points, because it's an "unsophisticated game of chance." Suddenly he's craving enthusiasm and spontaneity? A man whose preferred hobby is meal prep?

"Can you honestly tell me you loved me? Even in the beginning?" he asks me.

I shake my head, tamping down the hot frustration burning beneath my ears. "That's not how love works." I know what it feels like to be collateral damage to someone's doomed love story. I've never wanted that. I want what Rich and I have. The love of a nice, steady man that starts as a tiny seed and grows on you like vines. Though I suppose vines have a way of rotting the wood they wrap around—an insignificant piece of plant trivia that is now exceedingly relevant.

"It should be," he says, almost kind. Optimistic. Delusional. "Don't you want that too? Don't you want someone you can't live without? Someone you have to text to tell them you love them, even if they're only in the other room?"

"You're leaving me because I don't text you when you're in the other room? I can text you more!"

"But we never *want* to." Rich stands up straighter, emboldened by whatever he's about to say next. "It's time for me to go off on my own adventures. Like your friend Nathan—though I doubt I'll be so performative about it."

"Who's Nathan?" I ask, genuinely confused.

He shrugs. "Your shoeless friend. The one who lives in his car."

It takes me a second to connect the dots. "Do you mean Ethan?" I cross my arms, defensive. What makes him think *now* is the appropriate time to bring up the best friend I lost because my husband couldn't get along with him? "Ethan lives in a *van*," I bite out as the kindling of rage catches fire under my skin. Looks like I'm entering the anger phase of mourning this relationship with every loud, open-mouthed breath from Rich's punchable, congested face. Now that he's leaving me, I can finally take issue with the way he refuses to use his allergy medication and then complains about every symptom as though he's being personally victimized by the planet without recourse.

He only stares back at me, slack-jawed, because he doesn't care where my friend lives or whether I'll text him more. His mind is already made up. He's already gone.

"I'm sick of being lonely in my own marriage, Charley. I need adventure and passion and the spontaneity of the tides."

Again with the boats!

"I deserve to have someone fall for me, and I don't know if

you could ever let yourself do that. Or if you're even capable of it. You're too . . ." I watch him weigh his words before settling on: "guarded."

"Guarded," I say back, processing.

In my mind, I eviscerate him. I call him every name. I tell him that I've been lying about his second toe and it *does* look like a witch's knuckle. I insult his appearance with jabs so specific, they'd stealthily attack his psyche like self-esteem termites until he collapsed into nothing but an insecure husk of his confident former self. I scream that I never loved him, not because I'm incapable of it, but because loving *him* was an impossible task.

But I don't say any of this, partly because it's not true. Except for his toe. That toe is unnerving. But mostly because doing so would cede control of this moment to him.

He won't get that satisfaction. He'll get nothing but the "guarded" demeanor he used to love but has grown to resent.

Rich blinks first. He was never good in an emotional standoff. A checkered oxford shirt I bought him lies between us on the bed next to his splayed-open duffel. He folds it completely wrong, and I resist the urge to grab it from his hands and save him from himself one last time.

"I have to check in to a hotel. I figured you wouldn't want me to stay here while I search for a new place." When he looks up from his phone, his eyes are soft. Patient. Sad. He looks familiar to me again. That's the face of his I know best. "We had something good. It's hard to leave it behind for the possibility of something great. But I can't make you happy, and trying to is making me miserable."

I pinch the straw to remind myself it's there, the tangible proof of the life I had before Richard Warren.

"I care about you, Charley. I don't want this to get ugly." I nod, numb. "And Marlene never lets us forget that her son wants the place, so that part'll be easy."

He laughs—*laughs*—while bile fills my mouth. Because Rich isn't just *leaving*. He's toppling everything—my home, my finances—like he's the bottom row of the Jenga tower that's propping up my life. He's handing it over to *Marlene*, our next-door neighbor who kisses her adult son on the mouth and raises a suspicious number of dachshunds.

Anger pumps through my veins, and I lose control. For a split second, I'm the Incredible Hulk, and without thought or warning, I grab the shirt between us and rip it in two, a walloping grunt leaping through my throat like a battle cry as the fabric surrenders in my hands.

Rich's eyes are saucers as he takes in my strength, my passion. I watch a flicker behind his eyes, an electric current in something long burned out. I'm giving him exactly what he says he wants, letting my guard down and sharing a glimpse of the raw, unpolished Charley I hardly let him see.

But then he swallows and his face goes blank, and I know it's not enough. Our relationship might as well live in the drawer of mystery electronics between my iPod Touch and a five-year-old Fitbit that couldn't turn on if you boosted it with a car battery. Our marriage is dead and buried.

So when my husband of less than a year walks out the door with my extra-long iPhone cable, the four worst words in the English language glow behind my eyes like a neon sign: ETHAN POWELL WAS RIGHT.

Chapter 1

Divorced Zaddies
at Ruth's Chris

FRIDAY, NOW

WHY DOES MY phone assume all photos contain memories I wish to revisit?

BUILDING A HOME TOGETHER, the device proudly announces in white sans serif across a montage of our once lovingly appointed living room. I managed to snap the pictures when the moving crew began boxing away the books, the lamp, and the antique sideboard buffet Rich carved out as his own.

Because even though we bought more house than we needed and furnished it too quickly with nondescript typographical artwork and cold concrete nightstands in an approximation of modern-cozy that fell somewhere between a WeWork and a homier-than-average Airbnb, I needed to capture the image of it. Preserve the moment before my life dissolved into a puddle of sludge as something tangible I could hold in my hands, so in these months of divorce negotiations, I could use it to determine exactly what I, Charlotte Beekman, was owed. How many of Rich's collectible mugs and personal productivity books would it take to make me whole again? How many would make up for the promises we broke?

Because that's the truth of it, isn't it? A marriage is about promises.

But divorce is about *things*.

And argue over *things*, we did. Few people, aside from Kim Kardashian and Bethenny Frankel, can lay claim to a marriage in which the dissolution was more prolonged than the partnership. Now I'm just a divorcée, stealing glances of my past life in an iPhone montage at an intersection.

A car honks behind me, and I squint into the morning sun to spot the green traffic light. I shut off my screen and throw the phone back in my bag on the passenger seat before pressing the gas pedal, watching for rogue pedestrians as I turn into the underground parking lot of the Minneapolis high-rise I work in. It's the place where I spend most of my waking hours—and, occasionally, some sleeping ones.

The garage door shuts behind me, cutting off the familiar cacophony of downtown road construction. I glide my Prius past the conveniently located "executive parking" spots reserved for partners at my law firm and vice presidents of the various corporations with which we share this gray, boxy building. I settle for a spot in the nosebleeds that's partially obstructed by a load-bearing pole and requires just the right amount of courage and hubris to back into.

Parked, I remove my beverages from their respective cup holders—a travel mug of coffee from the Nespresso machine, a drive-thru Caribou iced oat milk latte, a Tetra Pak of iced tea, and two different stainless steel water bottles—and start the daily, nerve-racking process of arranging them in my arms like a German barmaid. Navigating the route to my office on the thirty-second floor without spilling a drop of my emotional support liquids involves a bit of juggling.

"Thanks," I murmur without looking up at the owner of the floral sleeve that holds open the door. The arm surprises me by snatching my travel coffee mug and a Stanley cup from my hands. "Whoopsie-daisy. Let me just sneak that right out of your hands there," its owner tells me.

"Stacy?" I peer up at my colleague's familiar face and glossy brown hair. Stacy Arroyo is an eager second-year associate with an aggressively cheery demeanor that I'm certain can only be counterbalanced by a dark pastime I have yet to identify. We are two people who would never choose each other as friends but have trauma-bonded after spending day in and day out in the same hellish workplace. I would lay down my life for this woman who says "whoopsie-daisy," and that's a fact I'm forced to carry with me now.

"Morning," she says, her voice ungodly chipper given the hour. Then her demeanor downshifts so suddenly, I nearly get whiplash. "AgriTech says they're cutting their legal budget."

"Were you staking me out in the parking lot to tell me that?"

She lifts her shoulder. "You don't like when I call you before work."

"Well, I don't like whatever this is either." I punch the elevator call button with my now-free hand.

"Why are you always dressed like a storm cloud? You're wearing gray on gray on gray. It's summer. Aren't we supposed to dress more casually? Or at least incorporate a pop of neon?" she asks, holding the elevator door open with her hip.

Today I'm dressed in a perfectly tailored gray suit and silk shell that I've paired with an eye-wateringly expensive taupe tote from The Row. I bought it in a retail-therapy binge sometime after Rich moved out but before I'd calculated how much of my stuff I'd need to sell to buy the house from him.

Still, I couldn't bring myself to return something I'd purchased in a rare moment of post-Rich optimism, and the quiet luxury of the smooth, supple leather makes me feel chic while eating breakfast tacos off a food truck. To remove it from its protective canvas sack, I need to hype myself up by whispering capitalistic affirmations like "This is an investment piece!" and "I deserve nice things!"

Despite these high-end staples, my coworker—whose enthusiasm for "tasteful" body glitter under the harsh workplace fluorescents has given her golden tan skin an iridescence rivaling that of the vampire family in *Twilight*—will forever see me as the grumpy Care Bear.

I frown. "I don't trust people who go too casual in a corporate environment. I don't need to see a man's bare knees in a place of business."

At Anderson & Gottlieb, I work with plenty of normal men who ask after my weekends in an appropriately disinterested manner before following up on the status of client files and shuffling away from me. But, as with any male-dominated industry, there are a handful of partners at my law firm whose energy teeters dangerously between condescendingly paternalistic and confusingly sexual, all executed with a healthy dose of plausible deniability. Advances are often subtextual and generally too difficult to explain in a way that would make for an actionable HR complaint.

All this to say, gray suits are a necessary defensive tactic.

"You said something about AgriTech?" I slurp iced latte from its rapidly collapsing paper straw.

"Yes," she tells me, leading the way to my tiny office, which is all windows, with no room for privacy or relaxation. "They want us to cap our fees or they'll stop sending work."

I barely suppress my groan. "If they want to spend less on legal fees, they should try getting sued less often."

Once we're safely in my office, I violently plop everything on my desk like I am both Miranda Priestly and the poor assistant who'll have to pick up after her.

"They're Bob's client. What did Bob say?" I ask.

Bob Champion is a managing partner with a gift for name-dropping washed-up politicians from the nineties. In the parasitic cesspool that is Anderson & Gottlieb, associates are trapped in a toxic, symbiotic relationship with partners in which job stability is dependent on how much those in power like and trust you. We *need* them to dump enough of their work onto us to meet our insanely high billable-hour quotas and live to fight another day. Bob is my whale who provides the endless supply of work that keeps my hours unbeatable, and I'm the tiny barnacle on his back he auto-forwards emails to in the name of "mentorship."

When I first joined Anderson & Gottlieb as a bright-eyed young lawyer, I immediately set my sights on Pamela, the only female partner in the patent group and a woman with the kind of severe black bob that seems to pass judgment on my bouncy blond blowout merely by existing in its inert perfection. Pamela rose through the ranks in the era of *Lean In* corporate feminism and seems permanently disappointed I'm not experiencing *more overt* sexism to the degree and frequency that she endured. No matter how many midnight calls I answered or miles I racked up flying all over the country at the drop of a hat, it never seemed to be enough.

So now I'm stuck with Bob because Pamela has a new

protégé in smarmy Paul, a fellow fourth-year associate so determined to push me out of this place that he spends his Sunday mornings endorsing me for things on LinkedIn.

Before answering my question, Stacy dips her head to the side. I'm not going to like her answer. "Bob said you'd handle it."

Unfortunately for me, I *can't* fall out of favor with Bob if I want to stay on the partnership track, and as a fourth-year associate, I'm completely at his mercy.

She doesn't miss my eye twitch. "My law school friend says Payne loves the work we've done for them, and they're hiring for multiple roles . . ."

I drop into my office chair. "We're not going in-house at a company that makes rat traps, Stacy. It's not that dire," I reassure her for the umpteenth time, because despite Stacy's commitment to her career, I know she has a chaotic streak that includes watching YouTube videos of workers telling off their bosses while she eats her bento box lunches at her desk.

"A & G is the safe bet," I promise her. "We've worked too hard here just to start over someplace else. We're playing the long game, Stace."

With Stacy, I'm always in this role: the slightly more senior associate who is yanking her up and out of this den of vipers by her pink chiffon sleeve.

She sets my drinks on my desk and moves to leave but then seems to change her mind. "Almost forgot," she says, wheeling herself back around to present me with a tiny black envelope.

I open it and analyze its contents. "Why are you handing me an expired gift card to Ruth's Chris Steak House?"

"It's *barely* expired, and I'm hoping it'll soften the blow of . . . you know . . . today."

The word she's not saying beats against my skull with a steady thump: *divorce, divorce, divorce.*

"Rich and I have been separated for over a year. Let's not make a big deal about the day the paperwork goes through, okay?" I hold up the gift card. "I appreciate the gesture, but I'm fine. Drink your own expired drinks tonight."

"Only the card is expired—the drinks are perfection—but I can't. Brady's mom's coming into town, so I have to pack all my stuff and pretend I live with my old roommate." Her voice is light, as though temporarily moving out of her apartment so her twenty-four-year-old boyfriend can defer an uncomfortable conversation with the woman who pays for his cell phone plan is just another quirky Friday night.

For months, I've wanted to shake her, warn her, or at least forward the invoices from my divorce attorney. See! it'd say in the body of the email. This can happen even when you marry the guy who has monogrammed towels and a metal filing cabinet under his desk that he *actually* uses to file things. Even men like this leave! You think you can go the distance with the dude who has to ask his mom to adjust his data plan???

Thankfully, a notification on my phone saves me from saying something I'll probably regret.

Ethan: I'm in the area, btw. It's been way too long and a little birdie told me you might be having a tough day.

Something old and neglected flutters under my breastbone at the sight of Ethan's name on my phone again. The one upside of divorce is that all your old friends who hated your husband come crawling back out of the woodwork. Ethan, my "shoeless friend," as Rich called him—though it should be noted that the barefoot thing was more of a short-lived teenage phase and less of a lifelong aesthetic—was one of the handful of guests who had something "come up" on the day of my wedding the way emergencies seem to materialize on bad dates as soon as the waiter offers dessert. As my best man, his absence was slightly more noticeable and initiated a year of silence that only ended the day Rich left and I sent Ethan a tonally confusing **Turns out, you were right** text message paired with a GIF of Kim Kardashian popping out of the bushes.

"What dude is sending you an 'in the area' text?" Stacy grabs my phone and examines the photo in my contacts. "Wait. Is this Man Bun from your bachelorette party? He was such a cutie," she says in an exceedingly wholesome tone. "I love this for you. Unless he's married. Is he married?"

"He's just a friend," I argue reflexively, because my oldest friend has never been a romantic or sexual option for millions of reasons, not least of which is that he's a musician who's been perpetually touring on the college circuit since we were nineteen, and I'm . . . well . . . me. "A friend who travels constantly and has been audited twice by the IRS. He's not the kind of guy you can sign up with for a vegetable CSA." I swipe my phone back from her.

"That's your immediate concern for a date? Whether you can see yourself eating locally sourced turnips together? You don't need to commit to a farm-share with Man Bun to rebound with him."

"He only wore it in a bun that one time," I deflect, despite the fact that I haven't actually *seen* him in years.

I suppose it's possible he still wears it in a bun. The thought of seeing him again, knowing for certain how he's changed outside of the grainy concert photos he's occasionally tagged in, sends a happy jolt through my ribs.

Ethan: Today's no good, but I can be around tomorrow if you need anything.

I roll my eyes to counteract the pitiful rock sinking in my stomach. I somehow let myself forget that "in the area" to Ethan can mean anything from a state park three hours away to a dive bar in a nondescript town somewhere outside of Lincoln, Nebraska. He's always hated being stuck in one place too long.

A third message appears.

Ethan: The little birdie is Lo. I don't STILL believe I can talk to birds.

I snort at that one, and, as though summoned, my sister, Laurel, is now FaceTiming me.

"I have to take this, Stace. Have a wonderful time lovingly deceiving your potential future mother-in-law."

She turns toward my door. "Enjoy the divorced zaddies at Ruth's Chris." She stops short, whipping her hair over her shoulder and holding up a finger in the universal gesture for *Sorry, one last thing.* "You're gonna talk to AgriTech, right?"

I loll my head back and find my already exhausted reflection in the window. How is it not even eight? "I'll make them sweat first, but tell Bob it's as good as fixed."

Once she's out of sight, I sweep the gift card into the wastebasket, because there's no such thing as a little bit expired, and a table for one at a chain restaurant sounds too grim, even for me. Then I pop in my AirPods and hold my phone level with my mouth like an octogenarian on speakerphone.

"Make it quick," I tell my sister, glancing sidelong at the surrounding cubicles from my see-through office. "I'm pretending you're a pesticide manufacturer."

"You have a booger," my sister says by way of greeting.

I raise my phone so I can glare at her properly. She's parked in her car with the phone propped on the dash, fixing her lavender milkmaid braids in the video of herself. Once upon a time we had the same honey-blond hair and fair skin, but her junior year of high school, she discovered box dye and has never looked back. Right now, it's more of a grown-out ombré, but she has the pixie-like features and unwavering self-confidence to make it look intentional.

Behind her, I can make out the hustle and bustle of a Love's Travel Stop, which tells me she's at least an hour north of her Saint Paul apartment. How early must she have started her day to already be outside of the Cities?

"Why are you FaceTiming me, Laurel? I'm at work."

"I needed to get my eyeballs on you for D-day. I was hoping to see you in some kind of revenge outfit or at least rocking a little tasteful cleave." She sounds disappointed.

"Please don't compare the day the paperwork goes through on my divorce to the invasion of Normandy," I practically beg her as I one-handedly type my network password into my computer.

Yes, today, this dreadfully ordinary Friday, is the day my divorce with Richard Warren is final. *Final* final. I'm a twenty-eight-year-old divorcée and officially the proud single owner of too much house. When I was married to a thirtysomething

man with an enviable hairline, homeownership seemed like
the obvious next step in my journey toward stability. Now,
when I drag my bins out on Thursday mornings, I worry my
neighbors look at me the way I do child pageant contestants,
as a tragic display of the trappings of womanhood without any
of the requisite life experience.

I glance down to see Laurel fighting with the credit card
reader on the EV charging station. "I meant more like 'D' for
'divorce.' 'D' for—"

"I know you want to say 'dick.' Just say 'dick' so we can
move on to—"

"DICK . . . ," she belts out, and because god is an asshole,
my AirPod falls out of my ear so Saroya, an aspirationally
gutsy law clerk who Juuls on Zoom calls, is within earshot.
Struggling with my AirPod, I mouth, "Client. Sorry," to Saroya, who doesn't seem to buy it but also doesn't really care.

Laurel *loves* calling Rich "Dick." When things were good,
it was a playful nickname between in-laws. When things got
bad, it was an accusation. Not lobbed against him but at me. I
was the reason she'd spent years following a bland and nondescript white man on Instagram who posted ill-lit photos of
food with captions like "hump day treat *drooling emoji*."
An account I still follow because taking the affirmative step to
unfollow suggests that unexpectedly scrolling past a picture of
a dim hand pie would be too painful.

What's more humiliating is at some point in the last fourteen months it *actually was* too painful and I had to mute him.

I shake away thoughts of my ex with Laurel's "DICK" battle cry ringing in my ears.

"I hate you," I say through a sigh.

"You love me," she responds in her normal, self-assured

way. Everyone loves Laurel, and no one knows that better than her. "And I deserve a little fun after the SAT course from hell. I swear, at least two parents think I'm one of those Lori Loughlin Varsity Blues college-prep tutors. Easton's mom asked again if I'd be dyeing my hair to appear more discreet when 'assisting' her son on exam day. She kept winking when she said 'assist.' You know, to avoid self-incrimination in case I was wearing a wire."

I nod. "As one does."

Laurel is that particular brand of inspiring high school English teacher lit majors aspire to be after watching the first half of *Dead Poets Society*. An embodiment of that aloof, chaotic energy seventeen-year-olds find intoxicating, she was voted Teacher of the Year so many times that her school instituted a policy of rotating eligibility. My sister, Laurel Beekman, is the FDR of Williamson Academy, and if I could purchase a bumper sticker to this effect, I'd slap it on my Prius in a second.

In the summer, she teaches SAT prep courses until her will to live outweighs her desire to pay her bills. That window seems to get smaller every summer. This year, she's made it to late June.

I hear the crumple of a convenience store bag on Laurel's end. "Obviously I wear a wire." I'm looking at my computer monitor, but I hear the unmistakable sound of Laurel biting into what I'm 90 percent sure is a gas station pastry. The girl's weak for shelf-stable bear claws. "But only for the benefit of my future biographers," she informs me between bites. "And to aid the police investigation when I'm tragically murdered by a serial killer, obviously."

"Stop falling asleep to murder podcasts," I demand, pulling up my work email on my desktop. "It's not good for you."

"Speaking of my gruesome murder . . . I have something to tell you, and I don't want you to kill me." I inwardly shudder—I don't possess the mental fortitude to be braced for a murderous revelation before I've finished my second beverage of the morning.

"What a windup," I say simply to lighten the mood, but then she doesn't say anything. She lets her pause swell into something stiff and surprisingly heavy.

She wouldn't be confessing something truly awful, would she? Not over FaceTime while she's perched on the hood of her car and I'm at work, fully visible to all my coworkers. With all we've been through together, she wouldn't do that to me. Would she?

"I'm actually headed up north . . . to see Petey."

That makes me sit up straight in my roller chair.

Petey. One of our oldest friends and Laurel's most stubborn situationship manages a hockey summer camp so far north that it's practically Canada. He must be between sessions. She must be looking to backslide.

Laurel's relationship with Petey is recognizable to anyone who went through a messy phase in their twenties. In college, they were combustible. Innocuous conversations about pizza toppings would erupt into incomprehensible, relationship-ending fights. She broke up with him so many times that she stopped telling friends when they reconciled, as absolutely no person with a functioning cerebral cortex could pretend it was anything other than a terrible idea to get back together with the guy she'd dumped twice on a single three-hour Mississippi River cruise.

I love Petey, I do. I've known him as long as I've known Ethan. He coaches youth hockey and always asks how my grandparents are doing and bought a truck because he genuinely enjoys helping his friends move. Petey on his own? An absolute sweetheart who's seemingly unburdened by the stressors of life and responsibility. But Laurel *and* Petey? *Together?* Total trainwreck.

"You didn't tell me you guys were in touch. Was the last time you saw him at my wedding?"

"A few times after," she says, obfuscating. "We picked things up after everything happened with you and Rich. We were just talking, but still, I didn't want to . . . Oh, no. Your nostril got all sad," she says, because apparently she's still watching me on FaceTime. "If you're not okay today, I can . . . I'll figure something out."

"I'm fine," I groan, though the words are more of a reflex than an honest assessment of my well-being. But this whole scheme is classic Laurel, and if she wants a foolhardy and misguided case of sexual déjà vu, far be it from me to stand in her way. "We've drawn out this divorce so long, I've basically forgotten Rich existed. Today will be just any other day."

"Really? I'm so relieved. I've been dreading telling you about the proposal."

"He proposed?" My voice cracks. Three sets of heads belonging to paralegals swing in my direction. I put on my best wobbly smile. *Nothing to see here.*

"Of course not. He won't even *date* me without a real commitment on my end," she says, correcting me. "*I* am. I'm driving up today to propose."

Dread clenches my gut. After my divorce and our parents' shitshow of a marriage, how could she even contemplate getting married? And to Peter Eriksson-Thao? A man with

Microsoft Clippy tattooed on his inner bicep? This has to be a mistake.

I swivel my chair toward the window for the illusion of privacy. "This all feels a little . . . impulsive. What if you—"

"Look," Laurel commands. "The timing, it's . . . bad—I'm sorry—but it has to be now. It has to be today. Or I might lose him for good."

"See? *That.*" I point my finger at her nose on-screen. "*That* is what I'm talking about. That's panic talking. You're not thinking clearly."

"I've never been more clearheaded in my life." She laughs. She actually has the audacity to laugh in a moment like this. "He leaves for his camping trip tomorrow, and I can't let two whole weeks go by without telling him I want to spend the rest of my life with him. He needs a gesture. It has to be big, and it has to be a real commitment this time." Her voice is resolute. I'm not talking her out of this on FaceTime, that's for sure. "But if you *really* need me today . . ."

If you need me, I'll sacrifice my own happiness in exchange for lifelong resentment toward you. That's what her silence is saying.

The next quiet thought belongs to me.

They'll never stay together long enough to make it down the aisle.

It's a cruel, ungenerous opinion I'm not proud of, but it allows me to muster the strength to say, "I'm fine. I'm so happy for you."

I hear her sigh with relief. "Thank god. I can't tell you how worried I was. If you could see my boob sweat. Actually . . ." She starts to move the camera to her underboob, but thankfully, another car needs the charging station and I'm spared the in-dignity of FaceTiming my sister's dampened tits.

After we end the call, I pick the Ruth's Chris gift card out of the empty trash can because, suddenly, an expired fifty dol-lars' worth of steak doesn't seem so pathetic.

She won't get married. I know this. Though Laurel's never lonely, she's always on her own. Hookups, relationships, and situationships flow in and out of Laurel's life like sticks on a river. They can never quite handle her current, and that's how she likes it. Between Laurel and the madness that is the wedding-industrial complex, this marriage will never come to fruition. I won't even have to be the bad guy.

She's fine. I'm fine. Today is like any other day, and it will be just *fine*.

Chapter 2

Hungover *Memento*

THE WINE WAS probably a mistake.

Well, the mistake was the three blueberry spiced mojitos I had before the wine, but adding malbec to the workload of my already struggling liver probably wasn't wise.

I shouldn't have introduced myself to the family celebrating their nana's eighty-fifth birthday as "the youngest divorcée in the restaurant." I definitely shouldn't have kept repeating that icebreaker throughout the night after it crashed and burned the first time.

When I blink open my eyes, the sliver of light peeking out from behind my blackout curtains pierces my eyeballs like they're little chunks of steak sliding onto a skewer. My fingers peel a crusty strand of hair out of my mouth but pause at the sight of Sharpie on my hand.

WET TED

It seems my night at Ruth's Chris Steak House took a turn and the subsequent hangover has plummeted me into a detective novel against my will. I wander toward my master bath to piece together the victim's final hours. The victim, in this case, is my head, which throbs like some particularly anxious soul pried my brain from its skull and squeezed it like a stress ball.

Who Ted is, why he is wet, and what "Wet Ted" is doing on my hand in Sharpie is something I cannot emotionally take on right now, but in releasing the contents of my stomach into the formerly pristine toilet bowl, the night returns to me in flashes, like hungover *Memento*.

I think I cried. I don't remember it, and I'm not typically a crier, but feelings have a way of creeping up on me when my defenses are down. I rub my forehead and massage the face muscles, which feel fatigued in the way they only do when I cry. But that might be the hangover. Or whatever I did after I put on my sports bra and leggings. And clip-in rowing shoes. Dear god, did I drink and row? Again?

Despite all the evidence to the contrary, I'm not much of a drinker. I don't like feeling out of control, and I rarely know where my car is parked sober, let alone the morning after a night of debauchery.

I have a vague memory of leaving my car at home and Ubering both ways, but I peek out the curtains to verify that there's a Prius in my driveway.

My little silver car is there. And so is a gigantic white cargo van.

I didn't steal a van last night, did I?

Okay, I'm 99 percent sure I didn't steal a van last night. People who aren't otherwise prone to grand theft auto don't itch for a joyride after only three blueberry spiced mojitos. And a malbec.

I grab my phone from the charger and pull up my email to

look for any clues about the provenance of the cargo van. Did I overnight a couch? I've been meaning to buy furniture, but I'd hoped to make a day of it at the Galleria's Crate & Barrel— wandering the showroom, flopping into one Lounge Collection configuration after another, imagining the possible futures that come with each small, seemingly permanent decision, like choosing between the boucle fabric and the linen weave.

Though I made those same mental calculations when I purchased my Restoration Hardware custom Cloud sofa with Rich, and look where that got me: the youngest divorcée in a steak house chain, drunk-dialing Wayfair because I secretly love a flat-packed bargain.

I find no shipping confirmations in my email and finally brave the driveway, where the front wheel of the van is gently crushing my azaleas. There's no driver behind the wheel. It doesn't *not* look like a delivery van, but something about the scene tickles a spot in the back of my head like a tiny thread on my brain stem, waiting to be unraveled.

I knock. There's no answer but the muffled rustle of a creature inside. I pause, and when the movement stops, I bang on the door of the van, the metal bellowing.

A male voice curses and slides open the van door with aching slowness. My limbs vibrate. It can't be . . . He wouldn't . . .

Hey, you. That little flicker in my chest recognizes him, and I know with devastating certainty that the person waking up in my driveway is Ethan Powell.

With a subtle lift of his chin, he reveals more of that face a *Pitchfork* writer once described as "obtrusively magnetic," and I lose all sense of time analyzing every new bit of him that is both exactly the same and completely different from the last time we were together. His face is as lit from within and sun-kissed as ever, with new lines etched by time and inconsistent sunscreen application. His hair is the same warm brown with new salt and pepper strands woven in. Though it's too short for a bun now. He must've gotten a haircut.

He pushes his hair back in that boyish, sleepy way so his steely-blue eyes collide with mine, and suddenly, I'm thirteen again. I'm under our tree, messing around with my dad's Canon and resisting the urge to photograph Ethan while he's strumming a couple chords to see if he "finds something." He never wrote songs, he "found" them, like they were hidden in the corners of his mind, waiting to be uncovered by a sunset or the chorus of rain beating against the windows or the sound of Petey and Laurel arguing over Mario Kart.

"Chuck." He greets me with a tilt of his head as he hops out of his dorm room on wheels, and suddenly, I'm eye to eye with Ethan Powell, the boy who at one point knew me better than anyone on the planet, whom I now keep in touch with primarily through memes and text message reactions. It's the sad, predictable trajectory of countless childhood friendships as one barrels into adulthood. Once upon a time, I spent every day with this boy and knew the exact noise he made when he slurped soup. Now I send him GIFs.

Which raises the question, why is Ethan Powell sleeping in my driveway?

"What are you doing here? At my house? In a camper van?"

"Well, good morning to you too. You look . . ." His eyes snake up my body like he's surveying damage to his car after a fender bender. I recall the way I woke up this morning and stiffen. He may be just as I remember, but nothing about me is the same. Last time we saw each other, I was about to get married. I was on a career upswing. I was looking at houses and had momentum. Now I'm . . . untethered.

Ethan's grin crinkles his face in that irresistibly charming way I've never been able to trust, as though he's a basset hound and I'm merely a person in front of him with sausages in her pockets. "I'm sorry. You look really bad," he says ruefully. "I shouldn't have started that sentence, but it's just *so* bad, I had to say something or—"

My laugh cuts him off. It catches us both off guard.

It's just such an *Ethan* thing to say. He'll tell anyone what he's thinking, 90 percent of the time, at least. It's that pesky 10 percent that's always been a mystery to me. When I think I've got a handle on him, he rips the rug out from under me and I'm left crashing to the floor.

"Your hair is, uh, mid-takeoff—" He reaches for my head, but I swat his hand away. "Are you in tap shoes?"

I look down at my clip-in rowing shoes and back up at Ethan. I'm not prepared to explain. "Yeah, yeah. You look like shit too."

He folds his arms with a sideways smile. "I can't look worse than you do."

"To what do I owe the pleasure of this very early morning visit?" *Or any kind of visit*, I don't say out loud, because I'm unreasonably excited to see my friend parked on my landscaping, and I'd hate to scare him away.

"I told you I was going to be nearby."

"And I never responded."

His head tilts, confused. "You don't remember responding?"

My stomach floats into my chest as my dehydrated brain tumbles around my skull searching for any inkling of what he might be referring to. My cheeks burn hot. "Obviously not."

Inside the van, I spy the sun reflecting against a kitchen cabinet handle and a fret of the acoustic guitar leaning against it as he yanks the door shut behind him.

"You texted me," he explains. "A lot." He pulls his phone from his pocket and scrolls through the damning evidence: a humiliating wall of gray text bubbles. All from me. Every so often he reacts to one or attempts to respond, but my messages move from one topic to the next at a breakneck pace.

"Oh god." I hand him back the phone. If I had anything left in my stomach, I'd vomit it up. Right there on the pavement.

His forehead scrunches the way it does when he's trying not to laugh. "Don't be embarrassed, Beekman," he tells me, pulling me into his arms with his signature warmth, which I've never been able to resist. I can't help but lean into it. "I like it when you drink and meme. And I would've come if it was one text or a thousand. I've missed you. It's been way too long."

I huff a laugh into the collar of his T-shirt. We're about the same height, so my face always ends up in his neck. I don't know if he still smells like sugar donuts or if my brain has permanently grafted that smell onto him over the years, but it's nice, whatever it is. He smells the way he's always smelled to me. It's comforting to know some things never change, even when the world feels like a current that's sweeping my feet out from under me.

"How long can you stay?" I ask.

His chin drops onto my shoulder. "As long as you need." His voice is steady and sure, and I feel my defenses slip a little. Then he says, "But . . . I'm playing at a festival in Grand Marais next weekend."

There it is.

As much as Ethan teases me about my devotion to my calendar and the routine predictability of my life, his bursts of spontaneity are far more tedious. I could set a clock to Ethan's wanderlust. Just when you're starting to get used to him, he's itching to take off. Love it or hate it, it's who he's always been. His restlessness is my unremarkable constant.

"But I have nowhere to be all week." He says it like it's an eternity. For him, it probably is. "Are you hungry? It's been ages since someone's complained about the way I order cereal."

I pull my head back so I can properly rib him: face-to-face. "It's not just the *way* you order it. It's *that* you order it. Who orders cereal at a diner?"

"Someone with celiac," he says, even though we've had this particular argument countless times before.

"You're still hopeless without me, aren't you, Powell?"

His smile is so wide it reveals his elusive right cheek dimple. "An absolute disaster."

Chapter 3

Clothing Is Merely an Extension of a Plate

S O, IT'S LIKE part taproom, part dystopian art installation, but there's cornhole on the patio." I'm in my bed, cocooned in a fluffy robe, scanning a listicle entitled "18 New and Exciting Bars in the Twin Cities" and avoiding eye contact with the farmer's breakfast that was waiting for me on the bed when I finished showering the hangover off me.

Ethan winces at my description of the nearby bar, shaking his hair out like a dog. "I'm fine sticking around here. You don't need to entertain me." He's shaved and fresh from the shower in a faded concert tee the color of an oatmeal cookie, which clings a little to the damp spots on his chest. I direct my gaze back to my laptop screen.

Even though Ethan grew up an hour north of here, I can't help but do that little song and dance reserved for all old friends and extended family when they come to town. That desire to take ownership of their life and justify every small choice—from where they live, to their career, to the quality of the nearest coffee place. Not to mention, structured activities have historically provided an off-ramp out of our stilted long-distance-friend demeanor and on to our ordinary, comfortable dynamic.

"You didn't eat your eggs." He observes the mostly full plate next to me. He insisted on making me something when he realized exactly how hard I'd been hit by both Ruth and Chris respectively.

"I ate the potatoes," I argue. He tuts and moves my now-chilly scramble to the dresser. He replaces the plate with his body, sprawling out next to me on my bed, where my laptop sits between us like a barrier wall. I'm really wishing I'd kept so much as a folding chair in my Broke Divorcée: Everything Must Go sale. It's hard to dip my toes back into this newly face-to-face friendship when he's so . . . present. Making me breakfast, using my shower and washing machine, dampening my pillow with his wet hair.

"What about mini golf?" I suggest in a rush.

"You and your itineraries," he moans with a full-body movement that causes his knee to nudge my laptop. "Are you going to force me to go to an escape room after? Or do you have a Groupon for an aerial gymnastics class? Are we going on a double cooking-class date?"

I snort. "I wish. I think I'd fall over dead if one of my dates actually planned an activity beyond staring at each other over boba tea."

It was only a *date*, singular, and to the man's credit, the boba tea was at my suggestion—there's something so non-threatening about meeting a man for boba tea—but I'd rather walk into an intricate spiderweb than disclose this statistic to Ethan, who's possibly the only hetero man to leave a dating app due to the sheer volume of sexual inquiries. I'd rather take the boba-date body count to my deathbed, thank you.

He leans closer to inspect me. "You've started dating again? Wait. Chuck. Have you been going to escape rooms with *men*?"

Now I groan. Once Rich moved out, dating was something I was *expected* to do. I was supposed to be meeting up with fortysomething men seeking twentysomething women, and share a bruschetta platter while describing our jobs and listing siblings.

Just as single women revel in watching their favorite formerly "smug marrieds" flounder on Hinge, married women *love* to shove their divorced women friends in the direction of divorced men. In the eyes of married women, we go together like pairs of worn socks, and if I'm not actively seeking a second husband from the pool of discarded suitors, their antennae go up with one whiff of my "comfortably divorced woman" aroma. Suddenly, I'm inherently threatening, as though I'm going to spot their man at a Super Bowl party loading up a Wheat Thin with the glob of jalapeño popper dip that dripped onto his golf polo and be overcome by the carnal desire to take him for myself. As though my friends' husbands, men who regard their clothing as merely an extension of a plate, are my best option.

It took only one uncomfortable date for me to pack it in. What was the point? I know how it ends: arguing over the antique buffet neither of us liked but that we can no longer part with now that it carries a perplexing symbolic weight.

So I *tell* everyone I'm dating, even though I'm not. The path of least resistance and all that.

I shake off my unexpected moment of self-consciousness, answering him with a breezy, "Escape rooms right out of the gate? Absolutely not. I watch too much *Dateline* to let a strange man lock me in a room and force me to solve riddles." I get up and grab a crystal tumbler from the bar cart next to my bed. "But one time, my coworker set me up with her uncle, who took me to one of those rooms where you break stuff with a bat," I explain, pulling a Brita out of the minifridge.

His smile is smug. "An *uncle*? Your coworker must hate you."

"He was a youngish uncle, okay? I didn't make Stacy bust out a family tree, but I think there were some remarriages and severed branches in play."

He shakes his head when I lift a cup to offer him a drink. "Are we not going to talk about how you have a bar cart next to your bed like a 1960s bachelor?"

I shrug. "It looked weird alone in the dining room without any friends."

Rich and I got an offer on the house fully furnished without even listing it. Word had spread through the neighborhood that the newly minted Warrens had gone kaput. It didn't matter that I'd never taken Rich's name. Those aren't the scintillating details that interest busybodies in the relationship postmortem.

Still, they were right about the house. Rich didn't want it. He'd never wanted it. It's one of those shiny new builds that are made to look like carefully built Craftsman-style homes but were produced by a single developer, so that every house on the block is more or less identical. He said it reminded him of one of those fake neighborhoods constructed for nuclear missile tests. *But you love it*, he'd told me. *And it doesn't matter, so why have a fight about it?*

He was good at agreeing when we were together. Less so once we were apart.

Rich was only willing to sell the house to me if I met the price and terms of the offer. So I sold all the furniture we picked out together that he insisted I take—partially out of spite, but mostly because I needed the money.

Everything I couldn't part with found its way to the master

suite. It's temporary, of course, but every other space in the house is punishingly empty. Everywhere I look in the chef's kitchen, the formal living room, the basement gym, I see empty space. My bedroom is my safe place. It's the only room where I'm not constantly aware of my score on the ledger of a relationship where I came up undeniably short.

"The minifridge is a newer addition. It got annoying walking downstairs for water when I had everything else in here. It's kind of nice, though, right? Like a hotel. And I use the space in the door for my liquid collagen, my facial creams, my serums . . ."

Ethan sits up. "How am I supposed to believe you're 'totally fine' when you're drunk-spamming my phone and becoming a full-blown 'bed person'?"

My eyebrows knit together.

"I'm being serious," he continues. "I worry about you. I only challenged you to that phone Scrabble game because I know you love beating me in board games, and you haven't taken a turn in over a month."

Something stirs inside at the thought of him refreshing the app, waiting for me to put electronic tiles on a board. It's the nostalgia of it, the childlike sweetness of biking over to your friend's house and begging them to come out and play.

"You have nothing to worry about. My bed lifestyle is totally under control."

"Lifestyle?" He grins too wide, and I immediately regret my choice of words when describing what is simply me eating chicken tikka masala with a towel on my lap.

"You cart a bed everywhere you go. You routinely bring women home to your van down by the river like a Chris Farley sketch and beg them to have sex with you."

He side-eyes me. "First, I play guitar—"

"Hands down, your worst quality."

"—so I've never had to 'beg for sex,' as you so eloquently put it, and second, I can do absolutely anything in my van that one of your khaki-clad house-men can do. I have a full bed and can even make breakfast on my hot plate."

"Wow," I respond, my voice flat. "You really roll out the red carpet for these women, don't you?"

"What can I say? I'm a caretaker."

He gives me that smug hot-guy look that drives me up the wall. Duty-bound to bring him back down to earth, I grab something from the dish next to the martini shaker and chuck it at him. "You are such a douche," I tell him.

He catches it in his chest like a football. Then he turns the object in his hands and looks up at me. It's a penis straw. *The* penis straw.

His expression, his voice, they're both cracking open when he asks, "You kept this?"

Ethan gives me the full force of his attention, which with Ethan is . . . intense. Absorbing. The birds silence. The world blurs. When Ethan looks at you, he *really* looks at you. It's a level of eye contact that requires getting used to, and, as it's been so long since I've been confronted by it, I'm more than a little unprepared.

I swallow down whatever's buzzing in my throat and put on my most casual voice. "Kept what?" The lie turns my stomach, but I don't want him to think my keeping it *means* something. Or that I'm still holding on to the things he said the night of my bachelorette party. Or that I thought that that moment was anything beyond Ethan being Ethan, unfiltered and pro-foundly unserious.

I can't read his face, and he doesn't say more. It's that secret bit of him I don't get access to. I hate that bit. But the moment is interrupted by a missed FaceTime call from Laurel that pops up on the bottom corner of my laptop screen.

Our conversation from yesterday bursts into the front of my brain. *Did my sister ask? Did Petey accept? Are they already fighting about wedding hashtags and the liability of animal ring bearers?* I'm both anxious to know and eager to avoid any acknowledgment that this proposal idea isn't an elaborate alcohol-induced hallucination.

I sit back down on the bed and type out a quick message.

Charley: sorry. missed your call.

I'm choosing avoidance. Like a coward.

"I didn't know phallic drinkware was still the bachelorette party favor of choice," he comments.

"In a campy, ironic sense. The last bachelorette party I went to also had travel-sized hibiscus-lube party favors I have zero use for. If you want to rummage around the bathroom for that, be my guest."

He shifts in the bed, his eyes brighter, like despite the hiccup between us, he's mostly back to his normal Ethan-y self. "I'm good. I actually make my own."

I wriggle on the bed, wincing both at him and at a hangover so bad that even my hair hurts. "Oh god, Powell. Could *never* be me."

He grins at the reference to one of our favorite games. In college, whenever I witnessed him wearing five-toe shoes or he caught me setting an egg timer before returning a guy's text (for very legitimate and scientific reasons), we'd look at each other and say, "Could never be me." Our gentle reminder to each other that we were both eternally undatable disasters and that you couldn't pay either of us to trade places with the poor souls forced to date us. It's funny in that melancholy way depressingly true things are funny.

His lips curl up higher until his smile pinches the corners of his eyes. "Really? Just for that?"

"I've said it before for less." I feel it happen. The nearly undetectable curtain of discomfort lifts, and we're *us* again. We're Charley and Ethan and it's just as it's always been. No more slightly stilted conversation. No more awkwardness. We're friends.

I think he feels the palpable shift too, because he throws the penis straw back at me and heads into the bathroom again. The tension in my shoulders releases.

"I just have one question." I hear his voice echoing from inside the linen closet over the sounds of backstock shampoo bottles colliding into each other. "Would you still be my friend if I told you I was Iron Man?" He jumps out of the bathroom in the gold-plated LED light therapy mask I bought during the same retail fugue state when I got the handbag I can't bring myself to return.

My lips twitch without my permission. "Seriously, my life is being held together by my Notes app and a punishingly thorough twelve-step skin-care routine, so if you break my LED light mask, I *will* kill you and no one will ever find the body."

"Ooh. Who told you ruthless Mob Boss Chuck is my very favorite Chuck?" He flops back on my bed, bouncing me and my laptop like a pool noodle in a tidal wave.

"I'm serious, Powell! I've thought about it a lot this past year, and I think I could be capable of violence if properly provoked."

He bobs and weaves his head away from me, my hungover brain sloshing around my skull. It takes a few seconds for either of us to register that my laptop is ringing.

I groan at the sound. Ethan and I are finally starting to feel like us. The last thing I need is Hurricane Laurel and her Petey drama. Ethan tends to regard their chaotic push-pull with an unearned gravity. Any discussion will undoubtedly unravel our day, devolving into lengthy dissections of breakup timelines, and I was starting to look forward to an afternoon basket of cheesy fries.

Ethan peers at me through my light mask. "Did I summon an uncle?" he asks, gesturing at the ringing computer. "Or the ex-father-in-law your work nemesis is setting you up with?"

"Stacy's not—It's Laurel. She's been on a FaceTiming kick since the whole . . ." I do a little *yada yada* gesture with my hand.

My marriage fell apart, my life exploded, yada yada.

He nods. "You going to get it?"

"I'm sure it's nothing."

"Answer it. I don't mind."

I hesitate but then suck it up and accept the call. Her face and lavender space buns fill the screen, framed by lush green leaves and imposing pine tree trunks.

"Lolo!" Ethan yells. His enthusiasm takes me by surprise. I look around out of instinct to make sure we're not bothering anyone and then remember we're alone in my room.

"Jason Voorhees?" she squeals back, which gets Ethan to finally remove the mask. Her face relaxes. "Ethel!" Laurel rarely calls him Ethan to his face, preferring to riff on the first letter. "This is perfect. You're both here."

"E's there too?" a familiar voice asks out of frame. The sound of it clenches my gut.

Maybe she hasn't asked yet. Maybe she changed her mind.

Laurel's head swivels toward the man off-screen. "See? I knew she was going to draw him out of whatever sad rest stop he was parked in. Did you listen to my voice memo last night about the spot we're camped by? Wet Ted's Canoe Outfitters?"

I glance at the words Sharpied on my hand. Well, that solves *that* mystery.

Ethan leans closer to the phone. "Is that Pete's arm?"

Petey pops into view. Laurel brightens as he presses his head to hers affectionately. At least they *look* happy. That's something.

"Hey!" He wraps his arms around Laurel and squeezes. "Hi. What's going on, E? What are you doing at Charley's?" Petey always says "hi" at least three ways and has never been anything less than genuinely ecstatic to see any person. Ever. The sweet doofus is so upbeat and good-natured, it borders on ridiculous. He busts into every conversation like a ripped Kool-Aid Man, shifting the equilibrium until everyone in his presence is grinning like an idiot. Petey simply has that effect on people.

"I have some free time before a festival next weekend. Then I might head east through Canada or maybe west to Montana."

He looks to me, as though seeking confirmation on his itinerary for Peter Pan–ing about the United States, but I ignore it. "Is there a reason for this call?" I hasten to ask. Anticipatory nausea sits in the pit of my stomach. I need her to put me out of my misery.

"Do you want to tell them?" They look at each other with a manic, electric energy that seems to crackle around them.

My stomach somersaults. "Tell us what?" I know what's happening. I can't *believe* it's happening, but I know it is.

Laurel breathes in deep, and any lingering hope I had plummets through the floor beneath me.

Don't say it. Don't say it.

"I asked Peter to marry me, and he said yes!"

So it happened.

Okay. It's okay. I expected this part.

"And we're eloping this weekend," Petey adds on.

Adrenaline surges through my veins, and I want to grab something, anything, but my fingers have turned into bricks.

Eloping?

"Finally!" Ethan cheers while my features arrange themselves into an *Are you serious right now?* face before I can stop it. My chest burns from the inside out until a red, splotchy stress rash blooms on my neck. And I know exactly how bad it looks, because I can see it in the stupid FaceTime window.

They can't do this now. It's too soon. The only thing that was stopping me from truly losing it was the knowledge they'd never stay together long enough to plan a wedding. I might be new to this whole "marriage is bullshit" thing, but Laurel was a founding member of the forever-single club.

She was mad at me—actually stopped speaking to me for three days—when I wouldn't self-fund a "Shes and Theys Only" compound for us to retire on. Her favorite celebrity coupling has always been Goldie Hawn and Kurt Russell, because they had "the good sense to keep the state of California out of their relationship." When I told her Rich proposed, she first responded, "We're too young to get married." Then, once the shock wore off, she opted for the more pragmatic "You know that you're much more likely to be murdered by your husband than anyone else. Statistically speaking."

But as commitment averse as Laurel is, she's just as passionate and impulsive.

"Elopement. Wow," is all I can bring myself to say. It's an abysmal recovery. I remind myself to breathe—in, out, in, out—until my thoughts slow enough to put a sentence together. "You don't think this is a little sudden?"

Laurel's face twitches with tiny glimpses of sadness and hurt that disappear with Petey's kiss to her cheek.

"It took fifteen years to get us here," he tells us. "I don't want to wait anymore. And with Lo and I camping this week before the next Timber Creek session, it feels like we're supposed to get married right now. Here." He gestures around them at their secluded spot surrounded by forest where no one would hear them scream.

Ethan nudges me with his shoulder. "We're so happy for you guys."

I feel each second tick by as time slips away from me. *She'll be married by the end of the day*, I think. I debate how effectively I'll be able to talk her out of this via FaceTime against other possible options: A well-timed heart attack? Interdimensional time travel? A light kidnapping? I'm still ruling out the gross misdemeanors when I stall by asking, "Have you told Mom and Dad?"

"Uh, no," she answers slowly, as though the very notion of calling our parents is insane, which makes sense because I'm not sure she's so much as texted our parents since I reminded her to last Christmas. "I don't think Derek or Mia needs to be part of this."

But I could be, I think. The idea tunnels into my brain, burrowing deeper with each passing second.

"Where are we meeting you for the ceremony?" The question pours out of my mouth in a verbal deluge.

Ethan eyes me because we both heard how they didn't invite us. It was very clear that my sister was simply delivering information and *not* inviting me to her elopement, but if I want to slam the brakes on this wedding, this might be my only way.

By the look in her eyes, she knows I'm up to something stupid. Reckless impulsivity might be a Beekman family trait.

Lucky for me, Petey is one of those people who foolishly believes humans to be innately honest and well-intentioned creatures. "That'd be perfect, Char!" Petey responds, a smile erupting across his face.

Laurel's eyes dart between her fiancé and the screen. "Are you sure? It's like five hours of driving, one hour of canoeing—"

"One *hour* of canoeing?" I can't help but object to that part.

"—and you've literally never taken a vacation. Ever."

"And what better reason is there to play hooky from work than you? My beloved sister," I ad-lib, anxiety jiggling my leg. "Come on, Laur. You need a . . . witness . . ."

She purses her lips. This is so unlike me. She knows it. I know it. But Petey—that sweet, sweet, hot dummy—doesn't. "Couldn't agree more!" he cheers.

Ethan peers at me in the FaceTime window, no doubt detecting the odd, manic vibrations bouncing off my skin. "But if you're looking for an intimate thing, we totally get it . . ." He trails off, providing them a much-deserved out.

"It'll still be intimate," I slide in, desperate to make this happen as the sweat pools in the palms of my hands.

"You really don't—" she starts to hedge, but I cut her off.

"Laurel, you walked me down the aisle. You can't *get married* without me."

The sentence sounds simple enough, but I watch my words smack her between the eyes. Try as I might to remain wry and self-deprecating, there's no denying that I drag my marital disappointments around like a three-piece luggage set, and now I've dropped them between us. I've made my divorce an obstacle, an anxious flyer staking out the boarding gate.

My sister's expression melts from guarded to guilty and lands somewhere near pitying. Which is fine. She can pity me all she wants. So long as she doesn't get married before I get there.

Because this isn't her. And if I can talk to her, face-to-face, I know she'll rethink things. She'll see sense. She'll have to.

I squeeze my eyes shut, begging shamelessly now. "Please. Promise you won't get married without me."

"Okay," she agrees, and relief crests over my body.

When things inevitably fall apart, she won't carry the pain and humiliation of a failed marriage when a breakup would suffice. Us Beekman women don't all need to make the same mistakes over and over.

"We can be there in six hours," I promise. "Seven tops."

Chapter 4

What Are You Doing on My Jeggings?

I THINK I WAS the only one who saw the boys when Mom pulled into the driveway.

The two of them were standing in the street in front of the brick house next door. The taller one was wearing a faded green jersey with a star on the front and holding a hockey stick. He had tan skin and dark hair that he was pushing out of his face when he yelled "Car!" at the shorter boy standing in front of a torn net.

That was when they stopped playing to look into our car window while my mom turned off the ignition. I knew the look on their faces well: the *Are those new kids?* look. It was the small-town equivalent of a celebrity sighting. I'd seen it enough times to know I'd never again be as fascinating to them as I was at that exact moment.

But then the shorter boy tilted his head and smiled—big and warm. He had the kind of smile that crowded out the rest of his pale face. It made me too aware of myself. Between the crusted drool on my chin from my seven-hour Dramamine-induced nap, the ginormous pimple on my forehead, and the once cute-messy bun that at some point in said nap had migrated across my scalp into something just regular-messy, I had no choice but to look down. He rubbed his buzzed head and looked away too.

My mom twisted over the center console to look at Laurel and me. "You're going to love the house," she said.

We'd been driving for an eternity. That's what Laurel kept saying. *An eternity.* But we'd finally made it to Lewellen, Minnesota.

"He sent me pictures of the place," she told us. "There's a big farmhouse table in the kitchen with a bell. Should I ring the bell for dinner every night?" Mom met my eyes in the mirror. She was happy, and I could see she wanted us to be happy.

But Laurel wasn't happy. "Who cares about this house? It's not like any of the stuff in it is ours."

Dad had gotten a position at the nearby college as a photography and film professor and was renting a two-bedroom house "fully furnished." I understood this to mean that the pull-out trundle and teal-painted dresser Laurel and I would be sharing were a *stranger's* pull-out trundle and teal-painted dresser, but Mom didn't like when we reminded her of that.

Mom closed her eyes and let out a long breath. "Don't say that to your dad, Laurel. It's rude."

"How is that rude? It's literally . . ."

Their argumentative jibber-jabber faded into the background like rain on a windshield. I looked for the boys again when I swung open the car door, but they were already gone.

Laurel sighed theatrically at the creak of the front door, and Dad spun clear of her, knowing his best chance at a warm reception was with me.

"My girls," he said, squeezing me hard enough that my legs lifted off the ground. Laurel's eye roll was so big, it got the whole neck and shoulders involved, and when he finally approached her, it was with a cautious, one-armed back pat that made her flinch.

Finally, he kissed Mom. It was one of those too-intense kisses I didn't like. He always kissed her like that after they fought, like he was a battle-worn soldier returning from war. It seemed so strange to act like that when the war was only ever between the two of them. The kiss was a stark reminder that we were in this furnished house in this tiny town I'd never heard of because my parents were "dating" again.

Mom had sounded excited about it when she first told Laurel and me. Laurel was *not* excited and made her opinions on the subject *very* clear. I, on the other hand, hadn't known what to say, but only because I hadn't understood what it meant.

Melanie Todrick, who was the fastest runner in seventh grade (until she got boobs), used to tell me all about her dates with ninth graders during Drop Everything and Read time.

"We go to Jamba Juice and talk about track," she answered, smacking her gum. "Or about summer camp, if they don't run track." She braided the ends of her long, shiny hair when she talked, and I wondered if older boys liked that about her. I always wore mine in a ponytail. "On dates, you have to get to know what the other person likes so you can decide if you want to go on more dates. Like to the movies."

I couldn't imagine my parents had anything left to learn about each other. For as long as I could remember, they'd argued and then made up. Argued. Made up. Until they stopped making up. I wasn't confident a movie and a Peanut Butter Moo'd smoothie would change things, though maybe old-people dates were different from Melanie Todrick's.

Pangs of anxiety fluttered beneath my ribs as Laurel and I waited in the driveway for our parents' kiss to end. The air was sticky and hot from the summer sun beating down overhead, and I could already feel beads of sweat building over my sunblock.

Suddenly, Laurel was right beside me.

"We'll be okay if this doesn't work, Charley. I promise," she whispered.

She walked into the house before I could say anything back, but for the first time since Mom told us about dating Dad and moving to this town, I was grateful to be sharing a trundle bed with Laurel. My sister's unshakable confidence had that effect on me.

"I have something special for you, Charlotte," Dad said, tilting his head in the direction of the back door. I followed him through the house and onto the deck. Wood planks creaked beneath my feet with each step. "I can teach you how to use it this summer," he said, holding up a digital camera that barely fit in my hands.

"That sounds good. But it's okay if you can't," I told him, anticipating how plans with Dad had a tendency to change.

He cleared his throat in a way that made me stand a bit straighter. "It's going to be different here, okay? I promised your mom it would be. I'm not going anywhere this time."

I nodded. I wasn't sure I believed him, but if my face showed any doubt, he didn't seem to notice. "The most important thing about photography is the light." He nudged my feet toward the edge of the deck and stood behind me, lifting the viewfinder up to my face. "If you only know light, you know most of it. And the shutter button. You have to hold it to focus, but first . . ."

He was going on about aperture size and framing my shot as I tilted the camera a little, searching for the angle where the setting sun didn't blow out the trees and houses but instead coated the world in an ethereal honey, when those boys appeared on the back porch seemingly out of nowhere. The one with the nearly shaved head waved at me in the viewfinder.

I took a picture of him without thinking, enjoying the satisfying click under my finger. Even though I didn't know the boy and probably wouldn't remember him whenever we moved on, it felt good to preserve that wave while it was meant for me. Magic. Like capturing a fairy in a jar.

"Do you guys live here now?" the other boy shouted from behind him.

"Yeah," I shouted back, because we did, and maybe it *would* be different this time.

"Good," the first boy said. "That's Petey." He pointed at his friend. "And I'm Ethan."

"Here two minutes, and you're already attracting the neighborhood boys," Dad cut in. I lowered my camera, feeling my face get hot. "I'm just messing with you kids. Why don't you two come in where there's air-conditioning and meet the girls. I'm about to put some hot dogs on the grill."

The boy in the hockey jersey opened his mouth to say something but the shorter one, Ethan, spoke first. "Thank you, sir," he answered. Then both boys crossed the lawn, wordlessly following me into the house and then in the direction of my new bedroom.

They watched me closely as though it was my space and they were waiting to see how they fit. I sat in the beanbag chair, pretending I always sat there like that.

They took this as their cue to plop themselves onto the lower trundle mattress. The room looked cramped with all of us in it. Somehow, in the ten minutes I'd been outside with Dad, Laurel had already managed to scatter clothes on every surface. Chipped teal paint peeked out beneath the explosion of skinny jeans, PINK sweats, and distressed band tees from concerts we hadn't attended. The curling iron Laurel used to achieve her perfect Serena van der Woodsen waves was already plugged in and staking a claim on the space in front of the single mirror. It wasn't turned on, though. Of that, I was mostly sure.

"Apparently"—Laurel swung herself inside the room, clutching the door frame for support, like her entrance was part of a dance—"'Minnesota Derek' cooks. Oh!" she blurted, eyeing the two strangers I'd collected from the backyard like they were the toads I'd hidden in the closet of our Florida house when I was nine. "Who are you, and what are you doing on my jeggings?" she asked, leveling an accusatory glare at Petey and yanking the denim-looking fabric out from under his leg.

Laurel was fifteen, and though she'd also never had a boyfriend, she was comfortable around boys in a way I, at thirteen, was not. She could be funny and enchanting and not at all affected by the way their throats looked different when they swallowed. I felt edgy around boys, like I was on one of those talent shows with a panel of judges, paralyzed by the pressure to impress as sweat collected on my upper lip.

"Is Derek your dad?" Petey asked Laurel, ignoring her jeggings-related inquiry.

Laurel was calling our dad "Derek" as a form of rebellion, but as Mom cared about it way more than Dad seemed to, she'd likely be switching strategies soon.

"Dad invited Ethan and Petey in for hot dogs," I said, answering both of their questions.

"Is that your camera?" Ethan asked, and I grinned proudly. He smiled at me like it impressed him. For a second, I felt guilty, but his expression was so warm and soft. The longer I looked at him, the more my insides felt like a microwave mug cake.

"Can I put some music on?" Ethan asked, pointing to an alarm clock sitting in the center of the bed. I unraveled the cord and wiped the docking station clean with my sleeve before plugging it into the outlet near my feet. Immediately, it came to life, glowing, beeping, and angrily blinking "12:00 AM" at us until Ethan silenced it by pressing his iPod into the docking station. He selected a playlist called "happier stuff," which was a lot of newer indie folk music like Bon Iver and the Decemberists, with the occasional appearance of men my dad listened to, like Johnny Cash and Leonard Cohen. None of it was markedly joyful, and since there wasn't a playlist called "sadder stuff," I assumed that the rest of his music collection was deeply depressing.

They asked us where we'd moved from and other new-kid trivia. Laurel and I asked about Petey's and Ethan's ages and hobbies. Petey was older than Ethan and starting high school but still a grade below Laurel. Ethan liked music and playing street hockey, but Petey took hockey much more seriously. His dad was the coach of his summer league.

"I wanna play in the NHL," Petey told us. "I'm applying to a boarding school up north, and if I get in, my coaches will be actual former NHL players. It's gonna be sick." He didn't sound boastful or like he was trying to impress us. He was sharing something essential about himself. Even so, Laurel did look a little bit impressed.

"Do you wanna go see something cool?" Ethan asked us.

"Yes!" Laurel agreed on instinct, just as I responded, "What do you mean?"

"I thought we were eating hot dogs," I added, to take a bit of the sting out of the fact that I did *not* want to go to a second location with a couple of boys I'd just met, even if they were starting to grow on me.

"I can't. I can't eat hot dog buns or anything the buns might've touched. Bread makes me sick."

"Why didn't you say anything earlier?" I asked.

"Yeah, bro. Why didn't you?" Petey swiveled his head toward Ethan like this was a familiar disagreement between the two of them.

He shrugged. "I'm fine. I didn't want to make it a thing."

"We can climb out the window," Laurel suggested, like it wouldn't be at all alarming for our parents to find the bedroom empty when they popped back in with a plate of hot dogs and potato salad.

"It looks painted shut," Ethan observed.

"I have a knife," Petey offered without missing a beat.

"You'll need swimsuits," Ethan told us, and Laurel instantly swiped a one-piece from the wreckage of her suitcase explosion.

"Where are we going?" No one answered me. "Why are we climbing out of the window?" I asked, trying again for *any* explanation.

"It's fun," Laurel finally responded from the closet. She was changing into her one-piece while Petey chiseled at the window frame, and Ethan was keeping watch for our parents at the bedroom door. This group was already a runaway train. "And this way, we won't need to explain to Derek that we don't want his performative Sitcom Dad lunch. It's a win-win."

"But . . ." My head pinged between the three of them, heart racing. "We're going to get into trouble."

Laurel emerged from the closet in a tie-dye swimsuit and denim shorts. She rolled her eyes at me. "Our dad left us to film a movie about penguins for two years without so much as a Skype call. I think we've banked enough paternal guilt to sneak out in broad daylight."

My heart smarted at the casual mention of how easy the two of us were to abandon. I looked for Ethan's reaction, but his eyes were on the hallway.

"Jesus, enough with the knife," Laurel instructed Petey, her new partner in crime.

He laughed. "You're sort of mean," he replied, visibly pleased. Together, they jerked the window open with an ear-piercing CREAK.

We all froze.

One second passed. Two. Then Ethan mouthed, *Go.*

————

They'd never told us where we were going, but by that point, it was too late to ask. We rode through the backwoods of town on a dirt path that was only slightly wider than a bike wheel, me standing on Ethan's bike pegs and Laurel sitting on Petey's handlebars.

"You can hold my shoulders," he'd told me, so I had. I could feel his shoulder bones under his cotton T-shirt, and this close he smelled like powdered sugar.

The trail was mostly flat until the very end. Ethan struggled up the hill before I finally hopped off. He didn't have time to get too embarrassed because Petey and Laurel toppled over in slow motion about a second later, and then we walked the bikes up the hill like that was the plan all along.

"Welcome to the falls," Petey said when we arrived at a lake surrounded by trees and a few houses we could just barely make out in the distance. A pile of bikes had been dropped at the base of a treacherous trail that led up the side of a waterfall with a sign reading: Lake Lewellen. No climbing, diving, or ice luging. A giddy squeal at the top of the hill followed by a splash signaled that the people of Lewellen were comfortable taking their chances with at least two out of the three.

Ethan and Petey nodded and fist bumped other kids all the way to the top as we followed behind. They told the kids our names too, but their voices could barely compete with the sound of water beating against the lake's surface in a frothy collision of waves.

"Why did you bring that big dorky camera?" Laurel said into my ear while we hiked up the steep path.

I didn't say anything but continued toying with the stiff strap so the camera would fall just so on my hip. As soon as I got it right, I wasn't sure where my hands should go and the process started over again.

"Hey," Laurel said, grabbing the hand that wasn't swinging the way a normal person's does because I'd made the fatal mistake of thinking about its swing. "They're just boys, Charley, and we're two fascinating *enigmas*." Laurel had learned the word "enigma" watching *Top Model* reruns and it'd become the only way she described herself. But this was the first time she was using the word to describe *me*. Even though I still wasn't convinced she was using it properly. "They're more afraid of us than we are of them."

I nodded and kept walking, feeling a little steadier with my sister's hand in mine.

Laurel could be like that sometimes. Though she mostly treated me like an embarrassing appendage, she could transform into a fiercely protective older sister at the first sign of a threat.

Petey wanted to jump first when we got to the top, which ignited Laurel's competitive streak. It wasn't that high up, but when I looked down at the lake, the bodies cooling off at the bottom looked like bugs to be crushed. There was no railing or lifeguard. No regulation high dive. It was a cliffside the Lewellenians had discovered through potentially deadly trial and error, the angry water foaming white beneath like a rabid dog.

"Wanna take pictures instead?" Ethan's head pointed to the camera dangling at my hip. "We don't have to jump today."

"I'm not wearing a swimsuit." He nodded as though he knew that wasn't the real reason I wasn't jumping but wasn't going to push it.

So we took pictures. At first, I pretended to know how to use the camera, but I gave up the act as soon as he noticed I'd forgotten to turn the camera on.

"It's cool you're teaching yourself photography. I taught myself how to play guitar."

"My *dad's* teaching me photography. He's a filmmaker, mostly documentaries. We used to travel with him on shoots all over, and now he's teaching at the college." I didn't tell him the part about all the times he *didn't* take us with him, because as an experienced "new kid," I knew that maintaining mystery was key.

"That's so cool. I've never left Minnesota. My parents own

the Donut Barn." He leaned his back against a tree and squinted up at the sun. "It doesn't give us a lot of freedom to go anywhere new."

"Do you have somewhere you want to go?"

He shrugged. "Anywhere, I guess."

He closed his eyes and lifted his chin like a dog stretching into the sun while I took more pictures. I liked the way the sun glittered on the water and made it look like a lit sparkler. The way Petey sliced his feet through the air like he was on ice skates as he plummeted to the water. The way the tips of Laurel's hair floated on the surface and surrounded her like she wore a crown. If there weren't people around, it might've made for more aesthetic photos, but the messy scenes most accurately captured the *feeling* of it. The start of summer and all the endless potential in the lengthening days.

With the camera, I felt outside of myself. Like I could exist in the present and still know I was making memories. The camera filtered the afternoon in sepia tones. It was one of those rare, perfect instances when I knew I was living in a moment I'd always remember while it was still happening.

The timer was running on our life here. Dad would leave, and then so would we. Maybe we'd follow him a little while, but eventually school and money would get in the way and we'd have to stay behind someplace that he'd promise to visit and then never would. I wouldn't have lazy Saturdays by the lake much longer, but with pictures, I could take it with me.

I was playing with the zoom when Ethan's shoulder nudged its way into the frame.

"How many freckles do you have on your arms?" I asked, zooming in and out. "Some of your moles aren't even moles. They're, like, clusters of freckles."

"Dunno." Without warning, he collapsed to the ground like a rag doll. "Count them. I'll wait."

The goofiness of this boy belly-flopping to the ground caught me so off guard that the spit-laugh I tried to hide from new people sputtered out from between my teeth. Ethan smiled like it pleased him to elicit something so embarrassing from me. I always figured there were only so many kinds of smiles, but I'd never seen a smile exactly like Ethan's. I wanted to take a picture of it again.

"I'm not sure I could count them if I tried. It's destined to be one of the great mysteries of the universe."

"I hope there's more out there to discover than my freckles." He sat back up. "I like that you're a girl Charley. The only one I know is the guy who owns the hardware store, but he mostly goes by Chuck."

"My dad says I was named after portrait artist Chuck Close, but I don't think that's actually true. No one's ever called me that at least."

"Okay, now I *only* wanna call you Chuck."

It was hard to explain what happened next. It was as though the air shifted. Something passed between us that seemed real enough to hold in my hands, like I'd look back later and identify it as the exact second Ethan Powell became my friend.

I lifted the camera and took a picture. I wanted to be sure I could take this feeling with me to the next place.

Chapter 5

Don't Be. Do.

THE MINUTE WE got off the phone with Laurel, I jammed everything within arm's reach into a weekender bag and shoved Ethan back into his van. Ethan didn't need to pack anything, of course, as we were traveling in his dwelling.

We've been on the road only forty minutes, but after an inconveniently timed bathroom emergency—I had to pee the moment we left my driveway and tried to will away the building pressure in my bladder with the power of thought—we're already off the rails and parked in front of a combination Kwik Trip / Dairy Queen Grill and Chill.

While taking off on a whim is simply a Tuesday for Ethan, it is *completely* out of character for me. My last vacation was my honeymoon. Rich and I spent five months planning every detail down to the service station stops on the way to Lake Geneva, Wisconsin, and I still ended it two days early, because I couldn't relax so far out of my comfort zone.

I was imagining every possible worst-case scenario occurring back at the office, in our house, or with Laurel. What if Pamela finally handed me one of the software startups I'd been begging her to put me on and I wasn't around to jump on it?

What if the ants made a comeback in the downstairs laundry room and established a new society in front of the dryer by the time we returned? What if Laurel got in another fight with her roommate and the treehouse Airbnb she booked wasn't the architectural wonder superhost Satchel promised but a literal children's treehouse of the Fisher-Price variety? Why hadn't Ethan texted me anything in days?

But here I was, my arms overflowing with everything Kwik Trip has to offer, stomping through the convenience store parking lot in the direction of Ethan's van home, feeling that same honeymoon anxiety starting to spike.

"Have you ever heard of a more Laurel-and-Petey thing in your life?" I ask, maneuvering my feet around a suspiciously hued Aquafina bottle lying in the parking lot like a live grenade.

"You mean besides the time they almost got married on a dare?" Ethan's question is rhetorical, and kind of rude, considering I'm mid-freakout. But he doesn't seem to register that from the driver's seat.

"Why couldn't they just keep their chaotic dynamic platonic like we did?" I parry through gritted teeth. Two can play the infuriating rhetorical questions game.

When I try to open the passenger door with the only two fingertips I can spare, the handle snaps back down. I try again, but there's no movement.

Ethan eyes my haul. "Oh good. You're still weird about hydration," he says dryly, stretching his arms through the window to take a couple of the water bottles from me, freeing up the hand that isn't cradling four extra-large Fiji waters and two lemon-lime Gatorades like a newborn baby.

I fling open the door and drop my goods onto the beige

leather captain's seat. The front control panel is oversized and spotless. Everything about it screams "new" and "luxurious," which are words I've never associated with camper vans. The buttons and knobs yell at me with all-caps abbreviations I don't recognize. I'd sooner assume I've been thrown into the cockpit of a small plane than inside Ethan's motorized house.

I push my sunglasses into my hair, and the sharp stab above my eye is instantaneous. "I'm still hungover, Powell, and I doubt the woods have a clean tap." I hunch in front of the passenger seat to tuck my bottles in every corner of available storage. My hip knocks a knob that kicks on a Minnesota Public Radio station, and Ethan switches it off.

His eyes drift down to the rigid set of my shoulders. "You okay, Beekman?" There's something about the timbre of his voice that turns it into a command: *Be okay, Beekman. You're going to be okay.* And then, suddenly, I am. Or my body is. My life, however, remains in shambles.

He's always had that effect on me, this steadying siren only I can hear. It's his incredibly specific (and useless) superpower.

I don't realize how choppy my breathing has gotten until it slows back down to normal. Ethan takes me in, deciding how he'll handle the woman in front of him. He must decide I'm well enough to meet with our normal antagonism. "This is a lot of plastic, Beek. Did you pack that Corkcicle bottle I got you for Christmas?"

"Oh good." I cut him off before he can step onto his up-cycled soapbox. Ever since a young Ethan watched a particularly incendiary rerun of *Captain Planet*, he's been a dogmatic—and somewhat judgy—advocate on behalf of Earth. "You're still weird about single-use plastic."

I unscrew my Gatorade and make a big show of taking a

sip. His brow furrows in such adorable irritation that I can't help but let a teasing smile creep up the corner of my mouth.

He fastens his seat belt with a click. "What?" He wipes his face self-consciously, as though my amusement is not to be trusted.

"I'm just enjoying you in your natural habitat." I gesture between the dumpster and the bike rack in front of us, which is securing various rusted-out parts, the sum of which does not add up to a whole bike.

"The Kwik Trip parking lot is *not* my natural habitat," he objects, reaching for the glove box. His arm brushes against my bare legs as he pops it open, and a satisfying tingle ripples from the point of contact. I've been so touch starved since my divorce that every swipe of skin from the FedEx guy or Barista Nancy or even Ethan has left me twitching for more.

But he tosses a bag into my lap, unaffected.

"A peace offering. Friends again?" He tugs the gearshift.

I turn the package on my lap and beam. It's chocolate, the individually wrapped ones with inspirational quotes. He began mailing bags of them to me in law school. My "study diet," he called it.

Sometime in the second semester of 1L year—when even the strong ones were starting to snap under the pressure—I fell into a bleak bout of anxiety-fueled superstition. I couldn't walk into a test without unwrapping a Dove Promises chocolate and reading the message. It wasn't that any of the wrappers were particularly insightful—they definitely weren't—but the ritual was essential. Reading "Calories only exist if you count them" or "Hands are meant to be held" just before opening that blue book and regurgitating everything I wished

I didn't know about the rule against perpetuities was a security blanket I desperately needed.

Twenty minutes before my property final, I realized I'd run out and called Ethan so he could talk me down.

Do they sell them at the bookstore? he asked me, voice crackling over the atrocious phone connection. He was somewhere near Vancouver at the time, opening for a big indie rock band on the Canadian leg of their tour.

It has to be one you send. It's dumb. I know it's dumb. I'm being dumb.

You're not being dumb, he assured me. *If you need a Dove Promise from me, I'll get you a Dove Promise. Just trust me, okay?*

The weirdest part was, I *did* trust him. It didn't make any sense to, but his superpowers were strong, even internationally. He had this confidence in his voice that soaked into my skin like rain.

Seconds before I walked into the exam, his text came through. It was a picture of his hand, and between his long, dexterous fingers was a chocolate wrapper that read "Don't be. Do," followed by a message: **I don't know what that means, but I know you're going to kick adverse possession in the ass.**

And I did. Even after I graduated, he still sent the occasional bag of chocolates from the road.

"Yes! How did you know I've been craving these?" I greedily pop open the bag in the passenger seat.

"I can sense it across continents." He pulls onto the frontage road headed north. The air-conditioning kicks back on, circulating the scents of sunscreen and the inexplicably happy basil plant that hangs over Ethan's kitchen counter.

"I don't know why you're so surprised about Lo and Pete," he says, checking his blind spot. His face is filled with such unbridled affection for them. If I didn't know any better, I'd assume this wedding was a good thing. "They were always going to get hitched like this."

"Don't say 'hitched,'" I beg around the half-eaten chocolate in my mouth. "It makes it sound even more unserious than it already is."

"I think you could stand to be a bit more open-minded about relationships. Not everyone needs to be . . ." He trails off, noticing the corner into which he's painted himself.

"Me and Rich?" I ask, finishing his thought for him. He has the decency to appear a little sheepish. "Look. Would I have liked my marriage to have lasted longer than a year? Of course. I'd also like to be farther along in my career and have the confidence to wear leopard as a neutral, but sometimes we don't get everything we want just because we want it. Regardless of my marital track record, I know my sister. I can tell she's not thinking straight. This whole wedding-crashing mission . . ." I circle my finger around the van. "It's for her. It's not as though I'm *excited* to reenact *Deliverance* with you. I'm trying to prevent my sister from making the biggest mistake of her life."

Ethan will never believe it—he has a soft spot for well-meaning disasters—but Laurel and Petey are doomed. This is the same woman who dumped a guy for being "suspiciously handsome" and who disappeared on more than one professional magician. But with Petey, she's even worse. She's never been able to take a measured, cautious approach. Each time they get back together always ends with her in a ball on her bathroom floor. This time, if they get married, someone will be left holding the bag when it all falls apart. I can't bear for that person to be headstrong, audacious Laurel. I don't want her to end up as disillusioned as I am.

I do a full ninety-degree turn in my bucket seat to face him, because I'm only going to ask this once. "What's it gonna be, Powell? Are you with me or not?"

"I'm driving you, aren't I?"

I shake my head. "Not the same, and you know it. Are you *with* me?"

He sighs the sigh of an Ethan who disagrees wholeheartedly but doesn't have the strength to fight me on it. I know it well. "What are you planning?"

Victoriously, I flip the visor down and uncap my lip balm. "Why do you assume everything I do is part of some sinister plan?"

"You know you're insanely easy to read, right?" His eyes flash between me and the road. My face gets hot. "Are you waiting until the officiant asks for objections or are you creating some kind of a diversion?"

"If whichever random they coaxed from a peyote circle to officiate this mess is taking objections . . ."

"Beekman, no," he protests, tapping his signal to change lanes. "As the de facto best man, I can't be an accomplice to ruining their wedding."

The words "best man" still chafe after the way our friendship fell apart when he was supposed to be my "best man." I trade my lip balm for a Gatorade and take a hard gulp. I'm desperate to quash the nausea and accompanying ache. "I'm gonna talk to her. That's all. *You* of all people should understand the necessity of that."

He squints as though debating whether to take me at my word. "Just talking? The normal kind? No legal tricks or cross-examination?"

I consider the question but opt not to answer. I know I can't tie a grown woman down and keep her from doing anything she wants to do, but I'd prefer not to make any promises I'm not 100 percent sure I can keep. "I won't make a scene. Just a simple, sisterly chat," I assure him.

He smiles like I'm ridiculous. "You think Laurel Miriam Beekman will be receptive to you accosting her—"

"Gently. It'll be a *gentle* accost," I say, correcting him.

"—at her own wedding? Or Petey, the guy with a tattoo of your sister's face on his left triceps, with the words 'My Khaleesi'?"

"That tattoo did not age well."

He ignores my commentary. "You need to trust that they're making the right decisions *for them*, Chuck. You can't control everything."

"Agree to disagree," I say, but when he glances sidelong from the driver's seat yet again, I give in the tiniest bit. "I won't have to say anything if they break up by the time we get there."

"I think they're going to surprise you . . ." He sputters out a declarative sigh—*I've said what I've said*, it announces. "But consider me in."

"Really?" I squeak with delight.

"Mostly because I'm genuinely worried you might die alone in the woods if I opt out, but your 'gentle' ambush is all on you. After that, if they still want to get married, you are letting them get married, got it?"

"I'm not going to kidnap her," I promise, popping open the kettle chips.

He holds out his hand in a Pavlovian response to the sound of a bag splitting apart. I place a pile of potato chips into his cupped palm. "You're capable of almost anything. It's terrifying," he says around a full mouth.

I tilt my head. "You love it."

"Yeah." Giddy relief uncoils my muscles and cancels out any remaining nerves. Ethan's on my team. All's right with the world. "This is not at all how I saw this weekend going, by the way." He passes me his phone. "Put some music on, will you?"

"Road trip DJ? Me?" I gasp theatrically. "This is so much power. You're not a little worried I'm going to let it go straight to my head and put on nonstop sea shanties? You must really trust me." I swipe around for his music app.

"No. I know you've never been interested in listening to men sing."

I scrunch my nose. "That's not true. I listen to *you*."

"Not according to your Spotify Wrapped," he says accusatorily, and now my gasp is real. "It's all Maggie Rogers, Lana Del Rey, Florence and the Machine, Beyoncé—"

"Ethan Powell! You are not allowed to comment on someone's Spotify Wrapped! It's the *most* vulnerable."

"You listened to an alarming amount of Phoebe Bridgers in 2024. I'm not supposed to remark on that?"

"I was getting divorced! Can you allow me one year for my sad-girl era? As though you're listening to anything more interesting." My finger jabs at his phone. "Jesus, Powell. Why is there a playlist called 'THE END OF THE WORLD'?"

"Oh yeah. Put that one on," he instructs, immune to my judgment.

I comply, tapping open the playlist. "I'm already so stressed about whatever's going to be on this."

To my surprise, I'm satisfied by its contents. It's a solid mix of artists I like and people I've never heard of. I put it on shuffle and toss his phone back into the perfectly sized compartment just below the A/C controls. I'm immediately put at ease by the hazy, ethereal female vocals. My eyes are closed as I vibe to the music, picturing us inside a movie montage.

The ping on my phone shoves me back to reality.

I groan at the email preview on my screen reading: URGENT! RESPOND ASAP!!!1! My eyes scan the body of the email. Then I unbuckle my seat belt and climb into the cabin. "Sorry, I need to handle this."

"Beekman!" He micro-swerves, elbowing my butt out of his eye line. "What the hell? I'm on the highway!"

"Huh?" I blurt unconsciously, stalling to close some mental browser tabs before I can begin to process language. "Oh, uh, Bob forgot a filing deadline, but he's 'on the boat,' which means he's already drunk, and I need to drop everything and e-sign a petition to revive a patent application. And I'm guessing that's what Stacy's spamming me on Teams about, but I can't open the app on my stupid phone."

He taps the brakes, sending me sideways into a mini Target haul, barefoot toe shoes, and a bulky camera bag. I recover quickly and steady myself on Ethan's headrest so I can grab my laptop.

"Seriously, Charley. Sit down. I'm not kidding. You can't wander around the place while I'm driving. Jesus."

"Okay. Okay." I sit back down.

"You're going to give me a heart attack." He clenches the wheel. "Why are you working? It's the weekend."

"Weekends and vacations aren't really a thing for me." I open my laptop and connect to the van hot spot.

"Don't throw up," he demands.

"I don't do that anymore . . . in cars," I add, because I *did* throw up this morning from alcohol. Completely different.

"I have a hard time believing you've cured yourself of your crippling motion sickness. Please wait fifteen minutes until I can get off the highway."

"I swear I'm fine."

But when I open Teams, the message waiting for me momentarily halts the flow of blood through my body.

> Stacy Arroyo: Did you see Paul's Insta Story? He was at Rich's surprise engagement party last night. You didn't tell me Rich was already ENGAGED. I would've given you more than an expired gift card.
>
> Stacy Arroyo: The party game was guessing how much bitcoin the ring cost. *vomit emoji* Was Rich always so douchey? No wonder he and Paul hit it off.
>
> Stacy Arroyo: Okay, now I'm looking at his sister's stories. I've viewed this party from every angle. I'm addicted.

I want to grab something, anything, so I clench the laptop that's already in my hands.

"You good?" Ethan asks, his normal crinkly-eyed resting happy expression sliding off his face.

I nod, frozen, adjusting to the reality that while *I* am a divorcée, Rich . . . isn't. There was comfort in the way his leaving me saddled him with the same fate. We were both failures. We'd both smugly announced to the world that we were ending the search for partnership only to take it back a year later. But *he* isn't divorced anymore. Not in the way I am. It's no longer his most current relationship status. He's some woman's *fiancé*. He left me and has already found someone better.

The shame hits me in the chest like a hot brick, and a familiar self-loathing burns into my skin. *Of course he left*, it says. *How could you delude yourself into thinking he would stay?* Rich couldn't even stay divorced with me. He had to fully excise me from every corner of his life. It's almost like being left all over again.

"Are you sure you're okay?" Ethan asks again.

I don't look up. "Mm-hm."

"You seem like you're lying."

"I'm not," I respond through gritted teeth as Ethan's fondness for saying the quiet part out loud grates against me.

But the longer I stare at Stacy's screenshots of my ex's engagement party, the more my insides sway, the images on my laptop shake, and copper-flavored nausea swims up my throat, settling behind my eye sockets.

Oh god.

"Ethan," I eke out through clenched teeth.

His head swings toward me. My stomach launches its rebellion.

"Pull over?" I ask.

But it's too late.

Chapter 6

We Know the Water Smells Like Eggs

AW, HONEY. I'M sorry," Ethan tells me as the last dregs of Gatorade leave my body. "Let it all out."

Standing on the side of the road, he's holding my hair back and rubbing small circles between my shoulders in a distinctly collegiate manner. But maybe that's a critical component of your entire life falling apart. Regression.

"Your poor van," I say, my face pointed to the grass. I'm not ready to go vertical quite yet.

"Don't worry about that," he tells me, his hand still on my back. "Worry about what's in your hair."

I grimace. "On my lap too."

He surveys the surrounding area. "There's a truck stop just north of us. If we're lucky, they'll have a shower where you can get cleaned up."

My shoulders sink. "A truck stop shower?"

"I usually shower at Anytime Fitness, but we're a little too far from a city for that. A truck stop is going to be your best option. Would you rather use my camping shower? It's ice cold, has no water pressure, and is fully open to the elements. Take your pick."

I momentarily weigh the prospect of a public nudity citation against exposure to staphylococcal bacteria and arrive at a verdict that surprises even me. Releasing a tiny whimper of resignation, I murmur, "Truck stop, please."

He rubs that spot between my shoulders again. It's nice. Comforting. Like when my mom used to make me those Lipton Noodle Soup packets when I was sick.

"That's my Chuck. So quietly heroic."

I don't care for the amusement in his voice, but as he just held my hair back, I'll let him have this one.

"I'm sorry about your upholstery." I avert my eyes from the soiled patch of grass and direct all my focus to Ethan's left leg. His muscular calf. His lightly suntanned skin. It's by far the strangest grounding exercise I've ever subjected myself to, but it works. It steadies me enough to lift my head.

"It's a wipe-clean vegan leather. It'll be fine."

"You're just happy because you were right about my car sickness," I say, finally looking in his eyes. There's a touch of schadenfreude tugging at his lips.

"Eh, but I wouldn't've minded being wrong." He disappears behind the van with my laptop and, about a minute later, reappears with a garbage bag. "I wiped off what I could. We'll see if a cup of rice is any match for your insides."

Yesterday, if you would've asked me what I'd save in a house fire, I would've pointed to the laptop inside this green compostable trash bag without hesitating. You think you know yourself, but then that alarm goes off and you're surprised by your own ineptitude.

My whole body recoils when I take the bag from him. "You think rice will help?"

"It brought your pink Razr back from the brink," he quips.

"Razrs are indestructible. They're a technological marvel. They don't make 'em like that anymore."

"All right." His palm finds my shoulder blades again. "Let's focus on you. We'll worry about the replaceable things later."

———

I take the shower key from the pretty young woman at the front counter, who seems only moderately irritated that I interrupted her reading of *Fourth Wing* with something as mundane as my cleanliness emergency.

"The shower's seven dollars. Keep your shoes on," she instructs, snapping her gum.

There's a giant red-haired man behind her restocking a row of tobacco pouches. "Don't come back here to complain that the water smells like eggs," he tells my reflection in the mirrored security camera. "We *know* the water smells like eggs."

And with that inauspicious disclaimer, their attention returns to sexy dragon riders and Cool Mint ZYN, respectively.

I'm not sure what I was anticipating from a truck stop bathroom, but it's somehow more grim than I would have thought. The space resembles a single-occupancy gas station bathroom (the kind where you're careful not to touch *anything*) with an avocado-green shower curtain drooping in the far corner. The dingy tile floor slopes inward to a drain at its center that's guarded by a particularly vigilant spider. There's no tiny bottle of shampoo. There's no shelf for clothes. There's not even a towel hook. Aside from the disconcertingly scorched toilet seat, there are no surfaces to speak of.

I can already feel the bile creeping back up my throat. I pop my head out the bathroom door, and the key clanks against the metal handle. I spot Ethan immediately and am flooded with relief.

He's leaning over the counter, all charming smiles, chatting up the woman behind the glass, who's been roused from her literary coma by his attention. She's twirling her hair, for god's sake. When she spoke to me, her entire body was an eye roll, but with Ethan, she exudes the small-town, effortlessly gorgeous energy of an undiscovered starlet. The scene makes my already sensitive stomach twist a bit more violently.

It's not as though I'm surprised. I've seen the effect he has on women. And men for that matter. Everyone is drawn to him and the way he moves through the world with an easy confidence. That, paired with his whole floppy-haired, eager-to-please Labrador retriever thing, is kryptonite to almost everyone. I'm only immune to its potency because I've known him since he had a buzz cut, gapped teeth, and a passing interest in close-up magic. Nothing can dampen an objectively gorgeous man's sex appeal quite like the memory of his thirteen-year-old self dousing my arm in lighter fluid while attempting to set a playing card on fire.

I'd be lying if I said that, from time to time, I haven't noticed my platonic best friend in ways that are undoubtedly *non*-platonic, but it always passes. Attraction might spark for a millisecond when he whispers into my ear during a movie, his hot breath kissing the spot on my neck that is biologically hardwired to send tingles down my spine, but then he immediately neutralizes it. He does or says something that reminds me that, at his core, he's still Ethan: allergic to preparation, monotony, and monogamy. The exact opposite of my type, which can be best categorized as a man who has strong opinions on German appliance manufacturers and always splurges on the extended warranty.

I clear my throat, hoping to get Ethan's attention without capturing the notice of the entire rest stop.

I'm only partially successful. Ethan swivels his head in my direction, and I watch Casually Stunning Counter Girl's face fall in the absence of his shine.

He jogs over to me, the aforementioned floppy brown hair flopping floppily. The whole maneuver is surely making Counter Girl weak in the knees. "What do you need, Beek?"

I flutter my lashes. "Could I possibly tear you away from luring that poor girl into your van? We have a situation."

"Don't *love* that insinuation, but you're in a fragile state, so we're gonna breeze right past it . . ."

I jerk my head toward the set inspiration for the movie *Saw* behind me. "I need your help in there."

"*There*, as in the bathroom?"

"No. *There*, as in the Portuguese consulate. Yes, *the bathroom*! There's no shelf. I need you to hold my bag and pass me my stuff while I shower."

He leans against the door frame to tilt his head through the opening. He peers around the room and comes up as empty as I did. He looks between me and the eerie room, the flickering fluorescent light catching on the edges of his jawline. "Can you set it on the floor?"

I have the patience of an absolute saint. "It's already been claimed by the largest spider I've ever seen. This is his house, and I'm gonna respect that."

His lips quirk. "You're so cute when you're petrified. Your nose gets all twitchy like a cartoon bunny rabbit's . . ." He takes my bag from my hands and strides into the bathroom, our arms brushing in a way that is surely raising his counter friend's eyebrows. "Never fear. I'll be your towel rack."

"Did I ever tell you that you're my favorite person in the whole wide world?" I'm practically bouncing with relief.

"Less talking. More showering. You still want to get to Petey and Laurel's campsite before sundown, right?"

"One thousand percent," I answer, slinking into the shower fully clothed, strategically avoiding contact with the mildewy curtain as though it's a red laser beam and I am the seductive art thief in an *Ocean's* movie. "I'm not taking any risks." I couldn't live with myself if Laurel married Petey.

"I think you're going to regret this attitude toward your own sister's happily ever after."

"When their divorce goes through this time next year, I definitely won't."

"Come on, Chuck. I know you're not actually that cynical."

"Oh, but I am. I'm a twenty-eight-year-old divorcée whose mom forwards her relationship advice from a Twin Flames Facebook group. Life has hardened me."

The way he pushes air through his nostrils spells out his thoughts. *Oof, Charley*, it says.

I peel off my T-shirt and pass it through the sliver of light between the curtain and the shower wall. It plops to the floor.

"Powell! The spider!"

"I'm not holding your vomit in my hands."

"I carried you on my back for three blocks after you stepped on glass walking through Zeta Kappa's foam party barefoot, and you can't hold a dirty shirt?"

"It was thirty feet, tops. And that party was basically a giant bathtub."

I shake my head even though he can't see it. "I can't have this argument with you again."

"I've got a garbage bag in my pocket, and I promise to make sure Felix doesn't hitch a ride with your clothes when we leave, okay?"

Of course he's already named the spider.

I pull my bottoms down and self-consciousness alights in my belly at the sight of my aggressively unsexy undergarments. I ball up the faded cotton and hide them in my shorts like I'm at the gynecologist. Then I toss them on the floor near Ethan's feet and yank the shower handle. Smelly, ice-cold water sputters onto my chest.

"Holy—" I cry out, just as Ethan says, "Whoa. That's . . . pungent."

When the heat of the water settles somewhere just below body temperature, I give up the fight and dip my head under the limp stream.

"I grabbed my soap from the van." His hand stretches through the opening. My eyes immediately lock on the tattooed flowers that climb up his forearm.

Something about seeing a male hand so close to my naked breast sends an unwelcome swoop low in my belly. I can't remember the last time a man's hand grazed my nipple. I think it was snowing.

I grab the bar from him, and thankfully, the feeling subsides when his hand disappears. "*Bar* soap? Is this a joke, Powell?"

"No plastic, and those giant bottles take up too much space." He laughs at my tortured whine. "I promise, I always rub it onto my washcloth. Never my body."

"If I find one curly hair, I swear to god—"

"I bought you a little bottle of shampoo from the counter whenever you're ready for it. I figured you might not be ready for the multiuse-shower-product lifestyle."

"You were correct," I answer, closing my eyes and rubbing the milky white bar into my palm. "Is that what you were doing at the front?" My voice is innocent. Mostly.

"Yes . . . what else would I be doing?" he asks, and I'm grateful for the moldy curtain that hides my reddening cheeks.

"That was a lot of chitchat over a bottle of shampoo."

I feel it first—the weight in my chest, the burning in my throat—before I know what it is. I'm jealous. I'm jealous of the woman, who minutes ago was just the cashier selling shampoo and scratch-offs but, with one look from Ethan, is now the physical embodiment of every way I'm falling short. She's a little bit younger. Her hair is just a little blonder. Her smile, eager. She looks easy and effortless when all I've ever done is try way too hard.

I know it's not a *romantic* jealousy—we've never been like that—but best friends are their own kind of soul mates. They're the people with whom we share our innermost selves. Ethan's known me best at nearly every stage of life. New people will never meet that nervous, optimistic kid, or the chaotic yet motivated college student, or the young professional with expensive suits and spotty dental coverage.

No one else will ever split my life into a before and after because they'll only exist in his after. They'll only know the person I'll let them know. But best friends get it all—our best selves and our darkest versions—even when they've never asked for it.

It's only natural to feel a little threatened by someone new when you have a friendship like that.

There's a self-satisfied smile in his voice when he responds, "Autumn was asking about my T-shirt."

"Autumn," I repeat, letting her name fill my mouth. It takes me a second to picture exactly which worn band tee he's wearing, but then the colorful figures come into focus. "Aren't you wearing a *Stop Making Sense* T-shirt?" I pause for dramatic effect. "You think the Sydney Sweeney lookalike is a big Talking Heads fan? Shampoo, please." I send my arm through the slit in the curtain.

Our knuckles brush as he takes the body bar and replaces it with a tiny green bottle of Garnier Fructis.

He clears his throat.

"She doesn't look like Sydney Sweeney. Sydney Sweeney doesn't even look like Sydney Sweeney."

I uncap the shampoo and the shower steam mixes with the scent of tropical smoothie. The aroma is a time machine that sends me traumatically straight back to a middle school girls' locker room. "There's no way she's heard of them," I tell him with certainty. "She looks twenty."

"She might've." His tone is defensive, but less for Autumn and more for the enduring relevance of David Byrne. "She doesn't look any younger than we do," Ethan adds.

"Can we just admit that that gorgeous young woman was looking to spend her fifteen in the back of your van with your small-batch tub of artisanal lube? Rather than existing in this alternate reality where twenty-year-olds know the words to 'Psycho Killer'?"

I cut the shower, and Ethan's hand slides against my ribs with one of his wide microfiber towels.

"I never said she wasn't flirting with me."

Something circles in my stomach—the last vestige of my

hangover? I'm not sure. But it's the reason I sound unsteady when I reply, "Sorry. I, uh, didn't mean to interrupt."

"You didn't. Well, you did, but I don't care." His voice is cool. Sure. Confident. "She's not my type."

"Oh." The syllable is more a puff of air than a response.

Goose bumps rise along the surface of my skin, and suddenly, I'm too aware of how intimate this is. Ethan standing on the other side of a thin curtain while I shower. Ethan's knuckles gliding against my wet skin as he passes me a dry towel.

"Not to mention . . ." He coughs. "When you have so many women beating down your van door, you have to be pretty selective."

My laugh jumps out of my throat and breaks whatever odd tension had been building between us. "You're delusional," I scoff, but I've never been so grateful for the reminder that though Ethan is *my* Ethan, he's also just a single guy I'd absolutely swipe left on if I ever bothered to redownload my dating apps.

"Do you think she recognized you?" I ask, wrapping myself in the towel.

Even from behind the curtain, I can detect Ethan's flinch at the mention of the minor celebrity status he achieved from his former band's only hit. "No. There's this, uh, look people get in their eyes. A *Did we go to high school together, or are you the guy that sang that one song that was in that one show that they parodied on* SNL? kind of look. If I never have to hear someone request 'Velvet Nebula' again, it'll be too soon."

"Hey, don't take it out on 'Velvet Nebula.'" I scrunch my wet hair into the towel, careful not to elbow the shower curtain. "It's a great song. I'll never forget where I was when Sutton and River finally kissed during the alien invasion at the end of season two. Then the music swelled, and my buddy Ethan was singing about the cosmic beauty of some random chick—"

He interrupts me with a groan so loud, I have no choice but to stop my shot-for-shot recap of *Aurora Falls*, the teen sci-fi soap that featured Ethan's song in a moment so beloved by girls that the world felt compelled to mock it ceaselessly in a way his band never recovered from.

It was the monkey's paw of overnight indie rock band success. His band, Lemonface, had a number one hit . . . and an *SNL* parody skewering the now-infamous teen soap moment. The group bagged a People's Choice nomination . . . and lost the award to Justin Bieber, who made fun of Ethan's earnest lyrics in his speech. Lemonface was beloved and reviled all in one moment they could never escape.

After finishing their first tour as headliners, the band broke up. Ethan was able to extend his fifteen seconds a little longer than the others by dating a slew of gorgeous, slightly more famous women, but ultimately settled into the college performance circuit, playing "Velvet Nebula" over and over for the age group who still appreciated it, albeit ironically.

I swaddle myself in his towel. "I love that song," I tell him, even as something deep inside me shrinks at the raw, romantic vulnerability of the lyrics and the idea of Ethan having someone significant enough to write *that* song about.

There's a particular cruelty in being friends with a musician. The reminder that you'll share decades of memories, secrets, and small, well-meaning lies, but all added up it'll never reach the emotional magnitude of even a two-week whirlwind romance. Fifteen years of friendship will never scratch the surface of whatever he shared with the girl who inspired "One More Night in Fiji."

Wrapped in the damp towel, I shake out my shiver and slip between the curtain and the glistening tile wall.

"Hey." Ethan's eyes widen with something like surprise, as though he's realizing for the first time that I've been naked for most of this conversation. "Oh, you have a little . . ." He gestures at his own cheekbone.

"Is it puke?" I squawk, searching the spot above the sink where the mirror should be and finding nothing but fire-damaged cinder blocks. I inwardly grimace at the prospect of reentering a shower that smells of warm egg salad.

He smiles. "No, it's dark, like eyeliner or something."

This seems plausible. It's highly likely I skipped the micellar water step in last night's skin routine when I was clipping into a rowing machine half in its bag.

I swipe my fingers along my undereyes. He frowns at my cleaning efforts. "No, you're missing it. Here." He takes his thumb and gently dabs along the ridge of my cheekbone. His face is close enough that I can make out all the tiny muscles tightening around his eyebrows with concentration. I pick a freckle on his forehead and stare.

"I'm sorry I'm such a disaster today. I don't normally, um, let loose like I did last night. Even after a shower, I probably still look like I got hit by a truck."

"No, you're always beautiful," he says, his voice low and gentle to match the weight of his thumb on my cheek.

"Okay. Now I know you're full of shit." I swallow, feeling each second pass with our faces this close. "I'm sure Autumn would just love this," I say, because the way he's touching me is just so unintentionally *a move* that not commenting on it almost feels like its own move, and I wouldn't dare project any sort of romantic intentions onto Ethan. "You know she's probably googling you right now."

"It's hard to google a name you don't know." He lets go of my face to rinse his hands. I keep my eyes on his forehead, hearing the rusty crack of the faucet handle, the splatter of water, and the high-pitched squeak of metal against metal as he shuts it off.

"Of course. She only knows you as 'hot van guy.'"

"Oh yeah?" He winks. As a rule, I hate when men wink, but Ethan objectively carries it off.

"It's funny," I start, my voice not sounding as casual as I intend. "Rich always pretended he couldn't remember your name. Or any critical details about you. He was always like, 'Your friend Aaron who plays his keyboard at state fairs.'"

His fingers gently caress the sensitive skin under my eyes. "Dude, these days, I *wish* I could book the Minnesota State Fair. Could you imagine?"

I could. There was a time when his band headlining stadium tours felt inevitable.

"It was his weird power move, like there were things about me and my life he couldn't make space in his head for."

Ethan doesn't respond. He just smirks.

"What?"

He pauses his work on my undereyes, and his cheeks stretch the tiniest bit farther. "You have, like, three friends, Chuck. The dude knows my name. Rich was threatened by me."

"Why would he feel threatened by you?" I ask, knowing exactly why I suspect Ethan wasn't Rich's favorite topic of conversation. When Rich and I were dating, every story of the old days had a way of looping its way back to Ethan, but from our honeymoon onward, his ire was definitely rooted in the way I drifted around the Airbnb that weekend like a zombie, checking my phone for apology texts that wouldn't come.

Still, I'm praying to everything holy that Ethan doesn't know that part.

He bobs his head, that smile ever expanding. "I don't know. You tell me."

I can't respond. I can only manage to stare at that forehead freckle. He chuckles. It's a warm, rumbly sound that shakes his chest, his shoulder, all the way to his thumb, so that I feel the tremble of his amusement at my temple.

I shut my eyes, unable to handle how he's crowding all five of my senses at once. The feel of his guitar-callused fingers holding my chin while his other hand draws careful circles under my eyes. The percussive rhythm of his steady breaths. His smell of sweat and sugar is so overwhelming, I can almost taste the salty sweetness on my tongue. Each piece could be too much on its own, but combined with the way he's looking at me, like I'm something delicate? Impossible to withstand.

The bathroom feels much too small all of a sudden, and I can't take another second of it. "You know, I think I wore waterproof mascara last night. It's probably not going to get much better than this." I take a step back from Ethan. His hands fall as he searches my face with the kind of penetrating blue-eyed stare that could make a smart woman do stupid things.

He swallows, nods, and searches for a place to put his hands.

"Can I . . . ?" I point to my bag. It's resting on his shoulder by the strap.

"Of course, here you . . ." He trails off, extending the bag toward me. I accept it with the hand that's not securing the towel over my breasts.

"I'll just . . ." I raise the bag an inch.

"I'll be . . ." He collects my clothes off the floor with the garbage bag like a dog owner bagging a turd but doesn't leave. My eyes drop to Felix the spider as we just stand there for another few seconds.

"I'm cold," I announce.

"Sorry, yeah," he responds, and then he walks out of the bathroom.

Since there's still no surface on which to set anything, I have to clutch my towel and clumsily swing my bag in front of my hips, one-handedly grabbing at my belongings in search of clothes.

While I'm doing this dance, wishing Ethan were still in here, the single shirt I packed flies straight into the toilet.

Chapter 7

===

Gently Used Animal Carcasses

Dear Charlotte Beekman,

We're reading <u>Persuasion</u> in English, and Mr. Farley gave us this assignment today where we can write a letter to anyone we want, but we have to do it while he STARES DIRECTLY AT US. He says he's not going to read them, so I could do another song ranking, but I wrote your name without thinking and I know you'd rather get a letter since you probably haven't recovered from my most recent ranking of every Arcade Fire song (which I still think is my greatest contribution to music ever, even if you're the only one who reads it).

Letters are so formal. Maybe that's why I haven't written to you yet even though my mom got your new address from the Ludeckis a few weeks after you left. That's the family that lives in your house now, by the way. I think one of them goes to the college, but I can't be sure. They have a six-month-old baby and basically never leave the house. Sometimes my mom has me mow their lawn, and they both wave at me from the window like hostages the whole time I'm out there.

I wanted to send you something on Facebook, but I'm still not allowed to have one yet. Do you have one? People at school ask me if you do. All. The. Time. You know there are people here who miss you, right?

DUDE . . . Forty-five minutes is a superrrrr long time to write a letter. I need to think of something else to say because Mr. Farley is watching, and his eyebrows are doing that thing where he looks like an angry Muppet.

I forgot you don't know Mr. Farley, because you go to high school somewhere else. What's it like going to school someplace else?

That was a dumb question. Sorry. I feel pressured to ask you something important because it's like the first letter I've written after two months, but the only thing coming to mind is did you see <u>Inception</u>? School played it on the lawn for homecoming, and I'm not sure if I liked it or understood it or just had a dream of Leonardo DiCaprio for several hours. I <u>really</u> need to talk to you about it.

My stomach is growling, so I'm gonna cut this short so I can get a bathroom pass and sneak down to the vending machines for chips.

From,
Ethan Powell (from Mr. Farley's
2nd-period freshman English class)

Dear Ethanius Potholomew,

It's kind of rude that you can use the weird long version of my name and I have no way to retaliate. I'm glad you wrote me a letter and not a list of songs I don't know and have to listen to because that's basically homework. Did you decide what song to audition for Jazz Band with?

First, let me answer your totally not dumb question. Going to school somewhere else is . . . weird. I'm not good at making friends here. I probably wasn't any better in Lewellen, but it was different there.

Now for your totally dumb question: Of course I saw Inception. Everyone did. At first, I thought I understood it, but then I tried to explain it to Laurel and then . . . it was like . . . I didn't? Then she saw the movie and tried to explain it to me, but now we're like, why was the top spinning at the end???

I'm sorry about how suddenly we left Lewellen. My mom says it was because it was the end of the month and staying longer would've cost more money. I don't know. Maybe that's the truth. For a while after we moved, I'd wake up at night to get water and think I was still in the house behind yours and walk into a closet. Then I'd realize I was dreaming and for a split second, it all seemed like a dream. That whole year. You. Minnesota. Everything. Like Inception! IS THAT WHAT IT'S ABOUT?

My dad's working on a new doc in Alaska. I haven't heard from him in a while, but he's like that when he's working. It's like we're all tucked inside a drawer and he forgets to take us out again. Which sucks, but also . . . it's whatever, I guess.

It's not all bad here. We're staying with my mom's aunt in Seattle, and she's paying Laurel and me to sell her "legacy" furs on eBay. She's been very disappointed by the lack of demand for her gently used animal carcasses.

I'm sorry I didn't write earlier. I don't usually keep in touch with people when we leave, but I'd like to keep in touch with you. Unless you wrote just for school. No pressure.

Is it weird I responded? If it is, just ignore it and know that I miss you and that Arcade Fire doesn't have enough songs I like to create a definitive ranking.

BOOM. Shots fired.

Best,
Charley (from the kitchen table)

PS: If we were there this summer, I totally would've jumped into the lake with everyone, and I want credit for that.

Charleston Chew,

I'll let your obvious play to antagonize me and Arcade Fire go because you know nothing of music or culture.

I got the lead guitar spot in Jazz Band, which is kind of a big deal for a freshman, but I'm not great at sight reading music yet. I REALLY wanted to audition with "Maggot Brain" by Funkadelic but at the last minute switched to Prince, which was probably the right move for Ms. Peters. My mom's been calling me Miles Davis ever since I got the spot, and I don't have the heart to tell her he was very famously <u>not</u> a guitarist.

Petey asked about you and Laurel when he was home for
Thanksgiving. He's still at that hockey boarding school up
north, which I can't believe exists outside of a <u>Mighty
Ducks</u> movie. I told him that I didn't know how you were
because the whole letter thing takes super crazy long and
he reminded me that email exists. Do you have an email
address? He said that he Gchats with Laurel sometimes, so
I'm guessing you have one too.

Mine is ethan8powell@gmail.com.

Regards,
Ethan (from the six-inch spot next to the register at the
Donut Barn)

PS: You get the credit for jumping in a lake WHEN you
jump in a lake and not one. Second. Sooner.

From: charlottebeek63@gmail.com
To: ethan8powell@gmail.com
Subject: Your email address is weird.

That's it. That's the message. Why is there an 8 in the
middle like a Zodiac Killer clue?

From: ethan8powell@gmail.com
To: charlottebeek63@gmail.com
Subject: Re: Your email address is weird.

Chuck—

Ethanpowell and ethanpowell8 were taken.

I kind of like it. It looks like an infinity symbol in the middle, like a superhero or a leader of a postapocalyptic society.

Have you read *The Hunger Games* yet? It's SICK. Like everyone dies. It's crazy. You'd love it.

—Ethan

From: charlottebeek63@gmail.com
To: ethan8powell@gmail.com
Subject: Re: Re: Your email address is weird.

Why do I want to read a book where everyone dies? Also, if we're rebuilding society, I'd prefer if I was the one leading it, but I'll keep the infinity symbol as a gesture of goodwill.

—Charley8Beekman

ELEVEN YEARS AGO

From: charlottebeek63@gmail.com
To: ethan8powell@gmail.com
Subject: Re: Re: You're an absolute nightmare

Powell—

Why do you have band practice on Sundays? I have no one to distract me from this college essay and have to resort to email.

I'm supposed to write about my biggest dreams, and all I can think about is how this house in Milwaukee is officially where I've lived the longest, but my mom still says it's temporary. She's been sleeping on a pullout for two years waiting for my dad to take us away and become the kind of guy who can stay in one place for longer than two minutes without getting bored. To him, our family is this interesting idea, but inconvenient in practice.

I don't get why my mom can't give up on this ridiculous dream of a happy family he doesn't even want. Laurel says the whole concept of monogamy is flawed, but then what about the Obamas? Explain them then!

It has to be possible for the right people to find each other and make it work. So maybe that's my big dream. To be in a power couple where we have a house that's ours and the jobs and the couch that's perfectly white and never gets dirty even though we have three muddy dogs and it all feels permanent, you know? Do you think that'll get me into college?

lol. lol. no. I'll channel you and write something about the environment.

—Charley

From: ethan8powell@gmail.com
To: charlottebeek63@gmail.com
Subject: Re: Re: Re: You're an absolute nightmare

Chuck—

I'm ashamed I ever thought your dad was cool. To my credit I was thirteen and had never met an adult man with a dangly earring.

I wish we could swap lives. Between the shop and this town, everything feels *too* permanent.

I got into this music camp in Northern Michigan. It's supposed to be great, but my parents need me at the shop this summer so my mom can finally get the knee surgery she's been putting off. Sometimes I feel guilty for being the third-generation heir to a donut shop who physically can't eat donuts.

Obviously, I want my mom to have time off to recover, but I also wanted this seemingly life-changing experience to maybe change my life. Sometimes it feels like my life is going on someplace else without me. This town's this fishbowl I'll never escape even though I can see through the glass.

I think I want to get a tattoo. Would you ever get a tattoo?

Also, is this anything?

www.soundcloud.com/lemonface/rooftop-comedown

—Ethan

PS: I don't know if you're kidding about the essay, but if you aren't, you should have me read it first. You should probably call me before you write anything about the planet you can't take back.

From: charlottebeek63@gmail.com
To: ethan8powell@gmail.com
Subject: Re: Re: Re: Re: You're an absolute nightmare

Your tattoo better be "Charlotte Beekman is always right" in curly font. Or maybe wildflowers, like the purple ones that pop up by the lake in the summer. Those always remind me of you.

And this song is OBVIOUSLY something! It's literally amazing.

Is the band *called* Lemonface? Are we sure about that name?

—Charley

Chapter 8

A Sampling of Balls

THE TRUCK STOP door clangs behind me on my way out. I cross the parking lot with my duffel under one arm and a toilet-water-soaked shirt in a plastic bag in the other.

"Don't say a word," I demand.

Ethan's leaning against his van, arms folded. The sun reflecting off the bright white paint casts him in a warm glow and spotlights his utterly deranged grin.

"Don't," I repeat, my voice pleading.

"Beekman." He says my name like a compassionate T-ball coach watching a grounder roll between a pair of children's cleats. "I would've given you something to wear. You didn't have to . . ." His eyes are glued to my new white oversized shirt, which reads "SEXY MOTHER TRUCKER" in capital letters.

"There was a mishap with a toilet. I'd rather not get into it."

The Sydney Sweeney doppelgänger was actually quite helpful in my time of need. When I tiptoed out of the bathroom, still wrapped in my towel, she directed me toward the only rack of T-shirts that weren't confrontationally patriotic.

I lift my plastic bag. "Should I stick this with the vomit clothes?"

"You fished it out?" He grimaces, and I know for sure that any fleeting moment of physical chemistry next to that shower is long gone.

"Duh, it's linen." I yank open one of the rear doors to search around for myself.

"You packed linen for a camping trip?"

I shrug. "It's summer. I wear linen in the summer. I don't want you to look at me differently or anything, but I'm fancy now." I toss my wet hair with an alarming degree of confidence for a woman who just fished her shirt out of a rust-stained toilet bowl.

"Oh, I know it. Here, let me." He unlatches something on the edge of the other door so both sides can swing open, exposing the mosquito screen that's protecting a mattress from the elements.

I hadn't really considered the lack of a traditional trunk. Every square inch of this thing is maximized for living space.

"I rinsed your clothes off at the spigot." He points to the putrid, rainbow-shaped rust stain on the side of the building. "That should help with the smell, but we'll have to line-dry them wherever we set up camp. I'll keep my eye out for a laundromat."

He pushes and pulls on something in the bed frame until it releases a long, sealed bin.

I'd always assumed that Ethan living out of a van would look more like, well, living out of a van. Messy, aimless, crowded. But Ethan's world seems intentional and well designed.

"I hate to say it, but I think your laptop might be cooked."

I laugh grimly. "Paul's going to love that."

"IT guy?" He ties off the plastic bag I hand him and stuffs it into the bin holding the other things I ruined today.

I shake my head. "My workplace nemesis. He'll stop at nothing to destroy me."

The back doors shut with a satisfying series of thuds and clicks. "Poor Paul."

"No 'poor Paul.' Paul sucks. The only crime I committed was starting at A & G the same day he did. For that grave offense, he sniffs next to me in the break room and goes, 'Was that you?' then slinks away like the little snake he is. He does that, like, once a month."

He removes my neoprene bag from my shoulder with a cough-laugh. "No, Paul, my guy."

"Right?" I climb into the passenger seat while Ethan secures my bag in the cabin.

"I was inclined to take his side," he says with a grunt, "because I know you're secretly a monster, but I've flipped. I'm on your side now."

"You're the worst person I know," I tell him in the flattest voice I can muster.

Ethan rests a hand on my headrest as he climbs into the driver's seat from behind. "You don't believe that for a second," he tells me before cranking the ignition switch.

We drive north on the highway that snakes along Lake Superior. Our van pokes out from the trees to view the shoreline every so often. There's some light weekender traffic, but not enough to ruin the drive. We're quiet for a bit, our chatter replaced by the music pouring from the stereo. I roll down the window to stretch my arm into the breeze like I'm in a road trip movie, but the mood is spoiled by the wind's low, obtrusive throb against the glass.

A familiar feeling grips my throat. Something like home-sickness. Nostalgia. Longing. It all mixes together in that wistful cocktail of feeling like you're losing grip of the moment even as you're experiencing it.

"Did I see a camera back there earlier?" I ask. "And your toe running shoes? I thought you burned those, by the way."

"You mean when you were traipsing around a moving vehicle, like a drunk girl on a Spirit flight, and then got sick, like . . . a drunk girl on a Spirit flight? Yes. There's a camera and barefoot toe shoes back there. I can't get rid of them. They're the only kind I can run in with my plantar fasciitis."

His eyes shoot daggers at my straightening legs, so instead of standing, I reach behind his seat, groping around for the guitar strap poking out of a nylon camera bag. When I tug on it, a Nikon swings between our bucket seats and plops into my lap.

"Careful," he intones. "I spent way too much money on that thing."

"Nah. These babies can take a beating. You should see the kinds of stuff my parents put theirs through." The weight of his camera sinks into my hands. It feels nice. It's been ages since I've broken out my sturdy DSLR camera, but it's also been ages since I was in a moment I felt compelled to keep.

I zoom in on Ethan until his profile is perfectly framed by the blur of sun-soaked trees whipping past. I adjust the shutter speed and curl my feet under me like a bird perched on a fence, repositioning my body so that the daylight floods his features.

"What are you doing?" he asks, curious but not exactly surprised.

I gently press the shutter and watch Ethan's eyes come into focus in the viewfinder. "Keeping this for later," I answer.

He shakes his head like I'm hopeless but he smiles anyway. It bursts across the tiny screen like a solar flare. It's exactly the moment I wanted. I press down my index finger and hear the burst of images the camera captures, and know without looking that one of them is *it*. One of those photos is *exactly* Ethan at this exact moment, and even once he leaves, I'll have a piece of him frozen in time, forever.

"There. Moment captured."

"Good," he responds, sneaking a glance at me swiping through his camera roll. "Searching for nudes?"

"I don't need to look for those. You've sent me plenty." I don't bother looking up.

He rears back but keeps his eyes on the road. "Are you referring to the medical photo I sent of a very troubling bruise *you* inflicted on *me*?"

I lower the camera. "If you pick up a woman from behind in a crowd of strangers, she's going to struggle. It would've been insane if I *hadn't* kicked you in the junk."

"You missed my junk—thank god—but your boot turned my inner thigh *green*."

"I know. I saw it in the nude you sent me."

"That was *not* a nude!" His laugh turns his cheeks bright crimson.

There's something that always shakes loose in Ethan when he laughs like that—that laughter that starts in his belly and bursts from his chest like a firework. It's as though, for the briefest moment, the small part of him he keeps for himself is on full display, and it's magnificent.

I shake my head, hiding my own reddening face with his camera. "There was a sampling of balls. Balls equal nude, dude."

He looks between me and the highway. "I'm worried about the caliber of nudes you're receiving from the local uncle scene."

"I *wish* there were some uncle balls in this camera roll. What is this lighting, Powell? Seriously, are these crime scene photos?"

"It's the camera," he says defensively. "They looked fine when I was using my phone but I wanted nicer photos of my custom van builds. The guy at the store said it would give me wide-angle shots, but the thing's a disaster."

"Please don't blame sweet baby Nikon for your ineptitude." I pet the camera at issue before plopping it back into the open bag behind his seat.

He grins, but then it slips. His eyes drift to my phone, sitting on the dash, which is flickering with notifications like a dying incandescent lightbulb.

"Sorry. That must be distracting." I reach for my phone with a groan, grateful I managed to take my picture before life crept back in. "What status do you think Microsoft Teams displays when you soak your computer in stomach acid?"

"Skull and crossbones?"

I don't respond, already absorbed in the relentless messages. Work anxiety whistles in my brain like a neglected teakettle.

"Why don't you use 'getting sick' as an excuse to take an actual weekend off?" he suggests, slowing to let a lime-green PT Cruiser pass him on the narrowing highway. "You must get a gimme for an act of god like this. It won't kill you to relax a little."

"I can't relax knowing I'm going to have seventy fires to put out Monday morning," I tell him, my sentence scored by the click-clack of my nails against my phone screen.

"Why can't people wait a day to hear from you? You're an intellectual property lawyer. No one is taking anyone's liberty away if you don't respond immediately."

I snort. "So?" I press my phone to my chest, allowing myself this diversion to brief Ethan on the intersection of capitalism and the American legal system. "When it comes to big corporate clients, the best lawyer is the one who responds to their email the fastest. I can be more capable and passionate than every other attorney on their payroll, but at the end of the day, general counsels of Fortune 500 companies will never accept anything less than immediate responses to the inane questions that pop into their heads at nine p.m. on a Friday night. It's a race to the bottom, and if I don't send that billable email during my friend's birthday dinner, Paul *will*. *And* he'll cc our bosses with a pointed postscript because he's trying to destroy me."

"And you like this?" he asks, as though it might be my preference to live chained to my email and in a constant grudge match with a guy who refers to his Rolex with she/her pronouns.

"Obviously, I hate it, Powell. Who would like this?"

I work exclusively for Bob, which means I work at the *whim* of Bob, and Bob loves the influence that comes with having a stable of clients with multimillion-dollar legal budgets. My days are dominated by kissing ass and churning out patents, not to help inventors, but to secure the financial interests of companies designing insecticides and internal tax management software.

"Why are you doing it then?" he demands.

This makes me pause. The question is so obvious, it's almost silly. Indulgent even.

I started down this path when my dad left. Again. We couldn't pay rent and had no choice but to sell the camera equipment he'd left behind. All of it. Even the camera I thought was mine. *I'll get you one of those Samsung phones with a built-in camera*, my mom promised.

Everything in my life had a way of moving without warning, even my camera. For so long, it had been this tether between the lives we had to pack up and leave behind. I had no control over where I lived or for how long or whether my dad would remember to call, but I could stop time. I could make the seconds that passed me by tangible and take them with me. But it turned out that even that stupid camera with its broken strap wasn't mine to keep.

When I was finally in control, I made a life that was immovable and married a man I thought wanted to share it. Computer science seemed like the most sensible major offered at Lewellen College, but law school sounded even safer. Intellectual property sounded safer still. It all seemed like the *right* next step at the time. And what else are we supposed to do besides take the right next step?

But it isn't all bad. In the distance, I can glimpse a version of my career I might love. One where I'm a partner or, at the very least, in control of my own time. I could choose clients with small software startups, people taking big risks and searching for a sliver of protection over their big ideas.

Ideas are ephemeral and startups fail, but patents? Patents last. They're tangible. Investors can hold it in their hands and protect their mark on an ever-shifting technological landscape. I've never been someone who can leap headfirst into the unknown and trust that a net will appear, but I know how to build a good net. Nets are my specialty.

"Because I'm good at it, Powell. Not all of us have the voice of an angel." I reach across the console to poke him in the side. He squirms and bats me away, and, like a good friend, I retreat. "Thank god some of us are good at the boring jobs so that other people can go around following their bliss."

"That's so noble of you. Remind me. Was it the general counsel of the rat-trap company who got you box seats at the Target Center or was that the guys at Cyberdyne Systems?"

I hold up a hand. "Okay, it was Payne, the rat-trap company—the other company you mentioned is from *The Terminator*—and the seats were for a WWE match called 'Tables, Ladders, and Chairs,' which is even less glamorous than it sounds."

His smirk unfurls between his cheeks. "Okay, I have. *so* many more questions."

"*Your* questions?" I toss up my hands. "What about *my* questions?"

"What questions could you possibly have for *me*?" he asks, eyes fixed on the highway stretching in front of us.

"Let's start with this van." I gesture at the impossibly chic interior. Between the crisp white kitchen cabinets, the walnut floors, and the Faribault wool blanket on the bed, the whole space is very Ralph Lauren–for–Ford Motor Company.

"What about it?"

"Your van is, like, nice. *Suspiciously* nice."

"Suspiciously nice," he repeats.

"Seriously, how can you pay for this?" I ask, reopening my bag of Dove chocolates. My stomach is starting to settle, and I'm ready to get hurt again.

He shrugs. "It's how I make money."

"As a van-life influencer? Should I be filming content for you right now?"

"No," he answers, rolling his eyes. "I renovate clunker campers and resell them to van-life influencers."

"I thought *you* lived in your van." That's how it looked on social media at least. We weren't exactly on speaking terms when his life went off-road.

"I do, for a little while. Then I sell the van and buy another one to fix up. But I'm hoping to hold on to this one for myself if I can swing it."

My eyes trail around the van's interior again. "That's a really good idea."

"I know it is. I've been doing it for . . ." He squints to perform simple mental math. "Over two years now? Should I be offended you're surprised that I'm able to come up with a solid business?"

"I'm not surprised. I just only ever picture you playing music. How do you run a business when you don't live anywhere?" I ask.

"I was working out of my buddy's place in LA for a while, but I did the last two builds out of my parents' place. They're getting older, and it's nice being around them more. Plus, it's closer to my gigs on the Midwestern college circuit."

"Never thought I'd see the day you went back to Lewellen," I respond, choosing a chocolate with performative concentration, while trying my best to conceal the way the memories of the two of us coming and going from that place pick at an old wound.

"It's not so bad," he says. Then he holds out his hand for a chocolate. I read the wrapper before handing it over ("Hug the sunlight!") and debate whether to say what's on my mind.

But I might as well have a ticker tape on my forehead publicizing my every thought.

"Say it, Beekman," Ethan demands, calling me out around a mouthful of candy.

I want to be irritated, but it's too satisfying to be seen this clearly again. The sensation carves most of the annoyance out of my voice when I spout out, "But you said you'd never come back."

My body waits for Ethan's response, desperate for him to tell me everything's different now. That he's staying. To skip over the part where the texts get further and further apart and his little **just checking in, Beek** messages get less frequent as he becomes impossible to pin down. Now that he's in front of me, I don't want to go back to mailed bags of chocolates after he thoughtlessly double-books himself for Petey's playoff game when Rich, who was still my doting new fiancé, pulled every string to get box seats for us.

When Ethan and I are together it's as though no time has passed. We're us. But then he goes, and he's still my best friend, but also, he's not. He gets distant and flaky. He becomes the kind of guy who feels comfortable sending a last-minute cancellation to my wedding via text, even though he's the best man.

It already aches—the way I'll miss him when he disappears on me again.

"I'm not, like, investing in property. I'm just visiting," he says dismissively, and I don't allow the rush of disappointment to settle into my lungs. The prospect of tying down Ethan Powell to a single zip code? Ridiculous.

"But the road life *is* hard," he continues. "I'd like to expand the van business. Play fewer college gigs. Get a cat. Live in the van for fun, not because I have to, you know?"

"Only you would live in a van because you *wanted* to."

The lowering sun reflects off his irises. "Say it, Beekman. You know you want to."

I smile, shaking my head. "Could never be me."

"There it is," he says, finding amusement in my utter predictability, I'm sure.

Something flickers across his face, like a momentary glitch in the system, but then he smiles, his profile exposing that elusive dimple that few can resist. Oh, to have that dimple in my arsenal. I'd probably rule the world. He turns to look at me, then back at the road. His eyes are bottomless.

The thought drifts through my mind. A dandelion in the wind.

So beautiful.

But it's gone just as fast and I chalk it up to the divorce, our proximity, the Eggland's Best shower, and my Dove-candy-coated nostalgia. It's not real. Our fifteen-year friendship depends on those feelings never amounting to more than a fleeting fantasy.

His eyes flash on me, intense. It's as though he's trying to read my thoughts—god, I hope he can't—but when he opens his mouth to say something, he's cut off by the loud gurgle thundering in his stomach.

I squawk. "Jesus! Is there a baby dinosaur in there?"

"It's fine," he says dismissively. "Just a little hunger pang. Can you hand me another chocolate?"

It rumbles again. My eyebrows raise. "I don't think a Dove Promise is going to cut it, bro."

"I have plenty of food in my kitchen, but we'd have to stop."

"Then we'll stop," I say simply.

"You gave me a mission, Chuck. You wanted to get to your

sister before sundown and there's only a few hours of daylight left." His voice is resolute.

"I love you for that, but I also have a mission, and it's keeping the only person who knows how to drive this van alive and satiated."

"Satiated?" His mouth tilts into a wicked grin. "Wow, that's . . . so descriptive."

"Shut up." I roll my eyes, though I suspect my face is turning the color of a tomato.

But he's already off to the races. "Such an evocative word choice."

"I didn't mean it like that."

He pulls off onto an exit. "Yeah?" He's relentless. "Then how do you mean to satiate me, Chuck? Because I have a few ideas and none of them involve food."

A choked "Uh" falls out of my throat. An unintentional glottal stop out of nowhere, because Ethan just made a sexual innuendo. About me. Us. The moment in the bathroom I convinced myself was all in my head replays in slow motion, and now I can only blink, manually processing my thoughts in single-syllable increments. *Me? Us? There? Here? Van? Huh?*

His eyes fall back onto the road. "I'm just messing with you. Chill." He says it so breezily.

"I know." I add an extra syllable onto the word "know" and say it entirely too loud. "Me too. We both were. Messing around. With each other, I mean. You know what I mean." I'm a computer that is spinning the wheel of death. "Oh, look, a road! You should turn," I shout with an incomprehensible urgency.

"I don't think it's public," he argues.

I'm sweating. Why am I sweaty all of a sudden? "If it's not public, why are there no signs?"

His forehead wrinkles. "What?"

"Turn!"

"Okay!"

He whips the wheel around and when we straighten out, it's as though I've popped the anxiety balloon. I'm breathing normally. I'm still sweating, but just the normal summer kind and not the *Oh my god, Ethan joked about having sex with me and now that's all I can think about* variety.

"Are we going to talk about what that was back there?" Ethan asks, a little too pleased with himself.

I give him a firm head shake. "I wouldn't count on it."

"Suit yourself."

Ethan's fingers grip the steering wheel tighter as the van rocks over the uneven dirt road that follows the Lake Superior shoreline. Tall grass on either side of us curves toward the center, narrowing the path. He rides the brake in an attempt to regain control.

"I don't think this is a road," I admit when the grass sweeps the passenger window.

"You think?" he deadpans.

His arms stiffen when something grabs his attention. He punches the brake, steering us off the path and onto a field. "Shhiii—" he starts through gritted teeth. The front tires lurch onto the grass. They roll and roll and sink until, suddenly, the van is no longer moving.

Ethan pauses. Taps the accelerator uselessly. Pauses again. "Huh," he remarks.

"What was that?"

His brows draw together. "A family of turtles . . ." He trails off, yanking the gearshift, then tapping the accelerator again. I turn to Ethan. I can feel his brain whirring. Panic flickers in his eyes before his confident smile snuffs it out.

"I'm sure it's nothing," he tells me.

"You have insurance, right?"

Multiple emotions war on his face. He turns off the ignition and hops out of the driver's seat, responding with a stiff, "I have insurance, Beekman."

I stare into the middle distance of Lake Superior for thirty agonizing seconds—I count them. I'm not looking at his facial expression when he finally admits, "So the turtles are safe, but the van . . ."

I jump out before he can finish to find him squatting on the ground in front of a tire that's lodged in at least three inches of mud.

He nods once with a delusional optimism I do not possess and strides back in the direction of the side door. "It looks like we've found where we're going to eat!"

Chapter 9

People Don't Full *Felicity* for Their Friends

M Y DORM ROOM was tiny and smelled like nickels. Luckily, my roommate had already lofted the beds, so that addressed my most immediate concern with the living situation. I had yet to meet Erin Gallagher but based on her decor, she had a singular interest, and that interest was horses.

"I'm still not over that you followed your *pen pal* to college. It's literally psychotic," Laurel chided me while fighting a collapsible milk crate that was refusing to cooperate.

"First, I followed my scholarship money to college," I argued, breaking down the crate myself and stuffing it under the desk that wasn't claimed by a *Black Beauty* tabletop calendar. "Second, Ethan's not my *pen pal*. He's my friend. People go to the same college as their friends all the time."

Laurel unzipped an overstuffed suitcase. Several rogue "going-out tops" mounted their escape. "People don't full *Felicity* for their friends." She said the word "friend" as though it possessed an ulterior motive.

"Who's Felicity?"

"Keri Russell, Charley. Get some culture." She rolled her eyes.

I wasn't sure what Keri Russell had to do with anything, but Laurel was a little bit right. There was more to my college selection than friendship and finances. It was also this town. College was the first choice I had that was all my own, and I didn't want to go to another strange place packed with people I didn't know. For once, I didn't want to be the new kid. I wanted to be recognized. I wanted to go back to Lewellen.

"Why are *you* here then?" When I'd suggested she transfer from Milwaukee Area Technical College to be with me at Lewellen, she couldn't wait for me to get the sentence out before she was ringing the registrar's office. "It wouldn't have anything to do with a certain sophomore on the hockey team, would it?" If she was going to reduce my college experience to chasing a boy, I could do the same for her and Petey, who was already making a name for himself on the hockey team as both the coach's son and one of the distressingly few Asian men playing the sport at the collegiate level.

"I would never move anywhere for a man." She straightens an already neat row of books on my desk. "Even one who watches all of my Snapchat stories and is clearly obsessed with me."

I narrowed my eyes. "Liar."

The door creaked and the tension between Laurel and me broke as Ethan and Petey burst into the Shrinky Dink of a bedroom, and suddenly, they were surrounding us with a megaphone and noisemakers.

"Beekman! Beekman!" they shouted in concert, their

amplified voices echoing around us like we were in a coffin. Laurel and I covered our ears, but it was no use.

And then, for the briefest moment, the world paused. It was Ethan and me, eye to eye, for the first time in too long. For years, my best friend had existed only in pictures—intangible two-dimensional images of someone older than the Ethan from my memories. When I imagined him—the sound of his voice, how his hands were always a little warmer than mine, the way his nose scrunched before he let out one of those laughs that exploded across his face—I was picturing the boy I knew back when. But the Ethan in front of me now wasn't a boy at all.

"You got tall," he said, smiling in a way that made me smile back.

He was finally close enough to touch, and the sight of him overwhelmed me. Ethan had always seemed to glow in the dark, but this was more than that. He'd grown into his limbs and transformed from a skinny, sweet-faced kid into an eighteen-year-old with a devastating smile and a jawline that could cut glass, and I wasn't prepared for how potent those developments would be in person. But since I couldn't very well *say* any of that, I accidentally negged him.

"You didn't. Get tall, I mean," I said back without thinking.

A boisterous laugh burst from his belly, surprising us both. "You think you're so funny. Don't you, Chuck?" He scooped me up by the waist and threw me over his shoulder. My chest simmered with giggles as my legs flutter-kicked behind me. Even with my feet in the air, I felt more grounded than I had in years. It didn't matter what Laurel had said. I knew in that moment that coming back to Lewellen was the right choice.

Petey, who was still chanting our names, took this moment as an invitation to start picking people up and sat Laurel on his broad shoulders, shouting, "Barn Party waits for no one!"

BARN PARTY, A Lewellen Welcome Weekend tradition, was exactly what it sounded like: an all-day party in a field abutting a barn.

Kegs sat on the ground next to pickups. Striped wool blankets lay strewn over truck beds. People were everywhere. A group of girls in matching T-shirts squatted together for a group photo. Boys in Greek letters were pitching a tent. Countless bodies were stacked on top of each other in lawn chairs, attempting to make the most of every available seat. A group in the center was commandeering the music with an amp so loud its vibrations shook the grass. A few cars were attempting to compete, blaring Rihanna, Kendrick Lamar, and a country artist I didn't recognize.

Binge drinking aside, there was something almost wholesome about it all. A Norman Rockwell portrait of Midwestern collegiate debauchery.

"This reminds me of the 'Party in the USA' music video," Laurel said before wandering off with Petey in the direction of a cornhole game.

Solo cups snapped under my feet. Ethan winced at the red trash scattered every which way. "So much plastic," he murmured.

"Is this your nightmare?" I asked.

He looked at me, his eyes bright. "Nah. This is the dream." He slung his arm over my shoulders, and I caught sight of his tattoo. It looked almost exactly like the flowers in the photo

I'd sent to him of the two of us lying at the top of the waterfall, our heads knocking together. The waterfall I never did dive off of. Maybe college could be my second chance.

Ethan and I took a lap around the field, sizing up the party, but still found ourselves irresistibly drawn to the people we'd arrived with. Laurel and I made it two rounds into a contentious flip cup tournament before getting knocked out of the bracket by Petey's hockey teammates. At some point, the RAV4 behind us started blaring "See You Again" through the open hatchback, so naturally, Petey wept as he recalled the plot of *Furious 7.*

"That's really beautiful, man," Ethan told him, comforting his buddy and validating his deeply felt opinions on the poignancy of big-budget action movies. But then a Demi Lovato song streamed through the speakers, and Ethan and Petey swiftly downshifted into what appeared to be an intricately choreographed dance routine.

Everything about the four of us together felt like old times, and still, I couldn't quite settle into our new dynamic.

For one, Laurel and Petey were *always* touching. If he wasn't stealing her sunglasses off her face in that way men tease women they're hoping to have sex with, she was "noticing" another one of the stupid tattoos he'd inked after losing a bet.

"Are those the lyrics of 'We Belong Together' encircling a DQ Blizzard?"

She traced the cursive with the tip of her finger, face equal parts disbelief and unfathomable arousal. He whispered something in her ear and she practically cackled. What could Petey possibly be saying that would make her laugh like that?

In the time it took Ethan and me to assemble our pop-up

tent, Laurel was on the hood of a car with her tongue down Petey's throat.

"Well, that seemed inevitable," I said to Ethan, pointing them out.

His hair fell onto his forehead in handsome wisps that made my fingers tingle with the urge to touch it. If for no other reason than to compare it to the feeling of his freshly buzzed hair in my memories. "Oh yeah, Petey lost his mind when Lo said she was transferring. You know he's, like, fully in love with your sister?"

I laughed. "What?"

"He compared her to a mermaid who would put a curse on a sea captain. But in a hot way."

"How . . ." Unease swirled in my stomach. "They hardly know each other."

He shrugged. "They know each other as well as we do."

Before I could fully consider who it was I didn't know as well as I'd thought—my best friend or my sister—Ethan began reintroducing me to old friends from middle school who pretended to remember me, my face vague to them like an old locker combination. When the sun went down, and he left to relieve himself behind a tree, I helped my new/old friends build the bonfire with a group of seniors who looked like honest-to-god adults.

"Here." The only girl who looked about my age passed me a long stick. "Just poke at the fire. As long as you look busy, no one will send you out into the woods for kindling."

"Ooh. I like that strategy," I replied, taking it from her. "I was planning to stare into the flames and look generally unapproachable, but this works too."

She laughed generously, the crackling firelight dancing on

her face. "Always good to have a backup option if the stick breaks. I'm Sadie, by the way."

"Charley."

"Oh, I know," she said back, flicking her brown bangs out of her eyes. "You're the famous Chuck."

"Famous," I repeated, hoping my tone didn't mirror the sinking feeling in my stomach. I didn't know of Sadie, but Sadie knew of me. She knew of "Chuck," which for some reason had me feeling like I was dangling over a ledge.

"You're Ethan's 'friend from Canada.'" Her eyes sized me up, and I had to summon every ounce of confidence to keep looking back at her with an unbothered gaze. "That's what we call you. We knew you were real, but Ethan's fun to tease. I mean, *you* know. He's so cute when he's annoyed."

"Yeah," I said, watching her eyes measure my response.

The truth was, I didn't know whether Ethan looked cute when he was annoyed because I hadn't been in the same room with him since the eighth grade. I only knew that *Sadie* thought he did. Sadie, with her Cool Girl bangs and her beachy waves that looked undone in a way that would've taken me hours but probably just *happened* to her.

I don't know *Ethan*, I thought. I'd followed a boy I didn't know to a place I didn't belong to anymore. Lewellen wasn't mine. There wasn't anywhere on earth that belonged to me. The world was constantly shifting beneath my feet, and I was sick of all the motion.

The silence between us was the loaded kind. It settled at our feet with flakes of ash as we prodded the flames with our sticks until Ethan materialized beside me out of nowhere.

"Laurel kicked one of Petey's housemates in the face doing a keg stand."

My face froze, processing. "What?"

"And Petey's, like, the only sober person at this party. He's gonna take Laurel and Seth home tonight. Seth is the—"

"The guy Laurel kicked in the face?"

He nods. "Do you want to head back with them or stay here with me?"

His hand clapped my back like he was shaking loose a rogue bite of hot dog from my windpipe. Sadie peeled her eyes off me to grin at Ethan. It showcased all of her perfectly straight teeth. Ethan acknowledged her with a nod, and something like jealousy slithered around my neck. She really was very pretty, with a sultry edginess that complemented Ethan. They made sense together.

"Let's stay," I told him, willing myself not to look at Sadie's expression.

A commotion seethed behind us somewhere. Ethan's attention drifted in the direction of the rising voices. "Uh . . . Beek . . ." he started, and I followed his eyes to an animated Laurel and Petey.

"It's not about the *label*. It's the *expectations* of the label." Laurel leaned deep into each consonant. With that one sentence, I knew she was starting to erupt. Laurel fought like a volcano: she provided plenty of warning signs to evacuate, but if you ignored them, there would be no escaping her destruction.

Petey hoisted either a teammate or a literal giant into the back seat of his SUV. "It's just a word, babe. There are no expectations." Petey's tone was teetering dangerously between mollifying and oblivious.

"Oh my god! I can't explain *the world* to you, Peter!" Laurel stomped in our direction, knocking me with her shoulder as she charged past. "I think we should call it. Whatever this is," she declared, gesturing between them. Petey's face fell.

She hesitated, and for a second, it seemed to the gathering crowd that she might take it all back. But she cleared her throat and said, "Leave, Peter. I'll stay with Charley. Your car is too crowded anyway." She turned away from him and kept walking.

"It'll be fine," Ethan whispered against my ear, somehow perceptive of the tension gripping my neck. "I'll be back in a sec. I'm just gonna . . ."

Ethan gestured toward Petey, who was pacing and kicking up hunks of grass next to his car. I nodded for Ethan to go and trotted after my sister.

"Laur, slow down. What's wrong?"

When I caught up, I hooked my arm through hers. She leaned her head on my shoulder. "Nothing's wrong," she said in that wet-throated way people sound when something is most certainly wrong.

"Did Petey do something?" I asked.

"No." She tried to turn her head away from me, but I out-maneuvered her. Her eyes were red with unshed tears. "He called me his 'girlfriend' . . . and like . . . we've been talking a lot more, but it wasn't . . . I mean, I guess it sort of *was*, but . . ." She hid her face with her hands.

I didn't say anything. Instead, I pulled her into my arms. She was stiff at first, like she wasn't sure she deserved it, but then collapsed into the hug.

"He thought by my coming here . . . But he didn't even ask, and I'm not . . . I don't know why I'm like this," she murmured into my shoulder. She was so quiet, and I wondered if I was even meant to hear her.

"Like what?" I asked.

"Poisonous," she answered, her voice wet and wobbly.

I'd seen my sister's dramatic side, but the way she was speaking now flipped inside my chest. *Poisonous.* "What do you mean?" I pressed her.

She pulled away from me, wiping her face with the sleeve of her Lewellen College sweatshirt. Then she lifted her head and revealed a completely different Laurel—bright, sunny, and unbothered. Her emotional heel turn flattened my stomach.

"It's nothing," she said with a straight-lipped smile. "Thanks for letting me stay with you guys tonight." Then she walked in the direction of a red Jetta blasting Fetty Wap, leaving me to wonder if I'd imagined the whole interaction.

AFTER A FORTY-MINUTE heart-to-heart with Petey, Ethan let his friend leave in an SUV packed with six or seven other hockey guys. I waited for him inside the tent, entranced by the glowing yellow light of the camping lantern. It was the kind that exploded stars in every direction.

"Is the lamp too 'try hard–y'?" he asked when he stepped inside. "I wanted it to be perfect."

I'd probably slept in as many tents and trailers as I had houses, often remote sites while my dad was shooting. It always felt special, particularly at night. There was this sense of anticipation for the next day, like the world was building up to something.

"I like it," I told him. He smiled as if that meant something to him. "It reminds me of that projector Petey had in his basement."

"Hopefully a little nicer than that," he muttered.

"Definitely. This one isn't stuck on 'strobe effect.'"

He straightened a bright red sleeping bag on the tent floor so that it was about a foot from a lavender one. "You know, the battery compartment eventually melted shut. We couldn't turn it off, and garbage collection refused to take it. Mrs. Thao had to bury it in the backyard."

I gasped. "Like a haunted doll?"

"Yes." His whole body lit up with excitement. "I kept calling it Chucky, and Petey thought I was talking about *you*. No one understood. This is why I need you back in my life." He shook me by the shoulders. My lungs fluttered. After the day together, I'd mostly adjusted to how he'd changed physically over the years—not the way that looking at him made my skin tighten across my ribs, but, you know, baby steps.

Still, I definitely hadn't accepted that *time* had passed. That Ethan had lived four years where I was only words on a screen and he was . . . him. The person everyone was drawn to and the Sadies of the world fell for.

A noisy unzipping sound announced Laurel's entrance into the tent.

"I was talking to this guy, Cory, and he didn't know what a nectarine was. What is *happening* with the men of today?" She starfished on the floor with a dramatic sigh.

"Really?" I said while nudging her calf off the pillow. I searched her face for remnants of her earlier distress, but she just looked like Laurel. An ethereal beauty with blue hair and a cracked phone screen. Charming chaos personified.

"Yes. And it's not even a quirky fruit."

"What's a *quirky* fruit?" Ethan asked.

"Kumquat," Laurel and I said in unison.

"Noted," Ethan responded through his snort-laugh. "Can you give my guy Pete twenty minutes before you start talking to the Corys and the Codys of the world?"

"Men will flow in and out of our lives." Laurel sighed. "It's important not to get attached. Charley, let me into your sleeping bag. I'm freezing."

"You smell pickled," I whined but still shuffled to make room, enjoying in spite of myself the comforting certainty of people behaving the way you expected them to. Minutes passed, the three of us lying side by side as we stared up at the simulation of a starry night, no noises apart from crickets and the distant murmurs of a dispersing party.

I squirmed under the weight of the quiet. "Sadie seems nice," I said, breaking. She didn't. She seemed weird and territorial, but starting something with Ethan's . . . "someone" wasn't going to serve me.

"Uh-huh." He stretched the syllables like he was waiting for me to say more.

"Who's Sadie?" Laurel butted in.

"Ethan's girlfriend," I answered, my eyes pinned to the lights dancing on the tent ceiling.

He groaned and turned to face me. The foot between our sleeping bags seemed to contract as an exhalation stumbled in my throat. "She's not my girlfriend. We're just friends who . . . *hang out* sometimes, but we haven't talked like that in almost a month." He said "girlfriend," "hang out," and "talked" like each word had alternate meanings I should know. "We're not like . . . a thing."

"We don't want to hear about your hookups, Edna. It's disgusting, and we're trying to sleep." Laurel retched performatively and rolled away so she and I were pressed butt to butt. At that moment, I felt a little grateful for my sister and her revulsion to Ethan's love life.

He and I exchanged smiles and I reluctantly closed my eyes, knowing one thing with absolute certainty: I wasn't jealous of Sadie.

To Ethan, Sadie would only ever be a girl he'd once liked enough to "hang out" with and was now distancing himself from in a crowded tent. Sadies would go in and out of his life like regrettable haircuts, and I couldn't allow that to happen to us. I was something better to Ethan. More permanent.

I was Chuck.

Chapter 10

A Reverse Benjamin Button Is Normal Aging

SOMETHING I LEARNED today that I never dreamed I'd need to know: in Rockland Bay, Minnesota, tow truck drivers will *not* pull your van out of a muddy bike trail in a public park—which is apparently where Ethan and I have found ourselves—no matter how desperately you plead with them.

"Little lady, you're not going to find a soul willing to drive a wrecker through a park without Alf's go-ahead." I suppress the increasing temptation to chuck my phone into Lake Superior at the words "little lady" and "Alf."

According to this driver—and the four other drivers who appeared above him in my Google search results—the scenic, unincorporated community of Rockland Bay lives and dies on the say-so of Alf Knudsen, a septuagenarian who's unreachable on weekends unless he's eating breakfast at the diner or watching the Vikings in his regular booth at the Pickled Herring.

After Randy hangs up, I kick pebbles into the water, imagining each rock catapulting directly into Alf's face. The fantasy is immediately pulverized by an anvil of guilt because Alf is probably a nice old man who loves this beach and wants to protect it from people like me—someone who barreled a mobile home down the lake's adjacent bike path.

Now that I've contacted every tow truck in the surrounding area, I try Laurel, but the call goes straight to her voicemail again.

My thoughts spin like a top on the edge of a table, already starting to fall into an anxiety spiral. What if I can't find a way out of this? What if I get there too late and she's already married? When it comes to Petey, Laurel doesn't know how to protect herself from heartbreak. She dives in headfirst every time and a little piece of her shatters when it falls apart. When this ends, I'm worried it might break her.

For a second, I wish I was still with Rich. Not because I miss him or love him or would even enjoy standing on this beach with him, but had he not left, I might still believe there's hope for the Beekman women.

Ignorance is bliss.

I stuff my phone in my jean shorts and stare hopelessly into the hypnotic swells of the water.

It's hard to explain the vastness of Lake Superior to people who've never seen it, but whenever I stand on the rocky, imposing shoreline and peer into the unending water, something changes inside me. My molecules rearrange themselves, and for a split second, I'm certain the dark waves will reach onto the shore and yank me under, as though I'm a bird or a boat or a shell. I'm an object that lacks the capacity to think or feel or perseverate on my full inbox and the echo of my living room. I'm just a thing, capable of being swept away.

I close my eyes, focusing only on the way the breeze hits my face and strands of my hair fly into my lip balm. I'm on the edge of the world, and the notion of that almost quiets the anxiety prowling around my mind.

A familiar hand meets my shoulder, and I let myself press against it. "Any luck?" Ethan asks. His mouth drifts to my ear to compete with the deafening crash of waves.

I shake my head. "Tony Soprano has nothing on the way Alf Knudsen has northern Minnesota by the neck. Which wouldn't be a problem if I could reach Laurel to tell her to hold off the wedding."

He purses his lips. "They must not have enough reception for a call. Petey read my text, so at least we know that *they know* we're not making it tonight."

I inhale through my nostrils. "Can this day get worse?"

He takes my hand but doesn't turn us away from the water. "Do you need to do 'dark side' or 'bright side'?" he asks, re-introducing one of our other old games: the "talk anxious Charley off the ledge" game.

I almost say, *She's already trapped*, but even that's not the "dark side" I'm most afraid of. Breathing in deep, I opt for the thing I can't always do on my own. "Give me the bright side, Powell."

He wraps his arm around my shoulder and ushers me from the shore like an adult coaxing a toddler away from a hazard. "So we're stranded on the side of the road—"

I cut him off with a snort. "You've gotten worse at this."

"I'm ramping up to it," he huffs, knocking my elbow with his. "So we got stranded—*beached*, if you will—"

"Hilarious," I deadpan.

"But that part's over now. We're done with the bad part,

and now I've made dinner, and then we get to fall asleep next to the largest freshwater lake in the world. This isn't some rinky-dink Lake Lewellen."

"And I have a lead on Alf's whereabouts tomorrow morning," I add, finally feeling the effects of Ethan's trademark bright side. "On Sundays, he eats waffles at the Grey Duck after church."

He gives my shoulder a squeeze. "See? Everything's coming up Beekman. Let's eat and worry about the rest of it tomorrow."

I follow him back to the van, pretending that hunger is all I have to worry about.

He's set up a pole behind the back door, and a single strand of café lights. Behind it are two camping chairs and a tiny propane grill. There are plates—actual *matching* plates with a navy stripe around the rim—filled with some kind of white fish, grilled broccolini, and a creamy rice thing that smells incredible.

"Are those slices of lemon butterflied into the fish?" I ask, pointing at the rest of the charred fish head still nested in a wad of tinfoil atop the grill. Its menacing eyeballs stare back at me.

"Branzino," he specifies.

I rear back. "You had a whole branzino hanging out in your camper fridge? And is this a risotto?" I lift my plate from one of the two camping chairs and inspect it. "How did you make risotto?"

He sits and shoves a forkful of rice into his face. "The Instant Pot," he informs me with a full mouth and pink cheeks. "It's tomato and Parmesan."

I sit, plopping the plate on my thighs, stunned.

"Here." He hands me an insulated tumbler of white wine.

"I'm stranded off a bike path, eating grilled branzino, broccolini, and tomato Parmesan risotto. This was *not* the way I expected my Saturday to go."

"I bet," he says, smirking. "Who's going to organize your freezer now that you're out here having the best meal of your life?"

"You think you're making fun of me, but that is my dream Saturday night." I bite into the perfectly flaky, expertly seasoned meal and let out an indecent moan. "My god, Powell. This is amazing. This tastes exactly like that Italian place you took me to in LA."

"Velluto," he offers, correcting me.

"You have all the ingredients to Velluto's branzino dish sitting in your van? What is your life?"

He glances at me and then away. "You caught me on the day I happened to go to the store."

"What store? Does Aldi carry whole branzino now?"

He rolls his eyes. "It's just a fish, Beekman. Do you like it?"

"I love it. I want to marry it, have its babies, and buy a cabin we complain about not visiting enough."

"Good." He laughs. "Then mission accomplished."

We talk comfortably about nothing, eating the most exquisite meal anyone has ever served next to a mud-bogged camper van. I drink the wine with small, tentative sips. My hangover might be gone but an aura of sensitivity continues to circle my skull.

I peer over at him under the gleam of the café lights and soak in all of his Ethan-ness. His easy posture, his dimples, the hard cut of his jaw, that laugh and how it ripples over my skin like a rock in a pond.

The breeze off the water flutters his hair, exposing the tiny silver scar along his hairline from when we collided on our saucer sleds in the eighth grade. At a house party in college, a girl asked him about it. He said it was from a bike accident. *Easier to keep people in the dark*, he'd told me the moment she walked away. *Not everyone needs to know that my friend Chuck is a secret daredevil.*

I nestle my wine into its cup holder, realizing all at once that *this* is the Ethan that the women in this van experience. Café-lights Ethan. Branzino Ethan. A man so beautiful it hurts and you'd do anything to keep him even after he's warned you he can't be kept. A perfect projection of a carefully curated, no-madic sexual fantasy as directed by Sofia Coppola. I almost want to take a picture of it, but this Ethan isn't mine.

"So is this how it usually goes?" I stretch my elbow over my chair and relax my head into my palm. Beads of sweat collect on my neck from the heat of the low sun. I'm warm and loose and feeling a little bolder than usual. "You grill her an *entire* fish . . . ?" Something swims in his expression at my prodding. "Set up these cute little twinkle lights? You say 'Just one night,' but do the absolute most, and then pick her stepdad up from the airport the next morning just to really confuse her?"

He plucks a fishbone from the tip of his tongue and tosses it into the grass. "I've only driven one stepdad *to* the airport, thank you very much."

"Powell!" I balk. "You're ruin-your-life attractive. You can't be this noncommittal while still doing your whole 'Ethan thing' and love-bomb them via acts of service. It deludes oth-erwise intelligent women into believing they can transform you into a monogamous grown-up with an immovable house like some sort of reverse Benjamin Button scenario."

The corners of his mouth tilt upward as a tiny ember of embarrassment flushes my cheeks. "I'm sorry. I stopped listening after you called me 'ruin-your-life attractive.'"

I wince. "I'm immediately regretting that choice of words. It's clearly going straight to your head."

He narrows his eyes, undeniably pleased. It's probably been ages since someone's both criticized and complimented him with such specificity. "You know, a reverse Benjamin Button is normal aging."

I refuse to acknowledge that he's read a lesser-known work of F. Scott Fitzgerald, though that's clearly what he's fishing for. "Is this even your first time helping a woman crash her sister's wedding or is this just another Saturday for you?"

He squints. "Third, I think."

I sigh dramatically. "And here I thought I was special."

My laugh starts light and playful—we're only playing—but soon, the sound disperses into the air like a puff of smoke, because he's looking at me with this increasing intensity. His eyes flash between expressions I can't decipher and others I can read plain as day. It's as though he's letting me peek inside his mind. I don't want him to look away, but I'm terrified to keep looking back.

"What makes you so sure you're not special, Chuck?" The tiny lift of his lips practically knocks me out of my chair.

"Ha ha. Very funny." Self-consciousness cracks through my voice. I'm the physical manifestation of lipstick on teeth.

His eyes don't let up, and that unfairly lovely gaze warms my skin like stepping into sunshine. "Who's joking?"

"Don't be that guy," I implore him.

That little shit is still grinning. "What guy?"

"That guy who needs proof that everyone in the room is

attracted to him. You're objectively beautiful, and I haven't felt the touch of a man since 2023." I put on a jokey, bawdy tone that I pray undercuts just how naked I feel at this admission. "It's not exactly an insurmountable bar to clear."

His face scrunches. "Twenty twenty-three?" Somehow, I've shocked him enough that he skates right past my *beautiful* comment. "That's not possible. You were still married in 2024."

"I was still married *yesterday*."

"But in 2024 you were, like, *really* married. You were . . . unavailable. You couldn't have . . ." He gestures all around us as though that clears up anything at all.

"Couldn't have what?" I goad.

He ignores my question. "Was it really that bad for that long?" he asks. "Why didn't you tell me?"

How do I begin to explain that I thought I had nothing to tell? I didn't even realize something was wrong until it was over. Sure, our sex life had been nonexistent near the end, but Rich and I were hardly sexual dynamos when we were at our best. A week would go by. Then two. And the longer we went, the more it started to feel like an email I should've replied to ages ago. Then, in a blink, it had been months, and I was too overwhelmed to press send.

I never felt bowled over by my feelings for Rich, but, to be fair, I've never been that way with any of my relationships. I wasn't built for love like that.

And how was I supposed to admit this *to Ethan*—a man who possesses so much excess passion he has no choice but to channel it into song? Even if I *had* realized something was off in my marriage, I couldn't have told him. A wall we don't talk about went up the day he missed my wedding. We were never going to have casual phone calls about the state of my relationship. He'd made sure of that. He lost that privilege when he picked a fight at my bachelorette party and abandoned me at the altar.

But as I'm not about to unearth long-buried arguments, I respond to his question with a simple yet meaningless "It is what it is" and scoop another perfect bite of risotto into my mouth.

"And no one else since?" he asks, incredulous. "The uncles?"

"Uncle, singular. Just one. I don't have some sort of uncle kink." I cover myself with a hot, sweaty palm as the mortification paints my face a deep shade of red. "Why am I saying all of this? I'm not even drunk."

"I'm surprised you're drinking at all after this morning," he observes. Unhelpfully.

I rub my forehead. "I was hoping the wine would help."

"What was wrong with the uncle, then? Singular." He's a dog with a bone.

I sigh into my camping chair. "I don't know. He lived in one of those apartments with vertical blinds and a balcony over a shared pool. In the parking lot, I saw not one but *two* middle-aged men installing car seats into Cybertrucks. I couldn't picture who we'd be together there."

"You didn't need to move into his Divorced Dad apartment to have sex with him."

To his credit, he doesn't roll his eyes, but he doesn't have to. The way I approach dating has always been Ethan's number one "Could never be me."

Back in college, I didn't have crushes on boys so much as rich fantasies of imagined futures with accounting majors in neighboring study carrels. I'd learn their likes and dislikes, all the while curating our every stage of life on my mental Pinterest board and presenting them with a pretty cipher: a girl who could reflect back the exact person they thought they wanted. A girl who seemed *rare*. Someone they couldn't afford to lose.

It wasn't something I was doing intentionally. I was addicted to feeling wrapped in the all-encompassing glow of someone's adoration. It was never real—they hardly knew me—but walking into a room and seeing someone's eyes spark as they identified me as someone worth claiming was too much to resist. I longed for someone to dream about a life with me the way I dreamed about a life with them. If I stayed distant, unknowable, they kind of did, and it was nothing short of magic.

By the time the clouds of early dating parted and the approval-seeking psychosis lifted, I'd usually decide that it probably wasn't in my best interest to cosign a car loan with a man who operated his television with an Xbox controller and had a pile of unopened mail next to his coffee maker just because he was cute and studying for the MCAT.

Ethan hated seeing the way I'd disappear around those guys. *He's not obsessed with you. He doesn't even know you,* he'd argue whenever I brought one of them around.

With Rich, it was different. We were so similar and wanted so many of the same things that at times I'd forget that his Charley and my Charley weren't quite the same. Over the course of our relationship, I revealed so many pieces of the real Charlotte Beekman, not always on purpose. She'd crack off during arguments and on bad days like shards from a broken mirror. Brief glimpses of a Charley who might hate playing pickleball on Saturday morning and isn't always agreeable— and, in fact, *usually* isn't.

I remember the moment he first realized who he was *really* looking at. We were playing Scrabble in the basement. He was quitting smoking again and using me as a distraction from the nicotine cravings. Rich liked to win as much as I did, so, naturally, I'd spent our entire relationship feigning disinterest in the epic high of triumphing over an opponent in a low-stakes tabletop game. But that Sunday morning, I was tired and over-worked and needed a freaking win, and he caught a glimpse of the real me. And he knew what it meant. I knew he did, because I'll never forget his face when he looked back at me as I preened over my triple-letter use of "K." It was as though he'd seen something ugly. *His* Charley was this beautiful, live woman and *I* was the Madame Tussauds wax figure taking her place.

Ethan has never understood how love and sex have a way of making me feel like I need to take cover. I've kept myself be-hind plexiglass, hoping someone would take a hammer to the protective barrier but too scared to ask for it. For a long time, it was easier to let people think I already was the woman I let them see. Then *I* could decide if I wanted to stay that way. But I don't have it in me to spend another decade waiting to be discovered as the cheap knockoff of myself.

"I know," I finally answer. "But I'm done with the whole dating thing. It's not worth it."

"And everything else . . . ?" He raises his eyebrows.

"Well . . . I'm not going to have sex with just *anyone*. I'm a rare treasure." I put on my best impression of a *very* serious person and to my delight, he lowers his head solemnly in response.

"Well, of course," he agrees.

What I don't say is that I'd *love* to be capable of enjoying sex with someone outside of a romantic relationship, but even after Rich left me, he continued to be the central figure in every subsequent encounter in a manner I couldn't stomach.

This man has a mustache. Rich didn't have a mustache. How will sex with a man with a mustache feel different from sex with Rich?

Rich left me, and yet he haunted me. The strangers I'd considered after him were, well, *strangers* and thus could only exist in opposition with him. I couldn't bring myself to share new moments of intimacy with the man who left me at the direction of a virtual rowing instructor, even if he'd never know about it.

"Charley." My eyes flutter open at the sound of Ethan calling me by my actual name. It's not often he uses it, and I like the way it sounds. "You're just giving up? Because of Rich?" He ejects my ex's name from his mouth like spoiled meat.

"I'm not giving up. I'm just recognizing the inherent flaws in relationships. You should be proud. I'm finally on your level."

Back when I believed in weddings and commitment and joint bank accounts, I'd thought some people simply couldn't be tethered. I'd seen enough men leave to be sure of that. But Rich was a cement block of a man and in less than a year, he'd floated away from me like a helium balloon. Because in a world of leavers and stayers, anyone is capable of becoming a leaver.

Ethan—who is here, for now—reaches for my hand. "You

can't let that guy . . ." He swallows hard. "Rich doesn't deserve to be the last person who's touched you."

My mouth goes bone-dry. I know Ethan's not suggesting
that he should be the *next* person to touch me, but the way he's
so adamant that *someone* should has my mind bursting with
images I have worked very hard to suppress over the years.
Our friendship is built upon the premise that Ethan and I, in
that way, are impossible.

It could never be me.

I don't do one-off sexcapades, and that's all Ethan has to
offer. If there are "stayers" and "leavers," Mr. I Have Nowhere
to Be All Week is the leaving-est leaver who's ever left. No
matter what happens next, he'll always drive off into the sunset, and I'll always live to regret it.

Still, I can't help but picture it: Ethan coming home in an
Oxford shirt with a messenger bag slung over his shoulder after a day at the office to my big empty house. We'd work side
by side on our laptops at the dining room table—a new one we
bought from Room & Board with AmEx points. We'd order
Hola Arepa for dinner before watching two episodes of *The
White Lotus* and going to bed. Then wake up to do it all again.

Whenever I try to imagine Ethan in my life, I can't help but
think of my dad and the way he looked whenever he'd come
back, like he was wearing a stranger's shoes he'd stolen from
the front mat. Like he didn't belong and was waiting for someone to call him out. Ethan would surely be just as miserable.

Ethan narrows his eyes, and I'm certain they could chisel
through my skull if he put his mind to it. "Do you—"

My phone beep interrupts his question, and I watch this
moment pass us by in real time like a cloud breezing past
the sun.

I lift the offending device. The work fears creeping up my throat settle when I read the notification. "It's my alarm to put on my light therapy mask. The Iron Man mask."

"You didn't bring that camping, did you?" He doesn't move.

I don't either.

He snorts, and whatever was just happening between us deflates into something less intimidating.

"Beekman, you packed no shirts but remembered to bring a gold-plated—"

"I'm on a twelve-week streak. I've come too far to risk fine lines on my forehead."

"You're twenty-eight. You don't have fine lines on your forehead." He climbs into the van, tosses me my bag, and then flops back into his folding chair.

"Duh." I unzip the bag. "Thanks to my hypervigilance."

He puts his hand up. "Fine. Whatever you're doing is clearly working for you."

"I use it every night before bed. The ritual relaxes me."

It's at that moment that it hits me. Ethan and I will be sharing a bed. His bed.

I strap on my face mask and press the button on my forehead until a red glow appears at the edges of my vision.

"You look like a mannequin that's been possessed by Satan," he tells me flatly.

To whichever demon spirit I've angered enough to deliver me to this moment, in this van, stuck in a literal quagmire with one Ethan Powell, I wish to repent.

Chapter 11

The Anticipation
Is the Best Part

SATURDAY, NOW

I N THE VAN'S kitchen, I slip into a pair of Ethan's boxer shorts and a faded band tee using my long-retired teen-girl Houdini tricks. Not since gym class have I undressed and redressed myself without revealing so much as an inch of skin.

Ethan pulls out yet another bin from under the bed and leads me through the rest of his daily cleanup routine. We deconstruct the dinner setup and not once does he bring up our conversation from earlier, but that one sentence loops in my brain like a sticky song lyric. *Rich doesn't deserve to be the last person who's touched you.*

We wash dishes and collect garbage, and when Ethan pulls a plastic toilet out of a cabinet and into the middle of the floor, I pee on it without complaining once, as though it will earn me some much-needed karmic goodwill.

I feel sick every time I think about the possibility of Laurel getting married without me, so I avoid thinking about it at all costs and pray that Ethan's right about Laurel's and Petey's willingness to delay this elopement. I feel even more sick when my phone stops connecting to Ethan's Wi-Fi and my email app dissolves into a black screen. In hopes of summoning a single bar, I lean my arm out the window and can practically hear my phone laugh at me.

When I eventually give up on technology, we cover the windows, brush our teeth, and prepare to spend the night lying side by side at an angle determined by the roll of a soup can he plops on the counter like a quick and dirty level.

I climb into bed first, squirming under the covers until I find the perfect position. He pulls a brand-new pillow out of a Target bag from behind his car seat. As much as I want to berate him for having the kind of single-guy home so hostile to part-nered domesticity that there's only *one* pillow, I'm too grateful for it to say anything.

When he climbs in, I discover firsthand just how compact van beds are and try to make myself tiny while lying face-up, like a corpse. He clicks off the lights and settles into the space beside me, the mattress groaning under our weight.

It's been months since I shared a bed with anyone besides Laurel. Fourteen, to be exact.

"This reminds me of college," he says. "Remember how I used to nap in your dorm in the middle of the afternoon and it felt totally normal?"

But I wasn't in the bed with you, I think.

"Are you saying this feels normal? Or that it doesn't?"

"It probably shouldn't feel so normal, should it?"

But it kind of does. I feel it too. No one knows me in the exact way he knows me. Why is that comforting and terrifying all at once?

I roll onto my side. Minutes pass with nothing but the sound of his breath. I anticipate each puff of air like drips from a leaky faucet.

"Don't think I missed in the shower how you admitted to watching *Aurora Falls*."

His voice is close. My silent chuckle puffs out from my nostrils.

"I watched your episode and got pulled in. It was strangely compelling—like *One Tree Hill* with an extraterrestrial spin—and your song was even more perfect for it on the rewatch."

"Who was your 'ship?" he asks.

I give the question more consideration than he probably expects. "Harper and Chase. But I had a soft spot for Reagan and Brooke."

"No." His head shakes my pillow. "They were so messy."

"I loved their mess!"

"The Thanksgiving episode when Brooke thinks she's carrying an alien baby?"

I snort-laugh. "Was she? I can't remember now."

"No, she was just training too hard for a gymnastics meet."

I pull the blanket tighter. "That show went so off the rails in season three."

"I love that it did. It was better for it. And Harper and Chase don't get together until season three," he reminds me.

"That's when it got bad. They had this perfect banter-filled sexual tension, and when they finally got together Chase got so boring."

"His brother was *just* probed. The guy's gonna be a little emo." He nudges my shoulder. I elbow him back but don't put any fight behind it. Our small touches aren't so playful in the dark, and I'm not sure what to make of that. "The anticipation was getting boring."

"The anticipation is the best part," I tell him.

He sighs. "Benson hated that we became synonymous with that show. I think it's why he wanted the second album to be all experimental and broke up the band when that direction didn't work."

Harvey Benson was the other guitarist, the self-appointed leader of Lemonface, and a man who didn't *believe* in paying loans because some Reddit forum had predicted that a *Fight Club*-esque bank-crippling cyberattack would inevitably "wipe the slate clean." It's important to note that Benson had two vehicles repossessed in the time I knew him.

"Benson's an idiot," I tell Ethan. "I love 'Velvet Nebula.'"

"It's a little sappy." His melancholic baritone tugs at my insides like a sad lyric.

"Do you miss it? The band?" I ask him, hearing my voice falter. There's so much about his life as a musician that he doesn't share, and a part of me worries that this piece of him, those hidden places behind his charismatic front, don't belong to me anymore.

He takes a long inhale before he answers. "Yes and no. I don't miss having only one-fourth of a say in my creative vision. All I wanted to do was see the world and write music. I didn't care about fame or recognition or even performing, really. If I could figure out a way to be a musician without being a 'musician'—some dude with a microphone, performing in front of a college crowd night after night, vamping about the Big Twelve conference—I'd literally jump at it.

"But I miss some parts of the band. I miss sharing things. I miss thinking about other people, if that makes sense? What someone else needs or wants. Every decision I make now is about me. Sometimes my parents, but usually me. I'm bored of my life being all about me."

His voice sounds different now. Loaded. I feel an echo beneath my ribs.

"I can relate," I tell him. "I'm bored of me too. Of my life. I thought it would feel different."

"What?" he asks.

"Rock bottoming."

He laughs at me, a full belly laugh that shakes the mattress. "Beekman, you have so far to fall before you hit rock bottom. Trust me."

"Well, I *am* sleeping in a busted-up van down by the river, so . . ."

"Don't talk about Lake Superior like that," he teases.

He pokes my side, and I nudge my heel into his shin as a warning. "Don't test me, Powell."

His hand drags up my back and lands a breath behind my shoulder blade. We're not touching, but the air around him is holding me close. The T-shirt I'm wearing snags under the flex of his fingers. I'm so aware of how each stretch of his muscles brings us fractionally closer under the guise of "getting comfortable." We're just friends sleeping beside each other on this tiny mattress in this efficient, minimalist van home. That's all this is—I *know* this—and yet I feel every twitch. Every facial expression. And I can anticipate the way he's working up to something and brace myself for impact.

"Do you ever think about . . . ?" He breathes in deep but then seems to change course when he says, "We've never talked about your bachelorette party."

This catches me off guard—his casual mention of the night we don't discuss, the tender cadence of his voice, like he's confessing something while still revealing absolutely nothing. Typical Ethan.

"We don't *ever* need to talk about it." I keep my voice breezy. A leaf dancing in the wind without an ounce of the anger or hurt that once clenched my throat.

I hope he never knows how much it mattered to me. How much the bullshit he spewed all over me that night affected me. His unfiltered assessment of my life cut so deep, but the worst part? He was right. He reduced my wedding to some childish affair born out of my own stubbornness, but he was right. It always hurts the worst when the naysayers are right.

That night, I was so angry with Ethan. Still, I never thought he'd bail on my wedding over it.

On the morning of my wedding, I couldn't bring myself to respond to the lame excuse he sent in his place over text—I didn't want to say anything I'd regret—but as time went by, the anger built around my heart like layers of thick paint.

Why did I need to extend the olive branch? I asked myself. *He was the one who attacked my life choices, then disappeared. My very best friend's only parting gift would be the plastic party penis straw he handed me at my bachelorette party.*

The decay of our friendship was slow and painful, like watching a limb rot off my body. Days turned to weeks—weeks to months—until I'd forgotten who wasn't talking to whom. Hurt and anger corroded my insides as my most important person fell away. Our friendship was this phantom that followed me around with only a phallic straw and discarded chocolate foils as proof that it ever existed in the first place.

But in bed with him now, I don't want to rehash it all. That's the key to preserving long-distance friendships. Pushing the slights and hurts so deep into the earth that the other can't spot them from the other side of the continent.

The silence is growing into something palpable. I have to put us out of our misery. "It was forever ago," I assure him. "And anyway, you were right. So it doesn't matter much now." A pitiful laugh vibrates in my throat.

His breathing is heavy. "But the way I just came out and told you . . . you know . . ."

"Trust me. I remember what you said."

His sigh is part laugh, part tortured exhalation. "Yeah. I imagine you do."

"I don't care. Really," I whisper, with such a quiet confidence I almost believe it myself. "I know what you were trying to do. Even if you had zero tact while doing it."

"Yeah," he agrees.

And as much as I want to let it go, I can't help but use this moment to make my own point about my sister.

"So you must understand more than anyone why I have to at least *try* to talk to Laurel."

"I guess it makes sense." He adjusts his position, shifting the mattress. "I'm still sorry I couldn't come to your wedding."

And stopped talking to me, I add in my mind. But it's possible he thinks I was the one who stopped talking to him. We were two stubborn people refusing to bend in a conversational standoff.

"I couldn't come," he repeats. His voice is thin, his incomplete apology draping over us like a gauzy curtain. Even the way he recalls it now—that he *couldn't* come—grates against me more than I'd care to admit.

The truth of it is this: my best man and I argued, and then

a woman who no longer follows him on Instagram (I'm not proud that I know that detail) got food poisoning, and he simply didn't show. Or maybe she was just a convenient excuse, but at the end of the day, he didn't *feel* like going. And Ethan doesn't do anything he doesn't *feel* like doing. He's always come and gone as it pleases him. It was my fault for being disappointed in a bird for flying away.

"Was it nice?" he asks, and something sweet blooms in my chest. It reminds me of the good parts of that day, how it wasn't all bad with Rich. Even the bad years have the occasional good days, and the bad days still have moments of sunshine.

"Wendy and Stuart had a great time." I smile, recalling Ethan's parents and how they stayed with me until the venue kicked us out. My parents were technically present but in one of their relationship's "off" cycles. For them, the wedding festivities seemed less like a joyful occasion and more like a series of interruptions to their heightening feud. But the Powells danced all night long and whispered "I love you" to each other during Paul Simon's "You Can Call Me Al." I adored the way his parents loved each other, out loud in this quiet and unselfconscious way that was truly for the two of them. It was different from my parents, who loved each other with a volatile frenzy, like they had something to prove.

Rich was so even, steady. I'd hoped we'd end up like the Powells, whispering "I love you" over coffee mugs. But when Rich told me he loved me in the morning, it sounded like he was reminding himself.

The day Rich left, the seas of boring husbands and petty fights parted to make way for a reconciliation with my best friend. Ethan was my first text. **Turns out, you were right,** was all it said. I sent it as Rich walked out the front door.

And just like that, I had Ethan in my life again. We didn't discuss the rift. We pretended no time had passed. I didn't want to hash out the hurt or run back the tape of my bachelorette party, because I had my best friend again.

"Does the wedding really matter if the marriage was a failure?" I sigh, searching for an adequate way to convey how relationships always seem to slip away from me like water through cupped hands.

I sink my forehead into his shoulder. His arm wraps around me, adjusting our bodies so that I'm perfectly curled into the crook of his neck. My hand falls onto his chest as his fingers gently comb the hair between my shoulder blades. The sensation cracks me open like I'm a soda can, releasing the tension building up my spine and replacing it with the effervescent fizz of anticipation. *Where will that hand go next? Where do I want it to go?*

We're quiet again for a minute, probably more, until he asks, "Did you love him?"

The simple question shouldn't conjure up the humiliation it does.

My pride wants to tell him that I always knew it was wrong. That's what divorced people say, right? Better to have ignored your intuition than to have never had any.

I knew Rich wasn't some big love, but I'd never wanted that. He was someone who could perfectly slot into my life and I into his. We never disagreed on anything. We didn't challenge each other. We couldn't hurt each other. I remember lying in bed with him thinking: *I could be happy like this so long as I don't think about happiness too much.* If I didn't dwell on the corners of our relationship where we didn't fit. The places in us that were dark and hollow. The parts of me that wondered whether he even liked me, not *loved* me, but *liked* me. *Needed* me. Asked things of me. And whether I wanted anything from him.

But somehow, despite the worries that circled and swarmed late at night, I was so sure Rich wasn't a risk. And isn't that all anyone is looking for in a love story—a person to keep their heart safe?

As much as I'd almost rather that Rich and I were broken from the start and that I didn't have the incontrovertible proof that someone could fall out of love with me in under a year— that would be a lie.

So I answer Ethan honestly. "I think I did love him."

I feel his frown in the strands of my hair. This bed is too damn small. "Then he was a lucky man."

I nod into the dark, a little dumbstruck. I blow a raspberry to defuse the solemn shift in energy. We're touching in too many places now—our shoulders, our knees, our knuckles— and nothing good can come from the vulnerability that's cloaking us like a blanket in this already stuffy van.

"I'm not sure he'd agree with you about the 'lucky' part." Ethan's pulse is racing beneath my cheek. It's terrifying. It's exhilarating. It's the greatest threat to our friendship, and I've never been so grateful for the dark.

Threat or not, he doesn't clear his throat or feign a yawn-stretch that'll unpeel his body from mine. Instead, he takes my hand in his and squeezes. Only once. Enough to remind me he's him and he's *here*, and all I want is to sink deeper into my best friend and let him hold all of my stiff broken pieces.

So I give in to how good it feels to have him this close. I pull myself onto my side to look at him eye to eye and find he's already looking at me, breath shaky. In the absence of the warm sun, his features look serious. Sharper. More intense. Like a black and white photograph.

"I don't care what that guy thinks." His voice scrapes against my skin like loose gravel.

My eyes have adjusted, and I can see how Ethan's tapered fingers look woven in mine. The way his purple loosestrife tattoo climbs up his forearm.

I got it because of you, he told me once.

His attention presses into me, until I'm hot and safe and terrified all at the same time. His tongue curls beneath his teeth, and I can't stop replaying our conversation under the twinkle lights.

Rich doesn't deserve to be the last person who's touched you.

And now his thumb is rubbing circles in my palm, and it would be easy—*so* easy—to get carried away with him right now. To be with someone who sees me in a way no one else ever has, to let him remind me what anticipation and passion and desire can *feel* like.

My body hums, and I think he feels it—the live tuning fork he's sharing a mattress with. His hand tenses. His flinty-eyed gaze flits between my eyes and my mouth like a compass on the fritz—up and down, up and down. His body doesn't make a move. He's waiting for me to decide.

But I don't want to decide. I don't want to be the one responsible for what does or doesn't happen next. I want his mouth to fall onto my skin like cool snow in this hot van. He'll just *happen* to me—every part of me—and it won't have to change anything in the morning. The sun will rise, the snow won't stick, and I won't have to risk the piece of my friend that's always been mine.

And that's when it overwhelms me. The years of loneliness. The searing pain of being this close to someone who understands me, after being married to someone I'm not sure ever knew me. The piece of me that's always wondered whether my best friend tastes as sweet as he smells. But with each breath, the possibility of something more between us slips further away, and I don't think I can risk another second of indecision.

So I press my hand against his jaw and tilt his face to mine.

And then I'm *kissing* Ethan Powell.

I don't know what I expected, but it wasn't this. This should be awkward. This should be *weird*. We should be staring regretfully into the whites of each other's eyeballs, wondering where our hands should go. But this feels . . . good. Right. Maybe because I keep my lips soft at first, testing the boundaries of what this is. But then his hands are in my hair, tense and grasping with a wildness I didn't know I liked until exactly this moment. All of my hesitancy falls away, and suddenly, my teeth are tugging at his bottom lip and his tongue is urging my lips to let him in. And so I do. *Of course* I do.

Because whatever *this* is, it isn't what kissing usually feels like. Kissing is supposed to be a clumsy precursor to sex, but Ethan's lips on my lips—and on my jaw and on my neck and along my collarbone—is downright *indecent*. He's kissing me like the world outside is ending, and I'm rising to meet him like I don't care if it does. How could I care about anything else when Ethan Powell is grabbing my hips so desperately that I hope it leaves a mark?

He's growling into my skin and following each of my tiny whimpers like a road map, and I'm greedy for more of *this*.

More earth-shattering touches that feel more intimate than sex with the man I married ever did.

More of being wanted and desired by someone who doesn't have to remind himself in the morning that he loves me.

But as Ethan's always had a way of reading my mind, he pulls his mouth back at that exact moment. "Who am I right now?" he asks through heaving breaths. He presses his forehead to my cheek and something about the familiar sweetness of it steals air from my lungs. "Am I . . . me? Or am I . . . not Rich?"

I twist away for air and stare up at the ceiling, my chest rising and falling so violently it might demand medical attention.

"I'm sorry." The apology might as well be an admission of guilt. "I . . . got carried away."

Even though the kiss wasn't entirely about my ex-husband— part of me is wondering (panicking about) whether this kiss was a decade in the making—it wasn't *not* about my exhusband. And for that, I feel sick.

He sucks air between his teeth.

"Can you forgive me?" The plea slips from my mouth.

I'm not the kind of person who lets emotions get the better of them, but right now, we're on a detour of a detour. This rescue mission was already a deviation from my real life. Maybe that's all this is: a much-needed vacation from my rational self.

"Of course. Could never be me," he says to himself with a laugh, but the utter truth of it sinks into my chest like a rock.

"I know what you mean."

I shift away from him two inches, settling into a more comfortable position, even though I want more than anything for him to hold me. I want his finger drawing slow circles on my pelvic bone until I can no longer bear the rivulets of need beneath my skin, touching me in ways he'd never touch his best friend Chuck.

I *want* to torpedo my life. For a second. If only to finally know what it would be like to feel out of control with him. But my friend who is always interested in trying just about anything has never seemed much interested in trying *this*.

"It was just a one-time slipup. I won't do it again," I promise.

My chest rises and falls while I hang on each of his deep breaths, in and out. "You will. It was never going to be just one time." He pauses, and I wonder if he's . . . professing something, if this simple kiss is the first domino in a collision of words and touches that'll lead to the two of us, side by side, in matching Adirondack chairs, watching our thirty-seven grandkids playing in the yard. My stomach swoops and spins like I'm at the top of a roller coaster, and I can't identify whether the resulting feeling is excitement or terror.

"I don't mean to brag," he continues, voice gravelly and too serious, as my heart darts around my chest. "But I have . . . skills . . ."

I pause. Silent. Stunned.

And then a spitty laugh explodes from my mouth and showers his face. I should be utterly mortified that I just threw myself at my best friend, but I can't bring myself to care, because the sentence that just fell from his lips is ten times more embarrassing *for him* than anything I could ever dream to say. I'm certain no one has ever experienced this level of relief from a man displaying such delusional levels of sexual bravado. "You're such an idiot."

"I'm just saying, I know what I'm doing." His smile is ridiculous and confident and so magnificently beautiful.

"Is that so?"

He puffs his chest out. "I've had a lot of . . . positive testimonials."

At that, I groan, but it's undercut by the fact that I can't stop laughing. It's only getting louder now, reverberating against the walls of the small space.

"I'm actually pretty impressed you were able to stop yourself without passing out from sexual frustration. That's not usually how that goes."

I shove him on the bed. "Stop," I beg as I struggle for breath.

His body shakes, and even in the darkness, I can just make out the edges of the silent laughter tightening his eyes. "Why is this so funny to you? It's true. There are, like, three things I know I'm good at, and this . . ." He takes pity on my respiratory system and lets his sentence go.

He stops teasing me, and when I regain control of my breathing, he rolls to his other side and settles into his pillow. "We good then?" he asks.

"Yes. We're good," I answer, wiping at my eyes.

"Good. Night, Beekman."

"Night, Powell," I say back, rolling into the mattress crack. I try not to examine the disappointment gathering in my throat.

The minutes stretch, and just when I'm crossing into the liminal space between asleep and awake, I hear Ethan's low voice against my ear.

"Next time," he hums, "it'll be because it's *me*. It's *us*. Okay?"

"Mm-hmm." My mind searches for the perfect pithy thing to say next, but I'm tired and that's more of Ethan's thing anyhow. Instead, I listen to his slow, sleepy breaths, matching his deep exhales with my own until the fatigue takes me away.

Chapter 12

Legally Blonde–ing
All the Way to Jail

SUNDAY, NOW

THE BANGING ON the rear window wakes me up.

"Police!" the voice calls out.

"Huh?" I murmur, my mind peeling away from the edges of sleep. It takes me a few seconds to realize where I am and that I'm completely cocooned in Ethan. His nose is on my neck. His hand is resting on my stomach. His knee is on my thigh like I'm his Charley-sized body pillow. I *really* try not to dwell on how good it feels.

"Ethan," I whisper-shout. "Ethan." I shove his muscled thigh, and that seems to do the trick. His groan is cut short by the fuzz pounding on the side of his house.

There's another bang at the window, and Ethan's eyes finally pinch open. "Shit. Can you pull up the window shade and check who it is?"

"He said he was the police." My brain, struggling to come online, finally registers that Ethan's shirtless.

Ethan is shirtless in bed with me, toned and tanned, casually rubbing a knot out of his opposite shoulder as if this isn't the strangest wake-up call he's ever had.

The banging gets louder somehow. He hangs his torso off the bed and reaches for the floor.

"Just make sure he is who he says he is before we open the door." The prospect that the man outside may not be a cop at all but, rather, a man impersonating a cop for reasons I now have no choice but to internally list (in a Keith Morrison voice) in order of gruesomeness sends shock waves up my spine.

Another knock jostles the mattress. "What exactly is your plan if he's not who he says he is?" My tone is both groggy and razor-sharp.

He sits back up and shrugs on a T-shirt. "I'll handle it."

I pause to assess whether his easy posture is comforting or if he's one of the delusional 50 percent of men who believe they could land a plane. For reasons I cannot explain, I arrive at the former and rip the magnetic blackout curtain from the back window.

The morning light is blinding. By the time my eyes adjust, three men are staring back at me: an elderly Black man, a young white man in a Minnesota Wild muscle tee, and a very real police officer.

Ethan shoots out of bed, knocking a worn leather notebook to the floor in the process. "So he is who he says he is," he observes, murmuring out the side of his friendliest, most puppy-eyed smile. He gives our audience a head tilt of acknowledgment and makes his way to the side door. "Just let me do the talking, 'kay?"

"Seriously, what was your plan?"

"Bear spray," he tells me before sliding open the door with a hard yank.

"You can't park here." The man's bellow reverberates through all one hundred square feet of the van.

I watch Ethan's profile squint into the sun from my spot on the mattress. "So sorry, Officer. We had car trouble."

Despite his request that I let him do the talking, my insides itch to get in the middle of this altercation. I don't know if it's the single semester of crim law I took or my inability to leave anyone to fend for themselves, but my legs cross the van on their own. Based on Ethan's lack of reaction, he seems to have expected as much.

"I can see that," the officer responds. His eyes flick over to me, sizing me up. I fix my bedhead ponytail and size him up right back, but I'm at a disadvantage considering I'm somewhat exposed in Ethan's holey concert tee and cotton boxer shorts. Officer Surly's ruddy complexion is mostly obscured by red facial hair and a pair of wraparound Oakleys that I'm guessing he'll also wear come wintertime on his multiple snowmobiles. I can't explain how, but I know with unwavering certainty that this man has uttered the words *My snowmobile—well,* one *of my snowmobiles,* whilst entering a meat raffle.

"Car trouble or not," the officer continues, "you're in the middle of a biking trail."

The older man huffs from over his shoulder, a bull pawing the ground to go toe to toe over municipal park regulations. "We have the trail marathon coming through here in two hours! Unbelievable."

The officer raises his hand. "Alf, I'm handling this."

"I said they can't be here, Billy. Randall and I can take it from here." The older man, who's wearing the shiniest silver polo Fleet Farm has on offer, gestures over at Mr. Exposed Armpits.

"Officer Louderman," the cop says, correcting the older man.

"Did you say Alf?" Ethan asks.

Alf? *Alf!*

My sleep-sluggish brain is ready to burst. "Wait. Are you Alf Knudsen?"

The man lifts his chin. "Yes."

"*The* Alf Knudsen?" Ethan repeats.

The man clears his throat, seemingly caught off guard by the degree to which his reputation precedes him. "Yes. Why are you asking?" The man's eyes dart between Officer Louderman and Randall for backup.

"And *you're* Randy from Randy's Towing?" I ask, grateful, astonished, and a little giddy, as if he's a long-lost family member, known to be as generous as he is exceedingly wealthy.

Randy doesn't flinch. Perhaps in Rockland Bay, this man is used to being received in the same manner as a celebrity crush. "Who's asking?"

"I'm Charlotte Beekman. I talked to you last night and begged you to tow us out of here. I offered to pay double."

"We were very concerned about preserving the integrity of the marathon," Ethan adds. He's laying his Good Midwestern Boy shtick on thick.

The older man wheels around to face his former ally. "Is this true, Randall?"

Randy sucks his teeth. "It was after seven."

"Pull them out of here!"

"The rims are all bent up. There's practically a tree in one of 'em," he whines back at the man.

Alf throws up his hands. "Then take the van to your brother's shop in Lutsen. I swear, Randall, you're even lazier than that father of yours."

Randy meanders back to his tow truck in no hurry, even at

the direction of Alf Knudsen, a man who previously inspired a Jimmy Hoffa level of obedience in local tow truck drivers.

I clasp my hands together. "Perfect. Everyone's happy."

Officer Billy frowns. "I'm not happy. You're fifty feet down a bike trail in the middle of a protected coastline. Whose van is this?"

"Mine," Ethan answers.

"Name, son?"

I position myself between Ethan and the police officer. "Is that information relevant to the matter at hand?"

"No," Alf responds at the exact moment the cop rips off his sunglasses and demands, "Now, who are *you*?"

"Charlotte Beekman," Randy offers up from the back of his rig.

I pull my shoulders back and harness the energy of Lawyer Charley when she's in her burgundy pantsuit that's tailored to perfection. "That's right. Charlotte Beekman with Anderson & Gottlieb. I'm this man's attorney."

"Jesus Christ," Ethan mutters under his breath. He grabs my arm with a grip that's begging me not to *Legally Blonde* him all the way to jail.

I change tactics. "Look. You want us off the marathon route, and we're on our way to a wedding—"

"Our wedding," Ethan ad-libs.

I swivel my head toward his. Apparently we're going for broke, the fake-engagement kind of broke. My eyes wander all around the freckles on his face and then skitter back to the men in front of us.

"Mm-hm." I inhale through my nose. "We're eloping in the Boundary Waters this weekend, but we've run into a little bad luck."

He pulls me against his side and I dutifully lean into him like a woman desperately in love with Ethan Powell would. His morning scruff scratches against my cheek, and for a millisecond, I forget myself and enjoy the crackle that travels across my skin at the memory of our kiss.

I clear my throat and make myself stand a bit straighter. "Officer, if you could give me and my, um, *husband-to-be* a little help, it would mean the world to us."

"A wedding present," Ethan adds, his eyes twinkling.

I direct all my energy to keeping my lip twitch under control.

Officer Louderman places his Oakleys on his forehead and tilts his head toward the van's sad front wheels. "Fine. But Randy's brother is an idiot. I'll have Randy take you to my guy a bit farther north. Tell him Billy sent you and you might get a deal on those tires."

Ethan's shoulders relax. "Thank you, Officer."

He nods back at us.

"Congratulations," Alf tells us once we're hooked to the wrecker. "It's a beautiful day for a wedding."

RANDY HAULS THE three of us and the van to a shop forty-five minutes north. Eventually, the road narrows through towering pine trees on either side as we enter the harbor village of Grand Marais, a vacation destination with a thriving art scene, bustling small businesses, and a coastal breeze that is as pleasant as it is hypnotic. It's the kind of place you visit and make genuine plans to stay. You ask yourself whether you truly *need* to be within an hour's drive of a Target or a Menards or even a supermarket. Maybe you could become the kind of person who values *experiences* over *things*.

I bet Ethan would thrive here.

When we pull in front of a darkened Brother's and Son's Tires and Auto Body, we're greeted by a Be Back Later sign that hangs below an intricate stained-glass window. Randy swipes Ethan's credit card through a chunky POS machine and unhooks the van.

"Kyle comes in around eight," Randy calls out through the window as his tires crunch over the pebbled drive. Then the tow truck disappears into the distance, leaving us alone.

"Do you think Kyle is the brother or the son?" I ask Ethan.

We hop onto the hood of the van so our bodies face the shoreline, but both of our necks are craned in the direction of the empty building.

"Aren't all brothers necessarily sons?" Ethan posits.

I peer at him in my peripheral vision, but his eyes are pinched shut. "What do you think happened to the father/ brother who connects the two?"

"I'm not awake enough for your word problems, Beekman. We still have an hour before this place opens. Should we explore a little?" Ethan tilts his head toward the town.

I adjust the strap on the pricey leather crossbody cell phone case I bought in a different retail haze (separate from the light therapy mask and designer tote one) and briefly consider whether I might have a shopping problem. "I need to find food before we do anything."

He twists his backpack around to his front and pulls out a Lärabar without looking at me. Which I find thoroughly annoying considering I'm painfully aware of why *I'm* avoiding his eyeline—the general humiliation, regret, and shame from kissing my best friend when he was trapped in a locked van with me—but I can't for the life of me understand why *he's* avoiding *mine*.

I rip open the package. "You are an angel sent from heaven."

"You always were easy to please," he hums.

The sentence does something to my lungs. "Should we talk about . . ." He finally looks over at me and it's too much. His slate-blue eyes bore through mine. I'd forgotten how intense those eyes could be. Like ice picks.

"About what?" he asks me, so infuriatingly nonchalant that he might already be enacting his ghosting protocols on me like he has on every other woman who's slept in that stupid van. *Like he did after my wedding*, I think before suppressing the unwelcome comparison.

"About . . ." He trails off. He's making me say it. I can't believe he's making me say it!

Two can play that game. I say *nothing*. My eyes stare back, daring *him* to say it. But he doesn't flinch as the silence stretches around us like sticky taffy, and I can't take it. I'm too tired. Too weak.

"We can just pretend it never happened if you'd like," I offer.

He tilts his forehead up to the sky, an animal lounging in a sunbeam. "That would be impossible."

I practically catapult off the hood of the van. "Hah! I knew you knew what I was talking about!"

He almost smiles, and I can finally take a breath. "As my legal representative, I was hoping you'd use your words."

"I said I was sorry and that it wouldn't happen again—"

"To be clear, are we talking about when you lied to a police officer or the time you mauled me in—"

"*Mauled* you! That is just . . ." I can hardly form a proper rebuttal. "That is . . . false! Just absolutely . . . You think . . . ?" Pebbles ping against the metal bumper with my pacing. "No. No. You're not putting this all on me. I heard *zero* complaints from you when we *consensually* touched mouths."

His top lip curls upward in a micromovement of amusement. I force my eye line to a spot on the bridge of his nose.

"Leave it to you to make kissing sound revolting."

My hands pin against my sides and clench into fists. "You kissed me back."

"Oh, I one thousand percent kissed you back," he replies. It stuns me. I didn't anticipate such an enthusiastic admission of guilt. I'm a deer caught in his headlights. "And when you do it again," he continues, "I'll kiss you back that time too."

How is he this relaxed? How many other women have this relationship with Ethan? Does he have "friends" he makes out with all across the contiguous United States? Dozens of Charleys, when I've only ever had one Ethan?

"Why do you keep saying 'when it happens again'? It *won't* happen again," I promise him.

He confidently hops onto the gravel drive. "It will."

I turn away and spot a crowd collecting in front of a building with wood slats and a white awning. "Then how about you wait here for that kiss, and I'll go find coffee."

"Charley." He catches me by the shoulders and swivels me back around. "It doesn't . . . ," he starts. His face twists every which way. "Everything doesn't have to mean *everything*, you know? It can be one thing for one of us . . . and then something else, and then . . . who knows? You know?"

This scene is humiliating. The way he starts and stops is like watching a boat parallel park. Mr. I Don't Do Relationships is letting me down easy between a mud-caked camper van and a garbage can painted to look like Marvin the Martian. I thought being left for a rowing machine while holding a plastic phallus was my rock bottom, but I hadn't known the true depths of my personal indignity.

"Look." I free myself from his grip. "We're now friends who've . . . kissed each other. But our friendship means too much to me to let that one minute become some world-ending thing." I couldn't handle it being a world-ending thing. Even if I'm one of many, he's so much more *to me* than that.

I start down the road, powered by avoidance and a desire for caffeine.

He follows me. "Hey." He knocks my elbow with his, as though he's not ready to let go of the time I made out with him in a broken-down van on a marathon route and got woken up by Alf Knudsen and his band of enforcers. "We 'touched mouths' for way longer than a minute."

I grimace. "'Touched mouths'? Disgusting."

"*You* said that." He lengthens his stride to catch up to me. "I was repeating what *you* said."

"I can still plead 'vulnerable divorcée' for every embarrassing thing I do for the next six months. It's my rolling affirmative defense."

He grabs my wrist. "You know I can't take you seriously when you speak legalese. You're like three kids in a Chico's blazer."

"Chico's?" I pull my arm back with a gasp. "I'm not your *mom*. My blazers are Sézane."

Do I have a spending problem?

I have no choice but to stop when we reach our destination and fall into line at World's Best Donuts, an old-school donut shop and an essential stop on any trip through Grand Marais per Midwest travel accounts.

"Is that supposed to impress me?" he asks.

"Is your endless supply of ratty band tees supposed to impress *me*?" I flick his shoulder, trying to get a rise out of him.

He eyes me up and down in a way we don't eye each other up and down. At least not when the other's looking. "But you look so cute in my ratty band tees."

The compliment immediately disarms me. I've always derived a bit too much pleasure from trading barbs with Ethan, but this sweetness? Absolutely lethal.

"Can you even eat here?" I ask, tilting my head at the store behind us. It's obvious I'm deflecting.

He shakes his head. "Nah. This is just for you."

Deep-fried dough, a love language.

"I'm getting Lewellen flashbacks of you at the Donut Barn." The memories flood my body with warmth. I suddenly feel too aware of my hands and take a step back.

Clearing my throat, I remind us both why we're here in the first place. "We should try Laurel and Petey again, just to make sure they're not legally bound to each other yet."

"You've texted them both thirty times. They've seen your wall of texts and are punishing you accordingly." He twists me around by my fingers to snatch the phone from my hand, and we collide with a delicious thud. "They'll wait, Chuck," he reassures me. "You don't need to overthink everything."

One second passes. Then two. We're nose to nose, chest to chest, fingers entwined around my phone. The energy between us zings across my front and down my spine. Last night, I wanted more—part of me still wants more—but this has to be enough. *This* is what forever with a guy like Ethan looks like.

Roasting each other in line for donuts. Close but not too close. Never close enough to hurt.

He removes a strand of hair from my mouth, and I *should* be laughing at this—the way it gently tugs at my lips is like something out of a movie—but the way his eyes are locked on mine is so open and intense. This doesn't feel like a choreographed move. But maybe *that's* the move.

We move as one, stepping back so that I'm up against the barn-wood siding—alone in a crowd of hungry people. What must we look like? Should I care?

"I'll always be your friend, Beekman. But I'm not going to pretend last night didn't happen. I'm not going to pretend that I don't want it to happen again." Something about his words— the way he says my last name, the way his eyes darken and his mouth moves—they make me feel naked.

Maybe we can't pretend we never crossed that line, but this, this new energy between us, is dangerous. Flammable. Explosive.

If I hadn't already had my mulligan kiss, I'd take it now. No question.

But he's not the one playing with fire here. What happens if we have another meaningless, messy make-out next to this family in matching tie-dye T-shirts waiting for a box of bear claws? By this time next week, Laurel and Petey will be having a relationship-ending fight over cabinet knobs in an Anthropologie, Ethan will be long gone, and I'll be alone—in my big empty house—replaying the way my friend's mouth felt on mine until I die. He'll have no problem dropping out of my life for the next adventure, just as he had no problem skipping my wedding. I'll be the only one left feeling the loss of him like a missing rib.

So instead of doing the thing my body craves like oxygen, I grab my phone from his hand and shove it between us, a sexual buffer. He instantly backs up.

"Do you think they'll have . . ." My mouth further detaches from my brain with each syllable. "A maple log?"

Ethan looks back at me. Like he's still deciding his next maneuver. Can he hear inside my brain? He seems all too aware of what he's doing to me, but he's been hiding so much of himself since the moment he showed up on my driveway. Again, I'm left wondering what he's about to do next.

Never breaking eye contact, he replies in a low, gravelly voice, "Do you want me to check? On the maple log?" Donuts have never sounded so erotic.

I nod and direct my focus toward connecting to the Wi-Fi of the neighboring bookstore. "That'd be great. I'm gonna try Laurel again."

Only once he's out of sight do I realize I'd much rather have a Bavarian cream.

Chapter 13

===

Colorado Is the Breakup Bangs of States

EIGHT YEARS AGO

OWEN TWOMBLEY STILL hadn't texted me since the "Pancakes and Personal Statements" Honors Lunch and Learn two days ago.

Owen Twombley was a fellow junior, an actuarial sciences major, and a possessor of cheekbones that made me weak. He wanted three kids, two dogs, and a second house in Door County by thirty. He was perfect and, prior to the Lunch and Learn, had zero interest in me romantically. That is, until I displayed a deep and expansive knowledge of fantasy baseball simply by agreeing with his opinions on the Astros' batting order and nodding at all the right times.

I was on day three of implementing my texting strategy, in which every message I constructed was more maddeningly cryptic, mysterious, and noncommittal than the last. With any luck, he'd read my words like they were a horoscope, finding in them whatever he wanted to until he was certain I was his forever kind of woman.

I itched for him to like me as much as I liked him. I already envisioned us whisking away to suburban Chicago over the holidays to meet his parents. But the passionate overtures I was anticipating were not yet forthcoming.

I shoved my silent phone into my back pocket. Ivan, the drummer in Ethan's band, was playing too loud for me to hear my own thoughts, let alone the notifications on my phone.

Lemonface was starting to get better gigs but, due to Ethan's Donut Barn work schedule, usually turned them down in favor of bars closer to Lewellen. Tonight they were playing at a college hangout that doubled as an Italian restaurant. There were too many families eating garlic knots for Ivan to be going *this* hard.

"We are Lemonface!" Ethan called out into the crowd. Though I still wasn't sold on the name, I hollered back dutifully, the lone wooer. He found my face in the crowd and sent me an embarrassed head shake. "Good night!"

After the show, I helped the band pack up the old minivan Ethan inherited from his mom. It took longer without Petey, who'd been uncharacteristically scarce since he'd been drafted to an AHL team and was now packing for his big move up to Edmonton.

"It's still early enough to head into Minneapolis tonight," Benson argued, throwing shut the door to the Dodge Caravan.

Ethan inhaled sharply through his nose, and immediately, I knew this conversation was gearing up for their standard fight about the direction of the band.

I stepped between them. "Ethan was supposed to drive me home. I have a practice LSAT in the morning."

"I thought you were like . . . computer-y," Ivan said to me, but before I could respond, Ethan was already pouncing on my excuse.

"I have to take her back to campus. Another time."

Ethan opened the passenger door for me. I stepped in, grateful I wouldn't have to explain to Ivan that, yes, I was "computer-y," but I was in the midst of a crisis over my postgrad future. Through my professors—most of whom were coders who'd been chewed up and spit out by dozens of tech companies—I was discovering that the tech industry was unpredictable and volatile. But the lawyer who taught my intellectual property seminar was a partner at the same firm he'd clerked for as a law student, his entire career at one address. His "home away from home," he called it. It sounded perfect.

"Sure, man. Whatever," Benson sneered.

And that was how Ethan and I wound up alone on the dirt road affectionately referred to as Pothole Alley back to campus.

"I don't have a practice exam tomorrow, by the way. I just figured you needed a hard out."

He sighed. "You were right." The band's forever sore spot was Ethan's shift schedule and his destiny as the Lewellen donut king.

"Worked out for me. Campus rides stop at ten and Petey's been MIA lately."

"He's been in Saint Paul. Wooing your sister."

"Really?" I asked, incredulous. I tried to imagine where Petey slept in the Frogtown apartment where Laurel was crashing to save money while student teaching. Last time I visited, she was sleeping on a recliner and using a T-shirt quilt as a room divider.

He clicked his tongue. "The clock's ticking, Beekman. He has to convince Lo she's actually dating him before he moves to Canada."

My eyes widened. "Well, that's a fool's errand."

"Love makes fools of us all," he said, then sang it to himself under his breath. He did that sometimes. "Is that anything?" he asked, referring to the lyric.

"Maybe? It kind of sounds like a Pinterest quote." He physically recoiled. "Speaking of love, how's the vet tech?"

He quirked his head to the side. "Who?"

"Quinn?" I attempted to conjure a name for the apple-cheeked animal lover who wore ribbons in her hair in a way that managed to look Parisian and not Minnie Mouse chic.

"Oh yeah," he answered, drumming his thumbs on the steering wheel. "That fizzled out. I was too 'unreliable.'"

"I told you to make up a different reason for forgetting to pick her up."

"We were watching *Survivor* and they'd just hit the merge. I literally could *not* leave your dorm room at that point. *You* would've understood."

Whatever phase of your early twenties involved bingeing reality competition shows for hours on end like casualties in a carbon monoxide leak, we were firmly in it.

"Let's watch more tonight. I can stay over." He looked at me and then back at the road. It was the first time he'd approached happiness all night. I almost wanted to say yes to see whether he'd offer up a grin.

I leaned my head back and rolled it in his direction. "Rain check?"

The light in his eyes went out again. "Busy with the mortuary? How's that going?"

"Owen Twombley is an aspiring *actuary*. No dead bodies in actuarial science, fortunately. They're more like sexy statisticians." I pulled out my phone.

Still nothing from Owen.

"Why do you call him by first and last name like he's a person of interest in a murder case?"

I sighed and stuffed my phone back in my pocket. "Because he's about to fall in love with me, and I'm getting used to the way 'Twombley' feels in my mouth. Thanks for asking."

His head tilted to the side. "Is he aware he's the mark in your patented man-catching system?"

"You make it sound like there are nets and hounds involved. I'm simply making myself mysterious and, thus, irresistible."

"You run your life like the navy, Beekman. I know exactly where you are at any moment of the day. You're the least mysterious person I've ever met."

My head whacked against the headrest as we lumbered over a series of mini potholes. "Okay. Ouch," I said, feeling the Smirnoff Ice from earlier in the night bouncing in my esophagus.

"What? It's true."

"No, no. Please, continue listing everything unattractive about me."

"Why is that unattractive?" he asked, fighting with the steering wheel over the rough terrain. "You're steady and straightforward. You're honest and stand behind what you say. Easy to read. You're like a clock."

"A clock?" I asked, because it was possible I'd entered a fugue state triggered by humiliation and had misheard him.

The car threw us from side to side like we were rag dolls as he doubled down, telling me, with a straight face, "Everyone needs clocks."

"Stop. I can't hear the word 'clock' again or I'm going to be sick."

"Are you carsick?" Alarm rang through his gruff baritone. "Are you okay? Should I pull over?"

"I'm fine," I gritted out, stabilizing myself against the bucket seat so I could look him in the eyes. "We're fighting now, by the way. *This* is a fight."

"Come on, Chuck."

"Don't you *Chuck* me. You're not getting out of this by being all charming. You said I was predictable—"

"I don't remember using the word 'predictable.'"

"—you called me unattractive and compared me to a *clock*—"

"I definitely didn't say 'unattractive,'" he cut in.

"How would you know?" I said. "You apparently have no memory of calling me predictable."

We barreled over another pothole. It sent my stomach straight to my face.

His eyes darted to me. "There's absolutely no way I'd ever call you unattractive."

"I heard it."

"Then get your ears checked."

"You said it!" I shouted.

"Why would I call you unattractive when I *obviously* think you're attractive?"

The sentence went off in the minivan like a gunshot. With the exception of my heart, which was confusingly fluttering up into my throat, we both froze.

That is, until the front tire cratered into a pothole the size of a small planet.

Ethan's arm shot out in front of me as my seat belt locked against my chest with a tight snap. "Are you okay?" His eyes met mine with a wild intensity.

"I'm fine," I assured him, but the tension in his face didn't abate until I wrapped my hands around the arm that was still braced against me like a guardrail. "I promise. I'm fine."

"Good." He swallowed and removed his arm.

We both faced forward for a second, catching our breath, until I shattered the silence. "I'm kind of surprised I didn't throw up."

His laugh broke free from his throat, and then I started laughing too. It was that hysterical, demented kind of laughter that comes from the hollow of your stomach—equal parts release and reminder that we were alive.

"Should we call Triple A?" I asked.

His laughter died. "I don't have Triple A."

"Okay, well, whatever insurance you have."

"Sure," he responded, but he didn't move. "What if I didn't have insurance? Hypothetically."

My brows drew together. "Hypothetically?"

"What if, hypothetically, I had insurance at some point and then didn't renew it? What would we do then?"

The fluttering in my stomach was replaced by a slow sinking feeling. "Like . . . as a thought experiment?"

"Or a problem-solving exercise." He waited for me to respond, but I only stared at him. "Cards on the table. It's not hypothetical."

I popped an eyebrow. "No shit?"

"Go ahead. Tell me how irresponsible I am. I'm a disaster, I know."

He threw his head in his hands and didn't look up again until I flung open the passenger door. "Wait. What are you doing?"

I jumped out and crouched in front of the tire. Relief fell over my body. The pothole wasn't nearly as big as it'd sounded.

I walked over to the driver's side and did the universal cranking gesture for lowering a car window. "If you cut all the way left, you can back out of it."

He stared at me for a long second. "You're not going to give me shit for forgetting to renew my car insurance?"

I shrugged. "I think you already feel pretty shitty about it. And this pothole really isn't so bad."

I climbed back in, and he stared at me, gobsmacked. "How do you do that?"

I laughed, a little self-conscious. "Do what?"

"Know exactly what I need when everything's falling apart."

I shook my head in a jokey, deflective way, because the explanation on the tip of my tongue was too embarrassing to say out loud.

I didn't want to tell him that I felt so close to him, I could detect his precise frequency. I could sense his tiny disruptions, when he needed me to match his vibrations or ground him to something steady. I was almost positive he felt that kind of closeness with me too, but couldn't bring myself to ask, because it'd be too mortifying when he responded with a confused "Huh?"

He closed his eyes, hit reverse, and miracle of miracles, we were free from the ruptured asphalt. We both cheered, but the joy was short-lived.

"What's that noise? Why is the car making that angry sound?"

"Goddammit," he swore, more defeated than I'd ever seen

him. "The gas gauge is broken. We're out of gas. I was supposed to get it fixed, but I can't afford it, and—"

"It's fine, Powell." I unbuckled my seat belt and interrupted his self-flagellating with a gentle shove to his arm.

We walked on the shoulder the whole way, Ethan insisting I stay on the side farthest from the road like Jimmy Stewart in a movie my mom would've fallen asleep to. I was just happy he remembered to wear shoes.

On the walk back, he carried both gas canisters, insisting they were easier to carry that way. "I'm evened up now," he said. "If you want to help, distract me or something."

"Okay," I said, biting into the Snickers I'd treated myself to at the gas station. "A little story time for you: this is not my first time walking to get gas in the middle of the night."

"Oh yeah?"

"It's my fourth time. My parents ran out of gas all the time. My dad mostly, but my mom's done it too. And it wasn't like the gas gauge was ever broken or anything. They would just ignore it. Or forget. I'm not sure." My voice took on that light affect it sometimes did when I talked about my parents. The kind that was perfected after sharing one too many "cute family anecdotes" that were met with expressions of shock and mild concern.

"Are they back together now that . . ." He wasn't sure how to ask it, so I didn't make him.

"Now that we're not in the way? I think so. They've been all over the country interviewing people negatively impacted by the opioid crisis."

"That sounds important."

I nodded because it was the part of my dad's life I couldn't argue with. His work always sounded sufficiently more important than everything else vying for his attention.

"Weirdly enough, my dad still takes off on her. Constantly. It's almost like Laurel and I had nothing to do with it, and it was always a 'them' problem." My attempt at levity fell flat. I still sounded too resentful, which I didn't like. I didn't want to care so much.

I cleared my throat. "So, anyway . . . as someone who's made many a nighttime gas station trek, I can say with authority that this was one of the more dramatic ones. Care to share why tonight sent you over the edge?"

"I'm seriously at the end of my rope. I swear, if you hadn't've been here, I would've left the minivan and walked all the way to Colorado. Started a new life there."

"It's not 'moving to Colorado' bad, is it?"

His forehead folded up like a taco. "What? Everyone loves Colorado."

"Colorado is the breakup bangs of states. No one in an emotionally stable place has ever up and moved to Denver." I nudged his shoulder with mine. "Spill."

"My parents bought an RV. I've been helping them fix it up. They're retiring and starting their next act. But Silver Lining Society wants Lemonface to open for them on tour—"

"That's amazing," I cheered, grabbing his arm and bouncing in a way that wobbled his delicate gas can balancing act. Silver Lining Society was an indie rock band on the come up. They'd played on one of the smaller stages at Coachella two years before and their most recent album was getting even more traction. This would be *huge* for the band. For Ethan.

"It *would* be . . ." He adjusted his grip. "If I weren't the manager of a barely profitable donut shop. Or if my band wasn't scoping out guitarists in Minneapolis to replace me. Or if the thing I did all day, every day wasn't literally trying to poison me. But my parents have worked so hard and have earned the right to see the country and have adventures. Meanwhile, I'm slotting into a life where there will never be any surprises. Just the same broken gas gauge, same life, every minute, forever, until I die."

"Wow," I said, letting his deluge of words wash over me. "That was . . . an extraordinary amount of self-pity all at once."

"What happened to my wonderful friend who didn't want to kick me while I'm down?"

"That was thirty-some minutes ago. Keep up, Powell. We're on to the harsh truths portion of this nighttime walk."

He laughed. "Fine, then. Lay it on me."

"Have you ever considered telling your parents about the tour? Or that you don't want to take over the shop? Or playing them 'Donut Holes and Claustrophobic Souls'? It's a fairly blunt track, lyrically speaking."

"It's a nonstarter. My grandfather *built* the shop from the family barn. That's generations of expectations on my shoulders."

"You're allergic to your family business. I don't think that was the family legacy Stuart Senior had in mind."

"My dad . . . it's the only thing he's ever wanted for me."

"Wendy and Stuart bought you your first guitar and the three other ones after that. They made custom shirts for your jazz band concerts. If music isn't at least *a part* of the life they want for you, it certainly won't be out of left field. Maybe they're not the only ones they want to see go on some adventures." I knocked his elbow with mine, offering a tiny jolt of human connection. He choked up on the gas can handles.

"Do you ever miss traveling all the time like your family used to? The adventure?" he asked.

My prepared answer, *Of course not,* was always at the ready. But something about the darkness and how vulnerable he was being with me tonight made me want to give him the other answer. The one that scared me. "Parts of it. I loved meeting new and interesting people. I liked the way every day was bound to be different. The energy to that lifestyle."

But I'd never felt like I had any control. Even less than the ordinary way that no kid ever feels like they have control. Being on location with my family, where our lives revolved around Dad, who treated us more like anecdotes in a charming story than a family. It was as though we were auditioning for a role in his life, always at risk of being cut. I desperately wanted my place in their lives to feel permanent, but it never did.

Even the good days vibrated with apprehension like the moments before an earthquake. I was always aware that the ground could shift under my feet. Being safe and stable and cared for wasn't compatible with my family's rootless existence. They could bend for me a little, but my parents' resentment would always be in the room with us like a family pet.

"You make me feel like that, you know," he said, pulling me out of the past as we approached the minivan.

"Insecure?"

"No." He stretched the vowel in a way that sounded suspiciously like "duh" and set the gas cans on the street. "Like every day is bound to be different."

"I thought I was a clock," I whined.

But then he did something wholly unexpected. He twisted

me around by the arm until we settled into holding hands, like a magic trick.

Tada.

He swung our hands between us. "I like how easy it is to read you. Everything's on your face. All the time."

My breath quickened. "Okay. What's on my face right now?"

He stared at me with eyes that bored through me. My chest rose and fell as I anticipated whatever it was he was about to say next.

"Chocolate. Or caramel, maybe?" He pointed at my chin.

Something sank through my body from my head to my feet. Relief, I thought. And a healthy dose of embarrassment, because no woman wanted a guy commenting on the mixture of chocolate and/or caramel hardening on her cheek. Even if said guy was just a friend.

I wiped at my face with my free hand. "Snickers," I explained, scratching at the messy hunk with my pinkie nail.

"No worries," he said, giving my palm a squeeze. "Now you're perfect."

"Cool," I said.

Cool?

But then my phone beeped, and beeped again and again, until the little *perfect* bubble between us popped like a balloon.

"Is it the undertaker?" he asked. I scrolled my phone screen, blinking fast.

Study group finally ended. Leaving library now.

There was an alumni mixer in the atrium and I stole us turkey burgers on pretzel buns.

Can I stop by your dorm, even if it's only to say hi?

Owen Twombley was gone for me—or at least a more dat-able, baseball-loving facsimile of me—four days ahead of schedule. This was the best part. Feeling that crush from someone new. Being possessed by the warm glow of what *could* turn out to be unending affection. Believing that we might be magic together because we were still fresh enough to be anything.

"The actuary," I said, correcting him. "He stole me a pret-zel bun."

"Contraband buns, huh?" He let his hand drop to pick up a canister of gasoline. "Could never be me."

He'd uttered that sentence to me a million times before, but tonight it sounded like a dare.

Chapter 14

Wet Ted Is a
Certified Hot Person

THE PILE OF Lincoln Logs comprising Wet Ted's is just as I imagined it. Ted himself is a different story. Ted is a certified hot person. If this tall, tan man in a T-shirt three sizes too small and with a face chiseled by the gods told me he was actually a supermodel who angered a vengeful witch while posing in a woodsy aftershave campaign and was now trapped in the Minnesota wilderness through some sort of hot, male equivalent of a Rapunzel scenario, I'd believe him.

Beyond his looks, Ted has the kind of capable charisma you join a cult to follow, and after two hours in the van—where I was very busy not having deep, carnal feelings for my most unattainable friend—such explosive sex appeal is the last thing I need to be facing.

"So this is like a 'buddy' camping trip?" Handsome Ted rubs his perfect scruffy beard, clearly fishing for something.

"It's a wedding," Ethan answers in his best service industry voice from his donut shop days: the one that's undeniably friendly but backed by a barely perceptible edge of open hostility. He hands the radio back to Ted. The man came through with a means to communicate with our formerly AWOL engaged couple. I'll give him that much.

"Need a date?" Ted's shameless. And hot. Did I mention Ted's hot?

I hold my breath, waiting to see if Ethan will jump in like a territorial duke in a Regency romance novel.

She's spoken for, he'd growl.

I'd storm off, yelling, *How dare you speak for me, Mr. Powell!* And then he'd kiss me furiously against an upturned canoe. He doesn't do any of that, obviously. He continues filling out the equipment rental release.

It's possible I've been watching *Bridgerton* in the wake of my divorce.

"Charlotte?" Ted asks. He folds his arms across his chest, flexing his pecs. It's an impressive maneuver that I've never before seen executed with such . . . gusto.

It's then I realize I'm staring at a stranger's pecs, and my last shred of self-awareness shocks the rest of my brain back to life. "Oh, no. No date," I answer after a short but embarrassing pause. "It's not a date function so much as a quarter-life crisis and the culmination of years of mistreatment as a teacher in the American education system."

Ethan mutters, "Jesus Christ."

"I'm hoping our arrival will inspire a short cooling-off period—"

"Do we grab one of the canoes out back?" Ethan interrupts me. "We're in a rush."

Ted takes the forms from Ethan and looks them up and down, scanning for deficiencies.

"Ethan Powell," Ted murmurs. Unease bubbles beneath my

breastbone as Ted's eyes ping between Ethan, the form, and Ethan again, like a pinball. "Are you that singer from that alien show?"

If Ethan could will the floor to open up and suck him to Earth's core, I suspect he would, but then he clears his throat, pulls his shoulders back, and assembles a fake smile. It's not one of his best. "Lemonface. Yep. That's me. Are you a fan?"

"God, no." Ted's eyes bug out of his skull as his expression melts from casual to panic-stricken like he's a Dalí clock. "Not that you weren't great. You were just more of my little sister's thing. She had a poster of you guys on her wall. She was obsessed with that show and played the soundtrack every morning before school. Can I get a picture for her?"

Ethan nods stiffly, and Ted hands me his cell phone to take the picture. I've been downgraded from hot girl to Instagram boyfriend in under a minute.

"We really need to be on our way," Ethan tells Ted apologetically. I hand the phone back to Ted and chase Ethan out the door.

Ethan lifts the first canoe he sees over his head. It's a neon orange fiberglass one. "Grab the paddles," he instructs, barely looking at me. I douse myself in bug spray and then follow his instructions. Quickly, we transition the boat into the water and row in tandem.

I notice the air first. It's a fresh, verdant breeze that's thinned out from the sticky heat into something crisp and light but no less warm. The pleasant air seeps into my skin, and I can't help but luxuriate in it, tilting my chin toward the sky, a flower curling into the sunshine. Rays of sunlight pour through the blanket of trees above me, making me squint. There are just so many trees in the woods. Which sounds idiotic, but that doesn't make it any less true.

"This is actually nice," I exhale to no one in particular, and then lower my gaze to the horizon, paddling onward.

At the first point in the chain of lakes where the water's too shallow, we heave the canoe over our heads. We have to trudge across the small spit of land before we can place the boat back in the water. When we're floating again, he hands me a map while oaring on both sides.

"I think we're headed in the right direction," I say.

He grunts in a very un-Ethan-y manner. Ethan's not a grunter. I put my map down and place my paddle back in the water. I speed up my strokes to keep us straight.

"Are we okay?" My stomach flattens from the humiliation of asking one of the most insecure and quietly vulnerable questions a person can ask another person, second only to *What are we?* "You seem . . . perturbed."

"Yeah, no. Sorry. I . . . Can you believe that guy? *Need a date?*" He mimics Ted in his best big, dumb oaf voice. "I was standing right there."

"What difference does that make?"

"He doesn't know anything about us. We could be the ones getting married for all he knows." Indignation powers each of his strokes. "And then he asks for a picture 'for his sister' after hitting on you right in front of me? Come on, bro. There's no sister. Just admit you watch the CW."

I sidestep the sister accusation because, frankly, I'm not sure how to unpack that one. "I don't think anyone would look at us and assume 'married couple.'" I pick up my pace. Drunken, indoor spite-row workouts didn't prepare me for an actual current.

"Why? Is it *so* impossible to imagine yourself married to me?"

"I can't imagine *you* married, let alone to *me*."

"Nice." He sounds genuinely affronted.

"I didn't mean it like that. I meant . . ." I dig deep for what might've been behind my reflexive response. "Okay. So if you saw Harry Styles renting a canoe with his . . . tax attorney, your first thought wouldn't be *Look at that happy couple*, right? It would be more like, *What series of weather catastrophes placed these two strangers in a* Planes, Trains and Automobiles *scenario?*"

"You think you're my John Candy?" He's somehow managing to increase his frenetic pace.

Out of breath, I guffaw, paddling furiously. "No, in this example, I'm definitely Steve Martin in both demeanor and appearance. Can you stop rowing like that? I can barely keep up."

He slows his strokes but not their intensity. What is his van workout regimen?

"It's not about attractiveness," I explain. "I know I'm attractive, but you and I are in different categories of people. You're a musician—"

He snort-laughs. "Not a successful one."

"People are drawn to you, Powell. You're the most fascinating man in the room and I'm the woman who takes her glasses off in a nineties movie."

His paddle drags. "You don't wear glasses."

"It's an archetype!"

"You're not . . ." The back of his hair sweeps across his neck with his head shake. "You have zero self-knowledge. It honestly astounds me."

I puff out my chest. "You find *me* astounding?"

"I find you annoying. Your whole 'thing.'" He laughs. "What did you call my thing? A floppy-haired Benjamin Button? Well, I'm over your whole 'I'm so ordinary' thing. It's tired. You're beautiful and funny as hell, and you're the only person I'd ever want to spend the night with during a series of travel catastrophes."

I nearly drop my oar. We've discussed each other's appearance before, but always in a jokey, distant way that's so cloaked in other insults, it becomes impossible to unearth the original compliment at the center. And after last night, every word between us is new territory.

"It was a *reverse* Benjamin Button. Your thing. And now that I'm hearing it again, you're right, it doesn't make a lot of sense." The sentence oozes out of my mouth like avoidant sludge. I pride myself on being someone who can stand confidently in a compliment. In a world where women are conditioned to make themselves small, agreeing that you're worthy of another's recognition is a muscle I've had to strengthen.

But after years of my only showing glimpses of myself, Ethan is one of the few people who sees all of me. The good and the bad. His words can penetrate, and I'm defenseless against it.

I suppress the impulse to further deflect, and let the rest of his nice words soak into my cheeks like sunshine. It helps that he's still looking ahead for the campsite marked on Ted's map.

We row for what seems like the length of a Scorsese movie. Every so often, I'm derailed by hovering swarms of gnats that always seem to be at face level and require immediate swatting, which sends the canoe sideways. When we eventually make it to the other side of the lake, we shove the paddles into the canoe and fling the thing over our heads, completely in sync.

Without warning, Ethan lifts the boat out of my hands and leans it against a tree.

I make a surprised throat noise and he turns to face me. His face brightens at something—the wind in the trees, or maybe the smell of petrichor in the air? The sky behind him perfectly matches his eyes. It's a gray blue stippled with swirling clouds that are turning over weather I can't predict. "Speaking of travel catastrophes, quick detour?"

He points past me. His face is all smiley wrinkles, dimples, and pure childlike glee.

"I only have you to myself for another quarter mile," he declares. "How about we make the most of it?"

My stomach flips.

"What did you have in mind?" My voice is embarrassingly breathy. *What is happening right now?*

He drops his hand to sprint in the direction of a clump of teenagers gathering at the edge of a gray stone cliff.

Absolutely not.

I sprint after him. "You're out of your mind if you think—"

"You need to get out of your head, Beekman," he calls back, refusing to break his stride.

"I will *crack* my head. That's what happens to people who plummet into rocky lakes."

"*Children* are doing it!"

"*Children* don't have fully developed prefrontal cortexes."

"You're cooler than this. I know you are." He faces me, walking backward on the narrow footpath. "I know you were scared back then . . . but it's different now." His words drop me on the top of that waterfall in Lewellen with him. Just two kids who had no idea that the world was going to kick them in the teeth.

I shake my head. "It's not—"

"Do you trust me?" he asks.

"Okay, you're seriously going to kill yourself walking like that."

He stops short, and it takes all of my lower-body strength not to collide right into him.

"Chuck?" He pierces me with that unfairly striking stare. "Do you trust me?"

"Yes." I say it without thinking, because that's never been a question for me. Of course I trust Ethan. He's Ethan.

My chin tilts up with a confidence I don't actually possess. Could I bring myself to trust him with every part of me? Even the dark places that repel love like opposing poles? What if I could? I know it's crazy, but even at the edge of a cliff, I feel safe with him.

His eyes dart around my face, like he might not believe me, but then he blinks. "Okay, then," he says.

We know we're at the right spot from the piles of clothes and towels dotting the jagged rock that juts out from the edge. There's no sign of the teens who left them there, which is troubling, but I refuse to dwell on it.

Ethan lowers his pack to the ground before stripping to his boxers. I keep my eyes on the water and follow suit, pulling down my shorts until I'm in nothing but underwear and a T-shirt.

"Wait," I tell him, reaching down for his bag. There's a fog bank in the distance, hovering over the enormous trees like a gauzy curtain in the sunshine. Our little rock seems tiny in comparison, the surrounding pines hugging the stone like a benevolent presence. On top of the forest, I can admire the way the trees and rock roll straight into the clouds. We're on the edge of the planet with water dotting the landscape, craters of serene blue. "I want to take a picture of this real quick."

"Without pants on?" he asks through a frozen jaw. The chill off the lake is getting to him.

"Is there a dress code?"

He sighs, like my brief interlude is derailing his perfect sequence of spontaneity. After a couple of shots, I stow the camera away, but I pause at the sound of my vibrating phone.

I look up at him. "This is torture. I have enough service up here to see that I have billions of emails coming through from Bob, but not enough to open them." Is this ledge the cork between heaven and hell?

His inhale flares his nostrils. "Put it away," he commands, and I throw the phone back in the bag with resignation.

"No more stalling, Beekman." When he says it, I can't help but *notice* him. The way he's standing close and how the light touches the lines of his bare shoulders, the smattering of hair on his chest and the way it rises and falls with his breaths.

I lick my lips and face ahead. He's right, I'm stalling. I don't mean to, but suddenly, we feel very high up, and I've already made the rookie mistake of looking straight down into the water. Fear rips through my insides like an invasive plant. This water is nothing like Lake Lewellen. It's wild and dark and bottomless.

"We shouldn't do this," I whisper, peering over the ledge, but I might as well be talking about this moment, last night, this whole damn trip. I'm never reckless like this. I'm never this out of control. My breath has grown ragged, and I'm failing miserably at concealing the unsteadiness of it.

"Look at me, Charley." Ethan's voice is steady, a buoy in choppy waters. "Charley," he repeats, grabbing my face, the tips of his fingers threading into my hair. His hands are so much bigger on my cheeks. Warmer than I'm used to. "I won't let go of your hand. I promise."

I nod, watching the bob of his Adam's apple. Intellectually, I know we'll survive this drop with little more than a bruised ass, but I catalog every crease in his face, the way his lip twitches, every small part of him, like it might be the last time I ever see it. I think he does it to me too. His eyes trail everywhere on my face like little featherlight touches.

We've been barreling toward this jump since the day we met, and now, after everything this year has thrown at me, I *want* to take this leap with him. I *need* to.

"Don't let go," I tell him, right before we jump into the air.

We kick our legs as though they might land on the surface and keep running like one of those water striders. We're weightless, existing somewhere between water and air, until the momentum and gravity split us apart, and Ethan plummets into the lake a half second before me.

He smacks the surface hard; the splash of his body against the dark water sounds like a cracking tree trunk. It's the last thing I hear before the freezing lake swallows me whole too, pressing me down like a needle through silk, silencing my senses until I'm caught by the water.

For the span of a single heartbeat, I'm disorientingly buoyant, as though I'm water too. The tension in my muscles spills into the surrounding liquid. By the next beat, my stillness is replaced by the instinct to kick myself back up.

We reach the surface at the same time, both of us gasping for air. He releases an exhilarated whoop and whips his hair to the side. "Holy shit. Can you believe that? Was it everything you imagined, Chuck?"

"I might've swallowed a bandage on the way down," I manage to say back, kicking my legs like mad.

"You're so full of shit." He gives me one of his big, toothy grins—his happiest kind—and it pulls my lips into their own smile. "You loved that. Admit it."

We just stare at each other. Him smiling at me. Me smiling at him. Both of us breathing heavily as our feet pump beneath the surface to keep our heads above water.

This look on his face is my soft landing. I can't tear my eyes away. My heart is beating like I've conquered Everest—I feel invincible—but the only thing I want to do is . . . exist. Be here, with him, in this moment for as long as possible. A place where I have peace.

But time keeps moving, my legs tire, and we have to swim to shore.

Out of the water, we follow the uneven, pebbled path in the direction of our clothes. I nearly topple back into the lake when my foot falters on a loose rock, but Ethan's there in an instant.

He grips my waist. "I got you," he says.

He keeps his hand there as I right myself. It doesn't mean anything, but knowing that doesn't stop my stomach from swirling like I'm at the top of the cliff again, leaning over the edge.

But my feet are firmly planted now, and his hand still hasn't moved. I turn my head and he's *right* there. We're eye to eye. I've always loved that about us. The way he looks at me dead on like he's bracing himself for whatever he's about to see, like I might still surprise him after all this time. Even though I never do. Ethan's maybe the only man I've ever truly been myself with, utterly transparent. No shields. No white lies to better package myself. Just me. He makes it safe to be me.

So what's another risk? I think as my veins course with adrenaline from my last leap into the unknown.

Slowly, I slip my hand around the slick skin of his neck, watching his response. He swallows hard but doesn't move. My eyes are slow and brazen as they drag up the column of his throat—a languid finger swiping a dollop of frosting along the side of a birthday cake. My rapidly shrinking self-consciousness makes me worry he'll laugh or wince or flinch at the way I'm drinking him in, but he doesn't do any of that. Instead, he licks his lips and, for a split second, I can almost taste him.

My thumb sweeps the top of his shoulder, pulling out a ragged puff of air from between his lips. My gaze darts back up to his eyes. Droplets of water sparkle in his eyelashes and tumble down the apples of his cheeks, gathering in the fine creases where his ever-present smile usually sits.

But he's not smiling now. He's not blinking. He's hardly moving. He's doing nothing but staring back at me with something like curiosity in those charcoal-rimmed irises. It's that look that does me in. Its uncharacteristic intensity that's only ever been directed toward me in these very specific circumstances. These *what if* moments I pretend not to notice.

I thread my fingers into the damp hair at the nape of his neck, hoping to ground myself so I don't drown in the two of us, our shared history filling my ears, my nose. It's all too much. *We're* too much.

"Chuck." He blinks his eyes shut—pure agony—his head still leaning into the press of my fingertips as though he can't help himself.

I know historically Ethan can handle friendships with an occasional benefit. He said as much at the donut shop. *Everything doesn't have to mean* everything. He's been daring me to cross this line all day. The question is, would it have to mean anything to *me*? What are the stakes of giving in? What are the stakes of not?

What if I end this trip without ever knowing for sure what it would be like to have him—really have him—just once, and to have someone who knows the whole truth of me want me back as fervently as I want him? Surely that's not more frightening than jumping off a literal cliff.

A breeze sweeps goose bumps up my back, but I'm consumed by this familiar discomfort of being on the precipice of Ethan Powell. The exhilaration of feeling as though something, anything, *could* happen—is *about* to happen.

But no matter how far this goes or how many lines we cross, he'll be gone in a week. He'll go—I *know* he'll go—and in that way, Ethan's not even a risk.

So I do the safest thing I've ever done and tilt my mouth to his.

"Me?" he whispers.

Our noses brush. "You." I want this moment, and I only want it with him.

That's all it takes. He dives into me without reservations. There are no quick pecks to test the waters this time. Ethan's mouth is hot. Slow. Responsive. He's learning me—no, he *knows* me. It's as though he's always known how I need to be kissed. Touched.

I notice every sensation. I catalog every bit: How my paper-thin shirt slides against his body, still sopping from the lake. The way he holds me so hard, as though he's worried I might evaporate in his arms like a dream. The sound of his tiny groans and how they rumble in my throat. How desperate it makes me.

His hands grapple with my waist, my hips, frantic as he anticipates my every mewl of pleasure, my every tiny, happy gasp. Ethan knows me better than anyone. I guess it stands to reason he'd know this too.

The taste of him dances on my tongue. It's sweet, like he snuck a bite of candy on our hike up the rocky path. It makes me greedy for more. More of this. More of everything. It all feels so present. So immediate. Already within my grasp. It's been a minute—maybe two—and I'm already consumed by possessiveness. My Ethan. Always.

My palms slide down his chest, and he, honest to god, moans into my mouth as he lets me revel in the feel of him, the firm ridges I've only ever glimpsed. But when my fingers reach the lowest part of his abdomen, he breaks himself from the trance.

"Charley," he says through heaving breaths. "How far are we taking this?"

"All the way," I say back, just as labored.

His grin presses into my cheek. "Yeah?"

"Yeah. Until you leave," I promise, tugging at the waistband of his boxer shorts. "Like you said, this doesn't need to mean anything."

"Wait." He grabs my wrist with a gentle hand. "Charley, stop. We're not having sex for the first time in the woods."

"Well, I'm not getting back into that canoe. I just paddled and portaged for an hour, and I'm planning to die out here."

His eyebrows curl inward in the most adorably frustrated way. He's a puppy who can't get his treat out of a Kong toy. "This isn't how I pictured it going."

I pull a face. He pictured it?

"We can have more time. We don't need to rush," he assures me, but his blown-out pupils mirror my fear-backed frenzy. The momentum between us is fragile. If we stop now, we may never start again.

I shake my head. "I'll lose my nerve."

"I won't let you. What if we—"

A twig snaps within earshot—the unmistakable sound of a hiking boot in the woods. Ethan pulls me close.

"Sorry to startle you guys," a man's voice says. "Are you Ethan and Charley?"

My legs nearly give out. Ethan at least has the wherewithal to adjust his shorts. "Yep. You with—"

"The lovebirds," he says, cutting Ethan off. The man who emerges is thin, pale, and mostly mustache. He's undeniably the type of stray Petey and Laurel would pick up in a campground. His clothes are tattered and threadbare in that style that toes the line between "obscenely trendy" and "lost in the woods—send help!" But, then again, I'm in a soaked-through shirt and underwear and Ethan is still at half-mast, so our house is made of the thinnest glass.

"Our site's not that far from here," he continues, gesturing west. "I can take you, but I'll . . . um . . . give you a second to dry off."

I salute weakly and scramble for my clothes, refusing to fixate on the possibility that either I've destroyed a fifteen-year friendship or my perfect, no-strings sexual encounter was just ruined by this man in a bucket hat.

Chapter 15

Are Zambonis Significant to Your Relationship?

ARE YOU FREAKING OUT?"

"No," I whisper to the back of Ethan's head. The word echoes judgmentally through the canoe we're schlepping on our shoulders. I'm not freaking out. I'm not.

"Don't freak out," Ethan suggests.

"Stop telling me not to freak out. Now I *might* freak out." I've been legally single thirty-six hours, and I've already jumped my male best friend twice. Perhaps a small panic is warranted. Prudent, even.

"It's only weird if you make it weird."

"How am I making it weird? Back there, I was the one saying it didn't mean anything while you were all like, 'Not in the woods, Beekman.' I'm not weird. You're the weird one." And now I'm whisper-yelling the word "weird" into a canoe like a lunatic.

"I'm sorry that I wasn't prepared to have *public* sex with you," Ethan argues under his breath.

"You live in a van," I hiss. "All of your sex is at least semi-public."

"Everything okay?" Jonah inquires over his shoulder. He

sounds about fifteen feet ahead, most definitely within earshot but honorably pretending not to be. I'll have to rethink my harsh take on men who wear bucket hats. "You can set your boat down with the rest of ours," he directs, and we follow his instructions. "They're just over there."

Voices carry through the brush, and for a split second, I wonder whether Jonah is luring us into a cannibal den, but then I hear the unmistakable sound of my sister woo-hooing over whatever feat of strength Petey is performing on the other side of the greenery.

Jonah pushes up a branch for us to climb under.

"You first," I tell Ethan, but he's doing one of those gentlemanly *after you* gestures, and our heads clunk together when we attempt to enter the clearing simultaneously with a mutual "Ope!"

It's possible I overestimated my ability to remain *casual* in a casual arrangement with my oldest friend.

Ethan leads me in front of him by the waist. I feel the heat of his proximity all the way up my back like steam on the surface of a hot spring. "There's no impending 'dark side' here, I promise. Just breathe, Beek." Then, with a sweet brush of his lips on my shoulder, he shoves me straight into the clearing.

———

Their setup is sparse: a few camp chairs, a couple tiny pop-up tents, and one *Naked and Afraid*–style leafy lean-to. There's a gray latrine, with which I'm avoiding eye contact, and a pile of logs set up around a small smoldering fire pit. It's not at all the spot I'd imagined for Laurel's spontaneous nuptials, and I momentarily wonder whether the purple-haired woman posted up in a collapsible camping chair is even her.

But then Laurel turns toward the source of snapping twigs and chattering voices, and there's absolutely no doubt that my sister's at this campsite.

"Thank god!" She stands and throws her canteen to the ground for dramatic effect. "I was starting to think you'd gotten eaten by a bear."

"There are bears?" I ask.

Petey's already charging at us. "Char-Char Binks!" He picks me up like I'm nothing and heaves me over the back of his shoulder. "Hey! Hi. You made it! You're soaking wet."

"We did. And I am," I tell his retired-hockey-player butt.

"E, can you believe we're doing this?" Petey asks Ethan. I'm still in the air, by the way, but no one seems bothered by that detail.

Ethan smiles, clearly over the moon to be in shoulder-socking distance with his best dude-bro. "Took you two long enough."

"Hey now. Every wrong turn is part of our story," Petey tells him.

"Put her down, babe. Her face is getting red." Laurel swats at Petey's arm and a bit of my thigh. "We need a group picture."

"Sure thing, babe." He finally plops me down on the ground and drapes his heavy arm around my neck like a shoulder yoke. "Harlow? Can you . . . ?" He gestures to a young woman with light brown skin who's reading a worn paperback on a blanket. She pops up, smiling brightly, and jogs over with a DSLR, her long dark braids swaying behind her.

"Say 'bumblebee,'" she instructs, holding up her camera.

The four of us repeat it back as the shutter clicks over and over, holding each other so close we can smell each other's sweat and feel each other's heartbeats.

The relief of being close like this, the four of us together again, flutters in my belly. Still, something twinges in my chest the way it does whenever we relive the past. Like we're touching the glass wall between experiencing ourselves as we are and remembering how we were.

"I like that better than 'cheese' for relaxing your facial muscles. And you can't look unhappy while thinking about a bumblebee. It's scientifically impossible." The woman lowers the camera and presses her hand to her collarbone with an elegance I find instantly intimidating. I have the posture of someone whose entire life is held together by nail glue and a bullet journal. I may not *actually* bullet journal, but I'm self-aware enough to admit that, energetically, I'm someone who'd buy a dot Moleskine in a moment of psychic despair and am thus programmed to find the woman in front of me equal parts terrifying and intoxicating.

"I met Lo and Pete yesterday, and I'm already in love with them. Harlow," she says, introducing herself. She seems like a Harlow, or at least someone with the beauty to carry off a name that should be reserved for nepo babies and skin-care influencers. "You must be the friends we're waiting on? Ethan and Charley?"

"Nah," Petey answers, squeezing us both tighter. "E's like a brother to me and Charley's about to be my sister. But the gang's all here now. So should we do this thing?"

My vision blurs at the phrase "about to be my sister." My eyes dart around at the group of strangers in search of my *actual* sister but everything's happening too fast. "Laurel, can we have a sec?" I ask her, but she doesn't answer. She's too focused on adjusting her braid in the reflection of Petey's aviators. My insides shake with twenty-four hours of pent-up agita.

"Jesus, Charley. Your teeth are chattering." Ethan's hands rub my shoulders.

I add his gesture to the "maybe this won't be weird" column but then notice something curious.

"Did you just call me 'Charley'?" I ask through my whole-body shiver.

"It's your name," he says dismissively. "Can we get a fire going first? We were in the water, and I think she needs to warm up."

I want to argue but it wouldn't do much good since I'm physically shaking. My body needs the entire world to take a breath while I catch up. Then I need a moment alone with Laurel.

The group of strangers works on warming me as one would a hypothermic Victorian child. I repeatedly try to break off from the group with my sister but am thwarted and shuffled back to the fire by the ragtag crew Laurel and Petey have amassed.

There's Harlow, the adventure photographer who every so often shoots our campsite for her YouTube channel, but also wraps me in the most luxuriously cozy blanket that's ever brushed against human skin.

There's Walter, a hedge fund manager from New York who's sporting a painful-looking sunburn after abruptly quitting his job six days prior to this trip. While meticulously applying a thick layer of topical ointment to his tender skin, he assures us no fewer than twelve times that he's *not* in the throes of a midlife crisis, but it's a bit "the man doth protest too much" after the third denial. By the sixth, it gets awkward, but somewhere around the ninth time, it becomes the most hilarious inside joke and will make zero sense to Stacy when I repeat it to her back at the office.

Finally, there's Jonah, the bucket-hatted near–sex interrupter who owns an artisanal pickling company and happens to be ordained.

After an hour, something funny happens. The strangers are no longer strangers but vacation friends—the kind you optimistically add on Instagram only to mute days later when you learn their feed consists of lengthy microwave pizza reviews.

Petey drags Ethan all over the campsite to show off his new camping gear to the tune of "Dude, dude, bro, no, seriously . . ." and "You have no idea how sick this thing is . . ." Ethan looks just as enamored of the new toys as Petey does. That wild, pitched-up laugh that only Petey and his particular brand of absurd humor can elicit bounces off the trees.

Around the fire pit, I continue brainstorming ways to corner Laurel without her realizing she's a bunny in a trap. Everyone else prepares a lunch consisting of s'mores, jerky, PB&J sandwiches, and other packable nonperishables Ethan can't eat.

Petey's scouring his bag for a shred of anything that won't make his friend sick. "I'm really sorry, man. When I packed the food, it was with Laurel in mind, and she eats like a toddler."

"Hey!" She swats his chest.

Ethan chews on another Lärabar. "Bro, you know I'm always good."

"You deserve way more than this." Petey's eyes scan the campsite. "Do you think we can hunt a deer or something?"

"Sit down," Ethan instructs with a laugh. He pops a marshmallow, one of the few things around the fire that's safe for him to eat, into his mouth and places another on a stick for me. "I'll roast it for you. I'm an expert at this," he brags, his gaze focused on the task at hand.

I assemble the other parts of my s'more and when he offers me the perfectly golden dollop of pillowy sweetness, I stare directly into his eyes, hoping he'll blink something profound in Morse code: *We'll always be friends*, or *Let's sneak off and get naked behind a tree*, or *Please erase me from your memories, you sex pest*. Just a sliver of insight into where we stood before we were interrupted and then imprisoned in this utopian commune that prohibits all private conversations.

Instead, my thumb goes directly through the burning-hot marshmallow.

"Holy—"

Ethan lets the s'more fall to the ground and presses my thumb between his palms. "Are you okay?" he asks. The rest of the group reacts all at once in voices that meld together.

"What happened?"

"Did you burn yourself?"

"Jesus, Char."

"Don't worry, Charleston. I've got an ice pack somewhere."

The last one was definitely Petey, because he runs up to me with one of those first aid snap ice packs. At the sound of its hard crack, Ethan releases my hand. The cold hurts and soothes in equal measure.

Jonah hands me a fresh s'more, which I accept with my left

hand. "We still don't know how you two got engaged," he says to the couple. Now that it's looking like I'll get to keep my thumb, the crowd is back to shining on Petey and Laurel.

"I ran onto an ice rink in combat boots and cutoffs and accosted him on a Zamboni."

The marshmallow in my mouth almost clogs my windpipe. Laurel eyes me with concern, but returns her gaze to Petey when I give her a thumbs-up.

"Cough it out." Ethan's gallantly trying not to laugh at my expense, my indignity a momentary détente in our awkwardness.

"Are Zambonis significant to your relationship?" Harlow asks as she pulls her long black braids into a topknot, her face affectionate yet confused.

Laurel eyes Petey in a way that says they've definitely banged on a Zamboni before, which probably should shock me but doesn't.

"Only in that it's where he was when I showed up to grovel for being such an idiot for so long."

Petey looks at my sister like the sun might literally shine out her ass. "Don't call my future wife an idiot, babe."

She beams back at him and rubs her hand on his knee. "See, the four of us met as kids—" Laurel starts.

"But I was immediately in love with her," Petey finishes.

She shakes her head. "Shut up. You were not."

"I was," he argues.

"But I wouldn't give you the time of day."

"But I kept trying." He smashes a kiss to the top of her head.

She looks up at him, this moment just between the two of

them. "I think I told you I'd only kiss you if you did a flip into the lake where we all used to swim."

He nods. "It was a *back*flip, actually, and I spent the entire summer perfecting it."

"Is that why we went to the waterfall every day?" I interject.

Petey looks momentarily startled that we haven't all disappeared into the mist. "One thousand percent," he answers. "I'm sure Ethan would've tried to serenade you in a treehouse all summer, but I needed to perfect my move."

Ethan squirms next to me.

Laurel beams at Petey. "But then he did it, and it was spectacular."

"And she kissed me," he says, eyes alight.

"But then he left for boarding school."

"And she moved all over the place. But then she followed me to college, obviously."

"No," she protests, but there's absolutely no fight behind it. "I followed my *sister* to college. My sister was following that one." She points at Ethan, and I want to disappear into the forest.

"No one believes that for a second, Lo," Ethan chimes in.

But his eyes trail all over my face, his brows trapped in the V of someone performing complex mental math. Now it's my turn to squirm.

"Semantics," Petey cuts in. "You were there—"

"But I was a twenty-year-old idiot who wasn't even sure what love or commitment looked like. I didn't . . ." Her tone downshifts into something serious—sad—and she grabs Petey's hand. "I was so afraid of . . . everything."

She breathes in deep, looking into the eyes of the man

beside her like he's the one who makes air, then turns back to her audience. "He never gave up on me. He made me work for it—he needed to see I'd grown before he'd risk his heart again—but he never gave up on me." I can't tell if she's so high on her lovesick feelings for Petey that these intimate details are spilling out of her like a club kid on Molly, or if this is one of those romantic performances our parents used to put on for dinner party guests. I'm not sure which I would find more terrifying.

The way Petey's eyes shimmer with emotion, I'm leaning toward the former, which the pit in my stomach tells me is much worse. "You don't give up on a woman like Laurel," he tells us.

"And I've never stopped loving Peter. Even when we were apart. It was always him. It always will be." The look on her face, like she's slipping into another world apart from the rest of us, makes my muscles tense up.

"It was always us," he agrees. "You can't fall out of a love like that. Even when we couldn't be what the other needed, it was there. Like a current under the ice."

She snorts. "Of course you have an ice metaphor for love. You're such a hockey coach."

"And you're *marrying* him," I interrupt, because listening to this story feels like ants crawling over my chest and I can no longer stay quiet. "It's just so funny because up until a few days ago, you didn't even believe in marriage." I laugh, as though it actually *is* funny, but beneath my lightness is a serrated edge. It's undetectable to everyone else—a Beekman family frequency. Her shoulders tense, but she doesn't look at me right away, the absence of her shine a gust of cold air.

Have I fallen into an alternate timeline where the two of

them *didn't* break up getting on a chairlift at Lutsen? The four of us had to ride up the rest of the mountain together, suspended in air with our snowboards strapped to our feet and Petey fogging up his goggles with hot tears. Am I the only person who remembers this?

Now I *know* I need to talk to her before she slips away from me and falls headfirst into disaster.

No one else seems to notice my shift in energy—apart from Ethan, judging by the way he's staring at me with renewed intensity—but internally, I'm crawling out of my skin. I can't keep sitting around wasting time.

I stand. "Laurel, can we take a walk?"

This isn't what she's ever wanted, and if I can only get her away from the camp bubble, her Petey fog, I might be able to get through to her.

But at the exact moment I stand, Ethan's facing me to say, "We should talk."

"Why?" Laurel asks me, just as I say to Ethan, "Can it wait?"

Ethan doesn't respond. He stares meaningfully like it should be obvious that it simply *cannot wait*. Apparently when you light a fifteen-year friendship on fire, people prefer a more immediate forensic evaluation of the crime scene.

My eyes dart between the two of them. I don't want to say something incriminating to either of them, but since Laurel is my immediate concern, I direct my attention to her. "Because I want to talk to you. About wedding stuff. Like flowers or whatever." Sure, it's a lie, but it's a necessary one—a fib—like when you hide your dog's arthritis medication in crunchy Jif.

Laurel narrows her eyes. "Harlow already made flower crowns. Which I know is a little Coachella-y, but my dress doesn't have a back, so we're leaning into that whole vibe."

Ethan tugs my hand, shooting a pitiful echo of seismic activity up my arm. "It'll just take a minute, Charley."

"Stop calling me Charley. You make it sound like I'm in trouble." I pull my arm away. "Laurel, are you ready?"

"Why are you being more neurotic than usual?" she asks.

A buzzing in the front zipper pocket of my bag interrupts our deadlock. "Crap," I murmur, reaching to silence it, but Bob's name lights up my screen like a threat as the top left corner flickers between a single tiny bar and the words NO SERVICE.

"It's my boss. I should really take this. If you can give me—"

"Who had under an hour?" Laurel asks the group.

Walter lights up. "Oh, me!"

"Pay the man," Petey commands over my ringing palm. Everyone besides me and Ethan stands to search through their belongings. "The service is horrible here, by the way. You have to keep walking east in the direction of the Lake Haslett RV park until you get another bar or you won't be able to hear anything."

My eyes bounce around the group. "Did you guys bet on when my phone would ring?"

Laurel tilts her head side to side. "Specifically a work call," she clarifies, followed by a chorus of "Yes," "No," and Petey's "It was more of a friendly wager."

"To be fair, we don't know you," Walter assures me. "But I *do* know what it's like being on that hamster wheel."

"My money's in my boot, but it's stuck," Jonah pipes up, sweating profusely from his spot on the log. "I think my foot is swollen."

Laurel ignores the hubbub, arching her brow at me. "Are you gonna get that?"

Then the phone stops ringing, answering her challenge for me.

"Walter technically doesn't win if she lets it go to voice-mail," Petey interjects.

"Laurel, walk?" I ask, but it rings again, louder this time. It's not *actually* louder but it *feels* louder with a rush of texts between rings pinging one after another like a buzz saw fighting a tennis ball launcher.

"Just take it," she urges.

I look between Laurel, Ethan, and the rest of the group, feeling the seconds ticking down on Bob's call.

"Gimme two minutes," I beg. "I need two minutes and then we'll talk, yeah?"

I run straight east to the sound of a single cheer and a chorus of groans.

———

"You better be dead in a ditch somewhere," Bob says without a greeting, though he generously waited for me to get a solid ninety yards into the woods with little more than a warbly, "Hold, please! Hold, please!" as reassurance.

"Good to hear from you, Bob," I reply through clenched teeth. "Hope you're enjoying your weekend."

"AgriTech called you twice, and you didn't answer."

"Sorry. My cell service is . . . unreliable. Did they call *you*?"

"I don't know what to say to them!"

My free hand forms a fist. I don't suggest he examine why it is he has no idea what's going on with one of his biggest clients, though I *really* want to.

"I sent you detailed notes from my call with them Friday.

It's attached to my email from yesterday—the one with a run-down of all your clients and what needs to be done while I'm out of touch."

"This isn't like you, Charlotte. You're usually one of the responsible ones. Focused."

His "praise" has a way of clenching my insides.

"Sorry. My sister's getting married." The number of times I've apologized to this man over the years for merely existing as a human is truly astounding. "I'll only be away until tomorrow. Tuesday at the latest."

"It's hard to justify your inattention when Paul is taking calls during his wife's C-section right now."

"That's crazy, Bob," I snap, because apparently I have more respect for my literal nemesis than myself. Sure, I can't stomach Paul, but I know he's obsessed with his wife and it has to be *killing* him that he's putting out minor administrative legal fires while she's giving actual *birth*. "You hear how that sounds, right? That shouldn't be expected of him, and he shouldn't feel like he needs to do that to earn your respect."

I brace myself for impact. I've never spoken this way to Bob before. Ever. I've *fantasized* about it. I've imagined the shade of red he would turn if challenged—vermillion—but I've never once been anyone to him besides Corporate Shill Charlotte Beekman, Attorney at Law. I accept his abuse with a decisive nod and then I beg for seconds. Bob knows that Ballbuster Charley exists somewhere deep, *deep* down—he relies on her—but I suppose he assumed I was too much of a kiss-ass to ever unleash her on him.

All these years I've worked for him, I've never taken a true sick day where I wasn't sniffling through conference calls. On my honeymoon, I was *so* available remotely that, to this day, no one at A & G even knows I *had* a honeymoon. Still, Bob is ready to lambaste me for taking a three-day weekend for my own sister's wedding.

I'm not sure I'll ever be enough for the Bobs and Pamelas of the world, and for the first time, I'm questioning whether I want to be. My best-case scenario is that in five years, *I'm* the person dressing down a twentysomething for daring to take a day off.

Bob's pause is interminable. My pulse trips on each of his hard breaths.

If he's playing pickleball right now, I swear to god . . .

"We'll discuss whatever's going on with you and your attitude the second you're back in the office, Ms. Beekman. For now, I need you to do your job and pick up your—"

"You're cutting out, Bob," I interrupt.

"Charlotte?"

"Are you there, Bob? It's the service out here. I can't hear anything," I lie. I can hear his nose whistling with each incensed inhalation.

"Charlotte!"

"Good luck with AgriTech." And then I end the call.

A week ago, Bob's weaponized incompetence would've sent me straight back to the office, wedding be damned. But now my blood is surging through my veins. Hanging up on a boss must rank somewhere between a jolt of adrenaline and a radioactive spider bite. I feel . . . good. Really good. Powerful even! Until my phone starts ringing again . . . so I do the unthinkable: I turn my phone off.

A text from Stacy pops up on my home screen as I power my phone down: **Found Rich's Zola website. It's a January wedding at the Como Park conservatory. BLEH.**

My first thought as I watch the screen turn black is, *I bet that'll be nice.*

After the years I've spent diligently following five-year plan after five-year plan, so preoccupied with the direction I'm headed in, I've *earned* this detour. One weekend of uncomplicated fun with someone I know will drive off into the sunset. So long as I'm out here, in the woods and off the grid, I need to just . . . be.

I stuff my phone into my pocket and practically sprint back to the campsite, wanting only to be near Ethan and, for once, not caring about all the reasons it could never be us. I want him to hug me like he did when we were kids and the world was moving too fast. When it felt like he was the only one who could hold my feet to the ground. I want him to kiss me and touch me for no reason other than that it feels good.

But he's not there when I get back. I see only Harlow and Laurel.

"Charley!" Laurel calls out first. Then her tear-streaked face emerges from between the trees.

I run to her without a second thought. "What's wrong?" My voice shakes.

"I can't get married today!" She grabs me by the shoulders.

Equal parts heartache and relief war in my belly as I pull her into my arms.

"I've got you," I promise her. "Whatever you need."

Chapter 16

In Search of a Good Time or a Minister

BEFORE MY SISTER can *Runaway Bride*, I pull her in tight. "We can leave right now."

"No." She presses her damp cheek against my ear. "I don't want to do it somewhere else. I wanted to do it here, but we can't with Jonah's swamp feet."

"Yeah, but—" It occurs to me that I have no idea what my sister is talking about. "Swamp feet?"

"Jonah has trench foot," she whines.

"You get it from not changing wet socks," Harlow explains.

"You're changing your wet socks, right? It was so gross." Laurel pulls her head back to look down at my water-resistant sandals and nods approvingly. "The boys are taking him to town for a doctor."

"Okay . . ."

"He's the only one who could officiate," Harlow explains.

"So no wedding *today*," I say with renewed understanding. Then I seize the opportunity. "This might be a sign from the universe. Let's head home. Take a beat. Plan a fall wedding in the Cities. Or a New Year's wedding, maybe? That could be fun. You could singlehandedly make New Year's fun again."

She tilts her head, as if weighing the option, then shakes it. "No, no. I'm getting married *here. Now.* While there's still energy and magic around it. If we have to plan it, I'll never want to do it."

Then you shouldn't do it! I scream inside my skull. God, I want to shake her, but this isn't my first rodeo with Laurel. Telling her not to do something will only make it more enticing to her.

"Let's meet up with the boys in town," Harlow suggests. "There has to be someone else who's ordained."

Laurel perks up. "Like a captain of a ship?"

"More like a minister or a judge, but sure. No bad ideas in a brainstorm," Harlow says encouragingly. "We'll find someone who can marry you guys tomorrow."

"I don't know if I'm up for it, guys." Laurel releases a dramatic sigh. "It's only two p.m. and this is already, like, the *worst* day. I was supposed to be getting married."

"Let's just chill here then," I suggest, my voice inordinately bright.

Harlow smiles mischievously. "Laurel, you're thinking about this all wrong. If you get married tomorrow, that means *this*—right now—is your bachelorette party."

"Ooh, I love hearing *that*!" Laurel titters, the conversation picking up speed in a direction I'm not sure I want it to go. "I can't believe I nearly got married without having a bachelorette party. Charley . . ." She faces me. "You're the self-appointed maid of honor. This is your job, isn't it? Nay, your duty?"

My eyes dart between my sister and Harlow, calculating whether I could successfully snatch Laurel and run. Then I remember I'm trapped in the woods without a car and am a whole-ass canoe ride away from civilization.

Laurel may be playing it cool right now, but I know her better than I know myself. Between her unresolved commitment phobia and rigid adherence to "vibes," she is one small setback away from calling off the ceremony herself. Something else will go wrong—I'm sure of it—and that means there's hope for her yet.

"Fine," I relent, because my best shot at stopping this runaway train anyway is by stalling it. "Let's go to a dive bar and see if we happen upon someone who marries people."

———

"Shot! Shot! Shot!" Laurel and Harlow slap their hands on the bar top as I down a Diet Coke shot at three-thirty in the afternoon. Initially, Laurel booed when I told her that even after cleaning up the campsite, canoeing for an hour, and walking from Wet Ted's to this genuinely divey dive bar, the sun was still way too high in the sky for me to start getting tanked on rail vodka when I've barely recovered from my Ruth's Chris mojito trauma.

But the more I lean into the "bachelorette" of it all, the less interested she is in identifying someone who can legally preside over a wedding ceremony. That, and I've let myself forget. That's how it goes with Laurel. I enjoy myself, lower my defenses, and forget that we're merely biding time before the storm. So while I should be bracing myself for impact, I'm double-fisting soda shots with a pint glass of water (I'm still me, so I require at least two liquids at all times).

Laurel taps her Coors Light on the bar top, clinks it against Harlow's can, and takes a long chug. After swallowing a tiny burp, she opens the floor for the tough questions: "Did anyone else notice that Wet Ted is, like, *super* hot?"

"Yes," Harlow and I respond in unison.

"I've put a lot of thought into this . . ." Harlow wraps one of her braids around her finger, and I find myself grinning in anticipation of whatever she's about to say next. Harlow is fun, and, against all odds, so is this obscenely musty bar that made my hands feel sticky on sight. "It's not just Wet Ted's looks. It's the *competence*."

"Yes," Laurel practically growls into her beer bottle. "I just know he could protect me in a postapocalyptic situation. That man could *Mad Max* me through a desert wasteland on his shoulders."

"No, it's more tender than that," I cut in, waving down the bartender, who's sporting a threadbare Vikings tee. "He's like Pedro Pascal in that zombie show with the little girl."

"That's what it is!" Laurel slaps the bar top. "You can just tell he'd care for you in this totally platonic way, which only makes him hotter."

I take my tiny refill from the bartender. "I'm sure Petey will appreciate you keeping it platonic when the zombies come."

"Oh, Wet Ted is firmly Plan B in a zombie apocalypse. I'm going with Petey all the way. Half the reason you get married is to have a built-in partner when society breaks down."

It's a nice thought. I used to think the same before Rich bolted. How would we have fared with a catastrophic event? Would he have zipped his Tesla out of town and left me to face the undead all alone?

Then my mind drifts to a dangerous thought: *What would Ethan do?*

"I need a platonic Wet Ted," I say, pushing out the image of Ethan and me as partners before it can have a chance to settle into the recesses of my brain. I don't need to corrupt something fun and low stakes by turning it into my disaster evacuation strategy.

"It would *not* be platonic with me and Theodore," Harlow muses, licking her lips as though she's prepared to eat that sexy woodsman alive. "I'd have *all* his apocalypse babies. It wouldn't be right to establish a new society that didn't have access to that man's bone structure."

I nearly spit out my Coke. "Should we call Ted and see when he gets off work?"

"Way ahead of you, Char." Laurel's already scrolling her contacts. She hops off her stool and heads in the direction of the exit with her phone to her ear.

"Oh, that reminds me . . ." Harlow sets her beer on the bar and grabs a mini tablet from her bag. "Gotta steal some Wi-Fi while I can."

"Ooh. Good call." I pull out my phone but stop myself before opening my work email. Boundaries are normal. Healthy, even. Surely nothing catastrophic will happen if I don't open my work email again today.

Instead, I distract myself by leaning over for a closer look at Harlow's tablet. I glimpse the footage she's uploading: sweeping overhead views of lush forests and lakes sparkling in the dawn light.

"Is this all from that little drone?" I ask, recalling the tiny black thing I spotted at camp.

"My baby is small but mighty. These scenic videos are my first love, but my 'day in the life' vlogs on being an adventure photographer get more ad revenue than my actual photography. Which used to bum me out, but, hey, the goal is the lifestyle, and *Athletic Greens* pays."

"Adventure photography? I had no idea that was a thing.

I'm so curious about how people find their niche in creative fields. My dad was a filmmaker."

"Well, I don't know how most people do it, but about two years ago I quit my corporate marketing job and moved into a pop-up camper I hitched to my SUV. And *my* dad is a forensic accountant, so at the time, he wasn't exactly thrilled . . ." Her laugh indicates that maybe she and her dad have gotten past this wrinkle in their relationship. "But I had to do it, you know. I never had time or energy for my art. It was soul crushing. But back then, I did have a lot more money. The money was nice."

"Money's like that sometimes," I agree, lifting my mini-Coke in salute.

She types on her screen for another minute. When she slips it back into her bag, her work seems to disappear, as though her income stream and sense of self are genuinely separate, and it is possibly the most unrelatable thing about this woman who already seems like a Free People ad come to life.

Harlow notices me noticing her and asks, "So you and Ethan . . . ?" She trails off.

In a humiliating twist, my body responds to the mere mention of Ethan. "Me and Ethan? We're not . . . We've only . . ." My head jerks in about six directions without permission. "We've been friends for years. Same as Petey and Laurel, but without the, uh, romantic undertones."

Or so I thought.

She pushes out her bottom lip. "With his Heath Ledger dimples and bedroom eyes? Those don't factor in at all for you?"

"I'm going through a divorce. Or just finished going through it, I guess. It's probably not smart to jump into anything."

She nods, unconvinced. "That makes sense."

I sip on my fresh shot glass of Coke. Memories of Ethan's

lips against mine and my hands in his hair burst in my brain like fireworks.

It's at the moment when I'm imagining Ethan emerge from a lake—full Colin Firth—that Laurel bounces back to our bar stools. "Good news, bad news. So Wet Ted's waiting for a camper with a nine p.m. reservation . . ."

I shake my head. "That won't work. We need to be back at the campsite or we'll be hiking in the dark."

She grins. "That's where the good news comes in. He needs to stay in for equipment pickup later tonight, but . . . we can bring snacks and come hang out with him and all of his hot friends, then lure them back to the campsite with us."

I cringe a little. "He told you his friends were 'hot'?"

She dismisses my skepticism with a wave of her hand. "Of course not, but hot people have a way of finding each other. I texted Peter, and Jonah is out of urgent care and checked into a motel. The rest of the guys can meet us at Ted's. It's perfect."

"Ooh. I love a joint bachelor-bachelorette party," Harlow adds gamely. "And one of them might be ordained!" She flags down the bartender to close out, and I try to conceal whatever the memory of a particular bachelorette party (and accompanying penis straw) does to my face.

———

"So you lived in Peru and you never did Santa Cruz?" Wet Ted's travel buddy Russell asks while handing me a LaCroix.

"'Lived' is a stretch," I respond. "I think I was two."

He shakes his head, a flirty smile creeping up his implausibly handsome face. "Still. It's criminal."

Laurel was very right about how hot people attract other

hot people. They must feel more comfortable with each other, the same way celebrities have an easier time making friends with other celebrities.

From the moment we walked into the apartment behind the canoe outfitter, Ethan had the role of "most interesting man in the room" all wrapped up. For the past hour, he's been trapped in a corner of astonishingly attractive humans, comparing adventures on the road.

Still, no matter where I am, I feel his attention on me, tugging me back into his orbit like I'm a rogue planet.

"Do you climb?" Russell's question breaks into my consciousness and I realize I haven't been listening to him.

"Climb?" I stall for time.

A hand snakes around my waist, and I turn my head to find Ethan. What does it say about me that my impulse is to curl into him like a cat?

"Charley's not a big fan of heights." Ethan's baritone voice vibrates against the shell of my ear. "Unless she's taking a photo."

"Are you a photographer like Harlow?" Russell asks. His eyes clock Ethan's possessive hand on my body—mine do too—and in a second, I watch myself plummet from *the object of Russell's desires* to *suspected cousin.* "What's Harlow's deal?" he inquires, chomping on a chip and eyeing Harlow, who's casually leaning against the frame of the open back door and looking arrestingly gorgeous while doing it.

I tilt my head in her direction, my heart hammering against my ribs from Ethan's prolonged physical proximity. "Harlow? Oh, she's very available."

What is this arm about?

"Very, you say?" He brushes the chip grease off his hands and does a practiced hair ruffle that gives him the perfectly unkempt look of a wilderness catalog model. "Wish me luck."

"Luck," I barely get out around the lump in my throat.

Ethan gives him a wave as he walks away. His thumb hooks into my belt loop and tugs me closer to him. Something raw and hot flips in my belly. The way his eyes cling to me is new and unfamiliar territory.

"You weren't enjoying that conversation, were you?" he asks, concern swimming at the edges of his face. "You had that look in your eyes. Like when strangers pitch inventions at you, *Shark Tank* style."

Ah, the joys of being the only patent attorney at a summer barbecue.

"You weren't interrupting anything." As if I could *think* with him touching me like this, all greedy and possessive.

His eyes search my face and must find something he likes, because he rewards me with a perfect smile that sends crinkles all the way into his eyes. God, I love that smile. The sight of it crashes into my chest like a hot rock.

"Good. How was your trek from camp with the girls? Did you point out the spot where we . . . you know . . ." He sits up on the kitchen counter, his hand dragging along my abdomen every step of the way. "Cliff jumped?"

His question is a provocation. He wants me to think about the kiss. The way he was pressed against me. How feral I was. How feral I still am. He curls his fingers around my hips, and I all but turn to goo.

This whole thing between us reeks of regrettable ideas, but that just makes it more enticing somehow. I don't usually regret things. Regrets require taking chances. But we've been teasing each other mercilessly for years. Something was bound to happen eventually.

I step forward between his legs, goading. *I can go toe to toe with you*, the movement suggests. I tilt my chin up, luxuriating in the way his jaw tightens at my unexpected advance into his territory.

"I didn't," I finally respond. "Laurel is in a highly suggestible state, and I'm not about to give her any new, reckless ideas. Accomplice liability and all that." It's so stuffy in this house packed with bodies. The walls are sweating.

"Accomplice liability, huh? Is it exhausting, the way your lawyer brain never shuts off?"

"This brain is how I earn the *almost* big bucks."

His head moves side to side, achingly slow. "God, I would kill to see you in action. I bet you're incredible." The word buzzes down my skin. *Incredible.*

This is how he gets, I have to remind myself. I've seen it before. When he's in front of a woman, he can't help but lay it on thick. He makes them dream it's real, that he wants it *all* with them, but in the end, he always drives away.

"So are we finally going to do something about this or what?" he asks, pointing between us.

"Do something about the way we're running dangerously low on beverages?" I deflect. "You should've let me buy *even more* Gatorade. It's yet another thing I was right about."

His grin widens. "Charlotte Beekman is always right. I have that tattooed on my rib."

I laugh. "No you don't."

"It's very small."

The air around us is thick and sticky, getting hotter by the second. It's as though I'm moving through honey when I inch closer.

"Prove it." It falls from my lips on a puff of air. "Lift up your shirt."

His gaze drops to the shirt I'm wearing. His shirt. "Only if you lift yours."

I lick my lips. "I don't have a tattoo."

His nod is heavy, his eyes hot. "Unfortunately, this is a *show you mine, show me yours* situation."

"That *is* unfortunate."

I hesitate, but then my fingers drag the soft fabric up an inch. Then another. He lifts his shirt too, revealing hard stomach and smooth sun-kissed skin.

Why can't we . . . why can't we . . . It's a partial thought, but that's all that comes together before he drops the fabric and covers himself up. "Fine," he says. "I don't have it, but I should." He takes a long, languid drink of his hard cider. "Careful, Chuck. You're getting dangerously close to daring me to get a tattoo."

Careful. Dangerous. Daring. Each word makes my stomach jump.

I stare him down, inhaling through my nose. He smells like apple cider and sweat. "I'm not Petey," I tell him in a hush. "And even he outgrew that."

He swirls his bottle, and I refuse to unpack why I find the movement so devastatingly sexy. "Not quite. When Jonah's foot went numb, Petey bet him we could row to the car in under thirty minutes. It took thirty-four minutes and now there's an outline of a foot on my guy's left delt."

"Wait, what?" I pull back an inch. It severs the flirtatious current flowing between us. "So he's camping for the rest of the week with an open wound? For what? A laugh?"

Is that gigantic man determined to never grow up?

Ethan grimaces. "He might not have thought it through, but Jonah was pretty scared and that Walter guy kept asking whether they'd 'have to amputate,' which was . . . unhelpful, to say the least. I think Pete was just trying to distract Jonah."

My eyes find Petey and my sister swaying in front of the record player. "Between Laurel and Shoulder-Foot, there are no adults in the room, are there?"

Ethan tugs my face away from the more chaotic Beekman sister. "Charley, Petey's a hockey coach who owns his own home and Laurel is an award-winning high school English teacher. They're gonna be fine. You don't need to worry about them."

"I hate this feeling," I groan, flopping my head onto his shoulder, releasing myself into the safety of leaning on someone. Or maybe just on him. "My stomach seizes up whenever I think about Laurel getting married. It's this . . . motion sickness. I can just feel everything's going to go to shit, and I don't understand how everyone else can't feel it too."

He places his chin on the crown of my head, so that I'm completely enveloped in him. "It's normal to want the best for the people you love," he tells me. "And it's even more normal for it to hurt when you watch them struggle for it. Or wonder whether there was something you should've done that would've made it all easier."

His T-shirt is so soft beneath my cheek that I'm overcome by one of those absurd childish thoughts that doesn't make any sense: *What if I lived here?* I think. *Right here, on Ethan's shoulder like a tiny parrot person. I could be happy like that.*

"Loving people is so unbearable," I whine, inhaling the scent of his neck like it's an aromatherapy candle.

He laughs into my head, and his exhalations ruffle my hair. "I know, honey."

I look up at him and catch the smile he reserves for only those intolerably happy moments. When everything is exactly right and your stomach is fizzy like uncorked champagne and the world around you glows gold. Or maybe it's that smile that casts a shimmering light everywhere I turn.

My eyes dive into his—pools of warm water—as he tucks a strand of hair behind my ear.

"Unbearable," he repeats.

But then he drops his hands, and it's as though whatever sensory deprivation they provided disappears with a harsh snap of the fingers. It's loud and hot, and suddenly, I'm back in a packed Lincoln Log apartment overflowing with people. I follow Ethan's gaze past my shoulder and spot Petey waving him over.

Ethan hesitates but hops off the counter. "Sorry. Best man duty calls."

The bubble bursts in more ways than one. He was my best man once, and the morning of my wedding he sent, **Margot's not up for it. Sorry, Chuck.** And then I didn't hear from him for a year.

I shift to the side and watch him walk away. Despite the unpleasant metallic taste swirling in my throat, I can still appreciate an impressive walk when I see one.

Petey whispers something to Ethan and then, after a quick

stress test, climbs on top of a chair and lets out one of those two-finger dog whistles, silencing the party.

"For those of you who don't know me, I'm Pete and the gorgeous woman in the crochet top is the love of my life, Laurel Beekman. And tomorrow, Lo and I are getting married thanks to our new buddy Ted, who happens to be ordained with the Official Church of Love."

The room whoops and cheers at the everyday heroism of the damp man who unites us all. My heart clunks.

"Love finds a way," Petey tells the crowd.

Ted waves sheepishly, murmuring, "Best forty dollars I ever spent."

"Earlier today, our officiant had a medical emergency. He's totally fine now—resting up at a hotel—but only because we were incredibly fortunate to have my oldest friend, E, there to carry the guy on his back for *half a mile*." Petey claps Ethan on the shoulder while everyone applauds.

I've been with Ethan all night, and he's never mentioned carrying Jonah to safety. He probably thought nothing of it. That alone melts my insides like an expertly toasted marshmallow.

"Because when it all hits the fan," Petey continues, "there's no one I'd rather have on my team. So let's raise a glass to my best man, Ethan, astonishingly bad flip cup player and the first person I'm calling if I ever get trench foot. Cheers to you, man."

A chorus of laughs and cheers trickles through the room, but it goes quiet again as Ethan takes his turn at the creaky wooden dining chair.

"I'll keep it brief out of respect for the fact that we're strangers to pretty much everyone here. Bet you didn't realize you were going to a bachelor party tonight, and now maybe a rehearsal dinner?" He looks over to Petey, then back to the group. "But I've spent the last few years on the road making a lot of meaningful short-term connections with people. I've gotten very good at keeping things light and detached, because it's . . . easy, I guess. And losing the people who matter is hard."

Ethan's eyes flash to mine so quickly I almost miss it. We're all hanging on his every word, but I let myself imagine this speech belongs to me. Each word nestles its way softly between my ribs.

"All we have is connection, right? All we are is how well we're loved by the people we care about and how well we love them back. Nothing else can be more important than that. And Petey's always understood that. He's taught me that nothing should matter more than that one person who makes you feel bigger than you are. Who makes every tent, every tiny mattress, every roadside service station, feel like home. The one who changes you and makes you dream about things that used to scare you."

Ethan's voice crackles with emotion. Just when I'm sure he's about to say more, he clears his throat and peels his eyes away from the crowd, looking only at Petey. "And that's what all of us strangers have in common today," he continues, voice light again. "We're in the presence of this all-encompassing, all-consuming, stupid love that's made fools out of Petey and Laurel for far too long and they're finally ready to do something about it."

Petey laughs, wiping up the happy tear that falls down Laurel's cheek.

"Many of us won't see each other again, but we're all part of this tonight. We're all a piece of this connection that's so much bigger than us. We're in a memory right now. At this moment." His gaze drifts around the room before finally settling on me, and this time, he doesn't look away. "So let's make it count. For them and ourselves. Cheers to the happy couple and all of the former strangers they decided to share their memories with."

The room erupts in cheers. Petey doesn't wait for Ethan to jump down, instead picking him up by the waist and carrying his friend around in a rough, rhapsodic hug. The room overflows with happiness. It makes me wonder whether Ethan's onto something. Maybe Petey and Laurel *are* part of something bigger than us all. Maybe their relationship is more real than anything I ever had with Rich, and that's why I'll never understand it. Maybe.

Maybe.

A friend of Laurel's would allow her this romantic blunder. They'd toast to her with all of these strangers. They'd wish her well and hope that the foreboding feeling gnawing at their stomach would eventually fade away.

But I'm not her friend. I'm her sister.

Ethan gets swallowed up again—the most interesting man in the room made brand-new by that speech. I stand frozen against the kitchen counter like a bystander, waiting for Laurel to appear in my eye line.

I cross to her, walking upstream in a crowd that's starting to spill out the door and into the glow of the lowering sun.

"We have to talk," I demand. "Now."

"We're all streaking," she responds without acknowledging my plea.

"Huh?" I must not have heard that right. "It's only eight. The sun's still out."

She breathes out a world-weary sigh. "It's the summer, Charley. We can't live and die by the sun."

"I think we literally can. You can't run around naked in the woods. You're an *educator*."

"I'm a *bride*, and I haven't even used that card yet. You used it all the time. You made me get, like, three vaccines. I got a Tdap for you." She pokes my biceps.

"That was for *you*. Rich's sister is anti-vax, and I didn't want you to get diphtheria from the flower girl because Kathleen listened to two-thirds of a podcast on mercury."

"We're in the middle of nowhere. What the hell else are we going to do besides get naked?"

About thirty other more appropriate activities come to mind in the form of a bulleted mental list.

Maybe my mistake was thinking there would ever be a *right* time to tell Laurel this whole thing—her engagement, her elopement, her insistence on running naked through the forest—is rushed at best and a colossal mistake at worst. "Don't you think we should slow down and—"

"Charley." She folds her arms across her chest. "This is my bachelorette party, and it's my turn to bride card. I'm bride card–ing."

I stare at her for a beat, then two, but the look in my sister's eyes is one I know well. No matter how I add it up, the answer will be the same: I'm taking my clothes off in the woods for the second time today. At this point, it's an inevitability.

"When I'm charged for indecent exposure, I'm sure the judge will be persuaded by the bride card defense," I whisper-yell through my teeth. "My underwear stays on." We shimmy past a man in a neon vest and nothing else to step onto the back deck.

She loops her arm in mine. "Have I told you lately that I love you?" She bats her eyelashes at me.

I face the sky, basking in every ray of harsh daylight that's still very much spilling through the summer foliage, and estimate how many friend requests I'll receive tomorrow from strangers who know the exact placement of my areolas. My money's on seven.

"I might hate you," I grumble.

"You love me," she chirps back.

Loving people might as well be an incurable disease.

Chapter 17

A Little Ceremonial Exhibitionism

THE "BRIDE CARD" is persuasive enough to get everyone's tops off and a fair number of bottoms too. Laurel and Petey lead the naked charge, which means I'm treated to his newest bum tattoos of Michigan J. Frog and zombie Bart Simpson, because again, the sun is out and will not be setting for another ninety minutes.

Ethan's wearing navy boxer briefs, a different pair from when we jumped into the lake earlier. Not that I noticed them then. Or now. I'm not even looking.

"Should I strip all the way down?" he asks. Can he read my thoughts? "You're staring at my underwear."

"No I'm not."

His smile is the annoying, self-satisfied one. "I thought you said you'd seen it all."

"I said I'd seen enough."

"Sure, sure."

"Stand in front of me. I promised Laurel I'd go topless for her little ceremonial exhibitionism, and I don't want you to . . ." I gesture between his eyes and my tee.

"You don't want me to see you? Seriously, Chuck? We're

going to be like that? Eight hours ago you were about to bang me up against a tree."

"Don't say 'bang.'" I cringe. "And the shirt was always going to stay on."

"You were planning to Winnie the Pooh it for our first time? Disappointing, honestly." He extends his arm and leans his nearly naked body against a neighboring maple. Heat burns at my aforementioned breasts and up my neck, blooming in my cheeks. He's enjoying this, making me squirm.

"Fine. I'm a gentleman," he says, backing down, but I don't feel like I've won anything. He's reading me like a book. A very simple book with only one line, over and over.

Then he steps in front of me, just as I asked. I step forward too, his back to my front with less than a foot separating us. His shoulders fidget, all of his previous bravado falling away. The space between us pulls taut. He seems to become equally aware of our proximity and what I'm about to do.

"Can you stay right here? So no one sees me, uh, take it off?" I keep my voice low, so that the sentence floats over his shoulder on the warm breeze.

"Mm-hmm," he hums, his voice unsteady.

I pull off my shirt. He's not even looking at me, but I feel him everywhere. My fingers are his fingers. It's as intimate as if he were doing it himself. I peel off my bra, covering my breasts with one hand and clutching my clothes in the other. "Okay," I breathe. "Keep in front of me, Powell. Eyes forward, okay?"

"If that's really what you want." The response runs up my exposed surface. Ethan promising *not* to look at my naked body might be more sensual than an actual perusal from any other man on the planet.

We both wait for my response, wondering whether I'll turn him around and ask him—no, *beg* him—to see all of me.

For a second, it feels like I might. For so long, I've been frozen midstep over the precipice of me and Ethan. Does everything with me have to be so complicated? This, me and Ethan, should be simple.

"Everyone ready?" Laurel calls out to the crowd.

Ethan clears his throat. Anxiety prods my lungs.

"Dark side?" My question cuts through my increasing panic.

She claps her hands together. "ONE," she hollers.

Ethan's shoulders roll back. "Uh . . . we all get arrested and register as sex offenders?"

"TWO," the crowd joins in, their shouts filling my ears like water.

I force myself to focus on Ethan. His shoulder freckles. The hair playing at the nape of his neck. The ropes of muscle trailing down his back. "Uh . . . no, actually." I feel the tight cord around my throat begin to unravel. "That's not a penalty for misdemeanor indecent exposure."

"Then I think we're gonna be okay." He stretches an arm behind him, fingers reaching for me. Before I have a second to reconsider, I remove the hand covering my chest and accept his firm, reassuring squeeze.

The throng cries, "THREE."

He releases my hand.

Petey's low baritone thunders through the trees. "EVERY-BODY RUN!"

A sea of skin takes off into the woods. I freeze, momentarily shocked by the chaos, the noise of a dozen or so near strangers howling naked into the lowering sun. It's so animalistic. Primal. I shield myself with my forearm and take off too.

My one-armed running gait is a bit clumsy, and I release my own little yell. It's the kind a child lets out when they're sledding down a hill, mostly fear and adrenaline but with a tiny jolt of joy. At last, the fear seeps out of my skin and is replaced by something like elation.

The euphoria of the moment overtakes me in waves until finally I throw my head back and shout out all my inhibitions, my pressures. I'm not a woman alone in an emptied-out house with a job that asks too much. I'm a shape in the setting sun. A set of lungs screaming into the heat. A pair of legs that can carry me any which way I want. I'm endless potential.

I tear the hand away from my chest so that the air can graze my nipples, before I pump my arms and break out into a run. We move as a swell of bodies deeper into the trees, free and wild and connected, just as Ethan promised in his speech. We're fragments of an unforgettable moment. I don't even have to photograph it to know I'll have it forever.

"AND TURN BACK," Petey calls out.

The whole pack pivots as one like a colony of bees. All except for one.

"Ahh!" Ethan shrieks from behind me.

I'm kneeling next to him in an instant, still moving on wild impulse. I scan every inch until my eyes fall on the way his hand is clutching his ankle. My vision tunnels, so much so that I don't notice how we've become an obstacle in the center of a nudist stampede and that my head is disastrously positioned at crotch height.

A hand connects with my shoulder first, then a knee at my back, until finally a dangling bouquet of flaccid penis and distended testes slaps the side of my face. For a split second, the sweaty skin sticks like a bug on flypaper, then it peels off my cheek when the owner of the rogue scrotum leapfrogs over my topless body. He buckles at the knees in front of me the instant he lands.

"Holy sh—" Russell cuts himself off, biting his own fist. His other hand is clutching his roughed-up genitalia.

"Are you okay?" I ask after him. He curls up into the fetal position, writhing in pain.

"Your cheek is so bony," he says accusatorily.

"You got some of my nose in there too," I respond, a little hibiscus LaCroix bobbing in my throat at the memory of Russell's balls against my face.

His body rocks back and forth like he's a giant baby entering the world in nothing but a pair of Hokas. Finally, he begins to uncoil when the pain appears to reach just-walk-it-off levels and he can stand.

"I'm so sorry. Are you okay?" I repeat.

"Ted!" He ignores me, calling out to his friend. "I need ice, Ted." He hobbles away from us toward Wet Ted's, behind the handful of stragglers.

"Your shoulder is bleeding." My scrape pulses under Ethan's stare.

"From Russell's shoe, I think." I position myself in front of him, leaning down over the ankle he's still massaging.

"It's fine," he says, pinching his eyes shut.

I sigh. "Let me look at it."

He winces. "It's twisted. What do you think you'll find?"

"Can you put weight on it?"

He lets out a childish huff. "How should I know? It literally just happened. You were there."

I swat his hands off his leg. "You must be in a lot of pain if you're being this big of a smartass."

That manages to extract a laugh from him, but then he jerks his head back.

Oh god, did I hurt him? "What's wrong? Is it tender?"

"Chuck. Your boobs are *right* there." He makes a show of averting his eyes.

I look down. In the shock of his fall and my collision with the penis, I forgot we were defectors in a seminude footrace. I pop my shirt back on and, after a moment of panicked indecision, stuff my bra in my shorts pocket.

"Okay, I'm decent," I tell him.

His eyes peel open one at a time. "This is *not* what I had planned for tonight."

"The naked run threw me for a loop too. Do you have a first aid kit in your van?"

Ethan doesn't get the opportunity to answer. Instead, Petey scoops him up like he's a toddler who's fallen asleep in the car, with one arm under his knees and the other braced behind his shoulders. "Don't worry, buddy. I'll get you to the campsite tonight."

"No, bro. Come on," Ethan whines, chagrined.

I grab Petey's elbow. "Absolutely not. He needs to ice and elevate his ankle. He can't lie on the ground in a hot tent all night. I'll stay with him in the van, and we'll paddle in with Ted in the morning."

"I'm really fine," Ethan protests from Petey's arms. We all ignore him.

"I can stay with him, Charley. It's no problem," Petey responds. But then Laurel gives him the most conspicuous glare

I've ever seen from her (which is saying a lot, as discretion is not one of her many strengths). Petey corrects himself, telling us that "upon further reflection," he needs to ensure his slightly tipsy fiancée gets to camp safely before sundown.

I've never heard the words "upon further reflection" fall from Peter Eriksson-Thao's lips once in my life, but I don't push back.

Petey sets a one-legged Ethan down in front of the van and backs away quietly like a naughty child. Then he and Laurel climb into a two-person kayak, and we watch them disappear on the water behind a spit of trees. From the water's edge, Laurel calls out from between cupped hands, "Don't do anything I wouldn't do!"

It's only then that I realize I've forfeited my last chance to talk to my sister on the night before her wedding.

———

"Ah, ah, ah." Ethan winces in pain at the temperature of the ice pack, at the firmness of the pillow under his foot, at absolutely everything I intend to ease said pain. His van is surprisingly well equipped. Although it should probably stop surprising me at some point how lovely a life this man has built.

"You're the worst patient," I admonish him.

"You're worse," he argues.

"I'm a perfect patient. I want to be left alone. I'm like a dog that hides under the porch and waits to die." I pat the swollen skin with my ring finger, and you would think I dropped a brick on him. "This is astounding. We're approaching foam-party-foot-injury levels, Powell. I was hoping I'd never see that disastrous human again."

"There was *so* much blood, Beekman. I was very high and thought I was going to bleed out on the sidewalk."

"Oh, I remember. You ruined my favorite jeans and made me promise to 'Liam Neeson' you, regardless of the coroner's 'confirmed cause of death.'"

His cheeks hollow out, like he's biting on them to keep from cracking up. "I won't be held responsible for anything I said on Benson's mushrooms. Those were basically lethal."

I grab his hand. "You kept yelling 'Confirmed cause of death! Confirmed cause of death!' like there would be an *un*-confirmed cause I ought to seek vengeance for."

"Which do you think was bloodier: the foam party or your bachelorette party?"

I move the ice pack around on his ankle with great importance. "I think it's a toss-up," I say quickly, hoping to seal up all the hurt that threatens to spill out at the mention of that fight and the year of suffocating silence that followed.

His eyes don't seem to register my inner turmoil. Instead, they find mine, giving me a look that turns my bones liquid. "Char," he murmurs, his thumb drifting up my wrist bone, then sliding all the way back down to the tips of my fingers. I feel that touch everywhere. Little pinpricks all the way down my spine. My mind spins with *what if* after *what if* and each of the resulting *but for*s.

"Please stop overthinking this," he pleads.

My eyes go to the ceiling. I feel his stare like the press of a hand. "Someone has to. You're *under*thinking this."

He pushes the ice pack off his leg and looks at his ankle, his hand, the counter, everywhere but back at me. Disappointment tugs at my lungs, because, for a second, I think I've done it. I've infected him with my fear and apprehension. I've ruined this before I even got a chance to *enjoy* it.

But then he whips himself back around. "I promise you I've dedicated a lot of thought to this."

His sentence hits me like a kick to the shin and words expel from my mouth. "I don't want to lose you again." The utter truth of it smacks us in the face like a swinging testicle. Still, the fear deep inside me beats like a drum. *Don't let yourself want something he can't give*, it says.

I know what this is and the bounds of what it can be. He's a nomad, and I'm a workaholic who desperately needs to pay off her mortgage on a very immovable house. We are the two least compatible people on this planet. But even knowing that doesn't feel like enough to keep me safe from the way this man could destroy me if he disappears again into a puff of smoke and an unsatisfying text message.

"You can't lose me. It doesn't matter what happens or doesn't happen, you'll never lose me. Do you get that? If this— what we've done—is enough for you, I can make it be enough for me. I *can't* push you away again. I won't."

Something changes in his face, an unknown emotion covering his naturally emitting light like a solar eclipse. "I'm serious. I'll take any shred of you you'll give me. It wouldn't have to mean anything, I swear." He lifts his thumb to my cheek and swipes at a tear. "Just tell me what you want, Chuck. I can't stand it anymore. Please, put me out of my misery."

I hold his plea to my chest like a physical thing, pressing it against my breastbone. Emotion coils around my throat; I'm overwhelmed by the panic of knowing I'm in a pivotal moment and not knowing whether it'll recast itself as a regret in real time.

"I want you," I whisper, and he doesn't make me say more. He inches his face closer and presses a hand into my hair, pinching his eyes shut like this small bit of contact is almost more than he can take. Every part of my body tightens. Every place we're touching—his fingers behind my ear, my hand on his thigh, his breath on my lips—is the turn of a crank.

There's no going back now.

He fingers the bottom of my shorts with his other hand, barely grazing the edge of skin near my inner thigh.

"Yeah?" The whisper of the single syllable cuts off the oxygen to my brain, and I'm not confident I'll be able to remain upright if he keeps going like this.

"Please," I whisper. We're so close, breathing together. "I've wanted this for so long."

It's exactly what he needs to hear. He closes his eyes and gives in.

His lips meet mine, velvety soft but so firm. Controlled. He has me—I'm safe—and I can fall apart into him. I tip my head back to let his teeth skate across my jaw. It takes everything in me not to cry out at the way the sensation sends fireworks straight through my abdomen. Still, somehow he knows—he always knows. His smug smile presses up against my neck. "I've been watching you drag your finger across your face right there for ages. You think I didn't notice?"

Did he catalog those tiny, seemingly insignificant parts of me? The same way I did with him?

"When you're concentrating, you brush the tips of your fingers right there." He draws on my jaw with his guitar-callused finger. "I've imagined reaching over and touching you right here hundreds of times. Thousands." He replaces his finger with his mouth, dragging his lips along my chin and down my neck.

"Can you feel how fast my heart is beating?"

"Yeah." His hot laugh vibrates against my skin as his hands grab at the bottom of my T-shirt. We break apart just long enough for me to pull it over my head and toss it onto the floor. In a moment, he's back on me, groaning between my breasts, fingers skimming my stomach. We're both so sweaty and hot, but it doesn't matter. We feel too good like this to stop.

When I tug on his hair, he nearly collapses into my chest. He looks up at me with wild, blown-out pupils. "God, Charley. You know, I've literally dreamed of you doing that."

"I've watched you mess with this ridiculous hair since you started growing it out," I tell him. "You think *I* didn't notice?"

"You like it like this. Remember, like, seven years ago we were at that music festival in Missouri . . ." His hands slide along my ribs, down to my hips, until he pulls me onto his lap so that I'm wrapped around him like a present. Those tapered fingers trail up my thigh. My hips roll toward him without any direction from my brain, every move of our bodies a perfect call and response. "You told me you loved my hair," he murmurs.

"I really do," I say on a gasp.

There's nothing inexperienced in the way he claims every bit of me, but I still feel like we're a couple of teenagers. Like I honestly might die if he stops kissing me. As though I could explode into pieces like glass under pressure. I'm certain I could kiss like this for hours—days—and never need more. I need no life outside of this moment. Nothing but a bed, water, and PowerBars for sustenance. I think I *get* the van life now.

His fingers skate against my shorts, finding their way to my zipper. He sighs out a needy breath, as though my fly is some sort of great elemental discovery. The sounds he makes—the desperate breaths, the bitten-off moans—give me this heady pleasure I didn't know was possible, and I nearly collapse at the mere sound of him losing his mind over me. Now that I've heard it, I'm becoming increasingly confident I could shatter at Ethan's sexually frustrated sigh alone.

Even with Ethan's sounds in my ears, his taste on my lips, his fingers traveling below my waistband, it's not enough. I squirm on top of him, searching for more points of contact, more of him, until he hisses in pain.

"Shit." I pull away. "I forgot about your ankle." I remove myself from his lap so that we're side by side again. Even though as I speak, my chest is still heaving hot, eager breaths, and he's essentially panting.

"So did I," he grits out, straightening his leg with a wince. "As incredible as this is, it still isn't how I imagined our first time together."

"It's so weird to me that you've thought about this before." I can hardly believe this is happening, let alone that Ethan's *pictured* it.

With a firm hand, he grabs the back of my neck and presses his forehead to mine. Something tender tugs beneath my ribs. "I would've gladly done this ages ago, but I was positive you'd immediately get all panicked."

I laugh into his cheek, because he's right about the panic part. Any other time in our friendship, a hookup with him would've sent me into a mental spiral of unending *But what does it mean?*s.

He pulls me into him again by the waist, apparently prepared to risk life and limb for sex with me.

I play with the ends of his hair as his mouth peruses my body, placing little kisses down my neck, between my breasts, and onto my stomach. "I'm not sure I'm your usual type," I whisper. Ethan's the king of friends with benefits, but I never would've imagined he saw *me* in that way.

"My type is you." He growls it against my rib cage, his words sliding smooth across my skin. "Last night was unbearable for me. You get that, right? I was so close to saying something, but you fell asleep."

"You can wake a girl up for something like that." I nudge him back but he doesn't let me go, looking up my expanse to level me with those stormy eyes.

"You're so beautiful, Charley. You're so fucking beautiful." He says it again and again like a prayer as he pulls down my shorts and presses his lips to my hip and then the inside of my thigh, allowing me to disappear into the feeling of being cared for and *known* in a way I'm not sure I ever have been before.

Sure, it'll end, but I push the fear of *how* it will end to the edges of my mind and commit to enjoying this while it lasts.

I revel in it all. The way his hair brushes against my neck. How he practically falls apart when I grab his face. That look when he's on top of me. As though it's always been this way, and it always will be.

Like he never wants to leave.

Chapter 18

Rhymes with "Endless Consternation"

I WAKE UP NAKED with my head wedged in the corner between the mattress and the rear door. We never bothered with the whole soup-can leveling trick. Or covering the windows. Instead, we had sex twice and then promptly fell asleep. Well, mostly. One of last night's many revelations was that I love touching Ethan Powell's body—the definition of his shoulders and back, the slope of his neck, the hair trailing his chest, the strong muscles in his arms. I couldn't bring myself to stop until I finally passed out from erotic exhaustion.

The best part was that I could tell he felt the same. One moment, he'd be grabbing me with a feral hunger that drove me wild. Then the next, he'd take his time. His fingers met my skin over and over with a reverent gentleness. It was one of the loveliest, hottest, most chaotic nights of my life, and, in the harsh morning sun, I'm a little disappointed that daylight didn't have the decency to stay lost awhile longer.

My bag is in the passenger seat where I threw it last night, and I dig out my last pair of clean underwear before throwing on a pair of Ethan's light blue boxers and one of his cozy

T-shirts, praying to all the available gods that the ceremony today doesn't happen, if for no other reason than I'd rather not wear a holey concert tee to my sister's woodland wedding.

When I slide open the van door, scents of cinnamon and coffee fill my nostrils. Ethan's playing the guitar again. I hesitate, hoping to catch a folky little riff before he notices. He looks up when he hears me and smiles. It's one of the larger, more ridiculous ones in his repertoire. Rays of morning light streak across his face, and he looks so damn beautiful that I almost say so out loud.

"Morning, sleepyhead," he greets me. "The sunlight woke me up, but I was hoping to let you sleep in."

"No luck." I step down onto grass, enjoying the dewy blades tickling my toes. He sets down the guitar and hands me a pouch of warm gluten-free oatmeal.

"Breakfast the morning after?"

"I made coffee too."

I bite the inside of my cheek to keep my face under control and focus on stirring my oatmeal. A tiny puff of steam releases into the air. "How's the ankle?" I ask.

"Can't complain."

I tilt my head in the direction of the guitar. "Are you playing something?"

"Messing around with something new," he replies, removing the instrument from his lap to lean it against the van.

I waggle my brows. "Were you writing a song about our coitus?"

He stands and walks over to me, wrapping his arms around the small of my back. I lean in too. I can't seem to help myself when it comes to him. "Yes," he responds. "But I can't think of a rhyme for 'full-on penetration.'"

I scoop a spoonful of oats into my mouth. "'Endless consternation.'"

"Flawless." His forehead crinkles, like he's working overtime to hide his amusement. "You should be the songwriter."

I swallow and drape my hands around his neck, letting my pouch of oatmeal dangle behind him. "So, *the* Ethan Powell has finally written a song about me?"

My comment turns the tips of his ears an adorable shade of pink. "I've written dozens of songs about you."

"What?"

"You'd have known that if I'd made it into your Spotify Wrapped."

The phrase "dozens of songs" shouldn't make my brain clunk around my head like a hunk of ice in a blender, but I can't seem to stop fixating on the *What will this mean?*s and the *For how long?*s and the *How will this end?*s and just simply exist in the present.

I bury my face into his neck, where he smells as sweet as ever. He can't read the anxiety on my face if he can't see it.

With his finger, he tips my chin to his, and my tension releases into the sheer pleasure of Ethan's mouth on mine, the way his hand cups my jaw. The way his body presses against mine and I press back. The physical sensation of being this close to him in every way is enough to overpower any whirring doubt.

"Nice shirt," he says, his voice a low hum.

"Sorry. I didn't have anything clean left. You can use my washing machine when we get back."

"You should keep it," he says, letting his lips drag along my neck. Pleasure crackles down my body. "Seraphina is a duo from the Bay Area. They've got this folky pop electronic thing going on. I think you'd like them. They're on the playlist."

"What playlist?"

"Yours. The 'End of the World' playlist. For when we have to rebuild society together. Remember?" I pull my face back and catch a glimpse of his breezy smile. "When I hear music I think you'd like, I add it to the playlist."

My stomach somersaults, and suddenly, I'm a performer in a community theater production of *Peter Pan* and an over-eager stagehand has just yanked me into the air by my waist. It's possible I leave my body, because what *is* that? Who curates secret playlists for friends they've imagined having casual sex with? What kind of fuckboy head game is he playing at?

"Charley. Don't." He squeezes my waist. The pressure of it brings me back down to earth. "It's not a big thing. I'm a musician with a weakness for curation and lists. That's all it is. Please, don't run into the woods."

"I'm not going to run," I promise. "I can't. I'm too sore from the nude five K."

Air sputters from his lips. "Good." He kisses me again, and I feel a bit more myself. Or whatever version of myself hooks up with Ethan in the woods. "Our canoe's still on the other side, but I saw Ted when I was making coffee, and he can take us over to the campsite for the wedding."

The wedding. I'd nearly let myself forget.

"But he has to work a couple more hours before his cousin can cover his shift."

"A couple hours?" I shake my head. "That's not good enough. I still haven't gotten Laurel alone."

"Chill." He groans into my bare shoulder. It's so addictive, stealing every touch like we're running out of time. It almost crowds out my worry about Laurel.

"You can pull her aside for a little sister time as soon as we get there," he reminds me. "I'll even run interference."

"You'd do that?" I ask, tilting my head to get a better look at his sleepy, sweet expression.

"It's still just a conversation, right? Then I'm on your team, Beekman." His words seep their way inside, sticking to me like chocolate syrup. *He's on my team now.* But I guess he always has been. "I'll tackle anyone who gets in your way. Even Petey."

"We both know you can't take down Petey."

"I cannot," he agrees without an ounce of wounded machismo.

Sun streams through the trees in bursts of light, dappling his face in the early morning glow. He looks like magic. He's a leading man in need of an equally enchanting costar.

"Oh. Don't move," I instruct. I inch back into the van, framing up the shot in my head. His body stays stock-still with the rigidity of a nervous child who has a spider perched on his nose. He relaxes a touch when I reappear with his camera.

"The light is incredible." The sun is that perfect tangerine hue we only get in Minnesota during these elongated hours in late June. When the light feels endless yet the days are still too short.

"These'll be perfect for your website," I say, my brows drawn in my "concentration face." "And they don't look anything like stills from a murder documentary."

Ethan's eyes grow wide. "I don't need to be *in* the photo. I'm selling *vans*."

"You're selling a lifestyle. You need to show people the person they want to be."

"And they want to be me?" He's incredulous but seems to find the idea somewhat persuasive since he's reaching for his guitar to complete the roaming-musician aesthetic. "Should I put a hat on or something?"

"And cover that nineties heartthrob thing you have going on? Absolutely not."

I move him to the mattress and position his arms around the guitar like he's an articulable Ken doll. The breeze kicks up, carrying with it florals and earthy notes of pine. It's my favorite thing about Minnesota summers. It falls through your fingers like warm sand. The minute you think it might last forever—that summer might never end—you catch that whiff of pine and you're transported to a dark December afternoon with the cold, crisp air scratching at your cheeks like a stray cat.

But I wouldn't want to hold on to it even if I could. The hot, sweaty days and bitter cold nights visitors find punishing are magical. The stark changes from season to season and complete transformation of the landscape serve to remind me that time passes, disappears even. And I wouldn't want to live in a place that would neglect its responsibility to gently remind me of how fleeting everything is.

It probably shouldn't surprise me how much I enjoy being in nature. It's how I spent so much of my time as a kid. I introduced myself to unfamiliar cities by capturing them with my camera. It didn't matter if I was dropped into places where I didn't belong. If I explored the woods, hiked along the shorelines, and traversed the unending city sidewalks, I could blend in. But whatever version of discovery this is with Ethan, I prefer it. It's nice to be someplace new with no agenda.

It's been so long since I could take a deep breath. I've been too busy with divorces and furniture sales and proving myself at work, all so I'd finally feel rooted to the ground. Somehow, I've neglected everything else I needed to flourish.

I move around the van, searching for the angles where the light hits Ethan through the open door exactly right. I frame up a few shots with his hoodie draped on the driver's seat so perfectly haphazardly it would've looked staged if I had placed it there myself. The space is vibrating with that pre-adventure anticipation. I get why people follow this hashtag. It's a fantasy of a new and improved sense of self. Van-life Charley would be patient, easygoing, and open to adventure. No partner would ever call me distant or guarded. I'd never be left for an idea, because I'd *become* the idea. If I only had a van . . .

"Can I play something?" he asks, growing impatient. "Or will moving ruin the fantasy?"

"Please play something. You look constipated all still like that."

He rolls his shoulders, his pre-performance tic that must connect him with his inner Bob Dylan. "Should I tie ropes to my wrists so you can more easily Jim Henson me?"

"Stop whining and pretend I'm not here."

He grumbles for a minute before falling into a riff, playing it over and over, slightly different each time. He always used to play like this in his parents' donut shop, building a song brick by brick until it sounded like an effortless explosion of melody. His lyrics were like that too. He'd start with something small— an interesting image or strange celestial metaphor that sounded right to his ear—then he'd build it out into something with meaning. It was beautiful to watch him work. It still is.

With a camera in hand and Ethan playing guitar, it finds me again: that feeling of being in a memory and bottling it with the perfect image, as though it's crystallized in amber light, so I might look back on it for years to come. His lips curl up in what isn't quite a smile but something better. It's awareness. Maybe he feels this too.

I know without looking that I've captured "the shot"—the version of this morning I'll want to hold on to. The dreamy foreground of him in the rising sun with the rocky lake shore in the distance. The depth of field renders the rippling current just out of focus so that the water looms behind, haunting him. The click under my forefinger is too satisfying for this not to be it.

I jump up beside Ethan on the mattress and close the mosquito screen. "That thing you were playing earlier was nice." I look up at him through my lashes. "It's good to hear you writing again."

"Chuck . . . ," he says accusatorily, his eyes on his guitar. "Did you snoop?"

My cheeks burn red hot. "I may have stumbled upon your secret songwriting notebook in our cop kerfuffle."

I flick through the camera roll in search of a distraction from how Ethan's face plunges my heart into a pool of warm water. I could drown in the bliss of being this close to him.

"You'll stoop to any level in your quest for nudes, won't you?" He sits there for a beat before putting the guitar down. "It's not much of a secret at this point, but yes, I'm writing songs again."

"Since when?" I ask. As far as I've known, Ethan's been blocked since Lemonface's epic rise and fall into the Velvet Nebula of stardom. His bandmate Benson, along with the slew of songwriters the label brought in, wrote their sophomore album, much to the dismay of listeners in possession of both ears and taste.

"The last couple of years." He says it as though he's not completely certain of the exact date he rediscovered his passion, and I don't buy it for a second. "Not having you in my life the way you used to be, it was . . . a shock to my system," he tells me, pulling a hand through his hair. "You've always had this way of shaking me by the shoulders and pointing me in the direction I needed to go, and without you, I forgot how to get up each day and breathe in and out. Just . . . exist. I was always a disaster when we were teenagers, imagining my future in that town—that slow life of waking up each day, clocking in and out at the shop, everything the same, day after day. I didn't even recognize myself in it. Our friendship was the one good thing I had there, and you were the only person who ever kicked me in the ass and told me to go for what I wanted. I'd begun to rely on you for that, and then suddenly, you were gone."

I suppress the impulse to jump in and soften his self-criticism. I stay silent, listening as he tugs me down onto the bed, our heads touching and our feet stretched on opposite ends like a bow.

"I flaked on a bunch of college shows and had to move back in with my parents to reset," he continues. "But I started writing again. It was cathartic. Ivan used a few of the songs on his album with his new band, and I cowrote some stuff with Seraphina." He gestures to the two women depicted in an artful line drawing on my boobs. "It's been nice to create songs and let them take on lives of their own outside of me. Writing was the part I always loved. Those relationships also helped me rebuild a stable of steady gigs, but I love not having to live and die based on the whims of Division Three college basketball banquets."

"I love that," I say, though it feels so insufficient. He curves his body toward me, letting his arm slide around my waist to land at the small of my back. We're so natural like this. It's hard to believe that we'll both be able to let this go in a matter of days.

"I was actually working on a song for Laurel and Pete. For a gift, kind of," he starts, but something in my face stops him in his tracks. "Say it, Beekman."

A small laugh spills out of me. "You cannot *gift* them a song. It's so 'oblivious guy at the bonfire with the acoustic guitar' and you've somehow managed to never be that guy."

"We have two hours to kill before Ted can take us out there. What am I supposed to do?"

"If that's the *only* way you can think of to kill time . . ."

Ethan considers for a moment, then moves closer so his forehead bumps against the tip of my nose. "Message received. You only want to use me for my body."

He pulls me into his chest, grounding me again and halting the buzzing anxiety in my brain. I'm so aware of the passage of time. The way each moment we're not touching is a moment wasted. He presses his lips to my wrist. It's so gentle. Warmth spreads up my arm like hot honey.

"To think I'd given up on this ever happening," he says, his voice low and aching. "Now that I have you, this whole other part of me has finally come alive, like the best things only exist when you're a part of my life."

I press my ear to his thumping heart and stare down at our clasped hands. "I don't want to run out the clock on this, you know?" My voice breaks on the last word. It catches us both by surprise.

"Hey." He pushes my chin up to meet his gaze. "There's no

clock," he assures me. "We can find a spot like this to park the van tomorrow night. And the night after." His lips travel along my neck. I groan when he finds the space behind my ear. "Can't sell this thing now. It's sacred ground. We'll keep driving forever if you want."

"That's nice," I say, referring both to the sparks skittering down the column of my throat and to the fantasy that we could live on an eternal road trip when I have an office of angry colleagues and a house I can't afford waiting for me.

But I'm still in that moment of the vacation where I'm playing pretend—imagining other lives for myself—and I'm not ready to stop. "I haven't ever thought of you and me as a possibility. I couldn't let myself picture it, knowing it could never happen."

"And now?" he asks, his expression so full of boyish longing. It's that dreamy, wistful look he used to wear when he talked about music or an imagined future outside of our tiny town.

"I feel alive too, Ethan," I tell him. Even though it doesn't do the feeling justice. The way my heart feels so tangible, I could tear it out of my chest and hand it to him. This indescribable pull toward him was nailed shut in a box in the deepest corners of my mind and I've busted it open with a crowbar. Nothing I feel for Ethan is new—it was always there—but now I'm consumed by it. His gravitational pull will yank me off a cliff if I'm not careful.

"You called me Ethan." His expression rearranges itself into something more cocksure.

"So?"

"I've never heard you call me that before."

My nose scrunches. "Sure you have."

His expression shifts—a storm changing direction. His eyes trail all over my face, staring back at me like I'm something to look at, a work of art to stand in awe of. It's how I sometimes catch myself looking at *him*. I drag my hand up to his collarbone, noticing the way the rhythm of his breathing slows.

I don't ask what this is or how this trip will change things between us. Instead, I kiss him, tangling our limbs as we grab hold of each other like our lives depend on it. Maybe because touching like this feels overdue after years of suppressing the occasional burst of fantasy. I know the weight of him, the feel of his skin, the press of his lips, from each and every time I thought about kissing him and didn't.

I'm so used to loving him, but loving him *like this* is all new, and I won't waste a second of it parsing out where the fantasies end and reality begins.

Chapter 19

A Combination of Brayden and Brody

I T'D BEEN TWO weeks since Ethan and I ran out of gas and Owen Twombley pilfered me pretzel buns like a man obsessed.

Though I was still swept up in his new affections, Owen was, at present, in Albuquerque for a student government summit. What was supposed to be my low-key weekend of laundry and *Survivor* had been upended by my postgrad sister whisking into town, newly single and ready to mingle. Whatever overtures Petey had made the week prior did not go to plan. Their flickering bulb of a relationship was off at the moment, so Laurel was falling into old patterns.

"I'm single!" she yelled into the mouth of Theta Delta's shot luge. We were on a fraternity porch precariously close to an indoor couch that'd been left in the rain since the Clinton administration. A poorly mixed mashup of "Hotline Bling" poured out the windows and onto the lawn of shivering women in bandage dresses and cold-shoulder tops.

Laurel swallowed her vodka shot and let out a woo.

"Charley, take a shot! Shot. Shot. Shot," she chanted, pumping her arm in a way that inspired the surrounding randoms to chant too.

I shook my head. "I'm not having a *Christmas Story* moment on a frozen liquor trough tonight."

"Boo." She threw her thumbs down with gusto, and, dear god, people were following.

I tugged on her puffer jacket sleeve and dragged her to the edge of the porch. "Stop that. We're at a fraternity. These people are very susceptible to chants. They'll repeat anything."

"I'm single, and you're ruining it," she said, pouting.

"How? By not being blackout at nine p.m.?"

"By being judgy. You're always so judgy."

"I'm not . . ." I didn't finish, because I *was* judging her right then and instantly felt guilty for it. "Let me find our ride back to the dorms. I made brownies."

"Magic?"

"No. Caramel."

She pumped her fist and murmured approvingly.

Just then, Ethan appeared on the trampled lawn.

"I don't know what a 'frat emergency' is," he said, jumping up the front steps two at a time and sidling up next to me with a gentle cup of my elbow, "but I didn't like the sound of it. I broke at least four traffic laws to get here. Also, I'm parked in a fire lane, so we gotta move."

"Of course she called you," my sister mumbled. "She always calls you. God forbid she be alone with me for two minutes."

I pressed my eyes shut. "Laurel, you're drunk."

"Let me get my bag, *Mom*. Then you can ground me for as long as you want." She ambled back into the debauchery while the base of my skull buzzed with irritation and dread.

"My god," I moaned.

Ethan's elbow knocked mine. "Hey, can we talk?"

"Uh, sure." I nodded, not sure what to make of a surprise *can we talk?* "Let's get Laurel home. Then maybe we can go somewhere?"

"Good. Yeah." His eyebrows curled into this worried-Labrador-retriever expression.

We waited on the porch as coeds spilled in and out of the door with the sounds of a booming bass line. Ethan wasn't saying anything. He looked nervous. Was he nervous?

I pulled out my phone, a reflex to feeling any social discomfort. Mixed in with the H&M promotional emails and unopened daily digests from the *New York Times* I'd resolved to start reading at the beginning of 2015 was an email notification from a name I saw biannually.

From: mia.beekman312@gmail.com
To: charlottebeek63@gmail.com
Subject: Norway album

Charley girl—

Surprise! We moved to Norway! We're with a research team following humpback whales. Absolutely incredible. Album attached. Can you ask your sister if it would kill her to respond to a message now and again?

—Mom and Dad

I typed up a quick response, sidestepping all talk of Laurel in favor of a school update she didn't ask for. Before I hit send,

I opened the attachments. There were a handful of stills my dad clearly had taken—action shots of whales flopping into the dark ocean, spraying water all around them like an explosion of stars—but the rest were photos from my mom's iPhone.

Derek laughing with some man in coveralls, one hand clapping the man's shoulder and the other clutching a tall glass of beer.

Derek wearing a camera on his shoulder, balancing over the edge of a fishing boat, his eyes slits as he concentrated on his mammoth subject.

Derek with his crew, pointing into the middle distance with an expression so self-important he gave candids of James Cameron a run for their money.

My mom wasn't in the pictures, and I couldn't help but pick apart the way she'd disappeared into my dad's life after he'd failed to be a part of ours. It was the only way for them to be together: someone had to recede.

I pressed send and closed out the window, feeling that particular brand of anxiety that swirled in my gut when I tugged on that thin piece of thread that still connected me to them, despite the way our entirely separate lives hardly ever crossed anymore. With my parents, I'd always be loose change at the bottom of their pockets: valuable enough to keep carrying but never prized enough to account for.

"You good?" Ethan asked.

I nodded without registering the question as I leaned my head through the front door in search of my sister. My eyes snagged on her chatting up some random dude who was lying on a stained sectional with two missing cushions. "One sec," I told Ethan before torpedoing down the hall.

I grabbed Laurel by the elbow. Her coat was nowhere to be found. It looked as though she'd wandered in to stay awhile with Fratty McFratterson. The hulking dude was wearing shorts with embroidered lobsters in the middle of December for chrissakes.

"Laurel, we're going. Come on." I didn't realize how drunk Laurel was until I watched her stand up. She was wobblier than a baby giraffe finding its legs.

"I'm Broden." Lobster Man extended his hand to me.

I sighed out a breath, because apparently I was about to exchange words with the man Laurel had targeted specifically to piss me off. "Broden. What an original name—"

"It's a combination of Brayden and Brody," he explained.

"Cool." My smile was more a presentation of teeth than a display of genuine kindness. I gave him a once-over, checking for distinctive scars I could use to describe him in a future police report. Broden was doughy and bloated in a fairly unremarkable way, but he had the full, pouty lips of a man who would open a credit card in your name, which, apart from Petey, was exactly Laurel's type. "Laur, shall we?"

She didn't respond. All of her faculties were dedicated to removing the baseball cap from Broden's head and putting it on her own, a drunk-girl pre-mating ritual I knew well. When she finally responded, the sentence flowed out in cursive, each letter curling right into the next. "Broden was telling me about his intramural Frisbee team."

I boxed the guy out to face Laurel and Laurel alone. "Can you not do the thing you *always* do, for once in our lives, please?"

"What the hell does that mean?" She dropped her hand from his chest like I'd struck her.

My remorseful eyes shot up to the ceiling. "Sorry, it's just . . . you said you'd leave, so let's leave."

She muttered something under her breath but still followed me out the door.

We piled into the back of the minivan, Ethan in the front seat flashing his hazards, the don't-ask-for-permission-ask-for-forgiveness of parking maneuvers.

"Charley, stop," she whined, fighting me off as I shoved her into the back seat. "I can't find my phone, and I won't leave without it." She tapped her screen with one eye pinched shut. "I'll call Broden so he can bring it out to me."

"Your phone is in your hand, Lo," Ethan said, checking his blind spot on his way out of the fire lane. "Whose hat is that? Brenden's?"

"*Bro*den's," Laurel and I said simultaneously, even though it filled me with an irrational fury that I knew the proper pronunciation of the name of a guy who was dressed like a Massachusetts Easter brunch.

"Where's your coat?" he asked.

"She's fine," I answered for her. "She's got her liquor jacket on." I fastened her seat belt with a sharp click.

"Edith!" She shot up, meeting the resistance of the seat belt strap. "We have to go back! That coat was a perfect Goodwill find. Irreplaceable!"

I pressed her down by the shoulder, but she bounced right back up like a toddler on a trampoline. "Once we find my coat, we can stop by the other party," she shouted through the van. Despite her valiant attempts at speaking at a reasonable volume, Laurel was drunkenly overshooting it.

"He's not here this weekend," Ethan cut in from the driver's seat.

"Who's not here?" she asked innocently, but, suddenly, the whole night—floating from sports bar to sports bar, pounding shots all the way to Greek Row, always scanning the room over my shoulder—was coming into perfect clarity.

"Pete's been in Edmonton since Wednesday," he told her, his voice sympathetic. "What happened with him, Lo? He wants to make it work."

"*I* wanted to make the best of the time we have left. *He's* the one who wanted to cut it off now."

"Couldn't you try long distance?" he asked her.

"He doesn't actually want to be in a long-distance relationship with me. He just thinks he does."

"You don't know what he wants," I argued, not because I felt defensive of Petey but because I was sick of Laurel blazing into my life and upending it like the Cat in the Hat with a bleached-blond shag (her current hairstyle of choice).

"So he can be handcuffed to his phone every second he's not on the ice in case I'm available for mutually unsatisfying Face-Time sex? Or so I can feel trapped in my room in the apartment I share with three other broke teachers? And then he can grow to resent me for never having time off to travel to his games?"

Her voice was a hard, bitter thing, but the words kept tumbling out of her. Boulders down a hill.

"Then I'll act out because I'll know he's unhappy. He won't say it—he'll never say it—but I'll *feel* every little moment when I disappoint him, and I'll hurt him. Because that's how I am, right?" She faced me, her eyes wild and frenzied.

"Stop it, Laurel," I choked out. The tears burned behind my eyes. I hated watching her crumble like this.

"Charley knows. I'm selfish, right? I'm selfish and dramatic, and not built to be with another person. Not for forever. Not someone like Petey."

Ethan's eyes were darting between his view of us in the mirror and the road. "Charley doesn't think that, Lo. I promise she doesn't."

"Well, then she's as delusional as our mother."

I fell deeper into my seat, debilitated by her jab and mortified that Ethan was here to witness it.

This was the problem with having sisters. They'd been there from the beginning. They knew your strengths, your weaknesses, and they knew how to deliver the fatal blow before you could even spot it coming.

"Enough, Laurel," Ethan told her in the voice he used for rowdy tweens at the Donut Barn. "You're drunk. You're going to regret saying all of this tomorrow."

But she wasn't interested in his words of caution. "You've met our parents, right? Their marriage is a joke. We'd've been better off if they'd never pretended they were capable of doing anything besides disappointing each other. Now we're cursed."

"We're not cursed," I butted in, because now I was pissed. "Mom loves trying to make a bad thing work and so do you apparently. If you would actually date someone who makes sense for you—"

"Like you and that Owen guy?" Laurel hiccupped. "You'll find a way to ruin it. It's what we do. We're ruiners."

"That's sweet, Lo," Ethan spat, putting the van into park in front of my dormitory.

Every part of my body was clenched. My jaw. My toes. My hands were fisted so tightly, my fingernails had pressed half-moons into my palms. I wanted Laurel to stop saying these things, but even more than that, I wanted them not to be true. *Was* I going to ruin things with Perfectly Nice Owen simply by being a Beekman woman? Doomed to be deserted or to disappear into an unequal relationship?

Ethan slid open Laurel's door, and I wanted to say something that would halt time. Turn it backward. Undo all the things we'd done and said that had placed us in this exact spot in front of the sidewalk where a nineteen-year-old stranger was vomiting into a bush.

"I'm not being mean. I'm being honest," Laurel said, digging through her purse for the pack of American Spirits she only smoked when she rode this particular level of intoxication.

Ethan unbuckled Laurel and pulled her out of her seat. "Said every mean person ever. You're lucky you're basically a sister to me, because I'm tempted to drive off with Charley and leave you on the curb to fend for yourself."

She fumbled with her Zippo lighter. "Someone needs to look after her once you're gone, and it's not going to be Owen."

I would've assumed her words were the ramblings of a drunken fool if not for the way Ethan's face crumpled.

"What's she talking about?" I asked, climbing out onto the sidewalk.

She rubbed her bare arms in an attempt to ward off the inevitable shiver. "The tour thingy," she muttered, cigarette flapping between her lips.

Apprehension slithered up my neck. My body knew *something* was happening, but it didn't know what.

Ethan grabbed my hand. "I was gonna tell you," he said. "That's what I wanted to talk to you about."

"Shit. Did I fuck up?" Laurel asked, chastened.

"Yes," he scolded, just as I said, "No, you're fine."

"I'm gonna smoke this where it's warm," Laurel interjected, looking between us and backing away in the direction of the heated bus shelter fifteen feet away.

"I wanted to tell you when we could talk. In private. I told my parents about the tour, like you said. It turns out, they've been thinking about closing the shop for a while. They knew it wasn't my dream, but they didn't want to sell it out from under me if I didn't have another plan." His eyes darted all over my face like he was desperate to decipher my expression. I didn't even know what I was thinking, so I couldn't imagine what my face was doing.

So much for being a clock.

I kept my voice light when I said, "I'm so happy for you."

His face changed, like I'd said something unexpected, disappointing even, but I couldn't tell how. He let go of my hand, stuffing his into his pockets. "Yeah?"

"It's all I've ever wanted for you." And it was true. I loved Ethan enough to want more for him than Lewellen. "When do you leave?"

"Thursday."

"That's soon. Not as bad as that time I skipped town the next day, but . . ." I forced my mouth to smile as a tear fell on my cheek. "We're always dramatically leaving each other, huh?"

"I guess we are. Will you email me? Like before?" He rocked on his heels, waiting for my response.

"All the time," I said. "I might call you occasionally, if you're lucky."

I looked over my shoulder at Laurel and opened my mouth to make any excuse to leave this conversation, which was turning me inside out, but without warning, Ethan grabbed me by the shoulders.

"Come with me," he said.

I blinked. "What?"

His eyes were wide and wild. He looked thirteen again. "Come on the road with me. You finished your last final yesterday. It's perfect."

"I have that LSAT course over break and then the spring semester starts—"

He grabbed my face in his hands. His whole body shook with a feverish energy. "Take a semester off. It'll be like studying abroad." His smile was so big and intoxicatingly frenetic, I wanted nothing more than to smile back.

"You usually get *credits* when you're studying abroad." I forced a laugh into my voice, an attempt to inject some sense of casualness into this increasingly uncasual conversation. What was he doing?

"Who cares about credits or LSATs? You're an incredible photographer. *Be* a photographer! With me. Come with me."

His words were the yank of a plug in a warm bath. I could feel the blood draining from my face. "What am I supposed to say to that?" I asked, my voice unsteady.

His eyes on me were too much. Too alight. Too pleading. "Say yes," he whispered.

I'd had countless fantasies of a man holding my cheeks and begging me to "say yes." Now it was happening with my best friend, and it sounded like more like "give up your dreams and lose yourself in mine." My heart was splitting, soaring and sinking all at once, leaving me mangled on the sidewalk.

His smile wavered. "Please," he begged soundlessly.

But I couldn't. I couldn't give up my life to follow him around as he lived out his wildest dreams. I couldn't be the woman he wanted. I didn't want to disappear. Not with him. The only right answer echoed through my empty chest like a gong. "No."

I ripped his hands from my cheeks, and in an instant, he backed away from me.

"What?"

Tears bit at the corners of my eyes. Mortification and shame were breathing against my neck like a monster perched on my shoulder. I took a shallow breath, hoping my face didn't betray how shattered I felt. "I'm not giving up my life to follow you around like some hopeless loser until you get bored of me."

"It wouldn't be like that," he pleaded, voice cracking. "Fuck." He grabbed at the back of his neck, looking up at the stars as though the universe were pressing in on him, and just as I was certain he was going to explode in every direction but mine, he dropped his hands to his sides. "I'm sorry. I shouldn't've . . . That was dumb. I'm sorry I suggested it."

I wrapped my arms around my chest. "It's fine."

He swallowed hard, still looking up at the sky, then faced me again to ask, "Can we forget I said all of that? Please?"

"Of course." I took a step forward to show him I really meant it. "Forgotten."

His hand cradled my elbow again. It made my heart do a sad little flutter. "Will you call me? Please."

I didn't answer, swallowing down the lump in my throat.

"I'll call *you*, then," he said. "You don't have to answer, but—"

"I'll answer," I promised.

"Good." He nodded as though convincing himself that we really were good. "Are you going to be okay with Laurel tonight? Do you need help getting her up to your room?"

"I've got it from here. Thanks."

He hesitated but then turned away from my dorm in the direction of his minivan. I tried not to watch Ethan walk away. Something told me I'd always remember it if I did, and I *really* didn't want to remember that.

I plopped down next to my sister on the bus bench, gutted.

"Full disclosure," Laurel told me through a hiccup. "I overheard the whole thing."

"Wonderful." I plucked her cigarette out of her mouth and threw it. "Those will kill you."

She reached into her pack for a replacement. "Die young, leave a pretty corpse."

"No," I scolded her, throwing that one too. "You're all I've got. You don't get to leave me."

She let out a sigh and pressed her head onto my shoulder. "That's why we're like this. So we'll always be around for each other."

"So you're always going to be this big a pain in my ass?"

"Probably." Her laugh was warm. Mollifying. "You know nothing happens when you graduate, right? You don't suddenly know what you're doing or who you are. You don't become an adult or anything. You're just the same shitty person, one year later, with more responsibilities and problems. My students look at me like I'm *so* mature, but I'm, what, five years older than they are? I have this recurring nightmare that one of them is bagging my groceries at Cub and sees that I subsist on Welch's Fruit Snacks and French bread pizza Lean Cuisines. And then, suddenly, *I'm* a French bread pizza Lean

Cuisine, and they're, like, stuffing *me* in a microwave . . ." She trailed off sleepily and dug her head deeper into my neck. Then, out of nowhere, she whispered, "I think I need to talk to someone."

"About your teenage boy diet?" I asked.

"About my brain, you idiot."

"Like a therapist?"

"Yeah," she hummed. She was falling asleep. "Or an astrologer."

I pulled my head back to look at her. She was so small curled up next to me, and it was as though I was sitting with every version of my sister all at once, even the youngest Laurel I could remember.

We sat there like that until a change in the wind shifted the stench of vomit in our direction. I grunted and heaved my sister up to carry her to my dorm.

"I'm sorry he's leaving," Laurel murmured.

My heart panged. "Me too."

"I'm sorry I called you a bitch back in his van."

"I don't think you did."

"Oh. That's good." She yawned. "I love you, Char Char."

"I love you too," I told her, because I did, and it felt good to have someone stick around long enough to let me love them close up.

Chapter 20

Eight Hours to the Winnipeg Petco

"I'M DEAD. I died last night. This is my ghost."

Petey might be thrilled to see us, but Laurel is visibly hungover, though still adorable in a pink halter dress and her largest pair of sunglasses.

"I might be a ghost too," I respond, sinking into the camping chair beside her.

"Did Ethan kill you with his penis?"

I shush her. "How did you know Ethan and I . . ."

"I didn't." Her pleased grin is so big and white, I can hardly look at it. "But now I do. Holy shit!"

I should play it cool, but I can't suppress the goofy smile that's been permanently plastered on my face since last night. "Keep your voice down."

"This is major." She sits up excitedly, before her hangover sends her back into the depths of the nylon chair.

"Do you need coffee?" I ask, moving my hand to block the blinding light that's refracting off the pond.

"Harlow made me some already. That beautiful baby angel of a woman."

I lower my own shades. "Still drunk?"

She shakes her head. "Feeling sappy on my wedding day."
The wedding.

All at once, I realize that *this* is it. We're alone. Her guard
is down. This might be my last chance.

"You don't have to get married today if you don't feel well,"
I tell her. Hardly my final thesis statement, but it's an inoffen-
sive start.

She swats away my concern with the flick of her wrist and
settles deeper into her camp chair. "No, if we don't do it today, it'll be this thing on our to-do list forever. I'd rather do it
now while it still feels right."

"That makes it sound like it'll feel *wrong* later."

Before Laurel can respond, Harlow bounces in with that
Russell guy, whom she apparently shared her tent with after he
socked me in the face with his scrotum.

"We're going to hunt for Wi-Fi before the ceremony," she
informs me. "Do you need to call into the office again?"

"Uh, maybe later," I respond. "I'm kind of hoping Bob'll
find a way to survive a single workday without me."

"Way to set a boundary, Char." Laurel's tone is sharp, and
it stings me a little.

My voice falters. "It's better than nothing."

"Do you know what you're wearing?" Harlow asks us.

I point to my boxer shorts and band tee. "This."

"You're not wearing that," Laurel objects.

I tug at my outfit. "What's wrong with it?" It's not the *most*
functional camping ensemble. There's a disconcerting breeze
coming through the cotton boxers, and my denim baseball cap
with "Ciao" embroidered over the bill costs more than is appropriate for attire I'll be wearing to poop in a hole, but otherwise, I've done pretty well given the circumstances.

"It's a T-shirt, and it's *white*. I'm not even wearing white."

I look down at my shirt. "It's more of a cream," I argue weakly.

"What else did you pack?" She wrestles the bag off my shoulder.

"My clothes had a run-in at a truck stop."

Fabric falls onto the nylon chair as she rummages. "Why didn't you pack anything nice?"

"I packed clothes appropriate for camping."

"'SEXY MOTHER TRUCKER'? Is that supposed to be a reference to Petey's upper-thigh tattoo?"

A derisive laugh spews from my mouth. I try to cover it with a cough but it's too late. "No," I say honestly. "I didn't know about that one. I swear."

"Is this funny to you? This is my wedding. You *invited yourself* to my wedding and didn't bring anything to wear."

"I didn't think . . ." *That it was* actually *happening*. I stop myself from saying it, but she sees the words written all over my face.

"I knew it." My bag shakes in her hands. "I wanted to think I was being crazy, and that maybe, for once, you could support me without needing to control everything. But no. You've been trying to corner me since the second you showed up here, because you don't want me to be happy."

"Of course I want you to be happy! But are you sure this wedding's a good idea?" I hate myself for the way her face falls. "It's just that . . . you don't exactly have the best track record with guys."

"Peter's not *a guy*," she argues.

"No, he's just *the* guy you were reeling from when I drove eight hours to rescue you from a Petco in Winnipeg."

My sister's jaw clenches. "You couldn't *wait* to throw Petco in my face."

"I was searched at the border at two in the morning. That's not when the *nice* customs agents are on shift, in case you were curious."

Harlow moves her lips but ultimately deserts our battleground without a word.

"That was eight years ago," Laurel yells, throwing up her hands as though *I'm* the ridiculous one in this situation. "Move on!"

"Oh, I get it." Blood boils up into my ears. I'm absolutely seething. "Because you gave me a Target gift card with thirty-three dollars left on it, I'm supposed to be over that by now?"

This is the scorched-earth way Laurel and I always fight each other. Nothing's off-limits. Every artifact of our childhood is primed to be excavated. Every argument is about *everything*, which means *everything* can hinge on the smallest bit of nothing. When you share a life with someone, it's impossible to let go of all the tiny little nothings when it counts.

"I'm not that person anymore. People change, Charley. Maybe *you* don't change, but other people do. I see it every time you look at me. You're waiting for me to—"

"To do something crazy and dramatic like marry your high school boyfriend in the woods?" My question is rhetorical. And cold-blooded. But I can't help myself. Fighting with my family always throws me into a fugue state of immature, unbridled bitchiness.

"No. You're waiting for me to be a mess. I think you're *hoping* for it. If I'm the mess and you're not, then we all fit into the same neat little piles we have since we were kids and you never have to question anything about your life."

I look around for someone to jump in and referee, but everyone's very busy pretending to be very busy. "I'm not . . . That's not . . ." I breathe in deep. I need to de-escalate this if I'm going to have any shot of getting through to her. "I don't think you're a mess, Laur. I think *this* is a mess. It's messy."

"You think Peter and I are messy? You and Ethan *just* rebuilt your friendship, and last night you were screwing each other in the back of a van! Now *that's* messy."

"You have no idea what you're talking about," I fire back, swallowing the scream attempting to break free from my throat. She's so off base. She's deflecting. She always does this. It's why fighting with her is infuriating. *She's* infuriating. How did this flip-turn into a dressing-down of *me* and my life choices?

"Oh, so you're not going to cut him off again when he starts being honest with you?"

"That's not . . ." Her accusation leaves me speechless. My fingers tingle with a mixture of white-hot rage and panic. I'm terrified, I'm rabid, and she's calm in the most maddening way. "This isn't about me and Ethan. This is about you and—"

"Do you seriously think I don't know Ethan's side of everything? Your bachelorette party? The wedding?"

Ethan's side of everything. The fragment worms its way inside my brain and burrows through all rational thought. The world pulses. My eyes dart to Ethan, but he's glaring at Laurel.

"Lo," he cautions her, coming around from the other side of the tent. He and Petey have been right there this whole time, within earshot. The whole Superior National Forest is within earshot the way we're shouting. "Stop. You don't know what you're talking about."

"Oh, I don't? You really think this time she's going to give up her life and move into your van with you?" She's refusing to let up, unrelenting, as each question presses against my breastbone like a forty-pound weight.

"That's enough, Lo." Ethan holds up a hand.

"Babe," Petey starts, seeming to recognize his fiancé at risk of going too far.

She throws up her arms. "Forget it. I need to clear my head." I watch Laurel march to the edge of the lake and plop herself into a kayak.

"Seriously?" My hands find my hips as we continue to devolve into our teenage selves. This argument might as well be a time machine. "Very mature, Laurel."

I look frantically between Ethan and Laurel, not sure where the most immediate damage lies. "I'm sorry. She just—"

He pulls his arms across his chest. "It's okay. Go. We can talk later." His voice isn't remotely reassuring, but for now, it's enough encouragement for me to do what I need to do.

I grab an empty kayak and paddle after my sister.

———

"Where are you going?" I yell once I'm finally within shouting distance. My shoulders are burning from the water's resistance and we've barely been at this for a few minutes.

Her gaze shoots over her shoulder. The paddle she's wielding almost drops into the water. "Jesus! You scared me."

"You can't row away from me," I call out. "We were talking."

"*You* were talking."

"You had a lot to say about me too, if you recall." Frustrated breaths expel from my throat with each stroke. "Can you stop? I've already lost one person this year over a particularly revelatory rowing incident and it's not happening again."

"This is a kayak."

She turns herself around to better berate me, paddling backward without missing a stroke, leading me to wonder if this is something she does recreationally. Does my sister like to kayak now? Why didn't she tell me about it? Or did she tell me and I wasn't listening?

"Why can't you be happy for me?" Her question skitters across the water.

"Happy for what? I *just* got divorced. The ink is barely dry, and you wanted to get married without me. You thought I'd be like 'Cool, Laur. Good for you'?" I gesture with my paddle. The resulting movement sends my boat a little sideways, cutting into its overall effect.

"Oh my god." Her mouth shakes with quiet rage, and she finally stops paddling. "Who cares about your stupid divorce? Thank god you're not still married to that boat shoe of a human. No one *wanted* you to marry Rich."

I now understand what it means to feel your blood boil. Not so much at what she's saying (I'd assumed as much) but the *way* she's saying it. Reducing my year of heartache and pain to something silly. I set my paddle on my lap, looking absurd in this giant red boat. I might as well be arguing about the dissolution of my marriage in a plastic clown shoe.

"But I respected you enough to let you make your own choices," she continues, ignoring the way my face is turning red. "But you couldn't respect me enough to let me make mine. And the worst part is, I *knew* you wouldn't. I knew from the second you showed up you were angling for something, but I got caught up in nostalgia and hope like an idiot."

Her pointed words jab me between the ribs, one after another.

"The only reason we didn't immediately elope in the first place was *because* of the timing with your divorce, but if I could do it all over again, I would've married Peter that day without ever telling you!"

"You wouldn't have!"

"I would so," she spits. "I would've married the crap out of him!"

What can only be described as a feral howl releases itself from my throat. At Laurel, the lake, my stupid paddle. I must look petty and childish. I may as well be calling out for our mom and crying about how unfair it all is. "You're so self-centered, Laurel."

"I get it." She punches her paddle into the air. "I was a horrible sister and you hate me."

Despite it all, I somehow manage a laugh. "Laurel, I *wish* I could hate you." I practically beat my chest with my palm. "It would be wonderful to write you off—but I can't because I love you and you're the only person I'll ever have."

It's so simple and primal, it decimates me.

She's my rock.

Our parents took off at the first opportunity. My husband left. It's only a matter of time before Ethan leaves. Laurel's the only person who's ever felt permanent. She's all I've ever had. But I'm not all she has. She's ready to dispose of me. She's leaving me behind for something better. For more.

My love for her pricks at my insides. I love Laurel with such untamed vehemence I have to keep it close. Otherwise, it'll explode from my heart like a defective box of thumbtacks.

I want to let her in, but she's not saying anything back. It's dangerous, the way fear can corrode, and I feel my defenses going back up in real time. "God, you're so desperate to leave me behind, aren't you? You can't wait to twist yourself into a pretzel so someone will keep loving you. You're no better than our parents. It's so pathetic."

She flinches like I've slapped her. I might as well have, because I know at this moment, even if we find a way past this, I'll never undo that flinch. I've struck her once, and now she knows I'm capable of it.

She considers for a moment but then says, "If you think any of that is true, you're a bigger idiot than I thought."

My eyes burn with unshed tears. I have no words, and that's the worst part, because I *hate* that. I hate feeling my emotions seep out of my body like sweat and having nothing to say. Nothing to do but sit in my own awful feelings.

I stand up, not sure what I'm about to say but desperate to say *something*. "Laurel—"

But I don't get to whatever I was ramping up to because my kayak flips over, and I topple into the water with a percussive flop.

My ankle catches and knocks against the boat on my way to the water's surface. The cold water stings against my shins, my belly, and the side of my face as though I've walked into a sliding glass door. The only difference is that shattered glass doesn't shoot up your nose the way lake water does.

I see the paddle bobbing in front of me when I come up for air and grab on to it. I dart my head around, but the kayak isn't anywhere.

"It's in the tree," Laurel tells me before I have to ask. She's headed for me at an impressive speed. Is she, like, *really* good at kayaking?

I squint up at her. "The tree?"

"The fallen tree to your left. When you went down, it flew in the other direction and got caught in the branches." I follow her finger and, sure enough, I see a moss-covered trunk jutting into the side of the lake with a long red kayak half in the water, half hoisted up by one of its branches. "Here. Get in with me. I'll take you to it."

She holds my paddle while I grip the side of the boat. "Not like that. Reach your left arm all the way to the opposite side," she instructs, and I clumsily follow.

I heave myself into the boat, drenched from head to toe, shivering as steady drips of water fall from my head in wet plops. My eyes wander between our chaos and the stillness of the lake, tracking the way we're drifting through the water, the world moving around us in slow motion.

"I can't wear white to your wedding now. So that's settled."

She laughs, a quick reprieve from our present fight. "You still could."

"It's a little translucent now."

"We've all seen your tatas. No modesty left in this group."

She looks at the tree line like there's something up there she needs to see. Then, apropos of nothing, she asks, "What are you more afraid of? Petey and I getting divorced or staying together?"

The question slices through me. The familiar refrain I've been repeating all weekend, *This won't end well*, is right there on the tip of my tongue. But that fear for her wasn't my immediate feeling when she told me she was proposing. It was loneliness.

"I'm not leaving you behind, Charley. I'm building a life with someone I love." She wipes her eyes with her wrist, and when she pulls it away she looks devastated . . . for me. Her anguish on my behalf is written all over her face. "You're so afraid of becoming our parents, you never became anyone. You never go for things you really want. You never take risks. It honestly makes me sad, Char."

My voice is quiet, and I can't even look at her when I say, "I'm taking a risk with Ethan."

"Are you, though?" she asks.

When she accepts that I'm not going to respond, she wades over to the kayak, and we free it from the tree with our paddles.

"I'm getting married today, Charley. You don't need to be happy about it, but I'd prefer if you were there. Not because I like you right now, but because you're my sister, and I love you. Understood?"

I nod.

She juts her chin in the direction of the neighboring boat. "Good. Now get out."

Once I'm seated, she hands me my paddle with apparent bitterness, which is a difficult emotion to convey with object work alone.

Then, before my paddle has even touched the water, I hear the first bloodcurdling scream.

Chapter 21

Wet Ted's Name
Is Ted Wetter

"WHAT HAPPENED?"
Everyone's surrounding a body lying on the grass just onshore. I scan the heads one after the other in search of Ethan's brown hair as Laurel and I drag the kayaks onto the rocks.

Petey answers me with a dazed expression. "Not sure. One second I was talking to E, and the next second Ted was screaming on the ground."

Relief swarms my chest—it's not Ethan—but my subsequent thoughts are swallowed up by another of Ted's raw-throated moans.

"His kayak went missing," Harlow explains. "He was looking for it and then . . ." She gestures to the ground in front of her.

My stomach drops. I feel Laurel's eyes at the side of my face.

"Is it bad?" Ted cries out to the surrounding bodies. "I don't want to look. Just tell me how bad it is!"

I break into the circle to find Ted, shirtless and curled into a rigid ball with Ethan kneeling beside him. I reach to pat

Ted's shoulder but retreat guiltily. "I'm so sorry. I borrowed your kayak." Everyone ignores my confession in favor of caring for the man who's on the ground, wailing in agony.

"It'll be fine, brother," Petey tells him. "We just have to get it off. Then you'll be good."

Laurel gasps. "Holy shit! Is that a bear trap?"

My eyes follow his leg all the way down to the red mangled mess of swollen foot and hiking sandal that's clamped between two metal jaws.

"Bear traps are illegal," Ethan informs Laurel. "Especially in parks."

"Well, it's here and crushing his foot, so—"

"*Crushing?* I can't look!" Ted whimpers, his head tilted skyward. Harlow hisses sympathetically as Russell gags over Ted's rapidly purpling foot.

I shake my head. "It's not a bear trap. It's a Payne small-animal grip trap. See, there's no teeth and the spring is still engaged to maintain gentle tension," I say, explaining the metal contraption.

"Gentle, my ahh—" Ted's wail interrupts his comeback.

"Why do you know that?" Laurel asks me.

"They're one of our clients. I wrote the patent appeal brief."

"Ted, I'm sure it's only broken," Petey says with what I'm assuming is the *intention* of comforting him, but based on Ted's face, it isn't the reassurance he's seeking. Still, Petey forges ahead. "You'll be fine. I've broken my wrist twice, and if I can handle it, you can handle it. You're Ted freakin' Wetter!"

"Wait . . . ," Laurel interrupts. "Wet Ted's *name* is Ted *Wetter*? Did anyone else know this?" Everyone, apart from Ted—who's still writhing on the ground—shoots her a look. She puts her hands up. "Not the time. Got it."

Petey's giant paws clumsily examine the trap. "Ted, buddy, I'm gonna tug your foot out slowly—"

"No." I stop him. "He'll lose a toe that way."

At the mention of toes, Russell retches, and Ethan tugs me down to foot level beside him. "Do you know how to disengage it?" he asks.

I nod. I know absolutely everything there is to know about the mechanisms of small-animal traps, and for the briefest moment, I'm grateful that Bob Champion has never done a single day of work in his life.

"Ethan, hold his foot still," I instruct. "We need to pinch this and pull the pin at the same time, and it should . . ."

The trap springs open, and Ted unleashes a scream that shudders the surrounding trees and shakes loose a flurry of squawking birds. If there are any campers within earshot, they are surely taking cover.

"Don't worry, Ted. It doesn't look so bad," Harlow says sweetly, but somehow, the foot looks even more malformed when free of the metal clamp. She turns to face the rest of us. "Russell and I will take him to the hospital for an X-ray and some pain meds. Can you guys pack up my stuff and leave it at Ted's?"

"Of course," Ethan assures her.

Ethan and Laurel grab Harlow's green canoe. Meanwhile, Russell helps Ted get comfortable.

"We should take my kayak," Ted directs. He's calmer but still noticeably pained and gripping his crimson-hued foot. "It's bigger. Charley, can you—?"

"That might not be possible," Laurel tells him on my behalf as she hands Harlow her paddles.

"It's a bit banged up. It's actually a really funny story," I explain, unable to meet his eyes. "So, it found its way into a tree . . ."

Ted's mouth drops open.

Laurel grabs the stern. "We handled it, Wetter. Don't you worry about a thing." She gives the canoe a double tap before sending it into the water with a shove. "See you on the other side, buddy."

"I don't think I'll be giving you your security deposit back," Ted calls out. "Any of you!"

And because that seems more than fair, Petey, Ethan, Laurel, and I wave apologetically as they float away.

And then there were four.

IT TAKES US a few hours to pack that crowded little patch of ground into nothing but memories. Ethan scours the campsite about twelve times in search of plastic wrappers and other trash. When he's satisfied, we drop our equipment off with Ted Wetter's teen associate and sit on the ground against the side of the building without a word.

"Well, you won, Charley," Laurel says, breaking the silence that settled onto our foursome. "I'm not getting married today."

Petey rubs her shoulder, ever the cheerleader. "Babe, we can still—"

Her smile is wild and wrong, a breath away from a worn-out sob. "I have no interest in memorializing this day. Charley made sure of that."

"This isn't . . ." I trail off. She's not interested in the nuances of my wedding objection or that I wanted *her* to be the one to call it off, not rabbit traps or trench foot. Still, she wants to be mad at me, and right now, all I want is for Laurel to have everything she wants.

I press my forehead into my knees as shame swirls in my gut. "I'm so sorry, Laur."

"I know you are." Then she pulls herself up from the ground and walks in the direction of her Chevy Bolt. I start after her, but Petey stops me with a gentle touch on my shoulder.

He gives me a quick head shake. "Not right now, Charles in Charge. It'll be okay, but . . . give her a little time."

He's so unjustifiably generous to me that I'm . . . annoyed. How dare this man be *nice* right now? How dare he care more about Laurel than his own, lightly battered, ego? It makes me look like such an ass. Which I undeniably am, because he's *right*. It kills me that he's right. It's more evidence that I might be wrong about everything else.

What if Petey and Laurel *are* good together and I've ruined everything? I know I didn't give Jonah trench foot or shove Ted into an illegal animal trap, but I brought spectacularly bad energy with me this weekend. I came here to ruin everything, and then everything was ruined. That'll be what we all remember.

The blood drains from my face, my fingertips, my belly, and out through my toes like air seeping from a hole in a raft. I'm emptied out and replaced with the certainty of one undeniable fact: It doesn't matter if, for the time being, my sister's name is still Laurel Beekman. I've already lost her.

THEY DRIVE AWAY first, then Ethan and I follow.

I release a heavy sigh of whatever the opposite of relief is. "I didn't want . . . *that*, you know?"

He pulls onto the main road. "Do you know what you did want?"

I sink into the passenger seat. "No."

"I think that might've been the problem."

I nod. Isn't wanting time to stop reason enough for a "speak now" wedding moment between sisters? But I know the answer is no. I'm the bad guy here. There's no way around it.

A heavy silence descends on the van. It snakes around my neck, tightening with each passing second. We drive and drive, until suddenly he pulls off.

"Pie?" he blurts into the quiet. The single syllable catches me so off guard, I actually jump.

"What?"

"I've been thinking about it and I don't think we can go any farther until we eat pie."

"Pie." The word comes out slow, like I might not be familiar with it semantically.

He nods. The sunshine glows against his cheeks. "These seem like pie problems."

"Pie problems."

"Are you just going to repeat everything I say or are you going to join me at the only pie stand on Lake Superior that makes a gluten-free crust?"

So then we eat pie. And we feed each other pie. And we kiss, and we laugh, and we act as though we're living a completely different day than the one I ruined this morning. We behave as we would were we driving *to* something rather than *away*. We ignore the reality of the situation and play pretend.

Every kiss on my knuckles, every swipe of his hair, is paired with an unspoken *just one last time*. We both know this is over, but neither of us is willing to acknowledge it out loud yet. Our relationship is a dog having its perfect last day on earth, and Ethan and I are somehow both the owner who knows they're headed to the vet and the unwitting basset hound with a heart defect who assumes this is just one of many more pup cones to come.

Winding roads turn to freeways and wooded landscapes to open fields. I enter a state of highway hypnosis and let the world whoosh past until we're finally parked in my driveway, where it all began.

"Harlow put us all in a group chat." Ethan's reading off his phone as I dequarantine my garbage bags of hazardous waste from the back storage. "Looks like Ted's doing fine. No broken bones."

"How is that possible?" I ask, heaving my weekender bag over my shoulder. It's looking a bit worse for wear. "Two of his toes were going the wrong way."

"Dunno." He shrugs. "He told me he's a retired ballet dancer, so maybe that's just his feet."

"Ted Wetter is a *fascinating* creature."

I head for my front door. Ethan goes to follow, then falters. In this game of reality chicken, it's the ultimate flinch. Any questions I had as to whether he thought this could go on fall away.

I let my bags drop to the ground. The computer hits the asphalt with a thunk that makes me wince. Ethan doesn't look at me. He just stares at the bags like I might yell, *Psych!* and throw them back in the van and drive into the sunset with him, vomit clothes be damned.

Dread twists my stomach the way it does in the windowless "bad news" conference room at my office reserved for personnel matters. Maybe that's why I feel compelled to take control of this meeting before it gets away from me.

"I can't go to the music festival with you," I tell him. Vacation is over and it's time to face reality.

"Okay." He inhales through his nostrils. "Do you have to work tomorrow?"

"I have to work every day. Most people do."

"Most people don't work *every* day," he mutters, closing his eyes. When he opens them, he lifts his head to face me. "We'll stay here then. I don't have that gig until Friday, but then I'm open for two weeks, so I can come back after." He's determined to keep this conversation breezy.

"Then what?" I ask, exhausted from pretending this could be something. I don't want to play anymore. I want to cry alone in my room. "We keep doing this friends-with-benefits thing forever?" It sounds ridiculous when I say it out loud. He won't stay. Who would? "Look. I know what this was, and I'm not about to force you into something you don't want, okay?"

He swallows his sigh, almost concealing it. "What is it you think I want?" he asks.

"Ethan, I'm tired. I need a shower. Can we just . . . ?"

"No. I'm curious. Who do you think you are to me?"

"I'm Chuck," I say simply.

He grabs my hand and clutches it, as though I'm so close to something. If only I weren't terrified of what that *something* was. "And who is *that* to me?"

I consider saying something flip or sarcastic. Something that would de-escalate whatever is happening right now on this stupid driveway that still has a hole from the truck that carted my ex's belongings away. But after my fight with Laurel, I'm emotionally spent. Empty. Scooped out of all feelings. What's left is that lonely, contagious ache.

"I don't know, Ethan," I spew bitterly, like an unstoppable plague of human misery. "The kind of friend you can bail on and forget about for an entire year, and then send a GIF of Nicolas Cage to like everything's normal." I swallow hard, pushing down the lump of grief suddenly building in my throat. The unprocessed loss of one of the most important relationships of my life. On top of another loss. And then another.

His hand grips mine for dear life but I don't stop.

"I'm the friend you can hook up with in the woods after you bailed on her wedding with a made-up excuse, because you know she'll always let you off the hook."

He drops my hand like I've burned him. "Seriously, Charley? That fucking wedding. I told you—"

"If you mention salmonella one more time, I swear to god, Ethan. You're my *best friend*. I know I'm pretty good about keeping my expectations of men to the floor, but I made you my best man at my wedding and you flaked because you wouldn't have a date? A woman you were casually—"

"She wasn't . . ." He shoves his hand through his hair and grips his neck. "Margot and I weren't even seeing each other anymore."

"What are you talking about?" For two and a half years, I've been reading and rereading that text, and it wasn't even true?

"I ended things with her the day of your bachelorette party." The look in his eyes strips me bare. "I couldn't go to your wedding because it was *you*. It was your wedding, to a guy who wasn't me."

My heart clambers up my throat, but I can't respond. I can't form words. I've been begging for a real answer, and now that he's giving it to me, I can't tell if I want to cover his mouth with my lips or my hand. His words recontextualize everything that happened after, knocking over each moment that follows like a row of dominos. Time stretches and slows. Everything's changing and crumbling all at once.

"And I was so fucking low, but I was going to swallow it," he continues, his voice breaking a little in a way that's breaking me. "Because you *wanted* to marry him. He was the kind of guy you wanted, who knew his credit score and had a house with one of those cupboards that's actually an ironing board that folds down. 'Could never be me,' right? That's our whole thing. That you could *never* see yourself with a guy like me."

That's not what *that* means. That's never been what that means. Not to me. *I'm* the undatable one. *I'm* the one who doesn't fit. But I can't force the words out.

"Then I was at your bachelorette party," he continues. "And you *looked* at me, and for a second, it was like I could see it all in your face. I saw . . ." He steps in close so my back is against the van. Just him and me and this haunted place. His gaze is warm and unflinching. It holds me like a cupped hand against my cheek. At that moment, I know everything, and I don't need him to say it. He *shouldn't* say it. I might not be able to walk away if he does.

"Charley, I think about you when I wake up. When I go to sleep, I dream about you. I try to outrun it, but wherever I go, it's already there . . . waiting for me. I can't escape the way I feel about you, and I don't want to, because even when I'm completely alone in the dark, you're there, and I can't ever let that go. You're . . . the moon to me, Charley . . . which I know sounds like some shitty lyric from a song I wrote about you, but that doesn't make it less true. I love you. I'm *in* love with you," he says, repeating the sentiment like it's nothing. Or like it's something I've always known—a principle of the universe he's simply restating. But the declaration steals the air from my lungs. We stand there in the quiet, staring at each other as time expands and contracts like a beating heart.

Intellectually, I know this is the part in the movie when I tell him I love him too—that I've probably always loved him—but my panicked heart is lodged in my ribs. I look down at my feet, gathering myself as fear clenches my throat. "If that were true—"

"It is," he pleads with me, his voice cracking.

I shake my head and gather up my voice like wreckage from a storm. "If it were, you've had *years* to tell me that."

He presses his eyes shut. "I *did* tell you. At your bachelor-ette party, I told you."

I don't recognize my laugh. It's hard and humorless. "I'm sorry, did you hand a party penis straw to me *before* or *after* your big declaration of love?" He steps back, struck. "That is such bullshit, and you know it. You said nothing!"

"I did! But you weren't ready to hear it, and it nearly destroyed us. Destroyed me." He shakes his head, sending his hair into his eyes. He looks like a cornered animal. "And I would've said it months ago if I'd have thought for a second that you wouldn't panic if I—"

"Ethan." It takes every muscle in my throat to keep my voice from collapsing into a soundless wail. "You let me *get married* to someone else."

"You don't think I regret that?" he grits out.

He kicks the rear tire like it's done something to him. How must we look to my neighbors, two grown adults passionately arguing beside a white van? Someone's surely reported this as "suspicious" on Nextdoor.

"Every day you were with that guy, you don't think it was killing me? I moved in with my parents. I tried to get the band back together—a band that I *hated* by the end of it. Thank god Ivan was already drumming for someone else and got me writing songs again or I would've gone insane knowing you were waking up next to that smug asshole every goddamn day."

"You abandoned me!" I cry out. "I thought I'd done something wrong. I was a wreck my entire honeymoon wondering what I'd done to make you leave me like that."

"How do you think *I* was, knowing you were *on* your honeymoon, Chuck? Why do you think I'm here now?"

"Because it was *convenient* for you," I say bitterly, pulling my arms over my belly. "It lined up with your schedule, and this whole weekend was happenstance. If you'd had a show somewhere else or hadn't been 'in the area,' you'd be professing your love to some other woman right now."

"I wasn't even 'in the area,'" he spits, his voice defiant. "I sent you that text from the parking lot of a Kroger in Atlanta after I bought everything to re-create the dinner we had in Malibu. Remember? You were wearing that red dress, and I all but begged you to move to California?"

I do remember it, but not the way he describes it. We were celebrating my passing the Minnesota bar exam. I'd spent *months* studying for a test that he casually suggested I throw away over a wine and seafood meal I couldn't even afford to split. I think I laughed at the offer.

"Then Friday morning," he continues, "Lo told me your divorce was final, and it was like a starter's pistol went off in my chest, and I just . . . drove. I bailed on an entire weekend of shows. I couldn't risk you starting your life over without me in it. I've always wanted this, Chuck. You and me," he whispers. "The way it's supposed to be." He takes my face in his hands, palms trembling against my cheeks, and god help me, I lean into them. "Let's just go somewhere. Leave this all behind."

A cold laugh wrenches itself from my throat. "Powell, this is all too familiar."

He drops his hands and takes a step back from me. "No, Chuck. It's not like that. I just want to . . . start something with you, someplace else. Someplace that's not your ex's house."

"It's not *his* house. It's *my* house. I went to great pains to make it *my house*."

"It's big and cold and empty. It's not you at all! Why do you even want it?"

"Because it's *mine*, Ethan." I jab my fingers into my chest with each syllable. "Because I own it, and it's not going anywhere. I'm sorry it's not a van with wheels that you can drive off in whenever you get bored."

"I haven't gone anywhere, Chuck. Not really."

"What are you talking about? Even right now, your big romantic overture involves flaking on the music career you've just rebuilt because you *feel* like it."

He rakes his hand through his hair. Watching him scores my insides. "I'm sorry I couldn't risk you getting *married* again. What do you want from me?"

"I want you to not be a walking red flag who's already halfway out the door!"

"I've been here the whole time, Chuck! Waiting like an idiot—sending you candy, singing songs that become punch lines on late-night shows—because you're never willing to *try*.

I could change everything for you and you'd *still* be determined to see this as over before it starts."

"Because I already know how this ends," I shout through hot tears. I try to swallow down the heartache, but it tastes too much of salt and sunscreen and misery. I wipe my snot with the heel of my hand. I'm a mess. *This* is a mess.

"Why can't we *try*?" He directs his plea to the sky. He can't even bear to look at me anymore. "When it stops working, we can try something else. We don't have to have every part of our future mapped out right this second."

"But *I* do, Ethan. I've always needed that, and being together means one of us is giving up everything, and I'm sorry, but I can't just 'try that on.' I'm not built for it. I'll never be able to do it, and *you* can't either."

He doesn't respond. He just stares back at me, devastated.

"It'll be Lewellen 2.0," I say. "That life you couldn't see yourself in? The clocking in and clocking out at some job you don't want? Every day the exact same? That's *my* life, Ethan. I would've stayed in Lewellen forever, but you left and it ruined the only place I'd felt at home. *You* were supposed to be my home but you felt trapped there, even with me. That's what it would be like with us. You'll feel caged and restless, and it won't be enough. Maybe you won't leave this time, but *I* won't be enough for you, and that'll be worse than being alone."

We sit under the weight of my declaration. Tears stream down my face. It's so quiet that I can hear his staccato breaths, and when he looks at me again, a wave of calm seems to flow over his skin.

"You know what's funny, Chuck? I just figured out why this has never worked. I actually want *you*, the *real* you. But *you* don't think I want you. Even though you're all I've ever wanted." His voice is quiet. Kind. Matter-of-fact. It's such an Ethan way of saying something so devastating.

He nudges my chin up with his knuckle so that I have to look at those magnificent eyes. "It should be me. Us. I *know* you, and that's what scares you so much. You can't put up a wall between us because I'm already a part of you just like you're already a part of me. We're too far gone for each other. You love me too. Even if you never say it, I know you do," he tells me, vaulting us both into the unknown. He knows I won't jump, so he'll jump for me. But it doesn't work that way.

The issue has never been whether I love Ethan Powell. He's right. I've loved him so completely without realizing it. It's whether I can keep *his* love, and how much it will wreck me when it goes away.

I step back from his hand. I feel its absence on my chin like a brand. "You'll *hurt* me, Ethan. You won't want to, but you will. And then I'll lose all of you." Losing him after finally having him will taint everything beautiful that came before. Memories with my best friend will turn to something rotten. Surrendering our future is the only way to preserve our past.

His face is destroyed. Looking at it punctures my lungs, and I can't take in enough air to say anything more.

"You don't believe that." Something about his words, the way his voice sounds, splinters off another piece of my heart, and I know I'll never forget this moment. I'm in another Ethan Powell memory. A bad one, but they don't all get to be good.

"You're so infuriating. You know that? You'd rather be right than happy. Every time."

I don't say anything back. I don't think he's expecting me to. It wouldn't make a difference anyway. He can see my every thought on my face, and I think I can see his too. There are no secrets or hidden thoughts. He won't do me the courtesy of providing plausible deniability as I break us. He makes me see all of him. It's as open-hearted as it is cruel.

"I'm sorry," I whisper. The truth is I'd love to be wrong about us. I just know I'm right.

I'm not sure he's heard me until he shakes his head and says back, "I'm not."

His stiff expression blooms into something gentle and warm. Loving. It crinkles his face all the way up to his eyes. I'm equal parts relieved and shattered just looking at it, and it occurs to me that this might be the last time I see it. Everything about this weekend has been a series of firsts and lasts.

His hands shake, and I pull them into my chest on impulse. "I'm sorry," I repeat. It's so inadequate, I have to laugh, and it's a sharp juxtaposition with the way I'm wiping my tear-stained face with the heel of my free hand.

I'm not sure who initiates it—I don't think I can bear replaying it to find out—but our lips are touching in a heart-breaking kiss that's sweet and slow and salty from our tears. I let it linger, long after the ache sets in, knowing this is it—the last time I'll ever be this close to my best friend. The last time his hands will caress my cheek. The last time I'll breathe in his air. The last time I'll savor the taste of him.

We stay this way for a good long while, clinging to each other, memorializing the press of our lips, my heartbeat slowing to match his steady pulse. It's devastating. It's everything. I don't want it to stop, and, still, I pull away.

He holds my face, his thumb trailing across my lips like he's memorizing them. Then he drops his hands and climbs back into the van.

I watch him drive away, admiring his profile in the glow of

the sun beating in through the windshield—the slant of his nose, the point of his chin, the smile lines etched in his cheeks—how he looks both the same and different at the beginning and the end. I don't need a picture. I couldn't forget it if I tried.

The van disappears into the horizon. When it's gone, I walk straight to the laundry room without stopping and wash the weekend off my belongings.

And then I'm really alone.

Chapter 22

Babe the Big Blue Tots

THE AX-THROWING BAR was my idea. I had no one to blame but myself for how terribly this party was going.

Like all bachelorette parties, the guest list was a collection of stray friends from various stages of my development: Stacy (new friend and work colleague), Rebecca (law school friend/ nemesis), Olive (one of those friends of unknown origin who appeared on a group chat and was somehow inaugurated into my inner circle without my knowledge), and Laurel, of course. Though they all knew Laurel and me, they didn't know each other. Or so we'd thought.

The guest-list snafu we couldn't have accounted for was that Rebecca and Olive *did* in fact know each other. They'd dated, actually. And it had ended badly.

"You *lost* my dog!" Rebecca shouted, throwing her finger in Olive's face.

Olive swept it away with the implied intimacy of two people who'd once shared a toothbrush. "His *ashes*!" Her ax whacked against the plywood target behind her with wild arm movements. "And I *found* them. But, noooo, we never talk about the part where I searched a Kum & Go dumpster for a Ziploc baggie of Sherlock Bones!"

"And how did Sherlock get in the dumpster in the first place?" Rebecca asked.

Olive sucked her teeth. "This is sooo like you. You're making the night honoring one of the sweetest women in the world *all* about you." Olive's declaration on my behalf was nice but fairly performative considering I wasn't quite sure how I'd met her, and no one has ever accused me of being *sweet*. It brought the whole friendship into question.

Rebecca laughed, because she *did* know me and was possibly still plotting my "accidental" death in the elevator shaft of the IDS tower. But before Rebecca could act on any potentially murderous impulses, Laurel ripped the weapon from her hands.

And that was when they confiscated our axes.

"Paula Bunyan's is a family establishment," a server in shorts and suspenders hissed.

"I'm the reason this didn't wind up in someone's skull!" Laurel insisted, indignant. Even though the party was a complete and utter disaster from moment one, my sister had nothing to do with its descent into madness.

"I think we should call it," I said, surveying the way our group had practically emptied out the place, including the exes, who'd taken their yelling outside. The only person who'd evaded the bar's notice was Stacy, who was parked next to the pull-tab dispenser, responding to work emails in noise-canceling headphones.

The party was over. Time of death: eleven p.m.

"No," Laurel whined, and tugged at my arms. "This was supposed to be the fun part. We can still crash a stranger's pedal pub. That was my break-glass-in-case-of-emergency plan."

I grimaced. "Pass. Can we put this party out of its misery, please? I'll settle up."

"Fine," she relented. "No matter what, you looked hot tonight. No one can take that away from you." She pulled me into a goodbye hug, then opened her rideshare app. "I'll make sure Drunk and Drunker find their way into separate Ubers. You'll be good getting home?"

I nodded and left her in our little lumberjack cubicle of partitioned plywood targets lining the back wall and headed for the bartender. Cedar planks covered every inch of wall space and filled the bar with the scents of a Norwegian sauna and stale beer. The place had recently opened up in the cursed part of a strip mall, next to an AMC, and would undoubtedly revert to a Spirit Halloween in nine months. Still, I was attracted to the idea of cutting loose in such a controlled environment.

THUNK.

My shoulders jumped the tiniest bit at the sound of an ax careening into plywood. I'd assumed the noise would fade into the background at some point, but it hadn't. The reverberations of cracking wood continued to hit me between the eyes like a ball-peen hammer to my lightly liquored skull. Every. Single. Time.

Still, I was disappointed that I hadn't gotten the chance to throw one myself.

THUNK.

I tried to close out the tab with the bartender, but the bar's grudge against our party was too fresh. A couple who'd been playing at the target next to ours came and went and still I hadn't received an ounce of recognition from Paula Bunyan et al. I was invisible.

The light of an Edison bulb refracted off the blade of an

abandoned ax like a neon sign reading THROW ME. YOU KNOW YOU WANT TO. I tried once more to get the bartender's attention—seriously, was I a ghost?—before wandering over to the forfeited target.

Ax in hand, I lifted my arms above my head. No one was looking. I let out a long stream of air between my lips, already wincing in anticipation of my ax's thud against the back wall.

"Beekman."

The voice behind me sliced deep into my core. I jerked backward.

"Are we seriously at an ax-throwing bar?" he asked.

He's here, I thought, my inner voice giddy. I turned around and there he was. Ethan.

He was dressed like an indie dirtbag in distressed jeans and a stained T-shirt. His arms were more toned than I remembered. They must've been forcing him to lift weights on that tour bus of his. It was like his forearms were flexing, even at rest. The floral tattoo I'd picked for him when we were eighteen was now framed by other botanicals in a complementary style, and he was wearing some expensive-smelling cologne I didn't recognize. Yet, even with all the changes, he felt exactly the same. Like home.

"Jesus, Powell. Don't you know not to surprise a woman with an ax in her hands? I could've thrown this at your head."

"You couldn't hit my head if I offered you a million dollars to hit my head."

"Think you can do better?" I offered him the ax. "Go on. Let it fly."

His lips curved up into a perfect sideways grin. "There's my Chuck. I knew you were still in there."

I pulled a face at the insinuation that I'd disappeared

somewhere, but he was too busy lining up with the bull's-eye to notice. His life had changed way more than mine had in the last few years. There was the tour with Silver Lining Society, their first album, their single that spent three whole days on the *Billboard* Top 100 after *SNL* parodied it, and the sophomore album that I . . . didn't totally *get*, but I was still hotly anticipating their next musical move.

For years, we'd texted almost daily. We FaceTimed, me in corners of the law library and him in the backs of vans and tour buses. We'd been each other's first call, until the calls from him started coming less and less frequently. I found Rich, and as a result, Ethan and I placed each other on the back burner, each hoping the other wouldn't scald from the lack of attention as we focused our energies on other, more tenuous parts of our lives. It was the unspoken agreement of our twenties: we'll neglect each other and call it "growing up."

Still, selfishly, I wanted it all. I wanted the career, the husband, the house, *and* Ethan. I wanted to stay the most important person in his life even as mine stretched to hold Rich. I knew it wasn't fair, but it didn't make it any less true.

Seeing him now, at this bar, I wanted to believe there were still parts of us that were the same, preserved all these years, to be excavated by each other alone. I wanted it to *mean something* that he'd come here tonight. That I was still the first person he wanted to laugh with and share secrets with. Now Ethan was here—proof positive that our friendship was still as meaningful to him as it was to me.

He let the ax go with a thunderous grunt. Maria Sharapova had nothing on Ethan Powell. Despite the deep vocalization, the ax landed about two feet right of the board with a disappointing thump.

"So close," I taunted.

He dug the ax out of the wall and handed it back to me.

"Your move, Lumber Jill. Show me what you got." He tilted his head toward the red bull's-eye.

And just like that, it was as though both no time had passed and years had come and gone all at once. I grinned and squared my shoulders in front of the target. With a deep exhale, I hurled the ax and watched it soar end over end until it landed dead center with an elegant thwack.

"That's right," I muttered triumphantly under my breath.

"Beekman!" Without hesitation, he picked me up and spun me around, his hand pressing against my bare back. "That was incredible!"

"I have a gift," I told him with a satisfied snicker.

When he set me down, I had to adjust the hemline of my slinky dress so as not to flash the bar queue behind us. "Tell the truth. Did you study? Did you practice?"

I considered lying but then didn't. I didn't lie to Ethan as a matter of course. "Fine. Yes. I've been watching YouTube videos obsessively, because I'm a nerd who hates to lose. It's why I'm a fantastic lawyer."

He leaned against the plywood partition and pressed his head to the side like I was simply too much. "You're a fantastic lawyer because you're brilliant and you're a badass. You're incredible at everything you set your mind to."

Something soft and nostalgic curled in my chest.

"So where's the rest of the bachelorette party?" he asked.

"Paula had to break us up. We were too rowdy. Except for my work friend, Stacy, who's by the bar taking our office's 'work from anywhere' policy extremely literally."

I pointed behind his ear, but his head didn't move. Instead, his eyes narrowed on me as though he was weighing all probabilities. "My instinct is to assume you're lying . . ." A group of a dozen or so men in matching tuxedo T-shirts bustled past. He stepped closer to my ear so his words could reach me through the increasing noise of the bar. "But the bouncer warned me there'd be a zero-tolerance policy for 'disturbances,' so I'm torn."

His smile loosened a bolt in my spine. I was at ease for the first time since I'd started planning my beast of a wedding. I couldn't help but relax into the comfort of being this close to my best friend.

"This night's been a disaster. Start to finish," I said, flopping my forehead onto his shoulder. "But I'm so glad you're here now."

"Me too," he responded. His voice sounded uncharacteristically thready.

Out of nowhere, the faux-tuxedoed men started hollering a fraternity drinking chant. Our shoulders jumped.

"Been a minute since I've heard one of those," I said, looking at Ethan's face and noticing with a jolt how close we were standing. For some reason, stepping back felt like an admission that being near him affected me in a way it didn't, so I kept my feet planted in place even as tension spooled in my stomach.

"I don't think I've been to a frat since that night I rescued you and Laurel from one."

"'Rescued' is . . . a verb. The wrong one, but—"

He leaned forward and looked straight into me when he asked, "Do you ever think about that night? Do you wonder what would've happened if you'd gone on tour with me?"

His face was serious, but he had to be kidding. "I would've bombed the LSAT and flunked out of school."

"Naturally."

"And then I would've been forced to sell my organs on the black market to make ends meet."

His eyebrow arched in a way that looked like a question but felt like a dare. "You always go straight to organ selling. Why is that?"

"My brain is weird? I don't know." I clapped my hands on my face to hide my hot blush. We were too close. It was too warm. He was too nice. It all felt so familiar and, yet, exhilarating.

"I like your brain," he said. He pushed a rogue strand of hair behind my ear. "I like lots of things about you." His gaze dragged between my eyes and my lips, down the gauzy mini-dress that Laurel had forced me into earlier that night. *Like sex*, she'd said. *That's what you're supposed to look like on your last night out as a single woman.*

I knew I wasn't *single*, but somehow, when she'd zipped up the dress, Ethan's face had appeared. Only for a millisecond. It was natural to wonder, I'd reminded myself, but I never let the intrusive thought settle. Ethan Powell was nothing but a fantasy. Not even a fantasy. An impossibility. And it was normal to ruminate on impossibilities. If there'd been a chance Michael B. Jordan would waltz into this bar that promoted a special called Babe the Big Blue Tots, I might've imagined him reacting to my outfit too.

I leaned my temple against the wall next to him, and he rolled his head to face me, matching me beat for beat. "You would've evicted me from the tour bus and sent me to the suitcase compartment."

"Benson got stuck in there by accident once."

Imagining that asshat trapped between roller bags sent a dart of laughter through my chest. "You're joking."

"Dead serious," he said. His forefinger brushed mine, but I didn't pull my hand back right away. He didn't either. We were two people, face-to-face, connected at the index finger in the strangest re-creation of *E.T.* ever conceived of in a Minneapolis ax-throwing bar.

"You might've written a song about me," I whispered, and it was as though I'd lit a fuse. The space between us crackled with dangerous intensity. God, why had I said that?

"Who says I haven't?" His eyes darkened, and I felt them everywhere. My pulse throbbed in the tip of the finger that was touching his.

"What's with all this chaotic energy, Powell?" I asked, injecting much-needed lightness into this confoundingly weighty conversation. "My money's now on you as the member of the bridal party who makes a scene."

His lips pinched, and I could almost hear his mind working. "I'm hoping to be the one who gets very drunk and pops out of the cake." Between his voice and his face, he couldn't seem to settle on a tone. Breezy or sincere. Nonchalant or wholehearted.

"People don't pop out of cakes at weddings. You're thinking of strip clubs."

"I forgot you opted against the Spearmint Rhino Gentlemen's Club in favor of the Nicollet Island Pavilion," he deadpans.

"You're *obsessed* with my wedding venue."

"I'm *fascinated* by this choice. I still can't think of you as married." His eyes narrowed. He was settling on serious, it seemed.

"Probably because I'm not. Yet."

"You're not. Yet," he whispered, drawing even closer. I told myself it was the acoustics, but I knew it was something else. The intensity of his half-lidded eyes. The quirk of his lips.

"You know, I came here tonight to tell you something . . ." There was a grit to his voice I'd never heard before—an intimacy—like we were talking in the dark, and suddenly, I wasn't sure I could get married on Saturday without knowing what he'd come here to say.

I held my breath, dangling out on a ledge of what was about to happen next. He didn't say anything at first, as though he was trying to read me. "Telling the time," he'd called it once. My heart pounded in my ears as his lips formed the first word.

"Don't—"

It was all he could get out before a stray ax came careening over our plywood divider and clocked Ethan on the back of the head.

———

Ethan sat beside me on the cot in a curtained-off area of an emergency room, holding an ice pack to the back of his skull and stinking of wound ointment.

"And that's when you were struck with the ax?" A younger nurse asked the questions while an older nurse typed the answers into the computer.

"It was an accident," he repeated for the third time, maybe fourth. "And it was the broad side of it. It's not like the blade got me or anything." No matter how many times he emphasized that last part, it never sounded reassuring.

"There was blood, though. Is that normal?" I was repeating things too.

"Head wounds, even superficial ones, tend to bleed," the

nurse informed us, just as the doctor had. As had the first tri-
age nurse we saw before they moved Ethan to this bed behind
the curtain.

Since they didn't suspect a concussion, they provided wound
care instructions and sent us on our way.

"Should I call us an Uber?" I asked when we stepped outside. It was late, maybe one in the morning, and, as we'd taken
the ambulance to the hospital, both our cars were parked at
the ax-throwing bar.

He pulled out his phone. "I can get myself a car."

I felt a bit silly. Why had I assumed I'd be going somewhere
with him?

"Were you going to say something? Back at the bar?
Before . . ."

He didn't look up from his phone as he typed in an address
I didn't recognize into the search field. "Huh? Oh. I, uh, was
about to . . . give you this." He plucked something from his
pocket.

I accepted it, confused. "Is this a penis?"

"A straw. You can't have a bachelorette party without a penis straw."

"Of course," I responded, blinking my disappointment
away. "Was this really what you wanted to tell me? That I
needed a phallic party straw?"

His jaw tightened. "No. I, uh . . ."

Someone brushed past us on the sidewalk, and when I was
starting to suspect I'd made the whole night up, Ethan tipped his
face toward me. I'd missed that face more than I cared to admit.
He dragged his head from side to side, his tongue in his teeth
like he was contemplating something, until finally, he spoke.

"Rich sucks."

Those two words drew all the sound out of the ambulance bay. It was actually pretty impressive for only a couple of words.

"I'm sure there's a more elegant way to put that, but my head is killing me, so I'm just saying it. That guy sucks." He drew out "sucks" into multiple syllables for emphasis.

"What?" I laughed, because what else were you supposed to do when your best man told you your future husband sucked days before your wedding? "What are you talking about?"

"He's *so* boring, Chuck. He's a pair of khaki pants with personhood. And he's always referring to himself as a 'foodie.' What *is* that? You eat food, bro. That's not a personality." Each new insult seemed to burst from his mouth like Pop Rocks.

My eyes bored into his, searching for . . . I wasn't sure what. A sign maybe. A signal that there was something I was missing that would make sense of all of it. He just tilted his head, like he was playing with me. Maybe he was. Maybe he thought this was funny.

"I thought you liked Rich," I argued.

"It's not that I don't *like* him. I don't *care* about him. I care about you, and you also kind of suck when you're with him."

"Nice." My mouth tasted like vinegar.

"I don't even recognize you with him. You're not *you*. You're this creepy yes-man . . . the wives . . . you know, like those wives that start out normal and turn into these agreeable automatons . . ."

Rage built behind my eyes. "Are you calling me a *Stepford* Wife?"

"Yes! Sorry. It's my head. The words are . . ." He scrubbed his stubble with palpable frustration. "You'd never show him up at an ax-throwing bar like you did with me tonight. Do you ever let him see the real you?"

Hot anger prodded my neck like a curling iron to the throat. Who did he think he was, telling me what I was and who I belonged with? "Did it ever occur to you that maybe *you* don't know the real me? I barely see you anymore."

A bullet of clarity shot through my belly. Ethan was no longer my best friend. Time and distance had contorted him into something else entirely: He was merely my *oldest* friend. A visitor in my life. The same way my parents were. He came and went with ease in a way I'd wanted to believe wasn't possible.

"Come on." The corner of his mouth lifted into a smirk, and I suppressed the urge to flick it. "Even you don't believe that. I know you better than anyone."

"I've changed." I wrapped my arms around my middle like a shield. "You don't know what I want or who I am. Not anymore."

He blinked, and something sad seeped into the edges of his expression. He was no longer playing a game. Whatever this was had turned serious. "If you marry that guy, you'll regret it. I know you will."

"You don't know anything. You're one to talk about 'sucking.'" Dear lord, why had he anchored this conversation in conjugations of "to suck"? "You bounce between women you don't care about to feed your ego."

He moved to push his hand through his hair, seeming to forget his bandage or that it was pulled back into a bun.

I lifted my chin at him defiantly. "And your hair looks dumb like that, by the way."

He looked me up and down without an ounce of the harmless, flirtatious heat I'd have bet my life had been there earlier. "Well, that dress is impractical."

"It's supposed to be!"

"If the world ends tonight, and everything distracting us disappears . . . there's no jobs, or music, or wedding deposits . . . is Rich still the person you want to be with?"

My heart folded in on itself. Over the years, Ethan and I had made zombie apocalypse plans in beanbag chairs and sad first apartments, joking about our doomed partnership in a postapocalyptic society, but that's all it ever was. A joke. Because we always failed to address the issue of proximity, primarily our lack of it.

"The world isn't ending tonight," I responded. "It's ridiculous to pretend otherwise."

I knew exactly what would've happened had I gone on tour with him all those years ago. I knew it as well as I knew my own name. I would've given up everything, only for the winds to change and him to leave me with nothing.

That would never happen with Rich. We wanted all the same things. We fit perfectly. Our lives were completely planned out. I felt safer just thinking about it.

Still, the sad, pitiful truth was that despite my vitriol, I loved Ethan too much to let him leave like this.

"I'm happy," I pleaded with him. "I'm in love with a man who loves me back exactly as I am now, and I want you to stand next to me on Saturday and be happy for me."

"And that's really what you want?" The question sank through my abdomen.

I swallowed. "Of course it is."

He put his phone in his pocket and looked ahead toward the empty ambulance bay, his smile cool and bright without a trace of the emotion that had been there mere seconds ago. "Uber's here," he said, his chin pointed in the direction of a blue Toyota Corolla.

I cleared my throat. "You need to be there early for pictures," I said, changing the subject, unwilling to dwell on the way my face was surely telling on me.

"Yeah, sure, but do you need a ride home?" he asked, ignoring my subject change.

"No, uh, Rich is picking me up," I lied. Guilt compelled me to bring his name back into the conversation one way or another. I hadn't done anything wrong but this fight felt like its own kind of betrayal. It had revealed starkly something I'd tried to hide from myself: the prospect of losing Ethan as my friend was more terrifying than the notion of not marrying Rich. Awareness slunk up my neck, and suddenly, I felt . . . gross. That full-body revulsion of touching a stranger's gum under the bus bench rolled over my body in waves.

"I'll see you Saturday, yeah?" I said, watching him climb into the car.

"Of course," he promised. "Wouldn't miss it for the world."

What was he seeing in my face right then? How sad and terrified I was that this could've been a relationship-ending fight and the only thing I'd have to show for it would be a party penis straw?

The car door clicked shut, but as I walked away, his voice echoed on the pavement behind me.

"Chuck!" He was yelling through the window, his body halfway out like he was a golden retriever on the highway. "I love you." It was as though the words dropped out of his mouth by accident.

I swallowed down the lump in my throat and pasted on my

breeziest smile. "I love you too, Powell," I shouted back through cupped hands.

His "I love you" spun around my temporal lobe, even though he was a dude with a head injury and didn't mean anything by it at all.

So I shoved even more nonchalance into my voice and said, "This is your final warning. If I see you climbing into my lemon buttercream cake, I'm coming for you. I don't care if you have a broken head."

His torso lurched forward, but he caught himself. His eyes lingered on me for an extra beat. "Lemon? For a cake?" He shook his head in that heartbreakingly familiar way. "Could never be me."

Never ever.

The scent of his aftershave was still on my dress as I opened my rideshare app. More than ever, I was so happy to be marrying Rich. He was the *would always* to Ethan's *could never.*

I looked behind me, just for a second, to watch Ethan's body slide out of the window and back into the car as it disappeared into the dark.

Chapter 23

The Fun Kind of Breaking and Entering

AT WORK, EVERYTHING has gone to shit.

Sure, my Monday disappearance didn't exactly set the place up for success, but while I was getting my heart stomped on in my driveway, Bob was hiding from the receptionist, who'd been fielding his angry client calls. Literally *hiding*. At some point, Pamela mounted a search team and caught him watching highlights of the US Open in the lactation closet.

So on Tuesday morning, I don't know what I'm expecting to greet me—acknowledgment, recognition, mild gratitude for my years of unrelenting service to his clients—but Bob has never been more of a heinous prick. I can't tell if he's embarrassed to have uncovered the depths of his incompetence or if he's just *that* entitled. No one asks about the wedding fiasco besides Stacy and, weirdly, Paul, who makes an appearance in the office despite having a two-day-old infant at home.

On Wednesday, Anders from IT delivers my new laptop in exchange for a garbage bag of rice and computer parts.

"It's set up like you had it before. Back to normal," Anders tells me.

The moment he's out of my office, I boot up my computer and stalk Ethan's van social media account again. He's been consistently posting the promotional photos I took over the weekend, but the newest image isn't that. Sure, the van is featured, but it's one I took of him while he was driving us to the wedding that never was. The night I kissed him in his van and he promised me I'd do it again. I know it's *his* camera, but I can't help but feel that that particular photo is mine, and he's carelessly exposing *our* moments to the light.

When Rich left me, I was listless. I was certainly grieving *something*, but sadness was harder to grab on to. Rich moved out and took with him the end of a possibility. I was grieving the unrealized potential of a life with him—what we could become if we were both a little different.

But without Ethan, I'm hollow. I'm emptied and splayed on the floor like a box of old photographs unearthed from the attic. I'm marred by memories of something so stunningly real and exactly right while an essential piece of my body has been pried out of my chest. I've lost something *tangible*. What Ethan and I had was something to lose.

There's a sad sort of beauty in the way grief goes liquid and takes different shapes to fill the body it's in. The emptier someone leaves you, the more your insides swim with their loss. Some endings are about mourning what's gone and some are about accepting what you never even had. The perfect husband. The perfect life. But perfect isn't the same as right. *Perfect* things can be all wrong. Losing something that was so imperfect in all the loveliest ways hurts infinitely worse.

I figure that so long as I'm drowning in the absence of Ethan Powell, I might as well internet stalk him with purpose and soundtrack the act with every song crediting him as a lyricist.

I made the playlist myself and it already has two saves. The Seraphina songs are particularly gut-wrenching. Heartbreaking poetry of lives never lived, paths not taken, and love lost out of cowardice. I've heard the album seven times already; each listen presses into a bruise on my ribs.

I hope he never knows I played him on a loop for days after he left.

I hope he sees he made my Spotify Wrapped.

Unable to spend another second wallowing, I punch out every browser tab one by one and do the one thing I've never let myself do: I openly cry at my desk. Loud, body-shaking, cathartic sobs. It's astounding how good it feels to audibly weep in a glass office where everyone can see and hear me but must carry on as though they're not physically disturbed by my behavior. I don't think I've ever felt so powerful. Is this how Bob feels when he berates a temp for stocking the wrong brand of nut milk in the break room fridge? The world around me is bending to my will. It's intoxicating.

But the party ends with a Teams message from Pamela that dries my eyes in an instant.

> **Are you CRYING? What is wrong with you? Have you LOST your mind?**

The rest of Wednesday is a blur of tears soundtracked by sad indie folk rock. Thursday starts with an elevator ambush.

"AgriTech is threatening to fire us again." Stacy's heels clap down the hall in front of me. When she realizes I'm not keeping up, she seems to consider stopping but instead only slows to half speed. She's suited in head-to-toe orange like a sentient

Creamsicle, while I'm in my depression slacks (which are just sweatpants I've ironed a pleat into).

"Good. They should. Tell them to do it," I goad, sipping on my Big Gulp.

She grabs the plastic cup and one of my other drinks out of my hands. "What's in your cup? Your breath smells like a movie theater floor."

I hiccup. "It's all the sodas mixed together."

She eyes me up and down cautiously. "Are you okay, sweetie?"

The question is too perfunctory to demand honest consideration, and still, it stops me in my tracks.

"Is this it?" I ask her.

She looks at me askance. "Is what 'it'?"

"Is this the thing we've been working toward? Is this what my dream was?"

Stacy's eyeing me as though she doesn't recognize me. Like I've possibly undergone a lobotomy. Which is fair, because my sense of self feels . . . off. It's as though someone's walked inside my head and moved all the furniture six inches.

"Partnership's the dream," she says simply.

"Being Bob is my dream? Bob is who I'm aspiring to? To be so afraid and stressed by my own job that I get slapped with an HR complaint for locking myself in the pumping closet? *That's* what I've sacrificed every weekend for?"

"Alrighty . . . how about we get you out of this very public hallway before you visibly unravel?" She peers over my shoulder and then coaxes me into a conference room. "You don't have to be like Bob to do his job," she tells me once the door is shut. "Ideally, you'd be nothing like him. He's not a good lawyer."

My butt slides down the glass wall, plopping all the way to the floor. I'm being unprofessional, but since the "crying incident"—which is already being discussed throughout the office in hushed, cautioning tones—I'm far past the point of caring about propriety.

"What is being a partner here supposed to do for me?"

She looks past my head with noticeable discomfort. "You want to work with more tech startups, right? Women founders? Marginalized founders? You'll need leverage to get the higher-ups to sign off on it. If you're a partner—"

"Then I'll be the partner signing clients who don't bring in enough money. Nothing will never be enough. All I'll get is a stake in a toxic firm filled with a bunch of overworked, underappreciated associates. Why do I want that?" I ask her, genuinely curious.

"I don't know, Charley. Why do any of us want it? Money. Security. Predictability. The devil you know and all that."

The devil you know. I hate this place, but I know it better than anywhere else, and if I give up enough of my happiness, I could have it forever. A relatively lucrative prison of my own making.

This is the bargain I've struck. I could've spent eternity in search of the impossible with Ethan, but, hey, if I stick it out here long enough, I might earn an executive parking spot. Maybe they could bury me in it.

———

Stacy recommends I work from home and I heed her advice, bringing my laptop into my bed with my Crisp & Green salad like I do every night. I'm a bed person now.

Hours go by. I'm cozy in my patent-drafting flow state. Nothing can disrupt me until something clatter-clatter-crashes at the other end of the house. Then I hear something that makes my blood run cold: a man's voice.

Every cell in my body tenses, as if I'm trapped in one of those dreams where I'm soundlessly screaming. A shriek is perched at the roof of my mouth. I lift my phone to call 911, but the device in my hand is a dead black brick. Darting my eyes around the room in search of a baseball bat or a particularly angular lamp, I find nothing in my sparsely furnished bedroom that could save me from an attacker. Nothing but a bed, a minifridge, and a bar cart topped with that damn penis straw.

Ethan's face flashes in my mind, and god help me, I want to grab the straw, if for no other reason than he'll know I died thinking of him when my body is found clutching it. Resisting the dramatics, I reach for the deceptively heavy mortar and pestle from my *Mad Men* bar cart and head for the stairs.

Every creaky step makes me wince. I could run out the front door and flee the scene, but I can't be certain the guy won't spot me making a break for it, and my system is coursing with too much adrenaline to think clearly anyway. Instead, I follow the voice, the rustling, the squeak of the rubber sneaker soles against the tile floor in my sunroom. There's nothing left to take and still I'm determined not to lose another thing without a fight.

My back is pressed against the wall beside the French double doors facing the empty great room. I breathe in deep. In. Out. In. Out. I swear to god, if I die alone in this house before I've even settled on a living room couch . . .

A woman's voice tells her coconspirator, "You're going to have to suck in your butt, babe."

Instantly, my stomach unwinds at the sight of my sister and her fiancé mid–B&E. "Holy—"

"Charlie Brown!" Petey's butt says. He's nothing but a pair of familiar legs dangling through my open window as Laurel fails to yank him by his tree-trunk thighs through the too-small opening. "Hey! Hi. How've you been?"

"What are you doing?" I lower my weapon and my entire body slouches in relief. "I almost killed you."

Laurel scoffs, shucking off soil from the plant she knocked over while making her entrance. "With that? Were you going to guacamole us to death? The Ring doorbell wasn't working, and you weren't answering your phone."

"And then Laurel got attached to the idea of breaking in." Petey grunts and squirms, fighting with the window until his feet find the floor. "Can you believe she's never done it before?"

"And you have?" Now that I've decided not to clock them on the heads, I set my muddling tools on the newly empty plant stand. My poor monstera.

"Just for team hazing. The fun kind of break-ins. Like this one."

"This"—I wave my arms around the room between the busted window lock and spilled potting soil—"isn't fun."

"Oh, don't be so dramatic." Laurel breezes past me toward the stairs. "We had lots of fun."

"I'll clean it up, Char. Don't worry." Petey looks around the room. "Where's all your stuff?"

Laurel answers for me, heading to the master without invitation. "Everything's in her bedroom."

"Like a dorm? Very cool," Petey says brightly. "You guys go talk. I'll take care of this window."

Laurel leaves Petey behind, trudging up into my room, where

she flops onto the bed. "Why didn't you answer your phone?" she asks.

"It's dead," I answer, hovering at the door.

"Dead?" Her eyes widen. "You let it go dead? This is much worse than I thought."

Laurel skates through her life with a perpetually broken phone. What right does she have to judge me? "So what?"

She tucks and rolls off the bed to rummage through my dresser. "You get physically anxious when *I* let my phone go below thirty percent. I can't count the number of times you've responded to a screenshot with one of those grimacing emojis."

"Because you do it all the time and the last twenty always goes faster than you think!"

"Ethan didn't make it sound 'cut yourself off from society' bad. What happened with him? Spill," she demands.

Hearing Ethan's name uttered so casually burns like lemon juice on a paper cut. Saying it might shatter me into so many pieces, I'll be trapped in my duvet for the rest of time. "He talked to you?"

"He asked me to check on you. Why do you think I'm here?" God, why does his unrelenting kindness hurt so much more than anyone else's cruelty? "I'm still mad at you, by the way," she says haughtily, wandering over to the minifridge. "Did you dredge up ancient history with him, or is that, like, an exclusively 'me' thing? Aha!" she yells, slamming the fridge door shut. "Halo Top. I knew it."

"It looked good," I respond, not sure why I'm immediately on defense.

"*No one* thinks it 'looks good.' It's ice cream that hates itself."

She's right. I saw it in the freezer section yesterday while I was wandering around Target in search of objects to fill the void: a faux-driftwood shelf I already hate; a wearable blanket; individually wrapped mozzarella pearls; yet another water tumbler; and, yes, slightly off-tasting dessert that can be reasonably consumed by the pintful.

"Did you break my window to come in here and criticize me?"

"I was worried that when *you* got around to reaching out, it'd be with baskets of expensive pears and apology flowers. *Thank god* you were too busy eating bed salads, because that degree of earnest contrition would've been *so* mortifying. The food waste alone . . ." She trails off, eyes still fixed to the Halo Top label. No one has examined the calorie content of diet ice cream with more drama than Laurel Beekman.

"Look," I start, because, right now, I'm willing to talk about anything—even this!—so long as it's not Ethan. "I didn't . . . I didn't want you to . . . *not* get married if you *wanted* to get married."

She shakes her head so hard, it becomes a full-body earthquake. "That sentence doesn't make any sense, Charley!"

"I didn't get in the kayak knowing I'd take out your officiant, okay? I only wanted to talk to you to see if marrying Petey was honestly what you wanted."

"Because you thought it was a bad idea, and only Charley knows what *good* ideas are."

"No," I argue. "That's not—"

"Why can't you acknowledge me for the person I am? You never miss an opportunity to remind me of the person I *was*, who was actually pretty great, by the way. Just with a lot of self-loathing and a tiny self-sabotaging streak."

"Self-loathing?" That stops me in my tracks. "What're you talking about?"

"You'll have to read my therapy journal for the answer to that one," she responds, moving from the fridge to the bar cart, and I've almost given up on the conversation when she says, "I didn't think I was a good person, Char. Like for a *long* time. I thought there was something rotten in me that would spread to anyone who got too close. Where people would love me and I'd hurt them—like Dad does."

"That's not . . ." I trail off, because it's so untrue I hardly know how to refute it.

Laurel's not rotting. She's almost too alive. She's bold and expressive, existing in vibrant Technicolor that makes everyone shine a little more by being near her. But how do you out-logic the illogical?

So I start with something simple and unequivocally true. "You're nothing like Dad."

"I know that *now*," she says, flashing her eyes to me before retreating to the protection of a mostly full bottle of St-Germain. "Not like *know* know. It's one of those destructive thoughts that'll probably lurk in the back of my head for the rest of my life, but I know that's what it is now. Whenever I was about to explode out of my skin and had to run away, I used to think, *This is that selfish and harmful part of you.* I wanted to protect everyone from it. I know you hate how I am sometimes, but—"

"I don't hate how you are ever," I argue, but her face is incredulous. "It's true. There's never a second when I feel only one feeling about you. In every moment, I love you and I'm exasperated with you and I want to be more like you. It's always all of it. All the sister stuff. That's why you and Peter scare me so much. You love him in a way that's so enormous and consuming. I think I'm going to lose you to it. Like you might drown in it the way Mom and Dad did. I can't lose you too."

She groans, but it's the lighthearted kind you do when you love someone so much it's infuriating. "Oh my god." She flops onto the bed next to me. "What our parents have isn't 'love.' Loving someone, *really* loving them, it could never be like that. And in what universe do you think you're going to lose me? You can't lose me. We're in this. We're stuck with each other forever, okay?" She pulls me tight against her side like we're kids again, waiting out a thunderstorm together. "There's more than enough of my love to go around for you and Peter because love isn't finite. It isn't a thing you have. It's something you do. Love is a verb, babe."

"Gross." My laugh is wet and snotty but no less relieved. "Is that something Petey says?"

"It's something my therapist says."

"I get it. You're in therapy. You're, like, self-actualized and shit and not walled off from loving everyone."

She pushes her feet under the blanket and snuggles up beside me. "Oh, you love harder than anyone I know. You're like one of those gorillas that doesn't know its own strength. What do you think that disastrous weekend was?"

"Fear? Delusion? Petty selfishness?"

"Shut up," she grumbles, dragging out the second word. "You could break a rib with the way you love. You've loved Ethan that way your whole life, and he loves you too. When was the last time you listened to his first album? It's . . . not subtle."

My fingers rub my temples. "Laur," I grumble. "It's not *that* obvious. You talk like every song is titled 'Dear Charley.'"

"Might as well be. They're all real confessional and yearny." Her nose scrunches at her own description. Laurel's musical tastes run toward explicit dance pop in which the word "sweat" is hypnotically repeated over a pulsating beat. "Face it. His songs are about years of pining, and, other than me, you're the only woman he's known for more than two minutes."

"Maybe they're about you," I deflect. Whether she's right or not, I don't think I can handle obsessing over Ethan's back catalog any more than I already am.

"I don't think he's in love with me. On Sunday, I asked him if I looked hot and he told me I looked 'healthy.' Like I was a great-aunt he had aggressively nonsexual feelings for. That album is all 'Chuck.'"

"It doesn't matter anyway. It could never be me."

She stares me down with pursed lips. "You're an idiot." She opens a tub of face moisturizer I fought off a preteen in Sephora for and helps herself to it. "He's not doing much better, by the way. It's not a Halo Top–level depression, but it's not great."

"You guys talking about the boat?" Petey strides in and makes his way to the bathroom sink without stopping. "Ethan's been talking about buying a Boston Whaler and recording an album using 'found sounds.' I try to be supportive, but . . ." Petey winces. "It's so grim, man. Oh, cool, a fridge! Is there food up here?" Laurel nods and rolls off the bed again.

"Have you seen Ethan?" Neediness cracks in my voice. Even the sound of his name hurts, but I can't help myself. It's the only thing I want to hear.

Laurel grabs the low-cal cookie dough dessert and a spoon

from the bar cart. "We're checking in on him constantly. I was sure he was handling this worse than you until we broke into your house, and now I think it's a dead heat."

She passes the ice cream to Petey, who takes it along with the spoon. There's something so intimate about it. The way they buzz around each other. Anticipate each other's movements. They're not all over each other but move in concert, never more than an inch apart, as though connected by a piece of thread.

"Charmander, this house is *sick*. I'm loving this weird kitchen-bedroom setup. Lo, we've gotta get a bed fridge." Petey passes the pint back and watches Laurel sniff cautiously but still shovel some into her mouth. The moment before he scrubs his face with his palm, I catch this private, amused smile he doesn't intend for me to see, and I know for sure: They are so sickeningly happy. They're in love, and it's not the tumultuous kind that burns hot and fast, but the soft kind that smolders, gentle and warm, and requires only a little attention. They're the real deal, and I've been too stuck in my own head to notice.

Petey nudges the shelf sticking out of my bag of situational-depression Target purchases. "Do you need a hand mounting this?"

"I'm an idiot." The words bubble over my lips, and in an instant, I'm crying again. For the past few days, I've been existing in a constant state of near weeping. "I'm sorry I ruined your wedding. I was so awful. Everything I said . . . I did . . ." Machine-gun breaths dart out of my mouth. "I was so wrong about everything."

Laurel sets the ice cream on top of the fridge and climbs back into bed with me. "Oh, I know, hon." She pats my back with just enough condescension for me to believe she's truly unbothered. The relief turns every bone in my body liquid until I'm nothing but a blob in my bed with my sister.

"And I wasn't really mad about any of it to begin with," Petey explains, perching himself on the edge of the mattress. "Obviously, I'm worried about my boy, but that's your guys' business. I'm never going to stop loving my Charley Horse over something like that."

I wipe snot on my sweatshirt sleeve. "Peter Eriksson-Thao, you are too pure for this world. And I ruined your one shot at happiness." The crying starts up again.

Laurel pats my back. "Okay, this is *a lot*." She squirms closer to me on the bed and squeezes me tight, pressing my cheek into her shoulder with her hand. "As much as I love hearing you admit that you're wrong—mostly because you *never* do it—it's all okay, Charley. We'll get married. We'll jump off that ledge when it feels right."

"Only you could make marriage sound even more terrifying."

She smooths my hair as she pulls back, her arms on my shoulders when she explains, "Nothing's that scary with Peter. We make each other brave."

It's so simple, the way she says it, and I'm still processing her words when something Petey said earlier pings in my brain. "Did you say Ethan was buying a boat?"

Petey nods. "And it's not like he has time for that kind of maintenance."

"It's an obvious bid for attention," Laurel adds.

"Is he planning to tow it behind his van everywhere he goes?" I ask, struggling to picture his life with an extra fourteen hundred pounds strapped to the back of it.

"He's selling the van," Laurel announces.

My eyes dart between her and Petey. "Why would he do that?"

She gives me one of her teacher looks that says she's not accepting any nonsense from me. "Why do you think, Charley?"

I shove the hope back down before it can ruffle beneath my breastbone. "It doesn't mean anything. Dad tried the house and health insurance thing for Mom and went back to his old life the minute it got boring."

Laurel screws up her face. "He didn't do that for *Mom*. His funding fell through for three projects in a row. He was broke. He *had* to take that job in Lewellen."

The two of them continue to discuss the perils of boat upkeep, providing me time to resurface after this flood of new information. The story I always told myself—that my dad *tried* to live a life for us but was destined to leave—isn't true. He didn't try at all. But Ethan *tries*. He's generous and loving and when he takes on something new, he throws himself into it without reservations. He's a stayer.

And now he's selling his van for *me*, without the *promise* of me.

I'm not sure how long I've tuned Laurel and Petey out, but when I perk back up, he's volunteering them to stay the night.

"We did a number on that window. You might feel safer if we slept over after . . . you know . . . scaring the crap out of you."

Even if he could fix it, it wouldn't matter. I don't feel safe in my own life after building my entire existence around that one criterion. Working my ass off at a firm filled with people I don't respect hasn't fixed it. Getting married didn't. Buying this house didn't.

I've been running scared for years, but rather than facing my fears down, I've been creating space for my insecurities and caring for them like little pets. Picking relationships and goals I could hold on to with one hand while keeping my shield up with the other, too scared to walk up to the edge and feel the rush of anticipation as the rocks tremble at my feet. And still I wasn't safe.

I was right to worry that Ethan would hurt me—he's the only one who truly can—but I don't feel safe in this life I've built without him. All that is permanent and certain is that I'm unhappy. Unless I jump off this cliff, I always will be.

And for the first time in a while, I really, really want to.

Chapter 24

That Sounded Super Murdery

I T TOOK ME a week to get the plan sorted. It felt longer because Laurel *would not* stop bothering me about each phase of the plan. Primarily because I hadn't told her any of it and, at present, she believes I'm in the middle of full mental collapse.

"So, we're going on a trip?" she asks, her eyes on Petey as though she might need him to tackle me at some point.

"Yes. All three of us. Like the old days."

"The *three* of us have never been on a trip together. Not without . . ." Realizing her error, she changes course. "We'll need separate cars. Petey has to head back to Timber Creek for the next session."

"We'll be fine. You and I won't need a car to drive back. I've made sure of it."

"Are you *Thelma and Louise*-ing us? Is this a road trip to our deaths?"

I laugh, a response she doesn't appreciate if her eyebrows are any indication.

"This isn't funny, Charley! I get really uncomfortable when you're uncharacteristically spontaneous."

"I'm not going to kill you. You just need to trust me."

"Please," she begs, eyes pressed shut. "Stop talking like the husband at the beginning of a *Dateline* special that ends with a meter reader discovering a troubling number of teeth behind a gardenia plant."

Petey rubs a circle between his fiancée's shoulder blades. "It might be easier to agree to this if we knew even a part of what was happening right now. A super-small part. Like . . . why does your sister need to bring her fireproof document box?" He works to keep his voice calm as Laurel starts to lose it. "I think that part's been a cause for concern for her. Would you say that, Lo?"

Laurel folds her arms across her chest. "It's only like the fifth-craziest thing she's done this week, but, yes, the fireproof box request is raising alarm bells for me."

"To execute my plan, I need your important legal documents handy."

"That." She points her finger at my nose. "Right there. That sounded super murdery."

"Again . . ." I plead, getting a little annoyed. "Stop falling asleep to true-crime podcasts. I promise I'm not murdering you."

She eventually agrees to get into the car with me, but not before saving my filmed criminal confession on her cell phone as "collateral."

We drive for hours without stopping—I half expect Laurel to check if I'm wearing a diaper. Little does she know that to get us to Wet Ted's on time, I prioritized love over my hydration addiction. Laurel eventually lets out a deep sigh of relief when she sees Ethan's van in the familiar parking lot.

"Thank god," she gasps out. "I was praying this whole thing was about Ethan."

Petey lets out a whoop. "Nice one. You had me going for a while. Between the snorkel and the goalie mask—"

"Red herrings," I confirm, anxiety tightening my skin at the sight of his van.

"And my document box," Laurel adds.

I shake my head. "That's still a critical part of phase two."

"Charlotte Beekman, are you or are you not reverse *Gone Girl*-ing me?"

Petey tilts his head like a confused puppy. "I don't think you can reverse that one, babe."

Usually I'd prioritize absolving myself of such criminal culpability, but my attention is transfixed to Ethan the moment he steps onto the grass. He's beautiful as ever in his simple T-shirt and shorts, face alight with his typical charismatic aura. The sight of him now is no different than it was two weeks ago . . . apart from the way my heart has now fallen into my butt.

He's here. He's really here.

I stumble out of the driver's seat, leaving my passengers behind as I force one foot in front of the other. So much careful planning, all in anticipation of this single moment. I smooth my dress and inhale before launching the speech I've been practicing for several days.

Yet, despite my preparation, my first sentence tumbles out in an inelegant squawk.

"I kept the straw!"

He frowns at my contextless outburst, the wind ruffling his hair. "What?" he asks, confused.

Fair.

I was supposed to build up to that. When I rehearsed this speech, I must not have accounted for just how much being in

Ethan's presence would unsettle me. Maybe it's that I expected him to be more affected by seeing *me* here, in the woods, unannounced. Seeing *him* feels akin to swallowing a beehive. At the sight of *me*, he's startlingly at ease, running a hand through his hair as if I were anyone.

On my inhale, I consider all the ways I've loved Ethan and felt loved by him. The years of messages, jokes, and restrained touches. The way being near him soothes my brain and lights me up all at once. The way he makes me feel normal and weird in all the best ways. His passion for life, the environment, music, and now, me. His fearlessness. His generosity. His kindness. His patience. Ethan's so tender and wholehearted. To be the person he gives all his love to, even if only for a little while, I'm almost certain would be worth any risk.

"That night at the hospital, you told me you loved me, and you were right—I wasn't ready to hear it. But I couldn't let you go either, so I kept it. I kept the straw." I pull the straw out of my pocket and use it to ground my thoughts. "Even when I didn't hear from you for a year, I kept it. I use it all the time, you know, which is insane because it looks ridiculous—I look ridiculous—but I can't get rid of it. It's my last piece of you, and I think you're one of the only people that's ever made me feel safe. You're this stabilizing force, and it keeps you with me even when we're apart and I'm missing you so much. It *hurts* how much I miss you, Ethan."

He doesn't say anything in response. He just stares, and it sends a strange twinge of anticipation through my abdomen.

"So I quit my job." My words are spewing out of my mouth and collecting at his feet in a jumbled mess. "Then I fully freaked out, because I can't pay my mortgage without a job. I mean . . . I couldn't pay it *with* a job. Now I'm hearing myself say the word 'job' a lot, and it feels like someone is scooping my lungs out of my chest, but it's fine."

This is not going at all the way I planned, but I can't make myself stop. "I'm honestly fine, because it occurred to me that I *hate* my house. It's big and cold and the air-conditioning does this clicking thing at night that drives me nuts. And that bed is so giant and empty, and I don't want to sleep in a bed you're not in, because I don't want to be anywhere you aren't."

His expression remains impossible to read. God, this is terrifying. Like I'm dangling over the ledge of a very tall building, waiting to see if the man of my dreams will yank me back into the safety of his arms or let me fall to my bitter end.

"So . . . since I can't pay the mortgage on a house I hate, and it's not like I have furniture or anything, it only made sense to sell it to my neighbor's son. I worked my entire life to put down roots, and I undid it all in a single week, but I kind of feel . . . amazing. Growing up, I always thought that it was the constant change that scared me, but it wasn't. To me, love was this . . . delicate thing. A rope that could slip right through my fingers if my feet weren't firmly planted on the ground and the conditions weren't exactly right, and it was up to me to *make* it right. But you . . ." I step forward, feeling emboldened by his nearness. "You love me, and it makes me braver. You make me feel like I can jump off cliffs."

His eyes trail all over my face. "Yeah?" His voice is so quiet. Reverent.

"Yeah." I chuckle, wiping at the tears forming in the corners of my eyes with the back of my wrist. "If you give me another chance, I know you'll wake up every day and love me, because you always have. Even when I didn't know it, I felt it."

In the way he treated me, accepted me, valued me. It was always there. I was simply too stubborn to see it.

"And I know I'm going to wake up every day and love you," I promise him. I won't have a choice. I've been doing it so long it's the only thing I know for sure how to do.

An ache settles over his face. *I'm too late*, I worry. *No.* I won't accept this as the end. Not without telling him everything.

"I have it all figured out, you know. Well, the broad strokes anyway, since I'm homeless and jobless. I'll have to return my car too, since that's a lease." I shake my tumbling thoughts back into place. "But that's fine, because I've recently come into possession of a gently used van home." He smiles a little. Just enough to make my stomach swoop. "I bought your van. I made the offer under an assumed name."

His brow furrows. "An assumed name?"

I nod solemnly. "'Sutton River' isn't a person. I made the offer with a fake email account."

"No." He gasps. "Two fictional characters from *Aurora Falls* aren't joining as one to buy a van from me?"

"I didn't think you'd put that together," I mutter. "But it's my van now. Our van. I don't want you giving anything up to slot into my life, and I don't want to twist myself into yours. I want to try something new, together."

His lips lift. It's tiny, almost imperceptible, but *I* can see it and nearly collapse in relief at the sight. It's a raft in choppy waters, and I grab on for dear life.

"But I'm not living in a van *all* the time. I need things like a home base and a mailing address. We could have a place together or I could rent my own . . . and I'll need a job, of course.

But I've been rethinking my whole career plan, asking around about remote opportunities, so we can take long trips or travel to your shows. It's not the natural next step for my résumé, but I don't care how our life looks on paper. It only needs to be right to you and me, because I'm just so pathetically in love with you."

I add on the last bit because I don't think I've mentioned that critical detail in all my ranting. I'm in love with him. I always have been. Even when I told myself it wasn't possible, it never stopped. My love for my best friend was a plant in hibernation, ready to bloom.

I take a much-needed breath, waiting inside his impossibly long pause, until he breaks the silence to say, "Okay."

What? "Okay?" I clarify, in case I missed a syllable. Or ten.

His face bursts to life with one of his familiar crinkly-eyed smiles. It's a privilege to know every one of this man's smiles, and I won't be taking that for granted again.

"Okay," he repeats. "That sounds good."

He steps forward and takes my hand, the meeting of our palms a period at the end of a sentence. His pulse speeds up until it matches mine in a single heartbeat.

"Just like that?" I had much more prepared. Hours of material. "You're not going to make me grovel or anything?"

He smirks. "That wasn't groveling?"

A smile ruffles my wet, splotchy face. "I practiced a whole penguin with a rock allegory in front of my mirror, where our friendship is this pebble, and—"

"You don't need to—"

"What about everything you said before? About how we shouldn't need to map out our whole futures and 'Why can't we just try things?'" I imitate his deep baritone.

"Is that what I sound like?" He clasps my other hand in his and pulls me close enough that our noses are only centimeters apart. My heart's been thumping against my bones like an animal in a cage since this morning. Only now, it calms. "You like to know what tomorrow will look like, and I think I can learn to go along with that. I just prefer when tomorrow includes me."

I twirl the strand of hair that flops onto his face between my fingers, and something heavy lifts from my chest. The armor around my ribs is cracking open and I can breathe again. Living without Ethan is so much more terrifying than the unknowns of being with him. "You're a critical part of my five-year plan."

"Can I kiss you now?" he whispers through his grin, and I tilt my mouth to his for a kiss that feels nothing like a dare, a challenge, or a risk. This kiss is a soft place to land. A beginning of an adventure filled with so many more moments like this one.

"So," he breathes into me when we come up for air. The buzz of his lips sends a trickle of heat down my spine. "I would very much like to carry you into the van right now and make up for lost time, but your sister and Petey are staring at us and—"

"Oh." I straighten and crane my neck to confirm that, yes, they're very much watching us. "They're phase two of my plan."

"Phase two?" He's as confused as my road trip captives behind us.

"You didn't think this was the *whole* plan, did you?" I tease. "I thought you knew everything I was thinking. I'm *so* predictable. Right, Powell?"

He shakes his head, his smirk blossoming into a full-blown grin. "Easy, Beekman. You surprise me all the time."

I face the car again, beaming at my sister's encouraging and perplexed face. "Phase two is the wedding."

Laurel cries when I show her my proof of ordination—fully weeps for two solid minutes—hopefully with elation and not in relief that the only thing I want from her document box is the Cook County marriage license she procured last time we were all here.

"This dress is perfect," she says, examining her braid crown in the mirror of Ted Wetter's bathroom.

Ted was pretty cool about the stolen kayak/animal trap situation when I called to check in on him after his accident and arrange the surprise nuptials. He was—understandably—unwilling to rent me boating equipment. Luckily, he pitched the perfect alternative and generously lent Petey a white button-down.

I smooth the skirt of the cream-colored silk dress I spotted in the window of a secondhand store in Linden Hills. Between the plunging neckline and delicate lace details, I knew it was made for Laurel the second I laid eyes on it.

"I'm glad you love it. I thought if the packing list included a white dress, you might catch on to my master plan. Though I guess I could've B&E'd your place, since that's a thing us Beekmans do." My smile slips. "Or Eriksson-Thaos now, I guess."

She grabs my hand. "You and me. We're Beekmans, Charley. A wedding doesn't change that."

That's when *I* start crying.

Petey knows the waterfall Ted is talking about based on almost no defining characteristics beyond *You'll know it when you see it* and *A sound bath of water and magnificence* and *It's absolutely sick.* But when we climb out of the van and see the untamed beauty of it—hear the chaotic yet harmonious cacophony of cascading falls—I *do* know it and it *does* sound remarkably close to a sound bath of water and magnificence.

Petey stares out at the torrent of water with his hands on his hips. "See? Absolutely sick."

Then all that's left to do is help two of my favorite people get married. No one gives Laurel away, because she's not going anywhere. She's using her enormous capacity for love to make something new with her best friend. I can't believe there was a time when I didn't want this moment for my sister.

Ethan eyes me the whole time like he's getting ideas, and that's fine by me. When it comes to him, I'm getting ideas too.

They exchange their own vows. Petey's involve a complicated hockey analogy that is surprisingly poignant, but Laurel's are simply, "I promise to run *to* you. With you. Always. To be as patient and generous with you as you've been with everyone you've ever met."

"And with that . . . ," I tell them when the rings have been placed and the vows have been exchanged. "By the power vested in me by . . . the internet, it is my great honor to pronounce you husband and wife."

Ethan steps on my decree with a raucous cheer that Petey can't help but join. My sister throws her arms around my shoulders and yells, "We did it!" directly into my eardrum. It's a clumsy end to an endearingly heartfelt ceremony.

"I forgot to have you kiss!" I lament once we've all signed the license. "How did I mess that up?"

"I'm sure it's still valid," Petey says comfortingly.

"Yes, but it's part of the tradition, and now you won't have that memory. You won't have any memories, actually, because no one was here to take pictures. I knew I should've let Ted do this."

"Charley." Laurel grabs my shoulder, coaxing me to meet her eyes. "It was perfect. Ted Wetter could never. I'm so proud of you."

"I'm proud of you too, Laur."

She looks back at me for a moment, happy tears building in the corners of her eyes, and pulls me into a hug that's a distillation of *all* our moments—girlhood and beyond.

"Enough sappy shit." She sniffs. "Go grab Ethan's camera and take some photos of my husband and me looking devastating next to a waterfall."

I take about thirty or so pictures of them holding each other, gazing into each other's eyes. I even snap a couple with her on his shoulders. Still, I know when I have *the* shot. Water is falling behind them in a dramatic curtain, they're nose to nose, and I've caught them in that fraction of a second before their lips touch. Laurel's eyes are closed and her face is nestled into his giant palm, but his eyes are open. He looks at her like a man possessed. That look says it all. My impetuous sister may be ready to settle down with the boy next door, but he still can't believe she's real.

"We need a sister one," Petey suggests, walking over to take the camera from my hands.

Laurel pulls me close in a moment that's a breath away from precious, but then she ruins it when she yells at her newly minted spouse, "That angle is terrible. Get lower, babe. We're going for fashion. *Drama.*" Only when Petey's cheek is to the ground is Laurel satisfied with his position. She releases him from his Instagram-husband duties after a few artful shots.

"Do the husband and wife have a song in mind for the first dance?" Ethan asks through the open driver's-side door. He's fiddling with the stereo.

"Play 'Velvet Nebula,'" Laurel calls out through cupped hands as Petey squeezes her waist.

Ethan's cheeks glow pink, and just when I'm sure he's about to pretend he can't find the track, the intro booms through his speakers.

I know every note of the first verse—every aching, yearning lyric—the way you remember a song in your bones no matter how long it's been. *Lost in time and space while dreaming of your face. I won't deny, I might be bracing for the one who will replace this heart of mine . . .*

He jumps down from the driver's seat and walks toward our sing-along on the grass as everything that's ever hurt about this song clicks into place. I freeze when he takes my hand, and Laurel and Petey join Ethan's twenty-two-year-old voice for the familiar riff, singing about that woman in his head—in his bed—even when they're galaxies apart. *Still her eyes, they're in the sky, at midnight . . .*

"In that velvet nebula!" The four of us scream-sing the chorus, jumping in the air holding hands and shouting the *Ah, ah, ah*s we've heard in TV shows, car commercials, and curated "feel-good indie" playlists. Petey picks Ethan up from behind, making his eyes bug out in gleeful astonishment.

"Lemonface, baby. Let's gooooo!" Petey hollers at a volume only acceptable in hockey arenas.

But we're all into it. Running up the pebbled lakeshore like children. It's almost too good to be reality. We're in a distorted image where the edges are fuzzy and the colors are saturated. We dance together, blurry orbs of who we were, who we are, and who we hope to become all at once. Uncertainty and fear of what comes next still exist, but this miraculous moment apart from time is real too. It only took jumping off a cliff to find it.

"So this song is about me?" I ask Ethan between the bridge and the chorus.

He spins me around, winding me up until I crash into his chest. "Yep."

"Laurel's right. It's not subtle."

His smile spreads into his cheeks, exposing his dimples. "I wasn't trying to be."

"Good," I reply, tilting my head sideways so I can drink him in. "Subtlety is overrated."

When the song finishes, Laurel takes control of the playlist. We jump and twirl, imbibing the champagne I packed early this morning.

"This was perfect," Laurel whispers into our hug through the passenger window of Petey's truck. The sun has fallen behind the trees in a watercolor of pinks and oranges, and it's time for her to leave. I wave as they drive off, wearing the bubbly, wet smile that's painted my face for the past hour, because it *was* perfect. This strange little surprise wedding was exactly them, and I love them. I'm going to *keep* loving them, knowing they'll keep loving *me*. We're a bunch of saps who can't help but be obsessed with each other. Distance and paperwork won't change that.

"What took you so long, Chuck?" he asks, pushing a strand of hair behind my ear. "I missed you so much, but 'Sutton River'"—he puts my alias in exaggerated finger quotes—"refused to meet me any earlier."

"The rest of the plan wasn't ready earlier," I counter.

"What were you waiting for? You quit your job on Friday and the house sale was basically a done deal Tuesday."

It takes a second for me to understand what he's telling me, but then it hits me square in the jaw. "Wait. You *knew* about the house sale and the job?" I shove his shoulder. He barely budges. "That's not fair!"

"Fair? After you quit your job, Laurel called me in a panic. Then I got this weird message about buying the van—which was so obviously from you . . ."

I stare at that smug smile of his in utter disbelief. "You already knew everything I was telling you. The *whole* time. And you let me make that humiliating speech?"

His hands find the dip of my waist. "I did. And thank god for that, because your plan was to ambush me in Wet Ted's parking lot with no warning," he complains, but his love-struck smile tells me he's not the least bit disappointed.

"I hate you," I say into his neck. He smells as sweet as ever.

His hands grip me tighter and his eyes dance all over my face as though he might not believe I'm real and in his arms after all we've been through. "You don't, though."

"I don't." I barely get the words out.

I can hardly remember a time when I was afraid of this. Of what would or wouldn't happen when I jumped into the arms of my best friend. I love him—I've always loved him—but I was so certain love was this fragile thing that would slice my palm when it inevitably shattered. But it turns out we're not so brittle, and I'm not that delicate.

"Wanna go home now?" He gestures with his chin toward the van. "Your name's on all the finance documents, by the way. Which was another tip-off that 'Sutton River' was an alias."

I pull him closer by the back of the neck. "I get it. I have no future in espionage."

"So, where do you want to live, Beekman?" he asks, pressing our heads together. "The van's too small. We'll have to start looking for places soon or we might kill each other. Or you might kill me, more accurately."

"Okay, rude. I can cohabitate in a van without resorting to murder."

He squeezes me. "Sure you could."

"You have no faith in me."

"Have you even taken a second to consider the dark sides here?"

"Nope," I answer, rolling my forehead along his. "It's bright sides only from here on out, Powell."

"Let's do a week," he suggests, his voice a little thick. "Then see where life takes us."

I step back and lead him to the van, enjoying the weight of our clasped hands the whole way.

"I could try that," I agree, sliding open the door.

Epilogue

Can We Keep the Physical Manifestation of Our Love With the Beer Koozies?

D ID YOU STEAL my straw?" I ask. It's not really a question but an accusation. More of a fact, honestly, because the man *definitely* stole my straw.

Ethan and I stare each other down in our kitchen—our immovable kitchen in our town house on Lake Lewellen. The van *was* too small, though I made it way more than a week. (Seventeen weeks, if we count the six days our engine conked out and we had to stay in a KOA, which I am 1,000 percent counting.)

The nomadic life is hard! And it's not just me who can't hack it. Ethan has fully leaned into his sappy sentimental side now that he has a permanent address to store cheesy mementos of our relationship. He keeps everything these days: gas station key chains that spell my name right, state park maps, every innuendo-emblazoned trucker T-shirt we stumble across. *We're only at the beginning, and I don't want to forget any of it*, he said when he handed the cashier at Yellowstone a twenty for a T-shirt that read OLD FAITHFUL BLOWS over a confoundingly sexual illustration of the geyser.

I don't think he knew how much that moment meant to me. The way he casually announced there was no ticking clock on this thing between us. It made me like the shirt more, even though I'd groaned for a solid ten seconds when he'd first plucked that ugly thing from the circular rack.

He's also pretty obsessed with Cat Power, the Maine coon kitten we found wandering around a Walmart parking lot somewhere outside of Bend, Oregon, and named after the singer-songwriter. Though she tolerates road life, her favorite spot on the planet is in front of our fireplace at home, and now that Ethan's writing songs—and no longer performing in bustling student unions during Rush Week—it's his favorite spot too.

We furnished the place slowly, picking pieces one at a time from antique stores and estate sales all over the country and decorating the walls with my photographs from our trips. Gone are the days of empty rooms and Airbnb-caliber art. Our home is intentional.

But that doesn't mean my boyfriend can just *take* my *things*.

"Powell," I caution. The forks and knives clank together as I scour the utensil drawer, searching for the familiar phallic novelty straw. "It's not in any of its usual spots."

He looks to the ceiling for strength. "This is an intervention. You've become desensitized to it. Last time my parents were here, you were just sipping away on that thing like it wasn't shaped like a penis."

I pull open the utility drawer next. Cat saunters between us, blissfully unaware of the brewing conflict between her humans. "You didn't throw it away, did you? It's the physical manifestation of our love."

"Please, Chuck. Don't give a phallus that kind of power."

I grab a sad metal straw from the empty glass next to the sink and thoroughly rinse it under hot water. "I let you keep your toe shoes, and this is how you repay me?"

Behind me, Ethan wraps his arms around my waist and rests his head on my shoulder. "The straw was indecent."

"Your Vibrams are indecent," I parry.

He sighs into my neck and I can't help but be a little giddy at the feel of him wrapped around me like this.

These are the moments I love most. The casual touches and dizzying banter that doesn't lead to anything else—when we simply exist together. It's those moments when I feel most rooted to the ground. Even when we're headed somewhere, I know *we're* not going anywhere.

He squeezes my middle. "It's not gone. Just put away. It's in that plastic bin in the garage with the camper plates."

I twirl in his arms to face him.

Once we accepted that a van was simply too small for two people to live comfortably in for more than an extended weekend, we decided to upsize. For a brief, irrational moment, I'd considered buying two vans that we could caravan on the highway, one after another, like charter buses on a ski trip. Luckily, we'd kept in touch with Harlow and Russell, who tipped Ethan off to a two-hundred-square-foot vintage Holiday Rambler, and after a fair amount of money and elbow grease, it's become my absolute favorite place to be . . . for two to three weeks at a time.

"I knew I loved you," I say triumphantly, draping my arms around his neck.

"Can we keep the 'physical manifestation of our love' with the beer koozies?"

"I accept these terms."

He tucks a strand of hair behind my ear. "No counter? You already put my Vibrams out there on the proverbial chopping block."

"Nah. Keep 'em," I reply, peering into his gray blue eyes. "I'm feeling soft today."

Today is Laurel and Petey's anniversary, which is sort of our anniversary. Though Ethan argues our anniversary is actually this one night we ran out of gas in our early twenties when, unbeknownst to me, he realized he was in love with me. I argue that knowledge is required by both parties to create an anniversary, not to mention his proposed date is in November, and November in Minnesota will test anyone's resolve. This year, we spent the entire month in Monterey, California, with Laurel and Petey, avoiding the harrowing transition from autumn to winter. Since my sister only forced my boyfriend to play Michael Kiwanuka's "Cold Little Heart" on his guitar about six or seven times while she looked woefully at the shoreline and pretended she was Reese Witherspoon in *Big Little Lies*, I deemed the trip a success.

"Do you have much work today?" he asks, his fingers absently stroking my back.

I shake my head. "I have to finish a reply brief, but it should only take me a couple of hours."

About two weeks after I bought Ethan's van, one of Stacy's law school friends connected her with an associate position at his much smaller—less dysfunctional—intellectual property firm. After settling in, she connected me with a position as a counsel attorney that offered the flexibility and autonomy of working for myself with some of the security of the law firm life. Now I get to pick my clients and work on projects that matter to me. There's no partnership path—something that used to be an immediate deal-breaker for me—but job security means something different to me now.

I spend my time with the people who feel like home. I work exclusively with and for people I respect. Sometimes I make art, not to live, but to fill me up. One day, I might find a way to make a career out of it like Harlow does. Or maybe I won't. There's no plan or agenda. For now, it's nice doing things for no other reason than that they make me happy.

My head droops to his shoulder, my spine a noodle in the face of his gentle ministrations. "The patent examiner was so egregiously off base with his rejection that I'm hoping my righteous indignation will fuel me for most of the morning. After that, I'm all yours."

"I love that for you." He plants a kiss on top of my head. "I have to finish mixing that thing for Ivan, but then I'm good if we want to go somewhere this weekend."

It takes everything in me to keep my face neutral, because I have a feeling about what this weekend has in store. "Yeah. Let's go."

Throughout the morning, Ethan shuffles between our shared office and the kitchen, Cat hot on his trail like a furry shadow. Meanwhile, I work on the back deck, thinking about everything other than the emerald ring I found in one of Ethan's five-finger-shoe monstrosities two days prior.

We haven't talked much about getting married, other than a few of those naked, late-night conversations when everything exists in the hypothetical. Somewhere between *If I turned into a zombie, would you kill me?* and *We should totally move to Gstaad*, Ethan whispered, "I know you don't want to get married again, but there's this caveman part of me that really wants to call you my wife. Is that weird?"

"You can just call me your wife if you want," I said back. "We don't need to be married for that."

"I can't just *start* calling you my wife. There should at least be rings involved, even if we never make it legal."

And now there's an emerald ring, and I'm sweating through my linen sundress.

"Charley, can you help me with something down here on the dock?" Ethan calls out just out of sight. I climb down the rickety wood stairs and follow the path to the water. Ethan comes into view. He's in one of his nicer shirts—one with buttons—and he's down on one knee.

"You're doing this now?" I blurt, then cover my mouth with my hand. "I mean, I thought you were doing this this weekend."

"What?" He shifts his weight on his knee, seeming unsure whether he's supposed to stay down there. "How did you know I was doing it at all?"

I lengthen my stride across the dock until I'm finally in front of him. "I found the ring in your shoes. Cards on the table: I also tried to hide them in the garage, but then I found . . ."

"I should've known something was up when you let me win with the straw!"

I kneel down in front of him, so I can look at him straight on as water builds behind my eyes. I start to take the ring, when—

"Wait!" I shove his hands back. "You didn't ask me anything."

"Oh, you're right." He closes his eyes, preparing what I'm

sure will be an incredibly moving speech. Then he opens them. "I'm sorry. I don't know what to ask in a nonmarriage 'marriage' proposal."

"It doesn't matter," I insist. My bare knees ache on the splintered wood, so I stand back up. "Okay. Ask me now. I'll pretend it's a surprise." I fluff my dress a little and take a deep breath.

"Okay . . ." Ethan looks up at me, his cheeks beet red in the sunshine. I love him so much that sometimes I worry something will take him away from me. My heart still squeezes a little whenever he comes back from a solo trip. At first, it was a ghost of old anxieties that he might disappear. Now it feels like something different, warm and reassuring. *Of course*, it says, *you knew it.* Love doesn't run out. It isn't finite, and having Ethan in my life is worth that dwindling fear that he might go away.

He looks between me and the ring, back and forth, until he explodes with laughter. "We are so bad at the big gestures." He pulls himself up to stand, wiping at his eyes. "This is tragic."

Something in the way he says "tragic," as though even our most disastrous moments are something magnificent, warms the inside of my chest. His eyes glisten, and his hand shakes as he wraps it around my left palm and slowly slides an emerald ring up my finger.

My heart thumps all the way into my throat, and I'm not sure I hear the question so much as watch his lips move when he asks, "Charlotte Beekman, will you let me call you my wife, so we can be this way forever?"

My eyes go blurry with tears. I don't even have to think. I have the answer memorized. I always have. "Of course. Yes!" I fling myself into his arms.

He presses our foreheads together. The electricity of the moment crackles down my spine. "Good." His sigh brushes my lips. "I got bands for us too. I know this won't be a legal thing, but I'd still like to exchange vows, even if it's just for us." That big, crinkly smile lights up his face.

"I'd love that." I nod. "But you know . . . it might not be so bad to get married again. To you. Like *married* married. If you want that."

He pulls back his head to look at me, his hands on either side of my face like I'm the only thing keeping his body from floating away. "It's all I've ever wanted, Chuck."

"Then let's get *married* married," I suggest through the happy tears. God, "in love" Charley is *so* emotional. I clear my throat. "We should probably do it soon. Your health insurance is *so* bad, and I think for tax purposes we could open—"

He shushes me with a kiss. "I love you, but can we put the five-year tax plans away, please? Let's play it by ear for the rest of the weekend. Get away somewhere . . ."

"Of course," I assure him, enjoying the way his laugh rumbles against my cheek. "You know I'd go anywhere with you."

ACKNOWLEDGMENTS

The funny thing about writing the acknowledgments for your second book is that you're *not* writing the acknowledgments for your second book—at least, not entirely. As I write this, my first book, *Four Weekends and a Funeral*, is only six weeks old! I could probably fill an entire (very boring and uncomfortably earnest) gratitude journal with everyone who made that book's release a dream come true, but I'll do my best to keep that part brief, because this is about *Anywhere With You* and everyone who played a part in this labor of love.

First, thank you to my incredible agent, Laura Bradford, who, along with her phenomenal team, is *the* reason I've written two (count 'em, TWO!) acknowledgments sections, and to Taryn Fagerness, who's brought my work to more places than I could've dreamed.

To my genius editor, Kate Dresser: you saw the potential in this story back when it was simply Van Life vibes with occasional snippets of banter. Thanks to your inspiring optimism and firm editorial hand, this thing somehow turned into a book I'm incredibly proud of. I couldn't have dreamed of a more positive or joyful partnership.

All the gratitude to Nicole Biton, the hardest-working publicist in New York City; Molly Pieper, marketer extraordinaire; the ever-dependable Tarini Sipahimalani; and to the rest of the Putnam team, particularly Ivan Held, Ashley McClay, Alexis Welby, Aja Pollock, Janice Barral, Tiffany Estreicher, Emily Mileham, Maija Baldauf, Meg Drislane, Chandra

Wohleber, and Sarah Horgan. You are all the best in the business, and I'm enormously proud to be a Putnam author.

To the writers who read and endorsed my first book— Neely Tubati-Alexander, Livy Hart, Naina Kumar, Kate Robb, Meredith Schorr, Farah Heron, Jessica Joyce, Tarah DeWitt, Sarah Adler, Alicia Thompson, Julia Quinn, and Abby Jimenez— you're all as brilliant and gorgeous as you are generous.

Endless thanks to the booksellers and librarians who lent their support to my books, especially Rachel, Ellie, and the rest of Content Bookstore; Caitlin and Lauren of Tropes & Trifles; Annie and Rachel at Magers & Quinn; Steph and Emily of Swoonworthy Romance Booksellers; Mae from Smitten; and every other professional book lover who's pressed an Ellie Palmer book into someone's hands and said, "I think you might like this."

All my love to Book of the Month (who selected my debut for their subscription box and made a hardcover version of *FWAAF* a reality), ARC of the Month Book Club (who bet on my debut MONTHS before it hit shelves), Bad Bitch Book Club (whose taste is always nothing short of impeccable), Minneapolis Beach Reads and Bubbly (who have truly the best in-person book club around), the Emilys at @bookedwith theemilys (who connected me with so many incredible readers), and every other book club that selected *Four Weekends and a Funeral* to read with your friends.

Many thanks to the people I didn't know a few years ago and now can't imagine my life without. Naina Kumar: You're the first person I trust with all my sloppiest first drafts and wildest ideas. I'm so grateful for your friendship and how you help me improve my work while inspiring me to keep going. Scarlette Tame and Ava Watson, what would I do without our delightfully unstructured Zoom brainstorming sessions? Perish, I'm sure. To Danica Nava, thank you for always being there to laugh with me about this puzzling industry. Thanks to the Minneapolis crew, Amanda Wilson, Kjersten Piper, Karsyn Zetah, and Elizabeth Armstrong, for being that perfect combination of brilliant and ridiculous. All my love to the friends in the group chats who keep me sane: Alexandra Vasti, Laura Piper Lee, Jill Tew, Myah Ariel, Melanie Sweeney, SF 2.0, Kitchen Party, and every writer who has brought me so much support and joy this past year. Finally, a very special thanks to all my wonderful friends who read early versions of this book and helped me make it better: Alexandra Kiley, Kate Robb, Amanda Wilson, Myah Ariel, Karsyn Zetah, Scarlette Tame, Ava Watson, and Naina Kumar.

To the Instagrammers, the TikTokers, the podcasters, the people out there shouting about books like Katelyn from @BookClubWithKatelyn, Steph from @StephsBookTherapy, Courtnie from @TheAnnexLibrary, Kasee from Longhand Pencils, Ada of @AdaGetsLiterary, Mylynn from @Hyperfix atedReader, Jenn Newman of @Jenn.Newm.Reads, Charissa from @CloveLetter, Bethany from @BethanysAllBooked, Ally of @AllysBookShopAroundTheCorner, Patty from @Tring GoesOn, Kendal from *Unofficial Book Club Podcast*, Tia from @TiaChu on YouTube, and *so* many more: What you do is MAGIC. Your reviews, posts, edits, playlists, and videos make authors feel seen and loved. You make us believe our work will find its people. For every one of you readers who's reached out to me or who's met me in person, you make this quiet, solitary job so lively and fulfilling.

Thank you to my loving family, especially my mom and my sister, and to my brilliant and hilarious friends. The emotional core of this book is centered on one woman's anxiety over how her relationships change with space and time. Thank you for proving to me every day that we can love each other just as well from far away.

To Chris: I love you. You're the best partner and the most phenomenal dad. You bring so much joy to our lives.

Finally, thank you to you, dear reader—there are so many good books out there, waiting to be read. Thank you for picking this one.

DISCUSSION GUIDE

1. From the first chapter, author Ellie Palmer notes that Midwesterners are stereotyped as being conflict averse. Between which characters did you see this quality shine through the most?

2. *Anywhere with You* opens with Charley's decision to stop her sister Laurel's wedding. Do you think Charley is justified in making such a call in love? How would you have responded in either scenario—first if you were Charley, then if you were Laurel? How would you define a sister's duty?

3. Charley and Ethan are complete opposites. Where Charley is a type-A queen, Ethan is as carefree and nonchalant as they (men) come. To what extent do you believe opposites attract?

4. Palmer spoils us with some swoon-worthy banter between Charley and Ethan. In which moment did you first sense their brewing sexual tension? What gave them away?

5. *Anywhere with You*, a beloved road trip romance, transports us through the Minnesotan woods. How is the road-trip trope known to foster intimacy, and to what extent does it manifest in this way for Charley and Ethan? If you were to embark on a similar road trip, who would you take with you?

6. Charley and Ethan have known each other since they were kids. Discuss whether such a robust history often hinders or encourages romance. In other words, to what extent does the progress of Charley and Ethan's relationship hinge on their early meet-cute?

7. After her divorce, Charley finds it easier to tell the frequently inquisitive that she's "dating around," even though she isn't. In her words, it's the path of least resistance. To what extent does society still pressure women to find love, and by a certain age? How does this interact with the stigma around divorce?

8. Charley and Laurel grew up observing a certain model of romance. Based on their present-day inclinations in love, discuss what they both took away from their parents' relationship.

9. Charley requests at least one year post-divorce to indulge in her Sad Girl Era. If you were in her position, which songs would be on your Sad Girl playlist? On the flip side, what would make up your Fall in Love playlist?

10. Having finished the book, where do you see Charley and Ethan now?

Author photograph by Morgan Lust

Ellie Palmer is the author of *Four Weekends and a Funeral* and *Anywhere With You* and is a prototypical Midwesterner who routinely apologizes to inanimate objects when she bumps into them. When she's not writing romantic comedies featuring delightfully messy characters, she's at home in Minnesota, eating breakfast food, watching too much reality television, and triple texting her husband about their son.

elliepalmerwrites.com
🅾 ♪ ElliePalmerWrites